NOTICES

Berserker God Copyright © 2023 Peace Weaver Press Inc. President Veronica Doran

ISBN 978-1-7381129-8-2

CONTENT WARNINGS

Please visit https://www.ursadaxwriting.com/content-warnings for content notes and warnings.

BERSERKER GOD

Brides of the Stone Sky Gods
Book Two
By Ursa Dax

Stone Sky God Name Pronunciation Guide

Skallagrim – SKAH-la-grim
Jolakaia – joe-la-KAI-ah
Koltar – COAL-tar
Koraba – koe-RAH-bah
Wylfrael – WOLF-rye-elle
Sionnach – SIGH-on-nock
Maerwynne – MARE-win-nuh
Rúnwebbe – rune-WEB-buh
Sceadulyr – shay-AH-doo-leer
Cynewylf – KOO-nuh-wolf
Heofonraed – hay-OFF-enn-rad
Vizhiri – viz-JHEER-ee

PROLOGUE

The stone sky god Skallagrim always thought he'd have more time. An affliction of immortals. Or perhaps just an affliction of a certain sort of male. The penchant to look fate in its relentless eyes, scoff, and simply tell the inevitable that it will have to come collect its due another day.

But even a god cannot push off fate forever. And even an immortal cannot escape the burning end when it comes calling.

I always thought I'd have more time. That was what Skalla said to himself when he felt his mind begin to blacken at the edges. They were the last words left in his skull before language began to dissipate like fog around him, inside him, until there were no words left but the broken echoes of what had once made sense.

I always thought I'd have more time.

Time to find her. The one mortal creature in the whole shuddering scope of the universe who could have saved him.

And saved everyone else.

When Skallagrim felt his mind start unspooling, when the mate madness first took hold, he went to the one immortal he could fully trust. The one stone sky god who knew him deeply, who loved him, and was, he believed, strong enough to subdue him. He went to Sionnach, his cousin Wylfrael's world.

But Wylfrael was no match for Skalla in his rampage. Skalla's berserker blood, inherited from his Bohnebregg mother, was an accelerant to the flame of mate madness. He became something formidable and terrible and not at all himself.

Wylfrael was defeated twice, evaded endlessly, until there was nothing and no one left to halt Skalla's cosmic riptide of rage.

No one...

No one except the one small, singular, mortal creature he should have been searching for all along.

His fated bride.

His salvation...

Or his undoing.

CHAPTER ONE
Suvi

Marta, Min-Ji, and I were in one of the caves of the new planet when the ship's alarm system began to blare.

"Another one?" Marta said, frowning and pushing up her safety glasses until they formed a headband for her kinky, dark curls. "We already had one this morning."

After what had happened to Torrance and the other soldiers on the last planet, we'd started running drills in this new world. Practice runs for if something like that ever happened again. If the sky turned to stone and some winged creature, brutal and alien and powerful beyond comprehension, came through, obliterating everything in its path. Whenever the ship's alarm system went off, we were to return to it as quickly as possible.

And if we weren't fast enough...

We'd get left behind.

Just like Torrance was.

That was three weeks ago. Three weeks since we last saw our friend in the ice and snow of the alien world we were all taken to against our will. Three weeks since the sky cracked open like it was made of earth instead of air. Three weeks since we retreated to this new planet, leaving her to die in the snow.

"Let's go," Min-Ji said, standing and brushing blue dust from the seat of her grey uniform's pants. Unlike that last planet we were hauled off to, this one wasn't plunged into the depths of snowy winter. The air here was dry and warm, no winter coats or snowpants required.

The lack of puffy clothing and snow made our steps quick as we trekked back out of the cave. We left all our stuff behind, as instructed for these drills, abandoning our tools and the little glowing samples of odd, bark-like fungi that grew in the caves of this world.

As we got closer to the cave's opening, the alarms blared louder and louder. But it wasn't just the bleating of the sirens that split the sky. That chaotic rhythm was underpinned by the sounds of...

Engines.

"Not a fucking drill!" Min-Ji shouted, breaking into a run at the mouth of the cave. Marta followed suit, grey boots flying over the hard, cracked ground, kicking up cerulean dust. Heart in my throat, I sprinted behind them.

Paska. Shit.

As a kid and young teen in Finland, I'd skated my ass off on the ice rink. But I hadn't been a hockey player for years, and my cardio wasn't what it once had been. The result was that the distance between my two friends – long-legged Marta and phenomenally fit ex-boxer Min-Ji – and me grew wider and wider with every step we all took through the dusty valley be-tween alien cave systems.

This area of the planet was essentially all caves and the space between them. There was one supremely large, wide valley, and the other valleys split off from it like tributaries of a river, with bulging blue caves lining them in-stead of shorelines. At the end of this extra-huge valley was the ship. I saw it gleaming ahead of Marta and Min-Ji and at the very same moment saw the reason for the alarms.

The air up above was hardening, just like it had over the last planet. The gold-choked alien sky of sunset became dense. Opaque. Solid. Matte and dark and not at all reflective.

It was only Min-Ji's screaming that made me realize I'd slowed way down, distracted by the cosmic fucking horror of the sky turning into stone. Sweat drenched the back of my grey tank top and beaded between my breasts. My breath burned in my lungs as I stared upward, suddenly unable to take another step.

When the hard stone substance in the sky cracked, it felt like something inside me cracked, too. Like bone was broken. My body split from skull to spine. Min-Ji screamed again, and I was pretty sure she said my name, but I couldn't look at her. Couldn't tear my eyes from the darkness of the chasm in the stone.

And the glittering behemoth that clawed its way out of it before diving straight down at the ground like a human might dive into deep water.

The force of that winged thing hitting the ground was catastrophic. A crater exploded between the others near the ship and me. The force threw me backwards to the ground, knocked every shivering breath from my body. Gasping, choking on the sudden, disorienting emptiness of my lungs, I fought to sit up, crawling backwards, further away from the cavernous hole ahead of me in the valley.

And further away from the ship.

I couldn't see Min-Ji or Marta now. Couldn't even see the ship. The planet-quaking power that had just pounded into the ground ahead set loose a torrent of rock. High caves and stone formations cracked and collapsed beyond the crater, creating a massive wall of blue and grey rubble that bisected the valley. Some of the falling stone poured into the crater, and I watched, wild with panic, hoping all the rockfall would subdue the alien thing at the bottom long enough for me to get to the ship before it left.

I should have known that was a stupid fucking hope. I should have known that I would not have been so lucky.

Because the thing emerged, dusty but unscathed, flinging boulders from its body as it climbed the way a human might shake off snowflakes.

It reached the top of the crater and stood to its full and dizzying height. *It's got to be at least two... two and a half metres tall...* It was huge and terrible and all fucking wrong, some disturbed mash-up of dragon and man. A two-legged, two-armed, two-winged beast with emerald scales and a tangled tumble of black hair. I could tell right away that this was not the same creature who'd come from the sky on the other planet. I'd glimpsed that one too, and it had had entirely different colouring. Stony greyish hide, silver-white hair, and black wings dotted with glowing lights.

This one had similar lights, though. It took a second for me to register the glow beneath the dust. But now that the sun was setting, shadows deepening and stretching, the lights on its body grew brighter in the ruined valley. Shining gold veined between the scales and all over its wings, glimmering like little flames.

The little lights illuminated its thick neck, its reptilian snout, and what looked like the sunken, ruined place an eye should have been

But it still had one eye. An eye bright with fathomless alien rage.

An eye fixed solely, squarely, upon me.

CHAPTER TWO
Skallagrim

D*rag body through the darkness.*

*Darkness everywhere. Darkness hard wet cold hot, **hot**, crush kill claw ruin.*

*Bleed. Drag body again and again and again. Drag up. Up up up. Hand in hard sky. **Crack.***

Down. Down like falling. Headfirst sucked right down to ground, into ground. Hard hole deep deep deep.

Word. A word for that. Word for bone drag down to ground. Energy attraction mass. Brevity cavity calamity depravity.

Down. Hard on top below and all around. Drag body out.

Stand.

New world. Same hot cold foul and fighting darkness.

Same same same.

Except...

*Not same. **Not same.***

Ahead. One single spot not-dark.

Darkness all around body. Inside body. Darkness as far as forever.

Until now. Until one little not-dark.

Another word for that. Shine sky eye blink bright night.

Not-dark not still. Wiggle worm crawl away.

Do not let it go.

Not-dark beneath body. Tendrils snap and lash.

Collides. Connects body to the not-dark.

And I can see again.

CHAPTER THREE
Skallagrim

I gasped, and it was like the very first time I ever took breath. I wrenched my head back, my eyes—no, my *eye*—wide and unblinking. My skull was going to split. I knew it. Could feel it. Feel the bone cracking, buckling, breaking under the pressure of the tsunami inside it. The ferocious wave, like a suddenly undammed river, filled me with sounds, tastes, thoughts, memories, *memories*. Memories when I had not had a memory in... in...

In I did not know how long.

I could not recognize it all, could not tell one memory from another. Could not place all the syllables joining and separating, words and not-words sparking into sound and then disappearing. It all crashed and took everything along with it, flooding through my head. A dauntless river, a wide and glittering river, a river that felt somehow familiar, like I'd swam in it, bathed in it, lived my entire life beside it...

My life. What life? *What life?*

What life had I lived once? Who had I been until now? There was someone before the darkness. There had to have been. Someone distant and discordant, someone whose name was nothing to me now but the sound of water crashing over rock, wind rustling through the tall reeds of some-where, somewhere, *somewhere...*

Knees digging into dirt, I groaned and closed my eye, clutching the sides of my head as the river slammed and swirled. If I let go, the bowl of my brain would crack and then shatter. And I'd fought too cursedly long to be obliterated now by nothing but the force of an entire life forgotten inside my own head.

It was all moving too fast. If I could just grab on to something, *anything*, maybe I'd be able to make sense of it all. Stop the river just long enough to snatch a single thought or word or sound.

There! There was a sound!

The sound of scrabbling through rock and dust.

I cracked my eye open, and for the first time since I did not know when, could see. Truly see. Forms and shapes and shadows and *light*. Light concentrated in the shape of a not-dark thing that ran from me. Feet flying. Arms pumping. Hair long and flowing like silver that comes from the sky at night.

I could not ever remember uttering a word out loud before now. Perhaps I never had.

But I did so then.

"*Little star.*"

It was a desperate rasp. A plea. An echo from the river. I could not tell if I recognized the voice or not. But I felt it come from my throat, so what else could that mean but that it was mine?

I panted and grunted on my knees, still clutching both sides of my head, and watched the bright creature as it ran. Everything hurt. Bone and blood vessel and sinew. Every part ached like my entire body had been stretched too thin for too long. Like each cell had been swollen, bursting, raging, brutal, berserk.

A word from the river, shooting out like an arrow took hold of me.

Berserker.

The further the creature got from me in this valley, the more my head hurt. And the blacker the edges of my vision became. The river receded, taking everything with it, until the crash of water was replaced by fever and fury and darkness so viscous, so vicious, that I nearly forgot how to breathe.

I did not know what that little star was.

But I needed it. It had taught me something, brought me back to something, and I could not bear to lose it or be lost again. It had brought me back to language and thought and myself, whoever in the cursed skies that was.

I tried to call it back. *Little star. Little star*. But the words never made it to my mouth. Something between my brain and my teeth had stoppered it all up. Already, things were disappearing. *I* was disappearing. And maybe I never even knew the words I'd wanted to say at all. I tried to remember, tried to slice through shadows until I reached the pure chaos of the river's churn. *Little... Little...*

Little not-dark. Do not run from me.

Limbs stretched and swelled. Scales rippled. Claws lengthened.

Power surged. Power that felt like anger, like hunger, like poison, like pain.

Drag body through the valley.

Darkness everywhere.

CHAPTER FOUR

Suvi

I ran blindly, not letting myself stop or look back. If I looked back, I'd see it. That formidable, terrible creature that had shattered the sky. The creature who could have been hunting me even now.

I hoped to hell I had enough of a head start. Something seemed to have hurt it, or at least shocked it. It had been practically on top of me, looming over me on all fours and snapping its feral jaws. When my hand had smacked against its chest in my attempt to get away, it had rocked back on its knees, grasping its head, whole body straining.

Rocks and dust sprayed from my boots as I sprinted. Fear made me fast, but it also made me clumsy, and soon my running was more like panicked stumbling.

I can't keep this up for long.

I choked back a terrified sob at the thought of what might happen when I stopped.

And the worst part of it all was that, while I couldn't afford to stop running, I was running the *wrong fucking way*. I was fleeing from the hulking alien monster, but I was also getting further and further from the ship. A snap of my head upward told me the ship hadn't lifted off yet. If I could only get to it...

Get to it, and lead the monster right to my friends?

I yanked my chin back down a split second too late, colliding with an outcropping of stone so hard it made my teeth rattle and knocked me flat onto my ass. I bit back a yelp as pain lanced up my tailbone. The pressure let up almost instantly, but there was no relief in that. Because I was being *lifted*.

It has me.

It has me, and I am going to die.

There was no fighting a strength like that. The power at my back was like nothing I'd ever experienced. Like a living, breathing, pulsing wall of iron. Even so, I tried—I fucking tried—kicking and wriggling and screaming and spitting. One massive hand clamped onto my abdomen, the other sliding up until the scaly palm settled into place at the front of my throat. Its hand was so huge that its fingers reached easily around my neck, meeting its thumb at the base of my skull.

It was an odd thought to have, in the final moment before my death. The thought of how nearly human its hand was, despite the monstrous size.

I scrunched my eyes shut, waiting for pressure. Waiting for the end.

At least I'd get to see her again sooner than I'd thought.

Elvi. Are you waiting for me, big sister?

But the end never came. Instead, the creature sank to its knees once more, dragging me along with it. It held my back against its chest with one hand while the other released my throat. It didn't stop touching me, though. That hand dragged upward to my jaw, passing over my face before sinking huge fingers into my hair. Tingles exploded along my scalp, and I shivered violently.

What the fuck is happening right now?

It wasn't hurting me, or trying to eat me.

It was...

Petting me?

It was making a sound, and I realized with a start that it was *speaking.* I had no idea what it was saying, but the sound repeated over and over in a pattern that could only be words, at least to my human ears.

"*Aerra bai. Aerra bai.*"

"Let me go!"

It was probably stupid trying to speak to it in English. Even if it could speak, that didn't mean it would understand. But even so, I did it again, and again, and then said the same thing in Finnish. *Let me go. Let me go. Let me go.* Maybe if I said it enough, forcing the words out of my terror-constricted throat, it really would let go.

It did not let go. But it did stop saying *aerra bai*, quieting, as if listening. It grew more still, too. I didn't realize how much that thing had been shaking until it stopped.

I still shook. My whole body trembled in its grip. The muscles along my back tensed and tightened against the solid strength of its massive chest and abdomen. I spasmed violently when the monster's snout moved down and brushed my cheek. Its breath grazed my neck, a heated fan that made goosebumps rise and pucker. The sweat from my sprint grew cold, and my clammy body shivered even harder.

My entire spine turned to ice when I heard the ship lift off.

"Let me go!" I screamed, my urge to fight renewed. I could not be left here. Not alone, not like this.

Whether it was a response to my sudden spasming, or a response to the new sound of the ship in the air, I couldn't be sure. Either way, the monster tensed, standing and hauling me right up along with it. It was so huge that, simply by holding me one-armed against its chest, my feet dangled and kicked a metre off the ground. I gripped its forearm, both marvelling and cringing at the metal-hard strength beneath those scales. Golden light glowed beneath and between the scales, spilling over my skin as I scratched and squeezed. That light was beautiful. And it was *warm*. Warm on my fingers when the night-drenched air was turning cold all around me.

The only warning I had for what came next was a leathery snapping sound behind me. But I didn't know until we were in the air that it was the sound of wings unfurling.

A scream tore from my lungs as we lurched into sudden upward motion. Both the alien's arms were around me now, holding me against its chest as we arrowed into the sky. We were going so fucking fast. Faster than the ship, which was now below us even as it ascended.

I wondered if they had me up on the viewscreen, or on some scanner in there. No doubt they knew what had become of me.

No doubt there was nothing they could do.

They could try to shoot us down, I guess.

Kill the monster and me all at once.

But that seemed less and less likely with every ferocious beat of the creature's wings. We carved through the night like a hurled knife.

Until suddenly, we stopped.

The alien replaced one of its arms around me with its tail, holding me firmly while it raised its newly free hand. Directly above us, the stars dimmed as if being viewed through thicker and thicker ice. And then I couldn't see the stars at all.

It's happening again.

The sky was blackening, hardening. Turning to stone once more, right before my eyes. And there wasn't a fucking thing I could do about it. Nowhere to run, nowhere to hide. If I made one wrong move, one single slip, I'd be hurtling down towards the ground faster than I could say *hyvästi*.

When the sky ahead was dense and coal-coloured crystal, the monster raised his gold and emerald hammer of a fist and smashed it. I flinched at the colossal crack of sound, then tried to quell the way my stomach flip-flopped in response to my movement that high in the air.

Just like before, a huge crack had opened in the stone. But this time, nothing came through it. Never mind flip-flopping – my stomach felt like it dropped out of my body entirely when I realized what was about to happen. That we were going to go *in*.

"No! Stop!" I sobbed, voice cracking as the monster beat its potent wings.

But it didn't stop.

It plunged into the abyss beyond that crack and it dragged me right along with it.

CHAPTER FIVE
Skallagrim

I barely knew what I was doing as I cracked open the sky. The words only came to me as I flew into the crack. *Sky door*.

I'd opened a door. I felt I'd done it many times before. The motions of the act were as natural as breathing. I did not know where the door would lead me. I had no name of any other world to call upon. I had nothing but my little star in my arms and the image of the river in my head. So I focused on that. On the river plunging and swirling and calling to me.

And it was like I conjured that river. Shaped it out of nothing but my own thoughts. Because when we emerged from the sky door, there the cursed thing was. Curving and serpentine below, blue and bronze under the setting sun of another world.

How I knew the sun was setting and not rising, I could not be sure. I just *knew*. Like I'd watched it disappear below that horizon, a thousand—no—a hundred thousand times before.

I hovered for a long moment, wings beating. I held fast to the little star and studied the river and the landscape that felt so foreign and so familiar and so out of reach even though I knew I could fly down now and touch it. Touch the water, the soil, the pebbles. The reeds and rushes whose tufts I could practically feel brushing my scales, the sensation something I was sure I remembered rather than imagined.

The river below us was calm. Its twin in my head roiled and raged, banging with watery fists, shouting the same thing over and over again. *You have been here before.*

I couldn't stay up in the air forever. Soon, I'd have to descend to this strange memory-scape. But something held me back, and it took me a long moment to realize that it was fear. Fear that I could descend, smell the land

and swim in the water, and that it would not make a lick of difference. That I could be in this world and know it without knowing it. Remember it without really remembering anything at all.

But, even though I could not recall my own name, I knew I was not the sort of stone sky god who held himself back in fear for long.

Stone sky god?

I could not spend much time chewing on that phrase, because the little star in my arms was moving. Shuddering and stretching and digging blunt nails into the scales of my forearms. I stared at its fingers against my arms. Slender and pale and tiny and soft. Its whole body was soft. Soft skin, soft hair, soft flesh over its bones. Soft little creature, so strange and so unlike myself.

"We're here, little star."

Where is here?

It did not matter. It did not matter because I'd caught this star and now, even though the sun had dipped and shadows opened their wings, there was no true darkness. For the first time in so long, too long, night was bright and clear with open-throated beauty. The reeds rustled, tufts and stalks shivering like the star in my arms.

I angled my wings and descended. And when I landed on the banks of the wide river, it was just as disconcerting and nostalgic as I'd imagined it would be. Because landing here felt like homecoming when I didn't even know what home was anymore.

Home...

I tried to assign an image to the word. But the only image in my frazzled brain was the one right in front of me. The face of the little star I'd just set down on tiny feet.

I was still holding it, my hands curled around the creature's narrow shoulders. I was not ready to let go of it. Not yet. Maybe not ever. Not when letting go meant darkness seeping back in. Not when it meant losing everything.

I needed this tiny, shivering thing with its white and grey eyes and its little nose and flat pink mouth. It was the answer to a question I did not yet have words enough to remember. The answer to something important.

"I do not know who you are, little star," I said slowly. "And I do not know who I am." The little star's eyes got wider and wider as I spoke, like it could not fathom a creature such as me capable of complex speech. I could barely fathom it myself.

The words felt old and new, difficult and true as I spoke them.

"All I know is that I cannot let you go."

For what it was worth, the little star did not try to go. It merely stood, trembling and staring, its liquid eyes tracking all over my face. Its gaze settled on one side of my face, above my snout, in a place I felt I should have been able to see out of. I released one of my hands from its shoulders, pressing my fingertips into a mangled void. There was a slight twinge of pain, like a wound not quite healed.

I had another eye. Did I lose it?

When? And how?

I let my hand fall from my face in consternation. I'd been so awe-struck, so relieved, at the little bit of light this star had brought back. But already my lack of understanding and memory began to gnaw at me.

I had the nostalgia of this river. The little star. One remaining eye.

And I felt as if I had nothing at all.

"Come with me."

There was little point in me actually saying the words. The creature in my grip could not have fought me if it tried. It was too small, too weak. It stumbled and cried out as I fastened my right hand around the back of its neck and led it forward towards the water. The water – the water ahead and in my head – had something for me. A key for the blackened box of my mind. If I just got in there, washed myself in it, submerged myself, maybe something would come back to me.

I was not willing to let go of the little star even for a moment, though.

So it had to come too.

The swaying reeds and rushes were even taller than the creature I marched before me. The puffed, fluffy tips of the plants grazed my scales and the bottom of my snout, a tickle so familiar that it practically itched.

The little star did try to fight me in the end. When we reached the sandy bank of the river and water sloshed over its feet, it yelped and careened backwards against me. I held it in place, then with a soft grunt, tossed it up over my shoulder. I didn't have the focus to fight with the creature. I needed to get into the water, breathe, and remember.

I also needed to maintain constant physical contact with the little star. So this would have to do.

"I just need to get in the water. Stop struggling," I murmured, wading forward as the little star bucked and wriggled. Its knees crashed against my chest, its hips bucking wildly at my shoulder. I clamped one arm across the backs of the creature's thighs, then fastened my other hand across its backside, holding it in place as I waded hip-deep into the water.

I stopped when the water reached my waist, staring down the length of the wide river, watching the way the sun disappeared and turned the surface to something silken and hushed. I felt myself frowning, the muscles in my face wracked with tension in response to the answers that I was sure were right there. *Right there* and just out of reach. This water meant something. The corresponding river raged inside my head, throwing images and words upwards, like the bones of lost ships hurled up to the storming surface.

For a fraction of a second, the river in front of me and inside of me converged.

The sun warms the Bohnebregg river as I wade in up to my waist. I turn back to see someone – a male – in the water with me. Behind him stands the palace on the banks.

"But you aren't even looking," the man says. His hair is bone-white, his eyes burning like pale blue fire. His wings, black where mine are green, rustle behind him, lit up by both the drenching sun and the bright blue points of his starmap.

"You aren't looking for yours either," I toss back at him easily. It's a conversation we've had countless times before. He's always been far more reserved and risk-averse than I have.

"I am younger than you," he counters. "I have more time."

I grin and thwack the water with my tail, sending a small tsunami crashing towards him. He does not even flinch as the glittering water explodes on his stone-coloured skin.

"Hard to believe you're the younger one. You sound like some wizened old crone," I scoff. He's always been this way. A serious, stoic worrier. I slosh water

at him again, more gently this time, trying to get him to ease up, to see that there is more time. There will always be more time.

But his gaze only narrows, his wings twitching with tension.

"You know what will happen," he says gravely. "You know what will happen if you do not find-"

He vanished.

So did the sun. And the palace.

I whirled, searching for him, but he was gone.

I knew him. *I knew him.*

What his name was, or who he was to me, I could not say. But I felt I knew him nearly as well as myself. That he was someone important. The place where my left eye used to be ached as I tried to keep the image of him fastened in my mind. My chest heaved, my breath catching in my throat. I clung to the only thing I could, the only anchor I had in this river – the *Bohnebregg river*. My little star.

I clutched at its legs, feeling like if I let go, I would completely cease to exist.

CHAPTER SIX
Suvi

I'd long given up on fighting the alien monster's hold on me. It was too big, too strong, and wasting my energy was pointless. Instead, as it dragged me into the river and held me on its shoulder, staring intently into the distance, I stilled. I carefully placed my palms flat against the muscled expanse between the creature's wings, lifting my head and staring through the curtain of my hair to get my bearings.

This landscape was nothing like where we'd just been. There was no sign of the caves or the valley we'd come from. No sign of the ship, either. The sandy soil was a golden beige instead of blue. And all the *water*. We'd relied completely on our ship's water supplies because there'd barely been any on the surface of the cave planet, let alone massive rivers like this. We knew from surveys and scans that the entire cave planet had been like that – mostly dry, with the only life forms being fungi and forms of bacteria. I gasped when, straight ahead, some sort of water fowl took off from a near-by bank, wings unfolding in a glittering array.

This isn't the same planet.

I gulped when that instinctive realization hit me. My rational mind tried to fight against it. I hadn't made it to the ship, so how the hell could I have ended up on another world entirely? I gritted my teeth, forcing myself to relive the moment when the winged alien had cracked the sky like the shell of an egg and pulled me through it. It hadn't felt like much of anything at all. It had been like stepping through a door.

But somehow, on the other side, we'd ended up in another sky.

And now, we were standing in a freezing fucking river.

Luckily the thing holding me was so tall that neither my feet at his front nor my head at his back were in the water. But even so, my boots and the cuffs of my pants were soaked from when the alien had first marched me into the water. And it was *cold*. I shivered, curling my hands into fists against the scales of the alien's back as I continued to crane my neck this way and that. Why it had carried me into this water only to hold me and stand there and stare at nothing, I had no fucking idea. For the moment, it didn't seem keen on hurting me, at least. *I'll have to get away from it the first chance that I have.*

But then what? My heart sank. I didn't recognize anything around me. For the briefest flicker of a moment, I thought we might have been on Earth. But that water bird was massive, with four spindly legs, unlike anything I'd ever seen or heard of on Earth. And the reeds and rushes were strange, too. They had fluffy tufts, reminiscent of something from Earth. But in those tufts at the top were hard, gleaming threads of what almost looked like metal. Like copper had been spun alongside something as soft as cotton.

We were not on Earth.

Maybe I was dreaming.

Maybe I was dead.

No.

My resolve hardened. There was no point in giving up and pretending this all wasn't real. I had to function under the assumption that my senses were feeding me accurate information. I had to assume that this was actually happening, no matter how little sense it all made.

And I had to survive it.

Almost as if reacting to my inner thoughts, the alien suddenly tensed and whirled. Its breath came quick and ragged, and its head swung back and forth as if looking for something. Its hold tightened on me, and I held my breath, terrified it would crush me with the strength of its hands or drop me in the freezing river.

It did neither. It remained still and breathing harshly for a long moment before trudging back onto the riverbank. My hair swung with its movements. Blood pounded in my head as I shivered again, more violently this time.

I didn't think the air was that cold, but the water had been, and the iciness clinging to my boots and legs was sapping the heat out of the rest of my body. When the alien had suddenly started and whirled, more water had splashed up the backs of my legs. Only my tank top and bra had come away from the river unscathed, but they were damp with cooled sweat from my earlier run.

Heat radiated off of the alien's body, but I tried to ignore it. I rejected the instinct to burrow against its back and started twisting in its grip once more. Surprisingly, its huge fingers settled around my waist and it set me on my feet. Between what felt like an entire body's worth of blood dumping out of my head, and the frantic, freezing, locking up of my muscles, I didn't stay on my feet for long. My knees buckled.

I never hit the ground.

The alien's claws shot out, grasping the front of my tank top. But the fabric was too thin, and its claws too sharp. With a horrifying sound, the garment tore as the weight of my body pulled backwards against it. The alien's wings curved forward, curling around both of us, creating a strange sort of hammock of flesh that I fell into with an *oof*. The alien cradled me – it seemed such a strange word to use for a creature so huge and brutal, but cradling truly is what it did – before it slowly lowered to its knees, adjusted the position of its wings, then deposited me on the ground.

It stared down at the ruined tank top in its claws then looked back at me. Instinctively I slapped my arms over myself. I still had my bra at least, but that didn't feel like nearly enough under the one-eyed gaze of the hulking creature before me. There was an exacting sort of intensity in the single golden orb of its eye. A hard and burning question in the gaze. Like it was looking at me, into me, and wordlessly asking who I was and what I was doing there even though it had been the one who'd brought me in the first place.

"What do you want?" I rasped through chattering teeth. The creature towered over me, unblinking as it stared. Its wings were still mostly around me, like a verdant canopy, blocking out the river and stars and sky until all that was left was that hard, alien body and strange, dragonish face. Something flickered in the eye, in the expression, and it opened its fanged mouth, once again stringing together sounds that really did seem like words. Whatever it said was ended, once again, with the uttering of *aerra bai.*

It had to be language. Especially considering the repetition of *aerra bai*. Whatever its motives, it seemed to be an intelligent creature.

Intelligent and powerful beyond belief.

It didn't say anything else, instead once again looking down at my shredded tank top. Its scaly brows lowered, and it turned its attention to my torso. I shrieked when, in an instant, both my wrists had been grasped in its one huge hand and torn upwards and away from my body. The alien held my hands over my head with one hand and, after dropping my tank top, used the other to poke and prod along my neck and shoulders, as if testing the solidity of my skin.

Fear pooled in my belly, and I stopped breathing when it brushed a knuckled between my breasts and down to my abdomen. It said something then, some sort of a deep grunt that I had no way of interpreting, before letting my hands go. I hugged myself and tried to scoot backwards and away from it, only for my back to hit the wings that still cocooned me.

"What do you want?" I asked again, this time in a whisper. It cocked its head. As it did so, its long black hair shifted, framing its strange, snouted face and tumbling in tangles over its broad shoulders and hardened pectoral muscles.

Once again, it spoke, and once again I had no idea what the fuck it was saying.

More and more, though, it felt wrong to think of the alien as an *it*. It had language. It walked upright like a human. And there was a deep, wild, inescapable intelligence in the harsh probing of its single golden eye. I sucked in a shaky breath, my gaze trailing over the brutal angles of its snout and thick neck, down over the scale-covered pectorals and rippling abdominal muscles. The alien wore no clothing, and there were no discernable genitalia between its bulging thighs. Maybe it was stupid to try to categorize this creature. Maybe it was foolish of my frantic human brain to search for a scrap of familiar context where none existed. But even so, I couldn't help the sudden and instinctive conclusion resounding through my body like a gong.

Male.

He felt distinctly male to me. And until proven otherwise, that's how I'd think of him.

It was so, so warm in the folded shelter of his wings. Heat poured off of him, sweet and disarming, like dark syrup. It rolled over my shivering form as I hugged myself tightly. When he didn't say or do anything else, I let my eyes drift over the glowing points of light twinkling all over his body, lighting up his scales like golden constellations. His scales were gem-like and so reflective that they multiplied the effect of the lights in the growing darkness, turning his body, from neck to tail, into a multi-faceted wonder.

If he hadn't been so terrifying, I would have almost called him beautiful.

He had none of the lights on his face, but there was a distinct and solitary glow in his remaining eye—a fiery amber that got brighter, nearly white in the middle, instead of darker like a human's pupil. I gaped when I realized that he had a thick fringe of sooty eyelashes above that eye, dusted gold with light from below. The lashes and the long black hair felt so non-reptilian, so at odds with his scales and wings and tail. Even the scales along his brow bone were darker, simulating eyebrows.

The sum of all the parts was... utter confusion.

I had no idea what to make of him or what to do about him besides the instinct bleating at the back of my head to get as far away from him as possible. But that instinct was at odds with my body's need to remain coiled inside the walls of heat his wings and chest had created. I tried to reconcile the two panicking messages – the messages telling me to stay warm and to run – and soothed myself, telling myself that I would figure out how to get away the moment fleeing from him was safer than being warmed by him.

I almost wanted to laugh bitterly. I wanted to punch him, or maybe the ground. Wanted to rage against the fact that this was what my life had become – that I'd been reduced to stacking my physical needs upon each other in order of importance, hoping the entire tower didn't crumble. That I'd become so calculating in regards to my own survival, prioritizing one bodily instinct over another. Staying warm came out on top. For the moment. But that would shift the second I needed it to.

The Scilla madeirensis can grow among hostile volcanic rock. The Sideroxylon spinosum has roots that go deep enough to find water in the driest climates, producing rich argan oil. The Cyrtanthus ventricosus only flowers after wildfire, bright blooms against ash, earning its name the fire lily...

The survival instinct was everywhere. Even in plants.

It was in me, too.

And wasn't that what Elvi had told me at the end? When she'd been in the hospital? She'd made me promise not to miss her. She'd made me promise to be brave and to live. Because that was the most important thing.

I'd thought that warmth, for the moment, was taken care of. But I'd presumed wrong, because before long, the alien was withdrawing his wings from around me. My bum settled on the ground, and I tensed and bit back a hiss at the sudden inward rush of cool air on my bare skin. I almost wanted to beg him to put his wings back how they'd been, even though I knew he wouldn't understand.

Maybe I can get away and make a fire...

Find a safer way to stay warm.

The alien suddenly straightened, staring down the river. Night was fully upon us now, stars creating a glittering canopy behind what appeared to be two moons, one much larger than the other. His attention, for the moment, was not on me. Mouth going dry, I began to tentatively scoot backwards and away from him.

But the soft rustle of my backside against the sand made his golden eye snap to me like a slingshot finding its target. A huge, scaly hand clasped my upper arm, dragging me to my feet. It didn't hurt, but the shock of the movement made me gasp. He eyed me sharply, scaly brow lowering as he peered downwards.

"What?" I said, trying to keep my voice from shaking. I still had one free arm, and I used it to hug myself, slapping my forearm against my breasts. The alien wasn't wearing any clothing at all, so maybe it was silly of me to adhere to any human forms of modesty, but it made me feel the tiniest bit better to be somewhat covered under his strange scrutiny.

He spoke again, then, and it made my head spin to have an alien trying to engage in conversation with me. He was trying to tell me something, to communicate. That had to be a good sign, right?

But then again, even psychopaths were capable of speech. Serial killers could talk, too. It didn't actually mean much, and that scared me.

Once again, he ended the string of unfamiliar sounds with *aerra bai*. I wondered if *aerra bai* was a phrase used in most sentences of his language. Maybe some kind of honorific, or a verbal form of punctuation.

"*Aerra bai,*" I repeated, entirely without thinking.

His nostrils flared, his eye focusing even more intently on my face. Clearly, I'd shocked him by engaging in his own language, but I wasn't sure I could have even helped myself from doing it. I was so desperate to understand this situation, to understand him. My human brain couldn't stop itself from poking and prodding at every edge of the problem, from sinking into the familiar back and forth of language even if that language was entirely foreign.

"Aerra bai," he repeated back at me, his voice a deep rumble. He raised his free hand, bringing his fingers and thumb close together, like he was pinching something tiny and invisible between his long claws. "Aerra." Then, he gestured upward with that hand. "Bai."

"Pinch... sky?" I said, frowning. Was he talking about what he'd done in the sky? How he'd brought us here?

It occurred to me how absurd this was. That I was so focused on figuring out some random alien phrase instead of thinking ahead to what came next. But the puzzle of figuring out this phrase felt somehow safer. Trying to understand a new word was more comfortable than deciding when I'd try to run from him and how I'd survive when I did.

And it definitely felt safer than thinking about how I would probably never see another human again.

Don't go there. Don't fall apart.

"Aerra bai," he said again. He was an alien, and I was entirely unfamiliar with his facial expressions, but there didn't seem to be any malice or aggression in his tone of voice. He wasn't snarling it, or growling it. The violence in him, the pure chaos of his power that I'd witnessed on the other planet, seemed to have been gentled somehow. Like he'd eased back from the edge of something terrible. I hoped it wasn't some tactic to get me to drop my guard. But then again, someone as strong as him wouldn't need to manipulate me into trusting him before he ate me. He could have killed me at any point.

But he hadn't.

He repeated the phrase again, and when I showed no new or obvious sign of understanding him, he suddenly crouched. He didn't let go of my arm, instead letting his hand glide downwards, clasping my hand firmly in his own. He grasped a fist-sized rock from the riverbed and held it up.

"Loirra pak." He tossed it down, then grabbed a much smaller rock, a pebble. "Aerra pak."

Big rock... Small rock...

I remembered the pinching motion of his fingers from before.

"Aerra! It's small, right? Little?" I pointed to the pebble, then used my index finger and thumb to indicate "a little" in a similar gesture to his.

He stared up at me, then did something that nearly knocked me flat on my curvy human ass.

He *smiled.*

Despite the foreign features of his face, there was no mistaking the expression. His snout pulled, revealing his fangs in a way that wasn't frightening or aggressive. His golden eye glittered. I was too dazed to smile back, and he turned his attention back down to the ground. His smile vanished, and he made a thoughtful grumbling sort of sound, rubbing at the underside of his snout with his free hand. His other hand was still wrapped possessively around mine, and I shifted back and forth on my wet feet, feeling antsy at the odd intimacy of it.

The alien stopped rubbing his snout and lowered his claws to the damp sand. Using a single claw, he started dragging deep lines through the sand. I recognized the two circles he drew but couldn't figure out where I'd seen them until he gestured at the sky again.

Moons. He's drawing the moons.

Around the two moons in the sand, he jabbed his claw downward over and over again, making a dozen or so little dots that I realized were stars. He pointed to one of the tiny divots he'd created.

"Bai."

"Aerra bai... Little star?" I made the pinching "little bit" gesture with my finger and thumb again, then pointed at his sandy stars before pointing up at the sky.

He stood with such sudden force that I would have stumbled backwards if not for the firm hold on my hand.

"Aerra bai," he said once more, and it felt like confirmation.

This time, I really did smile. I couldn't help it. It was so small, so *aerra*, but it was something. The tiniest little win. It made me ever so slightly less afraid.

He'd said something to me, and I'd understood him.

Now I just needed to figure out why he kept mentioning a little star. Was that important for some reason? Something about space travel? He kept repeating it, so it had to have some meaning to him.

I realized I was still smiling. The alien's expression had softened somehow. It should have been impossible in a face as brutal and alien and angular as his, but there was no other way to describe it. The intense brightness of his eye felt slightly darker, a crackling golden warmth instead of blazing flame.

"Aerra bai," he breathed, squeezing my hand slightly. His other hand came up to caress the side of my face, and my smile froze. "Aerra bai..." He sank his claws into my hair. "Aerra bai..."

He was looking at me and only me as he said it. He wasn't trying to communicate something about an actual star in the sky. It wasn't a message.

It was a *name*.

He was calling *me* little star.

The elation I'd felt at understanding him, the small victory of it, imploded around me. I grew colder, my jaw tightening with anxiety. There was no good or sane reason for this alien to be giving me some weird pet name.

There was no reason he should have taken me in the first place.

He wanted something from me.

Something that I promised myself he'd never fucking get.

CHAPTER SEVEN
Skallagrim

My little star looked unhappy. Its pink mouth thinned and twisted, and the openness that had been there a moment ago was gone. A sense of deep frustration throbbed in my river-smashed head. The frustration of not knowing where I was, who I was, or how to communicate with the one being in the universe who seemed to be able to ground me. I did not know what the little star was meant to be to me. Only that I could not risk losing it now.

"Whatever you are," I rasped, sliding my claws out of its hair, "you are important to me. You will remain with me until I can figure out why." *And until I can figure out how to remain in the light without you.*

I realized that I had essentially trapped this creature. It was not a mere animal to be trained or taken. Like me, it was conscious and competent, a sentient being. I had no name for its kind, but it was intelligent and emotive and starkly beautiful with its wide, wet eyes and moon-river hair. I was doing something terrible, maybe even unforgivable, by capturing it like this. Dimly, I remembered seeing a few others like it before we'd come here.

I took it from its people.

"There was no choice," I said forcefully, as if trying to convince both myself and the little star of that fact. The sudden vehemence of my tone sent a wave of tension through the creature, and it flinched in my hold. The movement made the covered swells of its chest bounce, its cushiony abdomen sucking inward with a tight breath.

Everything about this creature seemed so starkly in opposition to myself. Small where I was large. Soft where I was hard. Delicate. Silken. Sweet.

There was a word for it. An important one.

I almost seized it before it was lost to the river. I snapped my jaws in irritation, and the little star gasped again and tried to shrink away from me.

I was scaring it.

"I don't mean to," I growled. "I am not trying to frighten you."

I breathed out slowly and jerked my head away from the little star. I turned my attention to the river's edge, studying it. The moonlight was bright tonight and I caught sight of my own reflection in the still water.

I nearly reared back with the shock of it.

I'd forgotten what I looked like, but even so I knew I did not look like myself.

I forced myself to confront the creature staring back at me. One blazing, maddened eye glowed like an ember in the water. The place where the other eye should have been, where I was convinced I'd had another eye before, was a mangled, dug-out mess of tissue. My hair was a harsh tangle about my shoulders, and somehow I knew that was all wrong, that I did not usually wear my hair that way.

A braid. It should have been fragrant with oil, shining and combed and arranged into a long braid, then tied at the end with a sleek metal clasp.

That was how a Bohnebregg male of my standing wore his hair.

A Bohnebregg male...

I tried to hold onto that thought, to follow it through the murk to some sort of conclusion, to connect it to other information about my life or this river or this world. But it slipped away. With a foul, frustrated grunt, I thwapped my tail against the water's surface, shattering the image of a male I only halfway recognized and entirely rejected.

The little star said nothing, but I registered a tension in its hand as it tried to pull away from me. With a growl, I turned to face it once more.

"I will not hurt you," I ground out. "I know I have done wrong by you. But I cannot..." My throat ached, and my voice sharpened in response to the feeling. "I cannot go back to the darkness without you."

The little star stared back at me, mute and guarded. I forced myself to loosen my hold on its hand. Just slightly. Enough to indicate I did not wish to squeeze too hard.

But not enough to let it go.

"I will take care of you," I rasped. "I will protect you, honour you, put your life above my own. You are my salvation and I will let no harm befall you. But make no mistake..."

A deep, primitive instinct spread dark wings inside me. An instinct that whispered, *take, treasure, hoard.* My spine prickled and my blood heated.

"Make no mistake. *I will keep you.* No matter the cost."

CHAPTER EIGHT
Suvi

The alien led me along the riverbank for what felt like hours, never letting go of my hand. It seemed as if he was looking for something but he didn't even know what it was. Sometimes he would stop and look around, eye bright, as if on the verge of realizing something, only to jerk his head forward again with a deep growl and continue plodding onward. The only sounds were the gentle sloshing of the water, buzzing insects among the rushes, our footsteps, and the heavy scrape of his tail through the sand. I kept pace with him. Walking held the chill mostly at bay and gave me something to focus on. One foot in front of the other. Over and over again.

But I couldn't keep it up forever. I slowed and started stumbling more often, then limping, pain radiating from where blisters had formed on my heels in my wet boots. The alien noticed and scooped me up into his arms without a word. I should have fought him. I should have wriggled and scratched him and screamed.

But I didn't.

Adrenaline had abandoned me, left me limp and empty. I was cold and so, so tired. Everything hurt. And for a moment, it was easier to be carried by a monster than to continue being in pain.

But even the alien seemed to be faltering. Tension crept into his snout, and he walked more slowly than before. I thought of how he'd crashed into the surface of the other planet, how he'd created some sort of inter-planetary portal out of thin air, and wondered how much energy such feats would take. It all seemed to be catching up to him, his steps getting heavier and heavier. My heart sped up, my brain instantly beginning to examine all the ways I might use his new exhaustion to my advantage. Maybe he'd sleep, and I could creep away and... and...

And what?

I had no idea where I was or how to survive here. And it was unlikely I'd be able to hide from him for long. He'd pursue me, and even in his current state there was no doubt he'd be far faster than I was. Despair pressed down on me like fog, and I grew even more listless against his chest. I let myself sink into the warmth radiating off of him because there was nothing else to do. And maybe it wasn't too bad, maybe it wasn't too dangerous to relieve myself of a little bit of suffering. Just for now.

I must have dozed off for a while, because when I stirred and blinked my eyes, the landscape had changed. The river's shore had grown rockier, and instead of just reeds there were what looked like massive trees clustered a little ways back from the rocks and boulders. The moons appeared to be in a different position, too, assuming that we hadn't vastly changed course. I gulped and shifted, earning me a sharp downward look from the alien. I froze under his stare.

It scared me that I'd gotten so comfortable that I'd actually fallen asleep like this. Who knew where he was taking me?

Something told me even he didn't know.

He paused, turning his head this way and that, sniffing the air but never quite seeming satisfied. Eventually, he turned towards the trees, taking me with him.

The trees were unlike anything I'd ever seen before. They had huge, tall, tapered trunks. But instead of branches or leaves or needles, at the top were giant white puffs streaked with what appeared to be metal, just like the river reeds I'd seen before but on a massive scale. My botanist brain was too tired to try to figure out how the trees might have worked. The fluffy tops of the trees, silver-white and gleaming with hard threads under the stars, gave the grove an oddly dream-like appearance, like I was being carried into the hushed illustration of a fairytale story book.

The alien carried me into the centre of the grove. Shadows pooled here, deep wells of darkness between streaks of light. He put me down, and it was pretty gentle, which I hoped was a good sign for whatever was coming next.

"Now what?" I muttered, crossing my arms over my chest and shivering. Even though it was a relief to be out of his arms, I was already missing his heat. At least, my body was. My wet feet ached, blisters twinging beneath my socks. I rubbed my hands up and down my upper arms, hating the fact that I didn't even have a shirt anymore.

The alien didn't answer me. He peered around the grove with what seemed to be a vaguely thoughtful expression, then went over to a tree. He dug his claws into the side of the tree, slicing horizontally and then pulling downwards, tearing away a long, wide strip of what appeared to be a flexible sort of bark. I watched him in silence, lips pursed, as he did it again and again. Once he had several sheets of the stuff, he got to work arranging them together against the side of a boulder. He drilled holes in them with his claws, using long, durable blades of grass to bind the sheets together into a protective sort of lean-to.

Then he stood back and looked at me, something expectant gleaming in his eye.

"I suppose you want me to get in there," I tossed over, frowning at the lean-to.

He didn't reply. He simply cocked his head, his one eye locking even more tightly on my face. As if he could understand what I was saying if he only listened hard enough.

I shook my head, reminding myself not to get too comfortable with the fact that he seemed to be mostly conscientious. If he were really someone to be trusted, he wouldn't have abducted me in the first place.

I'd already been taken from everything I knew once, when Earth forces kidnapped me and forced me into this mission.

And he'd gone ahead and done it again. Only it was even worse now, because now I truly had nobody left. At least on the ship, I'd had friends. Other women in the same situation as me.

Here... I had no one.

No one but my alien abductor, staring at me with a single golden eye and waiting for me to crawl like a dog into the shelter he'd built.

Do I have any choice?

I could refuse, I supposed. I could scream at him, make him take me back to the planet where he'd found me. But even in the thickness of my grief and denial, I had to acknowledge that the ship had been lifting off. The other humans had likely moved on to another world by now, and there would be no way to get back to them.

And even if there was a chance, I just didn't have the fucking energy. I'd never been a fighter. I'd always been happier talking soothingly to plants than confronting other people. Elvi had been the strong one, the one who'd raised me even though she'd been only eight years older than me. When I'd been bullied, she was always the one who'd stood up for me. She was the one who put me into hockey to try to build some confidence in myself. *Paska*, even when she was dying, *she* was the one comforting *me*.

But she was gone now. And so were the last friends I'd had in this universe.

I choked back a sob and crawled into the shelter.

In the darkness, I huddled into a ball, too worn-out to even take off my soaked boots. I lay on my side, staring at the black underside of the wood wall of the lean-to. It was so dark that I couldn't even tell if things got blurred when tears filled my eyes. I blinked the moisture away angrily, hugging my knees to my chest.

Exhaustion became so visceral and thick that it was like a force outside my own body. It pressed down on me from above. It seemed like I would sink right into the ground with the bitter weight of it. My whole body hurt with cold.

A sudden sound made me stiffen, jaw clenching and eyes going as wide as possible in the darkness. A scraping sound, then a grunt, then the unmistakable drop of a hefty alien body behind me told me the creature had entered the tent. As he got all the way in, the golden lights scattered across his body cast a warm glow over the dark interior.

No way... he plans to sleep in here with me?!

His scales were as hard as metal. He looked more animal than man. Other than some signs of physical weariness, he didn't seem bothered by the cold at all.

I assumed he'd stay outside...

So what the hell was he doing in here?

I tried to remain frozen, but a vicious tremor wracked my muscles, forcing a sharp gasp from my lungs. The alien stilled at my back before muttering a sentence I didn't understand. A moment later, something thick and leathery and so warm I wanted to weep covered my entire curled-up body.

He'd draped one of his wings over me like a blanket, and heat was already seeping into my shuddering bones.

I tried to ignore the physical comfort of his proximity. Because he was the one who'd done this to me. The one who'd brought me here, dragged me into the river, and ruined my shirt. He was why I was cold in the first fucking place.

He was the reason for it all...

And he was the only remedy.

Other than a few lingering shivers, I didn't move. I didn't speak as he got into a more comfortable position behind me, his broad chest cupping my back, his thighs drawn up under my feet. Beneath his wing, he tossed his arm over my body, his forearm and wrist plastered against my own crossed arms, his fingers coming up to rest at the base of my throat.

Why was he holding me like this? Why had he brought me here when he seemed to have absolutely no idea where to go now or what to do with me?

"What do you want?" I whispered.

He gave me no answer.

And neither did my dreams when they came creeping in.

CHAPTER NINE
Suvi

I woke up slowly and then all at once.

At first, I relished the feeling of half-sleep. I was so warm. The blankets on our bunks on the ship were pretty sad, thin affairs. I wasn't usually this cozy when I came to. It was nice. I didn't want to wake all the way back up.

But when the blanket moved of its own accord, I did. My eyes flew open, not seeing anything but a wall of gold-spangled green. The alien's wing was still tossed over me in a warming embrace. So was his arm and even his tail. It almost felt protective.

Or possessive.

Probably the latter, considering he'd taken me from my people and seemed to have no intention of letting me out of his sight.

Is he asleep?

There was no movement behind me apart from the even rise and fall of his chest against my back. I turned slowly and carefully, heart like a hummingbird in my throat, until I was facing him.

He appeared to still be asleep. I'd been right last night – he really had exhausted himself with everything that had happened yesterday, and maybe whatever else he'd been doing before that. I paused to study him. It was clearly morning outside, as sunlight was spilling through cracks into the lean-to. It dimmed the bright effect of his lights, but not by much. Before I could stop myself, I reached forward and tentatively brushed one of the glowing spots on his chest. I breathed in sharply, feeling what could only be described as energy buzzing in that spot. The light was warmer than his scales, and it almost seemed to vibrate softly under my touch.

I withdrew my hand, feeling almost guilty for touching him, even though he was the one who'd come in here and smooshed himself up against me all night. Thankfully there was still no evidence of male genitalia – nothing seemed to be poking or prodding me from anywhere – and that was an immense relief. I began to wonder how his biology and reproductive system worked before I shut down that line of thinking like dropping a dark curtain on my own brain. I did not need to go there right now. What I needed to do was figure out my next steps.

Do I really risk it – trying to get away from him?

So far, this planet hadn't proved as hostile as I'd feared. I wasn't much of a survivalist, but I could probably figure out how to catch fish in the river. The cottony puffs on the plants could be used to make clothing or bedding. There would be no way to know what food here would kill me, of course, but I wouldn't have a better chance in that department even with the alien, considering I was a completely new and different species.

He hadn't really seemed fazed by how different I was, now that I thought about it. He didn't exactly appear to consider me an alien, not in the way I thought of him being alien, at least. Maybe there were bipedal, human-like animals where he was from. Maybe he thought of me as some sort of pet...

I stared at his sleeping face as these thoughts rolled through me. His thick dark hair was cast back from his face in a way that almost looked elegant, in a wild and undone sort of way. His brow was smoothed in sleep, his thick lashes cast downward on the right side of his face. On the left was the mangled pit of where the other eye had once been. I felt my mouth pulling in a sympathetic grimace because the wound looked like it had healed badly and it had to have caused an immense amount of pain. I shouldn't have felt sorry for him – I knew that. But I did. I'd always been like that. I was the kid who cried over things like flowers getting crushed underfoot.

I wondered who could have been strong enough—or trusted enough—to have gotten close enough to wound him like that. He'd crashed into a planet like an asteroid and clawed his way out of the hole unscathed, right before my eyes. Who could have possibly caused a being like him any damage?

Then I remembered that there were others somewhat like him. Like the being who'd appeared on the first planet, throwing tsunamis of snow against the soldiers like he was tossing bits of paper. I thought about Torrance left behind there, no doubt killed by him, and wanted to break down.

There was still no sign of the alien waking. My bladder throbbed. Cautiously and as quietly as possible, I scooted down his body, wriggling out from the canopy of his wing and the warm weights of his arm and tail. Frankly, I was kind of shocked that none of my moving had woken him. If he always slept this deeply, I might actually have a shot at getting away from him if I tried.

I decided that right now I'd start with something small: getting away from him long enough to pee in private.

I crawled out of the lean-to, then shakily stood. I winced, immediately regretting the fact I hadn't taken off my sodden boots last night. They felt awful and squishy and my feet were clammy and gross. I kicked them off and peeled off the damp socks, placing them all in a sunny patch in the grove of trees. I picked a tree on the other side of the grove, near the edge closest to the river, and went around it before pulling my pants and underwear down and crouching. I breathed out slowly and peed, using that quiet moment to take in my surroundings.

This really was a beautiful place. Everything that had been bronze and black and silver last night was now golden green. Long blades of grass and the stalks of the reeds and rushes near the river were lush and verdant. The rocks at the shore almost looked like slabs of marble, blue and gold streaking and swirling together. The sandy soil was golden brown, and the river ahead shone like a liquid mirror. Buzzing insects and the calls of cawing birds filled the air in a way that felt at once alien and familiar.

After crouching for a while, my legs began to protest. I hadn't thought ahead to what I'd use to wipe and sighed. One of the cottony puffs would probably work, but I'd have to get over there first. After a quick glance around told me nothing appeared to be ready to jump out and swallow me whole, I crouch-waddled out of the grove of trees to a patch of rushes, grabbing the tall green stalk of the nearest one and bending its fluffy tip down to my level. The cottony puff at the top was slightly tapered, shaped like the flame of a candle. I fingered the soft fluff of it, marvelling at the way thin threads of copper-coloured metal seemed to grow right from the plant it-self.

I examined the soft puff thoroughly, gently pulling it apart with my fingers and bending the threads of metal. The last thing I wanted was to dab this between my legs only to find out too late that there was some kind of stinging insect inside. Or to find out that I'd just put the alien version of a Toxicodendron species like poison ivy directly against my pussy.

But as far as my eyes and fingers could tell, the cottony stuff was just as benign as it appeared. I waited another few moments, making sure no irritation cropped up on my hands. I knew that something like a Toxicendron reaction could show up hours or even days after exposure, so I was still taking a bit of a chance, but there didn't seem to be any oil or sap coming off the soft fluff that could cause a problem.

I carefully peeled away the metal bits (because wouldn't jabbing myself with one of those just be lovely?) and quickly dabbed between my legs. My thighs burned, shaking beneath me after remaining crouched for so long. I dropped the puff, steadying my hands on my knees and preparing to stand, when a sudden crashing sound startled me, causing me to fall forward onto my hands and knees. Panicking, I wrenched my head backwards, only to find the alien standing at the edge of the grove behind me, his chest heaving with ragged breaths and his eye fastened to my bare ass.

CHAPTER TEN
Skallagrim

I'd forgotten what it was to sleep. I could not even remember the last time I'd done it. I had no idea how long I'd been in darkness, but in that darkness, I did not rest. At least, not like this. Not the way I rested wrapped around my little star. Clutching that small creature to my chest was a comfort that nearly defied words, and my worn-out body had immediately slipped into a deep, restorative slumber.

But perhaps the slumber was *too* deep. Because I did not feel or hear the little star disappear. I did not know if it had fled, or it was taken. I only knew, as I awoke, that something was very wrong. So wrong it seemed to screw my bones too tight against each other. A sense of terror gripped me. Terror that something had befallen the little star. That it was hurt somewhere, or dying, and that I wouldn't get to it in time.

And then I would be lost in the darkness once again.

I rose with a swallowed roar, sending the side of the lean-to crashing outwards as my wings snapped open. I wanted to run, to fly, to find. To appease the deafening dread with pure might and anger and speed. But I forced myself not to jump into the air. I lifted my snout and breathed in deeply, though rather raggedly, catching the sweet scent of the little star on the air, alongside another new scent that reminded me vaguely of urine. Both fresh.

I followed the trail, sprinting through the grove until I reached its edge and stopped.

There was the little star. It stared back at me from a position on all fours, eyes huge. My own eye was likely just as wide as it settled on the exposed backside of the creature. No tail obscured the sight of its plump, luscious flesh, its backside and thighs a creamy white that made my jaw ache. And nestled between those thighs...

A glistening area of ruffled pink flesh with a slit at the centre, framed with soft golden hair.

A strange tightness entered the area of my throat. And my groin. The river in my head crashed against a rock made of bone and sent droplets of water flying, each one a single word.

Female. Cunt. Wet. Rut. She. Her.

Cocks.

That's what I had. Cocks. Tucked away in my slit, I'd barely remembered them as I'd tried to reorient myself in a world and a body that made so little sense.

I remembered them now.

I tightened the muscles of my slit, ignoring the engorgement happening beneath with a hiss.

The little star, *she*, scrambled into a seated position, yanking up the clothing that had covered her legs and soft little cunt up until this point. We stared at each other, and I marvelled at the fact that even though I had not been touching her for some time, the darkness did not seem to be coming back for me as quickly as it had when she had first run from me in that rocky valley. It was as if being curled around her all night had filled me up in some way, like a rock being warmed by the sun so thoroughly it gave off heat even after nightfall.

I wondered how long I could go without touching her.

I was not willing to test it.

Even now my fingers were twitching to reach for her. My tail snapped back and forth as tension gathered in my spine. I crossed the distance between us in quick strides, bent, and clasped my hands around her shoulders, lifting her to her feet. I realized her feet were uncovered now, and I stared in fascination at the tiny, clawless toes while my hands stroked absentmindedly up and down her plush arms. The tiny, sensitive scales on my fingertips and palms prickled, registering just how deliciously soft she was.

My slit tightened against further swelling.

River help me.

I remembered rutting... someone. Many someones, I was fairly certain. I could recall no faces or names, but my body held the memory of the sensations from before the darkness. The hot, hard slide of my cocks against and inside flesh.

The more I remembered of myself before, the more complicated things became. It had been simpler mere moments ago, before I remembered concepts like *female* and the unmatched pleasure of spilling seed inside a wet, pulsing channel. It had been easier to touch her last night, back when she was simply my sacred salvation. She had almost seemed not entirely real to me, like she'd floated on another plane of existence far above my own. Something spiritual rather than corporeal.

But she was corporeal, alright. She was still sacred, still my salvation, still the star that had found me in the darkness the way no other light could.

But she also had a pretty, ripe cunt and that information was most assuredly *not* helpful. Because now, I had to balance even more against the knife's edge of my sanity. Balance the need to touch her to ground myself with the need to pull away before arousal surged too strongly. My head ached. My whole cursed body ached, my groin most of all.

My touch on her arms had become a caress, and I wrenched my fingers away. Colour bloomed in her cheeks and across her chest. *Mammary tissue. Teats. Breasts.* I remembered that now, too, as my gaze snagged on the supple, heavy swells of her chest.

She could have had a mate somewhere.

She could have had children.

I wondered what sort of male I'd been before. If I'd always been the selfish sort. Because I felt only the smallest twinge of regret at that thought before it was smothered under a jealousy that claimed her as mine above all others. Her mate could come for her and I would slit his belly before he even got close.

I must have indeed been a selfish sort of male, I decided. Because this kind of desire, this possessiveness, this need to keep her no matter whom it hurt, no matter whom I'd have to kill, did not feel unnatural in the slightest. It felt right, and I felt righteous.

I kept my eye on my little star and then walked past her to the water's edge. The sun warmed my scales in a way that felt like home. Without thinking or even realizing I could do it, I lifted my hand and a sheet of water rose with it. I inhaled deeply, stretching into this familiar and near-forgotten power. I did not think I'd done anything but smash things with my tail and my face and my fists in the darkness. I held the sheet of water suspended like a wall of crystal, watching fish swimming through the wall.

Within moments, I'd used my power to draw several fat fish from the suspended water and into my claws. I snapped their necks for a quick death, tossed them on a flat rock near my feet, then released my hold on the water. I did it slowly, carefully, so that the water was re-absorbed into the river with nary a ripple.

I quickly turned to make sure my little star had not gone anywhere. But she seemed frozen in place. One small hand was clapped over her mouth, her eyes gigantic, her pale eyebrows nearly at her hairline. I did not think she looked scared, exactly...

It bothered me immensely that I could not read her expression easily, nor could I ask her with words what she was feeling. It seemed wrong. Like I should have been able to comprehend her instinctively somehow, though I did not speak her language. My ears burned slightly, and I rubbed absentmindedly at my right one, as if by simply rubbing it I'd be able to make my own ear translate whatever words she used. Why did it feel like it had once been that way before? Like it had once been that easy?

Nothing's easy now.

At the very least, I could slice some blasted fish. I crouched, cleaning and cutting the first fish on the rock, preparing raw slices in a way that felt like muscle memory. I could already taste the white flesh even though I could not actively remember eating it before.

"Come. Eat," I grunted up at the little star. Now that I was growing more and more lucid, it felt a bit odd to keep referring to her as that. I wondered what her people called themselves. I wondered if she had a name, but found I had no way to ask.

When she didn't move, I tossed a strip of the raw fish into my maw and swallowed, indicating that it was meant to be food. It tasted exactly the way I'd expected it to, which was both comforting and destabilizing. I jerked my snout towards the other pieces from the first fish as I began to clean and cut the other two.

Slowly, as if against her own will, she edged closer, peering at the sliced fish and watching the quick movements of my claws.

She said something. It sounded like a question. My inability to parse the words made my jaw tick.

"Eat," I said again. I was finished slicing everything now, and I remained crouched and watching her.

She spoke again, and it sounded like the same question as before. But this time, she added hand gestures. She mimed rubbing two objects together, then threw her hands upward like two flying birds. I cocked my head, frowning and not having the faintest clue what she was trying to convey. She blew out a breath between tight lips then tried another gesture. She poked at the air then yanked her hand back, as if burned.

"You want fire?"

She pursed her lips and stared at my mouth as I formed the words. I grunted. We wouldn't get anywhere trying to describe what fire was to each other. Better to show her and confirm that was what she'd asked for.

I strode back to the grove, peeling away several more sections of bark. The bark was very flexible and naturally followed the curve of the shape of the tree trunk, allowing me to slice and then roll the sections into small tubes of wood. I arranged them in a pyramid on a flat rock near the fish. Something at the back of my skull told me I had no ability to summon or control fire the way I could control water. There was someone out there who could do it, I was sure, but if they had a name I did not know it. Instead, I focused on the tubes of wood, holding my outstretched claws above them and using a small amount of power to make them vibrate against each other. Soon, a wisp of smoke floated upwards, curling into the bright sky. Small flames appeared and then grew larger as the tubes of bark caught.

I added more wood and bark, and soon the fire was crackling and strong.

"There. Is that what you wanted?"

She grinned, showing tiny white teeth, and nodded her head vigorously up and down in such a way that seemed to indicate the affirmative. A small rush went through me, a piercing satisfaction that I'd understood her, at least a little. That I'd made her happy in some small way.

She hurried to the river and rinsed her hands thoroughly in the water before returning and grabbing some of the raw fish and placing it on the flat rock directly beside the base of the fire. Within moments the thin strips began to sizzle.

So, she prefers her fish cooked. I can do that.

I ate more of the fish raw, preferring it that way, then brought the rest over to be cooked, flipping the pieces with my claws, not wanting her hands near the flames. Once the first two pieces had developed a cracked, golden crust, I removed them from the heat and let them cool in my claws before handing them over. The little star paused, glancing from my face to my hands, before taking a piece. Her silken fingertips grazed my palm as she did so, and that tiny touch made every muscle in my body wind tight. I watched her closely as she ate, studying the muscles in her delicate jaw, the way her narrow throat constricted as she swallowed. I could see her pulse there, river help me. Her skin was so thin I could literally observe the trilling rhythm of her heartbeat at the sides and the base of her neck.

By the skies, she's breakable. It made me nervous.

She seemed to enjoy the fish at least, so that was something. I knew I was capable of feeding her and injecting at least a little strength into that ridiculously tiny body. After eating several helpings, she started touching her throat then pointing to the river.

"It's water," I confirmed. "You can drink it."

Assuming her kind drank water at all, anyway. I went to the river and used my power to raise a spout of water to my snout, taking a long sip. It was clean and good.

Her mouth twisted, and she moved her head back and forth. She pointed to the river again, then to the fire, speaking rapidly.

"The water will put the fire out," I told her slowly. She seemed to know about fire, but maybe she did not know that water would kill it? She seemed apprehensive about drinking water at all, so maybe there was no water where she came from.

Perhaps she wants me to put the fire out now... But then why touch her own throat and mimic thirst?

She started speaking again, pointing at the river then the fire, over and over again, and then miming cupping her hands above the flames.

Understanding dawned, and I felt like a fool. I'd told her that water would put out the fire, which she undoubtedly already knew.

She was asking for hot water.

"Cold water's better," I muttered, but I did not argue further. I drew a large bubble of water from the river then held it suspended above the fire. The little star watched in what seemed to be stunned silence, her eyes fixed to the orb of water above the flames.

I kept waiting for her to tell me the water was hot enough, but she didn't. It made me uneasy, thinking of water that hot going down her throat. Maybe her skin was more durable than I'd thought.

The water had been bubbling steadily and releasing steam for some time before she finally indicated it was hot enough. I levitated the orb of water away from the fire, but she made no move to touch it. She mimed burning herself again and shook her head.

"What? You're the one who made me get it this hot!" I said, frowning in confusion. The movement made the scar tissue of my left eye pull, and I grimaced. To speed up the cooling process, I manipulated the orb, making it into a very thin, flat rectangle of water that would release heat more easily. Once it had been suspended for some time and had no doubt grown tepid, the little star finally approached it.

She had no cup, and her hands would do a piss-poor job, I was sure.

"Just open your mouth," I said softly, twisting my fingers until the water had transformed into a suspended spout, ready to pour into her mouth. She licked her lips, her gaze flickering between me and the water, before she opened her mouth and waited.

She's thirsty. She just wants water.

I reminded myself of that as my cocks jerked behind my slit. There was something so softly submissive, so erotic about the way she'd opened her mouth to me, waiting for me to pour into it.

I focused all my energy on controlling the flow of the water instead of on the way the hidden place at my groin felt swollen and needy. Even with my intense focus, the flow of water was a little too much for her. Some of it gushed out of her mouth, coursing down her chin, throat, and breasts in shining rivers. The image of myself bent over her and quenching my own thirst by licking water from her skin with my forked tongue slammed through me so hard it felt like something that had come from outside my own mind. I pushed it roughly aside and clenched my jaw, praying to a god whose name I could not recall that she might be done soon.

But she was not done yet. In some instinctive attempt to guide the flow of water, she'd reached up to cup the sides of the levitating spout I'd created, her eyes closed. It looked so much like she was gently holding and drinking from a thick cock that one of my own almost emerged in response.

A spasm went through me, snapping my threads of control. The water lost its shape and fell in a sheet, drenching her face. Her eyes snapped open in astonishment and she wiped rapidly at her eyes before throwing me a betrayed glare.

"Please accept my sincerest apologies," I ground out. "It appears I cannot maintain my own power and imagine you sucking a cock at the same time. It has apparently become quite difficult to hold two different thoughts in my head at once."

Two different thoughts... More like two hundred. The river was still spinning and churning and belching up words and images and sensations at a wingbeat-rapid pace. I could not process most of it.

She blinked at me again. And again.

And then she laughed.

It started small. A tremulous sound that I feared was some sort of choking sob. But as it grew in strength, and her smile stretched her features, I realized what it really was.

"I suppose I deserve that," I said, my own grinning growing to mirror hers. It was impossible not to smile back. Her laughter was like light made sound. It made my ribs feel warm in the strangest way.

Taking a shaky breath and still chuckling, she began repeating a word and tapping her chest, smearing beads of water as she did so.

"Suvi. Suvi Harju. Suvi. Suvi."

"Suvi," I repeated, feeling the sounds roll around my mouth. I placed my hand over hers, sealing her palm to her wet chest. "That's your name, isn't it? You are Suvi."

Her nostrils flared, and the dark parts at the centre of her eyes blossomed.

"Suvi," she said again with a short nod.

I felt a smile on my snout once more. I'd wanted to know what to call her but hadn't had a good way to ask. But I hadn't needed to. She'd given it to me freely, handed me her name like a gift.

My smile curdled and turned cold when I realized I could not respond. She waited, gazing up at me expectantly, but I had nothing to give her in return.

I could not tell her a name that I did not remember.

Her laughter stopped, her open expression shuttering.

CHAPTER ELEVEN
Suvi

Maybe he doesn't have a name.

M I looked away, brushing water from my skin, though the warm sun and slight breeze was already drying it. I was aware of the alien's intense gaze on me, but I couldn't meet it. I felt weirdly hurt, maybe even embarrassed, that he wouldn't tell me his name.

He really might not have one...

But he had language. And he seemed like a person, if an extremely alien one. He understood the concept of names, because he'd seemed to grasp mine right away.

Which pointed more and more towards the fact that he had a name but just didn't want to tell me.

It was probably a good thing. A reminder of the power balance here. A reminder that he took me, stole me from my friends, and that he was not someone to be trusted even if he kept me warm and built me fires and used fucking psychic energy to control water and wood like the elements were a part of his own body.

He was doing it even now, like it took no effort at all and was the most natural thing in the world. I watched in stunned awe as he crooked his claws and raised a jiggly globe of water out of the river, dispersing it over the fire with a sharp hiss. It may have been my imagination, or a trick of the light, but it almost looked like all the golden lights on his body glowed brighter as he did it.

If he wanted to, he could draw up a tsunami and drown me in it.

I didn't think he would, but really, what did I even know about him? I had no idea the extent of his capabilities or what his true motivations might have been.

I didn't even know his name.

But he sure as hell knew mine. And now I felt like the scales had been tilted even more towards his side. Like I had even less power than before.

"Suvi."

The sound of my name in his alien rumble of a voice startled me. He stood at the edge of the grove, my boots and socks in his claws. He held them out to me in a very clear gesture. *Take them because we're leaving.*

I snatched my stuff from him in a movement that could only be described as petulant. But after everything I'd gone through, I thought I'd earned that much.

"So, what, are we just going to keep walking along the river again? Do you even know where you're going?" *Paska.* My socks were dry, but my boots were still very soggy. The thought of putting them on and walking made me cringe inside. But the only alternative would be having him carry me again, and I vowed that I wouldn't let that happen. I'd been too weak last night. I'd given in too easily.

I could be stronger.

I *would* be stronger.

It was nice and warm right now.

I'll walk barefoot for as long as I can.

That actually didn't turn out to be too much of a problem. Once we got through the rocky area by the shore, we were back on sandy banks, rushes dancing in the wind on one side of us, the river placid on the other. We didn't speak to each other, obviously. But even if we could have communicated, we likely wouldn't have had much in the way of conversation. The moment he'd refused to tell me his name he'd cracked whatever small thing had grown between us. He had reminded me that the only reason I was here and separated from my friends in the first place was because of him.

If I never saw a human being again it would be his fault.

So we didn't talk. Just walked, because it seemed like there was nothing else to do. When I wasn't looking at the ground to make sure to avoid any sharp pebbles in the soft sand, I was studying him in silence. He was such an odd jumble of contradictions. At times on our journey, he looked powerful and certain of his path. He seemed almost regal, like this land was deeply known to him, like it *belonged* to him. But then sometimes he just looked...

lost. Lost in the literal sense of not knowing where we were going but also in a much larger, almost existential way. Every once in a while, he'd slow down and then stop walking entirely, cranking his head this way and that, frowning at the river like it had just woken him from an important dream that he couldn't quite make out anymore.

I contemplated the possibility that not only was I trapped with an alien, but one who perhaps was not entirely sane. He certainly hadn't seemed sane when I'd first encountered him, and I chewed on the inside of my cheek with worry that he could descend back into that senseless, prowling rage again.

At least I didn't see any of that chaos in him now. Just an unnerving swivel between calm and confusion.

We stopped several times to eat and for me to rest. He seemed confused every time I asked for him to boil my drinking water for me, but he did it anyway, thankfully, even though he often turned away when I began to drink it. So far, neither the water nor the fish seemed to be having any adverse effects on my human body, one small mercy I could try to be thankful for. The alien ate a lot, but he didn't take much time to rest like I did. When I sat in the shade to take a breather, he prowled the banks of the river, hands knotted behind his back in a shockingly human gesture of intense, frustrated focus. Sometimes, when he seemed to reach a pinnacle of exasperation, he'd abruptly turn and stride towards me and put his hands on my body. He'd clasp my shoulders, or rub a few strands of my hair between his fingers and thumb, staring at my face like it could tell him what to do.

I was never really sure what he saw there.

Towards the afternoon, when I realized I was getting a sunburn and I started trying to ineffectually shade myself by holding my boots above my head, he noticed. Wordlessly, he lifted the wing closest to me and held it over my head as we walked, creating my own personal parasol of green flesh. His wingspan was very large, but in order to shade me fully he had to get quite a bit closer to me. I eyed him from the side, taking in the long, powerful line of his arm and the hard planes of his chest and abdomen. With the emerald scales so hard and shiny, his chest reminded me more of sculpted armour than actual flesh.

When we stopped for an evening meal at dusk, I let out a weary sigh and started regretting my too-proud-to-be-carried stance. I didn't want to rely on the alien, but maybe I was just making myself suffer needlessly at this point. My feet were throbbing, and even though I hadn't been wearing my boots, my blisters looked worse than before – angry and red. Fantastic. I didn't have a first aid kit and I couldn't even look at the plants to figure out which might have had natural antiseptic properties because I was on a fucking alien planet with no clue as to what was going on.

The alien built a small fire and boiled water for me, as had become our routine. But instead of letting it fully cool to drink, I directed him with limp gestures to dump warm water on my feet instead. He followed my pointed finger and when he noticed the redness, his eye immediately narrowed. In an instant, he was on his knees in the sand before me, gripping my ankles firmly and lifting my feet to inspect the blisters on the backs of my heels, the water levitating beside us for the moment.

"Yeah, this is why I have to boil the water. That river is teeming with bacteria my human body can't handle," I sighed at him. I should have taken off my boots last night, the moment I felt the blisters beginning to form. Sleeping with the soaking wet socks and boots when I'd developed open wounds on my feet had been a catastrophically stupid decision. Not that it had necessarily even been a conscious decision in the moment, but still.

Ugh. If my feet weren't so sore I would have kicked myself.

"Staring at it isn't going to help. Unless you have magic healing power on top of your interplanetary teleportation and telekinesis abilities," I muttered peevishly. I tried to pull my ankles from his grasp but it was no use. He was too strong, and I was too fucking tired.

His expression was unreadable as he examined my feet from every possible angle. Eventually, though he didn't exactly seem satisfied, he stopped his inspection in order to slowly let the warm water rinse my skin. I gasped, flinching against his hold at the hot sting of it.

He kept his hold firm as he controlled the flow of water, creating twin taps in the air that slowly poured over my feet. His thumbs gently rubbed my inner ankles. I realized he was softly muttering something, something that almost sounded soothing. He called me a little star again, and then his eye met mine.

"*Suvi.*"

Goosebumps broke out over my skin, and I swallowed hard.

"I wish I hadn't told you my name," I said quietly. "I wish you'd keep calling me *aerra bai* and that I could be just as unknown to you as you are to me."

But that was impossible now. He knew my name. He knew what I needed to eat and drink. He knew what my body looked like when it tore and when it burned.

He knew too much and nothing at all.

After rinsing my feet, he pushed my knees towards my chest, saying something that seemed to be a reminder to keep my feet elevated. He'd get no complaints there. I wasn't about to stick my newly-cleaned blisters in the sand. Leaning back on my elbows, my dripping feet in the air, I watched him as he sliced several river rushes at their stalks and brought them back. He pulled soft fluff from the cottony tops, avoiding the metal strands, and once my feet were dry he pressed the white stuff to the blisters on my heels, binding them in place with long strips of the green stalks. It was actually a pretty decent patch job. The cottony stuff was very gauze-like and he'd tied the strips of green stalks around my feet with a precise competence.

"Is there anything you can't do?" I said, gingerly placing the soles of my feet on the sand. "Seriously. You have the powers of a fucking god and yet here you are bandaging my mere mortal feet." I wanted to hold onto my anger, but I couldn't. I was too tired, and a part of me was pathetically grateful that he'd helped bandage my feet even though he was the reason the wounds were even there.

"Thank you," I whispered, my throat feeling tight.

I always found ways to excuse the people who had hurt me. It seemed this big green idiot was no exception.

I couldn't even call him an idiot, to be honest. There was no denying the fierce intelligence in his lop-sided golden gaze. He wasn't stupid. Brutal maybe, but not brutish.

Strong and stubborn Suvi made way for practical Suvi when the alien scooped me up into his arms once more. I didn't fight him. The sun was beginning to set and I was cold and he was warm and there was nothing else to be done.

He kept carrying me until long after the sun had set. I dozed off a little bit in his arms, not realizing just how much the day of walking in the sun had taken out of me until now. The rocking rhythm of his steps lulled me.

It was when those steps came to a jerking halt that I woke up once more. The alien practically vibrated with tension, staring at something in the distance. I twisted in his arms to follow his gaze. My breath snagged painfully in my throat when I registered the unmistakable shape in the distance.

On the top of a low, grassy hill ahead, bathed in moonlight, *was a building*.

CHAPTER TWELVE
Skallagrim

A *raider warlord's house.*

It was not the palatial home from my memory with the white-haired male in the river. It was not the house I was searching for, the one that felt like it meant something. This house was completely unfamiliar to me, and yet I knew instinctively what it was. I knew, somehow, that the main building would have housed a raider warlord and his family, the smaller rooms at the back serving as barracks for his mercenary followers.

I also knew, without exactly understanding how, that the people who lived there would be viciously territorial and likely would not welcome us.

I did not care. I was a stone sky god and a Bohnebregg prince, and if they did not let me in to shelter Suvi for the night then they would die for their disobedience.

A prince?

The word pinged around in my head. I ignored it with a grunt, opened my wings, and flew to the building.

I hadn't thought to warn Suvi first. She wouldn't have understood me anyway. But she gasped and bucked in my arms when I lifted off, clutching at me in a panic. I held her fast and tried to soothe her, told her she had nothing to fear.

My attempt at calming her earned me a sharp tug at my scalp as she pulled on my hair like it was a set of reins she could use to force me into landing.

In flight, the distance passed beneath us in mere moments. I landed on my feet before the house on the hill. Instantly, Suvi began to try fighting her way out of my hold. I did not let her go. Instead, I held her even more tight-ly and used my wings to create a shield in front of her, even though a spear would be snapped in midair before it ever reached us, a hurled stone or blade warped and crushed by my power. If I wanted to, I could collapse the entire building on the heads of whichever warriors were inside with nothing but a flick of my claws. River help them all if even one came close to hurting her.

My voice boomed with stark authority.

"I demand passage into this hall. As your prince, I lay my rightful claim upon your sustenance and shelter for the night."

The words slipped from my forked tongue without thought. As if I'd spoken them many times before.

"If you heed me, you will earn fresh metal. If you refuse, you will pay in both metal and in blood, as sure as my name is... is..."

Like a wind-battered candle in the dark, the words sputtered and went out.

Rolling my jaw in irritation, I gave up on whatever formalities I'd invoked and ploughed through the grass up the hill. The house had a large, pavilion-style room at the front, open to the air. Braided grass and cotton curtains hung threadbare and useless. There were no lights and I heard no sounds.

I kept Suvi wrapped up in my wings, even as she wiggled in defiance, using my power to slide open inner wooden doors. We passed through room after room.

There was no one here.

That was both good and bad. I wouldn't have to protect Suvi from anyone.

But there wasn't much of use here, either.

It looked like the place had been stripped bare. Like anything of value had been taken long ago and the structure abandoned. Even the empty house had not come away unscathed from whatever had happened – there were singed-looking holes in several of the walls, like something had blasted through and burned the walls while doing it. Ash and dust coated my feet and claws as I padded over the smooth, wooden floorboards.

Satisfied that no one was here, I finally let Suvi down in the largest central room of the house. She placed her boots down and looked around. I watched her in the gloom, observing her as she toured the perimeter of the room then ducked into another chamber. Like a shadow, I followed her.

She shook out an old blanket that she discovered in a dusty corner, then dropped it and jumped backward with a high-pitched yelp when something heavy landed on the floor with a thud. I quickly shoved her behind me, then bent to see what it was.

It was a leather belt with a stiff knife sheath attached. I pulled at the handle jutting out of the sheath and a long, curved metal knife slid out.

This style of knife, with its carved wooden handle inlaid with blue river stones and its deadly sharp blade, was deeply familiar to me. I stood, hefting the knife in one hand and holding the belt and sheath in the other. A deep, primal sense of satisfaction overtook me when I thought of putting the belt on. I had found it, I had claimed it, I would keep it. That was the way of things.

At least, I was fairly certain it was...

I sheathed the knife and moved to put the belt around my waist when my eye landed on Suvi and I halted. Something in my chest lurched, then went tight. She looked so small in this abandoned place. So vulnerable, with her soft skin and her little bandaged feet. Feet I hadn't even known to be hurting until tonight.

She watched me with gleaming, guarded eyes as I moved towards her. Her breath caught, her pulse fluttering in her throat when I leaned down close and looped the belt around her waist. I felt her breathing against the scales of my neck and chest, so gentle and warm, and a claw of desire curled low in my belly.

"Here, little star," I murmured, my voice sounding oddly husky to my own ears. "This is for you. Not that you'll need it..." My eye flicked up to both of hers. "Because you have me."

I did up the belt's buckle with practised ease, muscle memory taking over where conscious memory failed. Something told me that this was a child's knife and belt, because it settled easily enough around her soft abdomen, resting against the curve of her hips. It likely would not have even fit me. If it was a child's, that would explain why it did not seem to have been found and plundered along with the main stores of weapons my instincts told me a house of this calibre should have contained.

Suvi had a pinched expression as she looked down at herself. She shook her head in dissatisfaction, as if uncomfortable with the weapon. As if she wanted me to take it back. She fiddled with the buckle and then gave up with a sharp sigh when she found that she could not undo it.

"Keep it," I told her. It made me feel just a little better to see her with a weapon, even though, as I'd already promised her, she'd never actually need it.

She threw her hands up then went back to the corner, grabbing the blanket then plopping down on the floor with it. She lay on her side, facing the wall. Her back was to me, and despite my lack of understanding about many things, I at least could understand this. The message was clear enough.

She wanted to be alone.

Or, at the very least, she did not want to be near me.

Unfortunately for her, she did not have a choice in the matter.

I didn't have a choice, either.

For whatever reason, being away from her meant danger and darkness, and I would not go back. I stood, staring down at her still form, trying to calculate how much space I could give her while still being in contact with her all night. I had not really tested how long I could withstand not touching her. Every time I felt unease prickling at the base of my skull and darkness dancing at the edges of my vision during the day, I'd made sure to get closer to her, to stroke some part of her. I did not know if it was illness or madness or poison or maybe just the way I'd been made, but something had gone very wrong inside me and she was the only cure.

Bracing for rejection, I lay down on my side behind her, pressing one hand beneath the blanket until it rested lightly on her bare shoulder. She tensed instantly, then started wiggling forwards, closer to the wall and further from me, all the while trying to slither her shoulder out from under my hand.

"I'm sorry," I grunted, scooting forward to stay near her. "I have to touch you."

I worried if I slept too long away from her, that in my slumber I would not feel the darkness closing in. What if I woke in a frenzy and she could not calm me soon enough? What if, maddened and lost and afraid, I hurt her before I realized what I'd done?

That thought inspired fear like nothing else.

Perhaps she might need the knife after all...

To use against *me*. It wouldn't do much against most of my body. But if she shoved it into my eye socket, not faltering until she buried it in my brain...

At least it could slow me down.

It wouldn't come to that. Stone skies help me, if she would just stop trying to wriggle away from me like a river serpent...

But she had nowhere left to try to flee to. She'd reached the wall, the fingers of her hand splayed flat against it. Since we were in the corner, the tops of our heads abutted another wall. I gave up on my weak attempt at courtesy with that awkward shoulder-hold, and hooked my arm around her abdomen, trapping her firmly against my body. My tail hauled itself up over her legs, pinning her in place.

She stopped struggling and panted in my hold.

"Sorry," I muttered against her silken hair. "It has to be this way for now."

For now...

Maybe for always.

She did not reply, just kept breathing heavily. It made her breasts press and shift against my arm, and now that I'd gotten her still I had a whole new problem.

I was aroused.

She smelled so good and felt so good and all I could think about was the pink seam of her cunt when she'd been bent over in front of me this morning. This position was not helping. Her rump was currently pressed firmly against my groin. Or, rather, based on how events had unfolded, I supposed it was my groin that was firmly pressed against her rump.

In short, I seemed to have brought this entirely on myself. I could have come at her another way, maybe simply tried to hold her hand, instead of cornering her until I was forced to practically wrap myself around her to keep her from escaping.

But there was no changing that now. Here we were. Her, seething. Me, doing everything possible to keep my cocks inside my slit. Stone of the sky, how long had it been since I'd rutted someone, or even just spilled seed at all? I could not account for all the time spent in darkness.

Based on the protestation of my cocks, I wagered it had been a very, very long time. I ground my fangs against each other, trying to focus on other things – the press of wood into my side, the poke of the knife sheath against my thigh – so that I did not feel her body against me. So that I did not picture her bent, bare form in torturous detail while imagining the sudden deterioration of her clothing, the only barrier between us besides my rather overwrought slit muscles.

Lost in excruciating thought, I did not notice at first when Suvi had fallen asleep. Eventually I realized that the tension had eased out of her form and her breathing had grown slow and even. I exhaled tightly and rolled onto my back, keeping my upper arm flush against her spine, but at least creating some distance between the luscious shape of her backside against my twitching slit. I palmed my groin with a bit-back groan, feeling the engorged tissue behind the muscle, and resigned myself to a very long night.

CHAPTER THIRTEEN
Suvi

As soon as I began to wake, I knew that something wasn't right. My whole body felt achy and stiff, and when I moved my feet, I cried out in white-hot, pulsing pain. I was on my back, and I grew slightly aware of someone – the alien – sitting bolt upright beside me and leaning over my face. I groaned, shivering violently despite the heat pouring off of him.

Fingers ghosted over my forehead and cheeks, scraping sweaty hair back from my face. When I cracked my eyes open, an intensely focused alien face looked back, snout twitching and tight, golden eye dragging a panicky line back and forth over my face. He was saying something, asking me a question, following it up with my name. I groaned again, and let my eyes fall closed. Everything hurt, especially my feet. I was scared to even look at them.

He wasn't scared, though. Or if he was, he didn't let it stop him. He released my face and the sudden feeling of gentle pressure on my ankles was so painful I writhed and tried to twist away.

The alien grew very, very still. Trying not to vomit, I forced my eyes open to look at him, finding him with his eye trained on my feet which he held gingerly aloft.

Oh, fuck.

My feet were swollen and purple. The alien slowly peeled my pant legs upwards, revealing angry redness that had already started spreading up my calves.

Oh, God. Please, please, no.

I tried not to cry, because my head already felt like it was going to explode and the thought of crying made it seem like it actually would. But the sheer, desperate panic was undeniable. It bubbled up in my chest until I lurched up onto my elbows, leaned to the side, and vomited on the floor.

Infection. Now that I knew what was happening, I was convinced I could literally feel it sifting through my bloodstream. The feverish forward march of an unseen army, creeping all the way up my legs like ants. There was no medicine here, no antibiotics, no other humans, no *nothing*. Nothing except the alien who'd done this to me and who now had the gall to stare, frozen, down at my broken body as if stunned by the consequences of it all.

I was going to die here. I'd always suspected that, but now it seemed incredibly real. So close I could taste the acrid curl of it on my tongue.

My feet would go necrotic. My fever would get higher and higher. And then my organs would shut down.

I wasn't sure I could dream up a more agonizing way to end things.

I'd watched Elvi die, but she'd been asleep and pumped full of drugs. I wouldn't even have that small comfort.

"No," I choked out. I spit, trying to clear the last bit of bile from my mouth. Even staying up on my elbows was too hard, and it was only the quick shift of the alien's hand beneath my head that kept me from collapsing into my own vomit.

That seemed to have shocked him out of his stillness. Now, he was all movement, and it was explosive. He snatched me up into his arms, clutching me close and spreading his wings with a vicious crack. He didn't even bother walking out the door. He jerked his head upwards, and the entire ceiling cracked before blowing outwards off the house entirely. Sun blinded me, and I screwed my eyes shut as he took off into the air.

I huddled against him, fighting the urge to vomit again. I couldn't even be bothered wondering what he was doing or where he was taking me. I was too ill to feel afraid of how high we flew.

In the last dregs of consciousness, it occurred to me that we'd left my boots behind.

Then it occurred to me that I probably wouldn't need them anymore.

CHAPTER FOURTEEN
Skallagrim

I could not remember ever being so afraid. I flew like something terrible pursued me, like I would die if I stopped.

I would not die if I stopped.

But Suvi might.

I did not know what to do or how to help her. Concepts danced at the edge of my consciousness before fading like mist. Words exploded, sparks that lit up the surface of the river in my head – *fever disease medicine amputate* – but I couldn't string them together in any way that seemed to do me any good. That last word, "amputate," started to pound through me like an illness of my own and I flew faster, harder, so that I would not have to wonder if the knife at her hip would be sharp enough to do it.

There was.... someone. Somewhere. Who could help. I was certain of it in the maddening, contextless way I seemed certain of so many things these days. Therc had been a place, a person. People?

I chased the memory with my body, beating my wings hard while keeping Suvi safely nestled against my chest. I leaned into instinct, dove into the barely-there feeling that plagued me, the feeling that told me someone could help her, could fix this, if I could only find them.

I flew all day. I did not stop. Suvi drifted in and out of consciousness, and as the sun began to descend on the horizon, I feared that maybe I'd been wrong. That my memory had failed her, failed us both.

But then I saw it.

The bend in the river that I instantly recognized. Another tumult of words – *temple healer cotton goddess* – filled my head as I dove to the shore. I landed, twisting my head 'round, chest heaving, wings burning, feeling like

I was in the right place but that the place was not what it had once been. There was supposed to be something here. Something... Someone...

I wanted to roar. I wanted to smash something. I wanted to crack this planet down the middle until even the ancient core felt my rage. I wanted to apologize and run away and cut out my other eye in recompense. Because everything had gone wrong and I was the source of it all.

I did none of those things, because Suvi was shaking and burning in my arms, and river help me, I did not know what to do. I collapsed onto the sand, wings drooping to the sides, and cradled her close as I fought through my own dooming sense of helplessness.

Stone sky god. Bohnebregg prince.

Once, I had been powerful. Once, I had not been helpless.

I tried to reach back through my own mind, tried to reach for who I'd been before.

Maybe he was gone.

Fury overtook me. Fury at the fact that I couldn't remember a single cursed thing to help us. I could not take her to another world, because I could not even picture one. I could not return her to her people, because I'd seen them in their machine, leaving the planet when we did. There was nowhere left to go and no one left to turn to.

You promised her. You promised you'd protect her.

If she... stone skies curse me, if she died, and the darkness came back, I'd welcome it this time. I'd give myself over completely without a care for what happened after.

What point was there in trying to claw my way back to myself if she was gone?

What point was there in light, in lucidity, if it only illuminated what I'd lost?

Suvi whimpered, and the sound sent me shooting to my feet, as if by standing I could somehow help her. *Hateful, wretched fool.* I began to pace the river's shore, speaking softly to her even though I was certain she could not hear me and doubly certain she would not understand. My starmap vibrated, the golden points growing brighter. My power was responding to my emotional state, surging inside me as if preparing me for battle. But there was nowhere for all that power to go. I couldn't use it to help Suvi. It rose and fell, rose and fell, creating a relentless churn of shuddering noise inside my head.

The noise got louder and louder, bearing down on me until I stopped my pacing and whirled towards the river.

The sound was *coming from the water.*

The sun had fully set at some point during my frantic pacing, and a sudden blast of light from the surface of the water made me bare my fangs. Suvi moaned at the bright light aimed on us, and I swiftly covered her with my wings.

"Who goes there?" I hissed, backing up slightly. That putrid, cursed light. It kept me blind to whoever wielded it. With a snap of my jaws and an outward whip of my power, I crushed the source of the light. I blinked, getting used to the spill of the moons and stars as the only source of light once more, my eyes slowly focusing on a... a vessel.

A small boat was heading for the shore. The sound I'd heard was some sort of machine, a paddling propeller, built into the back of it. A lone hooded figure stood in the boat, and they appeared to be simultaneously steering the boat with a rounded lever while poking with their other hand at a smoking contraption that had to have been the light.

The vessel slowed. The boat touched the shore. The hooded figure prepared to jump to the sand.

Proclamations like the ones that I'd remembered at the abandoned house came to me unbidden. I spoke them into the air like a spell.

"You stand before a stone sky god and prince of this land. I compel you to state your name and purpose, as I have stated mine."

The figure jumped from the boat, landing gracefully in the sand. They did not get closer.

"But you have not stated your name. Nor your purpose," countered a voice from within the hood.

Impatience snagged in my throat. I almost entered a rage I would not have been able to easily drag myself back from. There was something wrong, something deeply offensive, about the way this person had answered me. Like they were breaking a code embedded in my bones.

I choked it all down, the anger, the feeling of being affronted. Pride and protocol that I could not even remember did not matter now.

Only Suvi mattered.

"My purpose... My purpose is to seek a medic... A healer... *Someone*." I grunted in exasperation. "I cannot remember... I came here because I thought there was something. Someone who could help. I have an injured..."

An injured what? What should I call her? Female? Friend? Star that reached out and split the black ooze that drowned me for so long?

"An injured person in my care," I finally ground out.

The hooded figure drew nearer, going slowly as if not to alarm me, dark red cottony robes rippling with the movement. They stopped a few paces short of me and pulled back their hood.

A snouted face startlingly similar to my own looked back, though the hair was worn very short. When the person spoke again, I instantly realized she was female. A Bohnebregg female.

"You remember correctly. You have come to the right place. It is here. You merely cannot see it."

"What is this?" I spat. "A riddle? Some sort of test?"

What in the blazes did that mean — I'd come to the right place but could not see it?

"Let me see the injured person."

"Let me see the place you speak of," I snapped.

Her snout dipped, then jerked sharply to the left in a gesture I instantly recognized as one of disagreement.

"I cannot do so until I verify what you've told me. The children of the cotton do not adhere to the royal order of Bohnebregg nor do we bend to the will of warlords. Being a prince means nothing here."

"How about the fact that I could crush your skull like a berry?" I seethed. "Does that mean anything to you?"

She inhaled sharply through her nostrils, but maintained her maddening composure.

"When I die our Mother will wrap me in cotton and bear me into her fields. If you inflict violence upon me, it simply means I'll meet her all the sooner."

River help me.

"Fine! Get over here," I replied. I gently pried my wings back, just enough to show Suvi's curled figure against my chest. "She's burning much hotter than she usually does. She has injuries on her feet that have worsened immensely."

A pucker of tension appeared on the woman's scaly brow, and she appeared to fight the urge to rear back.

"I did not realize you'd brought her from another world. That she was not of Bohnebregg."

"But you will help her," I shot back firmly. It was a statement, not a question. If she did not help Suvi, then she'd get to meet her Mother of cotton or whatever the cursed skies she was blabbering about before because I would wring her neck until it snapped.

She met my gaze and raised her snout, angling it sharply upwards to the right. *Yes.*

"We will try, Skallagrim."

CHAPTER FIFTEEN
Skallagrim

S*kallagrim.*
    The word felt like a crack of thunder. It exploded all around me, lodged inside me.

Skallagrim. Skallagrim.

I had a sudden tangle of sound in my head. People saying that word. A man with wings like mine and a woman with a snout like mine.

"That's my name." I felt like a bit of a half-wit as I said it, slack-jawed and gaping in response. I liked to think I recovered quickly enough, shaking myself back into movement and following the woman in her robes. We walked through rushes and long grass, parting the shivering sea of their stalks.

"You know my name. How do you know my name?" I demanded. "What else do you know?"

"Very little," was her rather irritating reply as she continued walking. "We do not keep records of the children of the metal here." She paused, as if deciding whether to continue or not, before proceeding. "You had a Bohnebregg mother and a foreign, stone sky father. One day you went into a berserker rage and disappeared from the world." Her eyes slid to me from the side before facing forward once more. "I have always heard that you are immortal. I suppose, considering how long you have been gone, that it must be true. But I have to say it is odd to see someone so old in a Bohnebregg body so young."

"How long have I been gone?" It was a milder, sedated way to ask the real question.

How long have I been in darkness?

"As I said, we have no distinct records of your mother Jolakaia's time. But it has been hundreds of strides of the Mother. Many generations," she added at my confused look.

Jolakaia...

A beautiful, haughty face appeared so clearly she seemed to stand before me. She had black hair, like mine, but bound and decorated with metal. She had called me Skallagrim, once. In the deepest and oldest of ways, I knew her, even though most of me had forgotten her.

"There are no records but you know my mother's name. You know how much time has passed," I growled, suspicions mounting. That did not add up, and if this woman had deceived me then she would pay dearly for it. "How do you know all this?"

For the first time, the woman's façade of calm indifference cracked. She hesitated, then took a slow breath, as if clearing her mind, or reminding herself of something important.

"I know all this because Jolakaia's brother, King Jolar, was my ancestor, and I grew up with the tales of our bloodline's glory." A bitterness twisted at the edges of her words, but then her tone returned to neutrality. "You and I are actually the most distant of cousins. Or, perhaps you are more of an uncle, considering your age. It's how I recognized you so quickly. There is a small, very old portrait of you in the home I grew up in, which is now my brother's. Although you'd likely think of it as your home. The one Jolar and Jolakaia's father built."

"The palace on the river," I said on a sharp inhale. *The one I've been searching for...*

"Yes."

"Is that why you are helping me? Because we are related?"

"No," she said with firm conviction. "I am bound by the Mother to help anyone in need."

"And are you helping me by leading me into nothing?" I snapped, impatience winding tight around my spine. "Where are we going?" We'd crested a low, grass-covered hill. Beyond it was a field empty of anything besides yet more grass and insects.

Suvi made a small sound of pain, and I lowered my snout, bumping it to her forehead. Her very hot forehead.

Do not worry, little star. I will find a way to fix this. And if this cousin or niece or whatever she is has wasted my time, then I will let you watch me end her when you wake.

"We are already here," was the Bohnebregg woman's reply.

"Are you quite well in the head?" Perhaps an ironic question from one such as me, but still needing to be asked. "There is absolutely nothing here!"

"There is nothing here for those who seek the way of metal." She turned from me, facing down the hill, then murmured a word. *Falreth.*

Somehow, I both understood that the word meant "cotton" and I simultaneously recognized that it was not a word of the Bohnebregg language. I had no time to dwell on the confusion of linguistics, though, because before my eyes a village – no, an entire city – was coming into view at the bottom of the hill.

She had not lied. She had not led me astray.

A surge of gratitude, maybe even something near affection, for this odd relation of mine made me feel just the tiniest bit sorry for all the times I'd claimed I'd kill her.

"What is your name?" I asked as we descended the hill, towards the gated wall surrounding the city.

She gave me a rather wry smile. "It is a familial name and one you already know."

We reached the tall gate.

"My name is Jolakaia." Her smile became more genuine. "Welcome to Callabarra."

CHAPTER SIXTEEN
Skallagrim

The welcome ended with Jolakaia's words. The gate was cracked open by someone – a Bohnebregg male – who instantly aimed some sort of weapon at my chest. My chest was where Suvi was held. My power licked out of me like fire, nearly unbidden, in an instinctive rush to protect her. The weapon, something long and tubular, was crushed in the invisible fist of my fury. The male, clearly startled, dropped the tube as if it had burned him.

"Aim another weapon at me or the one I carry, and I will obliterate this entire city," I said, my voice dangerously low and deadly serious. The male's eyes fell to my chest, then nearly bugged out of his skull when he saw Suvi.

"Jolakaia," he said suspiciously, "who are these ones? He speaks like a child of the metal and comes before us naked with no cotton to cover him like a heathen. You have revealed our position and-"

"Shut up," I said. The male looked at me in affronted shock. "Shut up before I crush your throat so thoroughly you can no longer speak. Or *breathe.*"

"Threats of violence will not get you very far here, Skallagrim," Jolakaia warned me. "We are compelled only by the Mother and the way of cotton. We do not fear death."

The shield of invisibility and the high wall and the gate and the armed guard said differently, but I saw no value in pointing that out right now.

"Skallagrim," the male breathed. "No. It cannot be. The one from the legends..." He gave his head a stunned flick. "Whoever he is, he is a child of metal and he cannot be granted entrance."

"I was a child of metal once too," Jolakaia said sharply. "He has come here in softness, to beg for help from the Mother's Hands. He-"

I had no plan to beg anyone for anything. If they could not be compelled by the threat of death, perhaps someone here with half a brain in their skull could be compelled by pain. I'd break a thousand bones if I had to until someone finally complied. Pull out ten thousand claws. Spill a river's worth of blood.

I refused to stand idle with Suvi suffering, maybe even dying in my arms, while some guard flung gibberish moral strictures at me. Metal. Cotton. Who in the blasted river cared?

My tail twitched. The points of my starmap buzzed.

I blew the gate off its hinges.

The guard very narrowly avoided being squashed by heavy falling wood. I supposed he should have thanked his cotton Mother for that. Personally, I thought it was rather a pity and probably would have lifted the gate from the ground and brought it down again, on his head this time, if I had not had more pressing things to attend to.

The seam of Jolakaia's snout had pulled long and flat, as if she were disappointed by something but not at all surprised.

We were standing in a large, mostly empty ring. Ahead was one more wall that encircled Callabarra, this one low enough that I could see the glow of the tall buildings beyond. From an opening in that wall, more guards poured forth, both male and female, about two dozen of them and almost all of them carrying more of the tubular weapons. Some of the weapons had begun to glow, emitting an ominous buzz of energy. I hissed, bared my fangs, and with a snap of power wrenched every weapon from every hand and pulverized them. Luckily, my power was as effective in controlling metal as it was water and wood. Perhaps I really was a child of the metal, whatever that meant.

Controlling flesh, however, was more difficult and yielded far messier results. As I held the group back from getting any closer to Suvi and me, I heard the distinct sound of several bones crunching even though I did not specifically mean to break anything – at least not yet. The three closest guards fell and clutched at various body parts. One of them was the original guard who'd accosted me at the gate, and when I saw the odd angle his leg was now bent at, I allowed myself to feel just the smallest slice of savage satisfaction.

This is what happens, came an inner taunt. *This is what happens when you defy your prince. A prince with the powers of a god.*

Somewhere, some sort of gong or bell was ringing. *An alarm.* Beyond the lower wall, my ears picked up frantic activity. Hurried footsteps, the slamming of doors, parents calling for their children. Someone cried out, "Koltar! The Mother's Eye!" Jolakaia breathed out tensely then spoke quietly to me.

"Rein in your rage, Skallagrim. Rein it in and present yourself calmly before the Mother's Eye. You have already done much damage here. We will help your companion, but if you continue in your rampage you will not be allowed within the inner walls. Your female will be taken from you in order to be saved."

"Let anyone come and try to take her," I hissed. The sentence was punctuated by the sound of another bone snapping somewhere in the group of guards I held back. It was unintentional, but it made my point rather nicely.

"I mean it, Skallagrim, calm yourself and-"

"And what? Your weapons will have no effect on me. Your walls cannot keep me out. I will pulverize a path through this city if I have to until I get what I need from it."

"Then what?" Jolakaia probed. "Do you really think we'll be able to attend your female with all due attention and all resources available if you are flattening everything we've built in a berserker rage? You have already injured four guards who now will need their own healing. Hurt any more people and all the Mother's Hands will be busy mending bones instead of working on this female. She is not of our kind and with her foreign biology she will take much more time and expertise. You must realize that!"

My heart pounded so painfully hard that I felt it in my eyes – or my eye, and the hollow of the other. It was as if part of me could hear her logic, but another scratching and slavering part wanted to reject it entirely. *Curse words,* that part said, *curse logic, curse the consequences of my actions and destroy. Fight and fight and fight until you get what you desire or there is nothing left.*

"The Mother's Eye!" The call came again from within the city's wall, much closer this time.

Jolakaia gave a small hiss.

"There's no more time. Koltar is about to pass through the inner wall and find us. If you want to get your female help with any sort of quickness, then you will calm yourself, *now*, and release the guards from whatever hold you have on them."

Then she squeezed her eyes shut, placed her hand on my shoulder, and started to pray.

"*Mother, wrap him in cotton. Wrap the metal's edge so that he may find his way without cutting his path through this world. May he be durable and flexible and staunch all wounds and...*"

Though it went against every bristling instinct that shaped me, I did as she asked. Just as a new male wearing golden-yellow robes came through the inner wall, I released my hold on the guards.

But unlike Jolakaia, I did not pray.

And I did not repent.

CHAPTER SEVENTEEN
Skallagrim

The male in the deep yellow robes surveyed the scene with eyes set deep above his snout, his brow low. Everyone looked at him, to him, and it was obvious to me that he was some sort of leader among these people. Koltar. The Mother's Eye. The guards slowly collected themselves and their crushed weapons. At least, those who could stand did.

"Honoured Eye, he-"

Koltar silenced Jolakaia by raising his flat palm then closing it into a fist. "I have heard much of it already."

"Perhaps you should be named the Mother's Ear, then," I hissed. "If you can hear so well then hear me now. This female will be healed. *Immediately.*"

He jerked his snout up and to the right. "She will be." He said it rather blithely, and for some reason the words did not reassure me but rather made me angry.

"Then let us pass!"

He eyed us for one excruciatingly long moment, then jerked his snout again in agreement. The guards who could walk freely clustered around us, two of them flanking Koltar and a third one placing his body between Koltar's and mine as I followed him. *As if that would do anything*, I thought peevishly, *if I really wanted to kill him. I broke some of their bones without even meaning to.*

Imagine what I'd do if I meant it.

I adjusted Suvi in my arms. She made a small, pained sound that sent my guts twisting in my belly. I kept my wings firmly around her, protecting her and blocking her from prying eyes – of which there were many, peering from windows and doorways and the alleys between tall, lit-up buildings –

but I made sure not to smother her too much. Her shivering body was already so much hotter than usual, and I did not want to make it any worse. I bumped my snout to the top of her head, rustling the fine hairs there with my breath.

I was a half a head taller than anyone else here, with longer legs and a much stronger purpose propelling me. Koltar and the three guards leading the group moved maddeningly slowly. After treading on the hem of the black robe of the guard ahead of me for the fourth time, I hissed in vicious annoyance. He stiffened, but did not look back at me. And I supposed it was not really his fault. He was behind Koltar and Koltar walked with what almost felt like aimlessness. Ambling along like we had nothing to do and nowhere to be.

"Calm, Skallagrim," Jolakaia urged quietly from close on my left side. "We are nearly there."

"We had better be," I snapped, loud enough for Koltar to hear me, though he did not appear to register the words.

It became clear fairly quickly that the city was arranged in looping circles, built outwards from something at the centre. *This must be the temple*, I thought as we reached it.

The temple appeared to have been built around two of the largest trees I had ever seen. Their trunks were so thick at the base that even if someone with a wingspan as large as mine stood opposite me, we would not have been able to reach our wings around and make contact with each other. The trunks tapered smoothly up into the star-dappled sky, their puffy, metal-threaded tops looking as large as clouds above. The two trees marked a sort of entrance – like an archway that did not bend and meet at the top. They were two natural pillars behind which a beautifully constructed, multi-level building sprang up.

Passing through the trees led us into a walled courtyard. The claws of my feet clicked as I walked. In here, the ground was smooth and hard with interlocking river stones, gold-veined blue. Ahead was an obvious entrance into the temple, a large, rectangular opening with cotton curtains hanging, illuminated by golden light behind them, somewhere within.

Wordlessly, I started walking faster, forcing everyone out of my way as I did so. Jolakaia yelped in surprise, and I heard several sets of running feet behind me.

"Skallagrim! You must be robed in cotton to enter the temple!" Jolakaia gasped. "You cannot-"

With a bit back sigh, I adjusted my hold on Suvi, freeing one hand just enough so that I could snatch at a curtain as I passed it. I ripped it down with one fierce tug without halting my forward motion. I slung it over one shoulder as I walked, tossing part of it back between my wings and sliding the other part gently under Suvi, creating a billowing, untied sash. Apparently, my sash was not good enough, judging by Jolakaia's stammered complaints behind me, but at this point I did not give two immortal stone sky shits. The fact I'd bent this far to these people's will at all was beyond the realm of comprehension.

Something told me that, once upon a time, I never would have done any of this.

I would have flattened this place in an instant, the first moment the guard raised a weapon to me.

If it had not been for Suvi.

"Take me to the healers," I barked at no one in particular. I kept walking through the large space, curtains behind me (what remained of them, at least) and the smooth wood walls of the inner temple ahead. Two small figures – older children or young teenagers – who had been crossing the room nearly jumped out of their scales, swivelling their heads to me.

"Not you," I hissed at them. I already felt like I was dealing with children all around me right now. No need to make it literal.

Thankfully, Jolakaia seemed to have somewhat recovered from her conniptions over my lack of dress. Sounding rather harried, she said, "This way," pulling ahead and leading me through another set of curtains on the right. This took us into a windowless hallway. Despite the lack of windows, it was still very well-lit by intricate sets of narrow tubes built into the hall's ceiling.

"We are heading towards the medical wing of the temple," she told me. Her robes jumped and fluffed about her ankles as she jogged just ahead of me. "I think it would be best if she were ensconced in one of the private rooms."

"Of course, she will have a private room!" I snapped. Why in the endless stone sky did Jolakaia think I'd possibly allow Suvi to be shoved into some common sickbay? *Fools. Fools everywhere I bloody turn.*

Fools behind me, too. While it was not the whole group who'd escorted us, two guards were trailing us through the hall, claws clicking in rapid succession on the stone floor.

Suddenly, Jolakaia stopped directly in front of me, and it was only the refinement of my reflexes that kept me from completely toppling her. She slid open a set of doors I had not noticed and we stepped into a small room.

It was a plain rectangular space, also windowless, as I could tell it was situated well within the temple. But like the hallway, tubes of light along the ceiling kept everything softly bright. There was a door at the other end and a bed in the centre of the room, surrounded by various contraptions of metal, glass, and wood that I had no names for.

"Put her on the bed," Jolakaia urged me.

"Where are the healers?" I growled. It was still only Jolakaia with me in the room, the guards standing in the doorway.

"I am one of them," she said brusquely. She waved her claws towards her robe. "A red robe means I'm one of the Mother's Hands. Put her down."

I did not want to relinquish Suvi. My heart chanted, *hoard, hoard, hoard,* but I forced my muscles to unlock and laid her gently down. She moaned when I let her go, like my little star did not wish to be parted from me, either, and that tore at me. Her head lolled towards me on the cotton sheets, her eyes cracking open and looking dazed.

Instantly, without even realizing I had fallen, I was on my knees before her. I bent my head, levelling my gaze with hers.

"I am here, Suvi. I am here with you and I *will not let you die.*"

Her lips, cracked and pale instead of their usual smooth pink, parted, but she made no sound besides panting breath.

I did not know when I'd started touching her again. My hands skimmed shakily over her forehead, her cheeks, her jaw. Jolakaia buzzed around the room, rolling contraptions this way and that. She struggled to attach several tiny cotton circles attached to flexible metal tubes to Suvi's chest, then hissed in frustration.

"Everything I have is for Bohnebregg biology. These sensors are supposed to be held in place between scales." She tossed them onto a tray. "I'll skip the diagnostic and monitoring equipment entirely since it won't tell me anything useful. She obviously has points of infection on her feet so I will treat them like Bohnebregg wounds and hope that it works."

"What do you mean, *hope*?"

"I will do what I can and I will pray to the Mother," was all she said in reply. She rolled over another contraption then met my eyes above its metal surface, her expression grim. "I suggest you do the same."

CHAPTER EIGHTEEN
Skallagrim

Jolakaia kept her promise. I heard her prayers, murmured under her breath as she positioned her machine. This contraption was a large, upright ring of metal lined with sections of tubing on its inner side. It had hinges in three places, like the ring could be unlocked and opened up, two sections sprouting out from the centre one like wings. Jolakaia did not open up the ring, merely positioned it at the foot of the bed. She rolled up the sleeves of her robes and fastened them at the elbow with unseen clasps, grass-green scales on her forearms gleaming in the room's gold-hued light from the tubes above.

"First, I will use the Mother's Light on her feet."

"Mother's Light?"

She jerked her snout towards the ring.

"It harnesses the power of light to clean wounds. Then, I will have her take a tincture, to help clear the infection from the inside."

"Should we not administer the tincture first?" I asked. As concerned as I was for her feet, I was far more worried about things like lungs, heart, and brain. Those were the things that, when they failed, would kill a mortal man, and I imagined that they'd kill a little star, too.

But Jolakaia jerked her snout in disagreement.

"I need her lying on her belly to expose her heels to the light. I don't want her vomiting it back up."

I grunted, then stood as Jolakaia gently but firmly rolled Suvi over. Her movements were decisive, competent.

"How long have you been a healer?" I asked her as she helped Suvi turn her head to the side. I circled to the other side of the bed so I could keep Suvi's face in my sights.

"Since childhood," Jolakaia replied, hurrying down to the other end of the bed. She had to use some sort of fluid from a glass jar to remove the cotton from Suvi's heels because the pus and dried blood had made everything stick. "I used to tend to my father's soldiers after raids. We never had equipment like this, though," she said about the metal ring. "Metal was used to pad my warlord father's hoard and to fashion new weapons. Never to build machines that would heal the men who'd injured themselves fighting to retrieve it for him."

She pulled Suvi's feet down until her knees were straight and the fronts of her ankles rested on the inner tube of the ring.

"That was when I first became disillusioned with the way of metal. When my father died, my brother Joleb took over his army and hoard. The things I ignored or found I could stand under my father's rule, I could no longer tolerate under my brother's. I left my familial home and walked the river for many days, prostrating myself before the Mother until Koltar found me and brought me into Callabarra."

Jolakaia tapped something on the ring, and the inner tubes lit up with brilliant light, blue instead of the warmer yellow that illuminated the temple and the city streets.

Instantly, Suvi jerked, using more force than I'd seen her exert all day. Violent tremors wracked her body, and Jolakaia instantly splayed her large green hands down on the backs of Suvi's calves to keep her from pulling away.

In her weakness, Suvi could not manage a scream. The high-pitched, whimpering keen that crawled from her throat had me digging my claws into my hair, eye wide. It was a sound of pure, primal panic. A noise made by an animal caught in a trap.

"You're hurting her!" I bellowed, claws flexing spastically against my scalp. I whipped my hands down, forming fists without even meaning to do it.

I'd smash it. Smash the ring, then Jolakaia, then this whole cursed place because Suvi's pain, her suffering, was worse than my own. I could not take it. *I could not take it.*

"The pain is necessary," Jolakaia was saying, her eyes trained on the trembling legs she held in place.

I barely heard her. My own heartbeat, echoing behind Suvi's agonized whisper-moans, filled my ears. Every muscle lurched, swelling, bulging, stretching until my joints ached. My claws felt tight at the tips of my fingers, my scales bunching and bristling.

"Jolakaia!" came a call from behind me.

Jolakaia's eyes went to the doorway, then to me, and then widened.

She straightened, but kept her hands where they were while Suvi writhed beneath her hold.

"Skallagrim!" she shouted. "You must control yourself! If you enter a berserker rage now, we are all doomed. Including her." She gestured to Suvi with her snout. "*Especially* her."

I panted, chest heaving, heart feeling too large for my ribcage. My starmap buzzed insistently, begging me to draw upon the power that was rising inside me, a black river about to overflow its banks with nowhere to go but outwards. Until everything was drowned in it.

Even her. Especially her.

The echo of Jolakaia's words lanced through the darkness building in my brain.

I reeled, falling to my knees, wings spasming, tendons crackling.

"Little star," I begged, not daring to touch her in case I hurt her even more than she already hurt. My claws dug into the bed, slicing instantly through the sheets and mattress in front of her turned face. I trembled nearly as violently as she did, shoulders hunching forward.

"Little star, precious Suvi, show me the way. Show me how to stand by you now without destroying everything." My words felt mangled by my aching throat, and I hated myself for asking her for anything while she choked out her tearless sobs of pain.

You are weak, I hissed in silence to myself. *She hurts because you brought her here. She hurts because you do not know what she needs. She hurts, and it is your fault, and even now you cannot master yourself without begging for her help.*

Strength bloomed in my tightly leashed limbs. More strength than any mortal creature would ever hope to wield.

And I had never felt so weak.

Suvi's keening ended with a shuddering gasp, and her face suddenly went slack with relief. Jolakaia had turned off the light. My cousin-niece rolled the contraption away from the bed, her yellow gaze narrowed and fixed on me as if waiting for me to explode and kill us all.

"I will not..." I blinked away darkness and allowed one solitary fingertip to crawl over the ruined mattress and make contact with a bit of Suvi's hair. Just her hair. So that if I cut it, at least it would not bleed. "I will not rage. I will restrain myself."

Jolakaia remained quiet for a long moment. Finally, she said, "Even though I told you to, I knew you would not pray to the Mother. I thought that maybe, instead, you would pray to the Father, but you don't."

She paused, her eyes finding and lingering on the place where my fingertip fervently stroked a single, silvery strand of hair.

"You pray to *her*."

CHAPTER NINETEEN
Suvi

❝ *Minulla on huono olo*," I groaned. "I don't feel well." I didn't know if anyone was there to hear me. I didn't even know what was wrong with me. Only hoped that somebody could help because I felt more unwell than I ever had in my entire life.

I was lying on my back, but not for long. Strong hands beneath my shoulders and my back lifted me, then leaned me back against something warm and solid so I was half upright. I moaned in complaint, begging them to let me lie back down, but fingers closed around my shoulders, holding me there, as something cool and hard was pressed to my lips.

On instinct, I shut my mouth as tightly as my eyes and shied away. The fingers on me gripped harder, and something firm bumped my cheek. Someone's breath skimmed over my skin.

"Suvi."

I stilled.

It wasn't the use of my name that felt so familiar, that penetrated the thick, heated fog around me. It was the voice itself. A gruff, cajoling rumble that I recognized somehow. I *knew* that voice, I was sure I did.

And I decided to trust it.

I let the firm, breathing thing at my cheek bump and guide my head forwards again. The cool thing – the smooth edge of a glass cup, I thought – returned, and I parted my lips for whatever was inside. Thick liquid tasting of mud and bitter herbs slid into my mouth and I choked it down, stomach roiling. Luckily, there wasn't too much of it to drink. When the cup came back, it contained only water. I managed a few sips of that before I pulled away, the back of my head relaxing against whatever I was leaning against. The headboard of a bed? A wall?

No, walls stayed still. They didn't adjust to my every movement as if trying to cushion me better. Walls didn't expand and contract in time with the breath ghosting across my face and neck.

Words were spoken, words I didn't understand but in a language I was sure I'd heard somewhere before. There must have been a second person, because only a few of the words I heard came from the voice I knew, and each time I heard that voice, the living not-wall at my back vibrated.

A chest.

The new and unfamiliar voice said something else, then what sounded like clicking footsteps expanded in my ears, getting closer, before retracting into little points of sound that eventually disappeared. I tried to pry my eyes open, but I was too fucking weak. I let out a small moan of complaint. Like the sound I'd made had exerted some sort of electrical current, the hands on my shoulders and the chest at my back and whatever breathed against my neck all twitched in unison. Fingers slid down my arms, then my hands were taken in two larger ones and held together in my lap.

I was being hugged from behind. By... *someone*. Someone big, someone with a voice that conjured up fever-distorted images of rivers and rocks and fangs.

"Who are you?"

I wasn't sure if I managed to whisper it or I only asked it inside my own head. When the other person answered, they didn't tell me their own name. They simply said mine.

Over and over and over again.

Like an anthem. Like a prayer.

The echoed repetition of my name wrapped in that deep, river-rock voice followed me as I slipped into sleep.

The next time I woke, I didn't just feel sick. I felt like I was on fire. My feet, specifically, though the agony made my entire body burn and spasm. I tried to move, *had to move*, but someone was holding my legs. Someone was forcing me to stay still while they held my feet in a fucking fire.

I'm being tortured.

My head arched back as I bucked, eyes flying open. At first, nothing but white filled my vision, and I panicked more, thinking I'd gone blind. But the white was not vague or cloudy or uniform. I could see details within it. Threads, and torn areas. It was fabric.

I was staring down at fabric stretched over... a mattress?

The sheets on the ship were grey. The sheets in my bedroom back home had been blue.

So where the fuck am I where the fuck am I where the fuck am I?

I couldn't puzzle it out. Didn't have the brain space for it. Every ounce of my energy and mind was occupied with pain, and the drive to get myself out of that pain obliterated everything else.

I groaned, putting everything I had (which admittedly wasn't much) into pulling against the holds on my legs. Someone said something sharply from near my feet, and the hold on me tightened. I tried another tactic. Instead of simply pulling my legs, I tried flopping down on the bed and rolling over so that maybe I could twist out of the other person's grasp. But as soon as I lay fully down on my stomach again, a hand – a new one, a third one – came down firmly against my back before I could roll anywhere. The hand on my back was huge, spanning my shoulder blades and pinning me in place. I wrenched my head to the side and finally saw something other than white.

Green and gold filled my vision. At first, I thought I was looking at some sort of jewellery, or maybe a piece of armour, like a helmet, inlaid with gems. But then the emeralds and shimmering gold took on a more familiar shape.

The shape of a brutal face with a gouged-out eye and a snout that I'd once seen making words I didn't recognize in a voice that I did.

A snout I could picture smiling.

"Help me," I begged him, feeling instinctively that he was the sort of person who would help me if he could. I knew he'd done things to help me before, though I couldn't think of any examples as agony burned holes in my brain.

Maybe someone was holding his feet in the fire, too, because his snout tightened and his brow contracted in what looked like raw, devastating pain.

Whether he couldn't help me or wouldn't, he didn't. He just stayed where he was with his hand on my back holding me down and looking like it hurt him to do it. His other hand sank into my hair, massaging my scalp with tense and twitchy fingers, like he was barely holding himself back from pressing harder and puncturing my skull. He muttered unintelligible strings of words at me, his voice scraping and low.

"Who are you?" I sobbed.

Had I already asked him that once? Twice?

Maybe I had asked him ten times. A hundred times.

I could ask a hundred more and I would never get an answer.

I closed my eyes and screamed.

CHAPTER TWENTY
Skallagrim

The next few days passed in a painful haze of Suvi sleeping, then being awoken by the bright torment of the Mother's Light on her feet. Seeing her that agonized and being so helpless to do anything to stop it changed something inside me, though I could not quite say what. I only knew, as I knelt and held myself back from smashing the light and Jolakaia and everything else in this city, that I would not be quite the same man as I had been before.

Not that I even knew who he was.

No new memories came to the surface of the river. I didn't even bother reaching for them. All I cared about, thought about, in those first blurred and breathless days was Suvi.

I grew to love and loathe the Mother's Light contraption, because though it caused Suvi immense pain, it seemed to be working. Every day, Suvi's wounds healed a little more, the brutal redness in her flesh receding. At the end of the third day in the temple, Jolakaia jerked her snout in satisfaction and declared that Suvi would not lose her legs. A hard fist in my chest that I did not even realize had been clenched this entire time instantly let go.

"Thank you," I said, standing but placing a palm on Suvi's bed, overtaken by the unfamiliar and debilitating sensation that I was about to fall over for no discernable reason.

Jolakaia jerked her snout down and to the left.

"Thank the Mother," she replied. "Her cotton staunches all wounds."

I grunted, turning my attention back to Suvi. At the door, the two pointless guards (always there, and always two, though the guards were not always the same ones each day) straightened and muttered, "Honoured Eye."

Koltar, as he had done several times over the past few days, came to hover obnoxiously in the doorway. The first time he'd done that was during one of Suvi's Mother's Light sessions, and my nerves had been so ragged that I'd snapped open my wings, starmap blazing, and bellowed at him to *GET OUT.* He had eventually left, but without any sort of hurry or fear in his eyes and that had bothered me even more than the original intrusion.

Jolakaia turned and greeted him respectfully.

I glowered and growled, "What?"

"I come merely to see how she fares under our Mother's care," he said smoothly. "And to ensure that you remain wrapped in cotton while you're here."

At first, I thought he meant literally. I gestured impatiently down at myself. Sometime on the second day, I'd been relieved of my tattered curtain sash and had been given my own robes. Since I occupied no real station in the temple and had no official role besides some hostile combination of guest and conqueror, my robes were undyed white cotton—the colour that children wore.

But Koltar just jerked his snout *no.* "Not your clothing, Skallagrim."

Ah. More of this "wrap your metal in cotton" nonsense.

"I have maintained peace," I muttered, eye narrowing. Barely even aware I did it, I took a step to position myself between Suvi's bed and Koltar's gaze. "If I were not cottony enough for your liking, you would not need to come all the way down here to discover it. You'd know it by the sounds of falling walls and snapping bones."

He made a non-committal sound deep in his throat then remarked, "The four you've injured are doing well, by the way. The bones have been set and the other Mother's Hands say the breaks should heal in time. Though Nakib may have a permanent limp."

I rather savagely hoped that Nakib was that first, most annoying guard who'd tried to keep us out at the gate.

I wondered if Koltar could guess at my lack of contrition. He stared at me with green eyes in a blue-scaled skull, as if waiting for an apology and already knowing that he would not receive one.

"I suppose that is all I will get from you today," he finally said. "That is fine. You calmed under the Mother's influence at the broken gate, and that satisfies me for now."

I gave him a questioning look, and he jerked his snout towards Jolakaia.

"You only calmed when she put her hands on you and prayed. Proof of our Mother's infinite benevolence."

Jolakaia suddenly made herself very busy checking on Suvi's feet, avoiding my gaze. After another long, vastly irritating stare, Koltar departed, taking the two guards with him out into the hall to speak with them about some other matter.

I turned to look at Jolakaia even as she staunchly kept her eyes turned away.

"I did not become calm because you prayed and your goddess answered. I forced down my rage because of the logic of your argument – that only being calm and entering the temple would help Suvi."

"Yes. I know."

"So, all that putting your hand on my shoulder and begging the Mother...?"

"It wasn't just for Koltar's benefit," she said quickly. "I pray all the time. But... often I pray inside my own head. The words do not need to be spoken aloud."

I hissed out a low laugh. *Clever.* She knew I was reining in my anger and violence already, but having that happen during her prayer would make it look more real, more reliable to their leader, if it appeared to be the result of prayer and the Mother's intervention instead of my own control. It made me look more like one of them.

"Is fooling your Honoured Eye part of your holy life? Surely lying is not part of the way of cotton."

Her snout tensed.

"No, it is not," she said slowly. "But I am one of the newest followers to the way of cotton and I humble myself before the Mother as one imperfect and often lost." Then, rather tersely, she added, "Besides, it worked, so maybe you should spend less time questioning me and more time thanking me."

I laughed again, louder this time, just as the two guards returned to their posts. Suvi stirred in an apparent reaction to my voice, and I sobered instantly, crouching beside her bed and brushing damp tendrils of hair away from her face. Her temperature had returned to something a little less disastrously feverish, though she was still weak. Without opening her eyes, she said something I did not understand, then appeared to fall back to sleep.

"Why can I not understand her?" I wasn't asking the question of anyone in particular, but Jolakaia answered from behind me.

"I can't understand her either. She's not speaking the Bohnebregg language."

"That's why I can understand you and Koltar and the others, then," I said without turning to look back at her. I was too absorbed in watching the way Suvi's skin changed from pale at her brow to pink at her cheeks, like the blush of light warming the horizon at sunrise. "This is the language I've spoken all my life."

"Yes. That and, I imagine, your father's language. The stone sky tongue. Although..."

The rolling of wheels and clacking of metal told me Jolakaia was rearranging things in the room somewhere behind me. I did not rise to help her. I simply watched the way Suvi's silver-brown eyelashes rested in the hollows above her cheeks.

Were those hollows *too* hollow? I frowned, leaning so close my snout nearly touched her tiny nose. Her face looked more drawn than before, and my frown deepened. Getting food into her was nearly impossible. The best we'd been able to do was get her to take sips of rich broth cooked in the temple's kitchens.

"Although," Jolakaia was saying as I tied myself into knots wondering how long Suvi could go without eating solid, chewable food. I did not want any of her softness – the heavy roundness of her breasts, the gentle padding at her hips and stomach – receding in hunger.

I did not want her taking up less space. It felt too much like disappearing.

"I am surprised you do not understand her. I thought you'd be able to."

That had me finally turning around. I kept my knuckles firmly anchored against Suvi's cheek but cast my attention back to Jolakaia. She was polishing that hateful saviour, the Mother's Light ring, with a spare bit of clean cotton.

"Aeshyr can understand any language he runs into. I assumed it would be the same for you."

Aeshyr...

The name meant nothing to me. Not even the vaguest sense of recognition rippling through the river.

"Who is Aeshyr?"

"You do not know him? He is another stone sky god. Like you."

"No, I do not know him," I muttered, rather testily. "I barely even know myself and had to rely on you, a near stranger, to tell me my own mother's name. Why in the depths of the river should I know him?" I snapped up to my feet. "Wait. How do *you* know him? Is he here?"

If he was here, maybe he could tell me more about myself, more about what had happened and where I'd been. More about who I'd been before...

But Jolakaia shut down that frantic line of thought with a sharp jerk down and to the left with her snout.

"No, he is not here. He hails from the world of Riverdark and only comes here when he wants to trade. Apparently our metal is useful to him. It's his spell that hides Callabarra."

Riverdark...

Now there was a word that rippled through me with recognition. *Riverdark. Mages warlords blood magic alchemy...*

Still, I was fairly certain that I did not know this Aeshyr. I did not think he was the man I remembered with the snow-white hair and the starmap bluer than the river we'd both stood in once.

I supposed it did not matter if Aeshyr was not even here to begin with.

"Anyway, he has something that allows him to understand all language," Jolakaia said. "He gave a piece of it to Koltar, so that they can speak more easily when they trade. I assumed it was a stone sky invention. But perhaps it is something from Riverdark instead."

I grunted, her words prickling familiarity in the most irritating of ways.

Nearly remembering something was like hovering on the edge of orgasm. Constantly reaching, stretching, aching for something *right there* but out of reach.

Bloody unbearable.

I ground my fangs together.

"How often does he come to trade?"

Jolakaia put down her cotton square on a tray before lifting her hands in a sort of *I don't know* gesture. "He is immortal. With such a stretch of time before him, he uses it differently than we do. There is no regularity to his visits. He has only come here once since I have been at Callabarra, and I have been here nearly six full strides of the Mother now."

"Strides of the..."

"One stride is four hundred and eighteen days."

"Right," I said. "Four hundred and eighteen. I knew that... But..."

"Children of the metal call them years. That is probably what you'd remember."

What a useless collection of junk my memory was turning out to be. Remembering that a Bohnebregg year was four hundred and eighteen days but not remembering how many of those years I'd spent in darkness.

At least that darkness had not yet come back for me. Being near Suvi was still sustaining me for whatever reason, and I brushed my knuckles once again over the impossibly silken curve of her cheek in silent thanks and wretched self-loathing. I stole her, I saved myself and perhaps a thousand other worlds, but now she was starving and fevered and weakened and I could do nothing about it but stand here and stare and watch her waste away.

"She is improving, you know," Jolakaia said gently. "Her wounds are healing and the infection has receded. She takes more broth every day and her sleep is far less fitful."

Fitful. That was one word for it. Nightmare-plagued was probably more apt a phrase. For the first few days, when the fever was at its worst, Suvi cried out over and over again in delirious agony, saying words I did not know but that I thought might be names. *Torrance. Elvi.*

Perhaps names of the people I'd taken her from. People she still searched for in dreams.

People I had no idea how to find if I'd even had the vaguest inclination to return her to them.

Which I didn't.

"Who is she to you?"

My inhale was sharp as I once again tore my attention from Suvi to look at my red-robed relative.

Over the past few days, Jolakaia had asked that question a thousand times with her eyes but never once with her mouth. Until now.

I'd asked myself just as many times. Probably more.

"Salvation," I muttered after a brooding silence, because it was what felt most true.

Jolakaia's snout pulled in a frown, and one of the guards, a female robed in black, piped up from the doorway, "The only true salvation is in the Mother's-"

Shoulders bunching with tension and starmap buzzing, I used my power to slam the door shut from across the room, cutting off her words.

Jolakaia sighed. "She is right, you know. True salvation lies not in the fleeting brushes of mortal life, but-"

"Fleeting?" I could not keep the vibration of dangerous fury from my voice. "*Mortal?* My life is neither of those things. The shadows that consumed me were neither of those things. You yourself said I've been gone for generations. Hundreds of years lost in violent darkness. So spare me the righteous blathering when your Mother so clearly chose not to spare me from that. There was *nothing* in that darkness, Jolakaia! For years I could not even *see*, could merely fight my way through it with no thought to how much blood I spilled. I went from a prince of this land to a maddened beast and there was no relief, no way to come home, no *salvation*," that word came out on a hiss, "until *her.*"

I stabbed a claw downwards to where Suvi lay in her bed, and Jolakaia rather wisely snapped her snout shut.

"Suvi is my only saviour. The only star left in a sky I'd long since given up on seeing with clear eyes again," I growled. "I will devote myself to no other. There is no altar I will kneel before but hers."

If my words offended Jolakaia, she did not show it. Instead, after absorbing my remarks, the corners of her green snout pulled in a slight smirk.

"We do not actually have any altars here, you know."

Actually, I did not know. I hadn't seen any other parts of the temple besides the courtyard and hallway on the first night because the only thing that mattered to me was here, in this very room. Jolakaia came and went – she had other duties to attend to in the temple and a wife out there in the city – but I remained.

The lack of antagonism in her reply deflated my anger somewhat, and with a tight jaw I turned and got down on the floor, placing my snout upon my folded fingers on the mattress.

Snout to face, I gazed at Suvi. With hard stone beneath my knees and the exquisite brush of mortal breath upon my scales, I knelt before the only altar in Callabarra.

CHAPTER TWENTY-ONE
Suvi

For what felt like an eternity, the only thing that punctuated the sick, sleepy haze of my existence was the pain of fire on my feet. But even that eventually stopped, leaving me in a mind-numbing state of confusion that didn't get any better even with longer and longer periods of wakeful lucidity. There was no window in this room, and even though there was unfamiliar equipment, there was nothing that looked even remotely like a clock or a calendar. My sense of time was absolutely shot.

Everything was eerily, maddeningly constant.

Especially him.

In the throes of feverish nightmares, I could pretend I'd dreamed him. Maybe even pretend I'd dreamed everything that had started with my abduction from Earth, when military men had come for me and forced me into the service of our original human mission. But every day (at least, I assumed days were passing somewhere out there) I got a little stronger and a little more myself. And reality settled more firmly all around me. I was still here, on an alien planet, with some half-dragon-looking giant staring endlessly at me with his glittering golden eye.

Every time I woke, he was there. Sometimes kneeling, sometimes standing. But always, always there.

And he wasn't the only one. There was another alien who looked quite a bit like him, with a snout and green scales, but this one wasn't as tall or broad-shouldered, and it didn't have wings. This other one wasn't here all the time, I didn't think, though it was hard to really keep track. One thing I did notice, though, was that even though I couldn't understand them, they could clearly understand each other. I caught snippets of conversation in their alien language but didn't bother trying to untangle any of it. I could barely keep my eyes open most of the time – trying to learn a fourth language was, at least for the time being, out of the question.

One question did crop up, though, what I thought was approximately three days after the sporadic burning torture in my feet had subsided. *Where the fuck am I supposed to pee?*

It was the first time I'd been lucid enough to even be aware of the sensation of a full bladder. I lay in the bed (which was becoming more and more obviously some kind of alien hospital bed) simultaneously wondering when I'd even consumed enough fluid to need to pee and trying to decipher where the hell I'd been doing my business this whole time, because I was positive I hadn't left the bed. I gingerly shifted my legs then flinched, noticing something between them. Closer inspection made me think it was a leather pouch, or maybe even some sort of cleaned and processed animal bladder.

Oh God. I've been pissing and shitting in a fucking bag.

Thankfully it seemed to be empty, but that just brought up the even more cringe-inducing question of *Who's been emptying it this entire time?*

My eyes slid to the alien male. My slight movements hadn't yet drawn his attention – he was currently too busy staring moodily at some big metal ring thing. But when I fully sat up and groaned, head swimming, he straightened and pivoted instantly, sending white robes swirling around his long, lizard-like feet as he advanced on me.

"Did you always have those robes?" I croaked, trying to focus through the red-tinged throbbing of my head. "I thought you were naked before."

And then, as if in a horrible anxiety dream and not my painfully real fucking life, I looked down to see that I was now the naked one. I gasped, clutching at the thin white blanket that had slithered down to my hips and yanked it up over my bare breasts.

"Where did my clothes go?" I whisper-shouted in a hoarse voice. *Paska,* now I remembered I'd already lost my tank top outside, but I'd at least had trousers and panties and a bra, all of which were now mysteriously nowhere to be seen. "Did you take them?"

I took several shaky, deep breaths, heart slamming and cheeks burning. I tried to rationalize with myself. I appeared to be a patient of some sort.

I'd obviously been very ill and injured. Maybe it made sense that my clothes were gone.

But those ideas didn't bring much comfort. My stomach flip-flopped at the thought of being naked and vulnerable and completely unaware of what was happening to me for so long.

For what it was worth, the alien dragon whatever-he-was kept his single eye trained relentlessly on my face. He didn't let it dip even for a moment to my bare chest when the blanket wasn't covering me. His scaly brow was bunched in concentration, maybe even concern, as his golden gaze raked across my cheeks, leaving a trail of warmth in its wake.

I guess I'm an alien to him, too. Maybe he doesn't care about my naked body. It probably looks all weird and squishy and fleshy to him, anyway.

With a weakening flush, I remembered with vicious clarity that he'd already seen my bare ass and pussy when I'd been bent over in the sunshine outside, and he hadn't ended up doing anything weird then, either, though he very well could have if he'd wanted to.

With that somewhat reassuring and deeply embarrassing thought in my head, along with the increased complaining of my bladder, I weakly kicked away the leather bag thing and wrapped the blanket awkwardly around myself.

"I have to pee," I said thickly, fighting wooziness and clutching my blanket-dress. "Where do I do that?"

Mr. Dragon Dude obviously hadn't been peeing into an external bladder this whole time, so there had to be somewhere nearby I could go. I was weak, but now that I was awake and at least somewhat with it, there was no way I'd be able to relax enough to pee in my bed the way I'd obviously been doing up until now.

The alien balked when I limply heaved my legs over the edge of the bed and let them hang there. He swung his great snout towards one of the room's doors, his expression furrowed with alarm, and it was so clearly a *maybe-we-should-wait-for-the-doctor* look that it made him seem nearly human. But he wasn't human. He was well over seven feet of green-scaled, glowing alien muscle with wings sprouting from holes cut raggedly in the back of his robes.

Nope, not human, and probably not even halfway trustworthy considering he was the one who'd abducted me in the first place. But in that moment, he was just about all I had.

"I have to pee," I said again. I adjusted my blanket so I could hold it with one hand, then pointed over at the leather pouch abandoned on the bed beside me. "I have to pee and I am not doing it in that bag."

His brilliant eye lurched from my face to the bag to the door and then back again, an uneasy triangle of movement. I was pretty sure he knew what I wanted but he obviously wasn't jumping into action to help me. Instead, he just stood there, a great green and gold slab of silence.

"Fine," I muttered. I'd find the bathroom alone then. If I stayed here much longer, I really would pee myself, and after all the pain I'd gone through and the fresh hell of finding myself naked under his alien stare, that was just one humiliating step too far.

I hardened myself with the intense, almost bloodthirsty knowledge that I would find a fucking toilet even if it killed me, took a shallow breath, then hopped down to the ground.

Maybe the fever had cooked my brain a little more than I'd realized, because it never dawned on me that my legs wouldn't be able to hold my own weight until they didn't. They didn't spare me a single second of strength, so I couldn't even say that they'd buckled. It was like they weren't even legs at all. As if sometime during my stay in bed all the muscle and bone in the lower half of my body had dissolved into mannapuuro, a Finnish semolina porridge.

Two huge hands closed around my waist. My *bare* waist. The protection of my blanket was now a useless heap on the floor, leaving me completely exposed. The alien locked one arm around my back, drawing me close – *Oh God oh God that's way too fucking close* – until my entire naked front was plastered against his robes. He leaned forward, snout at my throat, chest sealed to mine, dipping me back like I was his dance partner. My ribs felt like they were full of bees and my head felt like it was full of sand and I couldn't have struggled out of his grip even if I'd wanted to. All those thoughts about him maybe being trustworthy, about him not caring about my body, evaporated in a terror-stricken instant, replaced with *stupid stupid Suvi you were so damn wrong.*

I should have just stayed in the bed and peed in the bag.

"Let me go," I gasped.

But what a pointless thing to say.

Because I'd asked him to let me go before, hadn't I? And he hadn't done it then, either.

His arm was like a living band of metal against my back. His inner forearm held firm in its place against my spine, his fingers curling around the base of my skull as he leaned me so far back that the ends of my long hair brushed the floor.

I can't let him get me down to the floor. Once he's on top of me, it's over.

I put every morsel of strength I had left into fighting his hold, and for a disorienting moment, I actually thought I was successful. But after shaking my heavy head and blinking a few times, I realized that he'd merely straightened up once more, drawing my body along with him. We were upright again because of him, not because of anything I'd done.

One of his arms was still strong against my back, holding me steady.

The other was held slightly aloft, the white blanket that had been on the stone floor a moment ago hanging like a flag of surrender from his fist.

Oh.

He'd just been reaching down for the blanket and trying to make sure I didn't fall at the same time.

Using only one arm and the assistance of his thick tail under my ass, he plopped me back onto the bed once more, then got to work securing the blanket around my shoulders like it was some sort of cape. He tied two corners of the blanket into a knot at the base of my throat, and I had to admit it was pretty impressive the way he was able to work so quickly, with such deft and capable movements, without even looking at what he was doing. His eye was suspiciously expressionless, his gaze blank and firmly fixed somewhere above my head.

Once the knot was tied, he gave each side of the blanket a firm tug inwards, as if shutting the curtains on too-bright sunlight, before he finally risked a glance down.

"Thanks," I said weakly, tongue feeling heavy and sticky in my mouth. All I'd done was get out of bed and I was already exhausted. I hadn't even taken a single step! Helpless despair threatened to overwhelm me, but I fought it down. I wouldn't be able to do anything at all if I completely fell apart and lay back down. There's a Finnish saying that Elvi used to remind me of all the time, especially when I was young and she was trying to break me out of my shell for hockey: *A brave man gets to eat the soup.*

If I wanted my soup, or, in this case, getting a trip to the bathroom, I'd have to grit my teeth and keep on trying.

"I have to pee," I said for what felt like the hundredth time, blinking back tears of irritation. "I'm going to go do it."

As if anticipating me jumping down again, the alien moved liquid-quick to hold me back, settling his huge hands firmly on my shoulders. He said something, jaws opening and closing very close to my face – close enough for me to realize for the first time that he had a dark blue split tongue moving in that mouth.

When I didn't answer, he heaved a sigh and lifted one hand from my shoulder. Using two fingers as tiny legs, he mimicked a walking motion through the air, pointed at me, and made a hissing sound of disapproval. Then he jerked his snout towards the bag.

The message was clear. *Humans who can't walk have to pee in the bag.*

"No," I said, shaking my head until it felt like my brain swam inside my own skull. My hair was greasy and limp, flopping in stiff tangles. I tried to scoot off the bed once more, but he stopped me again. He made another rumbling hiss sound, then looked to the still-closed door like he'd done before. He stared at it, as if willing someone to open it and come through it, before apparently making up his mind about something and scooping me into his arms.

I gave a reedy yelp of surprise as he hefted me easily against his chest, like I weighed barely anything at all. I scrambled to keep the sides of my blanket-cape tight across my front as he crossed the room to the other door. It slammed open without him even reaching out to touch it, and I *felt* that power in him, felt the lights between his scales heat up and vibrate against my body as he did it.

Thankfully, he hadn't opened a door into a prison cell or dark base-ment. It was, despite its alienness, so very clearly a bathroom that I almost burst into tears.

The toilet was a smooth bowl of gold-veined blue rock built into the floor. The alien carried me over there with swift strides, got down on his knees, then helped me into a wobbly crouching position. He remained behind me, hands as solid as rock on my waist, holding me steady as I fought to keep my cape from trailing into the bowl.

"OK, I'm good," I said, panting slightly, arms quivering from the ordeal of keeping my blanket tight enough so that it covered me but also wouldn't get drenched by my own pee in the toilet. "You can go now."

The alien didn't move.

My cheeks blazed, and my bladder twinged painfully.

"Look, I'm shy, OK? I couldn't even pee in a public restroom if someone was in the stall beside me back on Earth. So I really just need you to go now."

Still no movement behind me. No words of response, either.

The alien knew what I unfortunately knew, too – that I'd probably collapse the second he let go.

"How about this?" I asked, wriggling in his hold until I was on my knees straddling the bowl. I kept one hand on my blanket, then placed my other palm flat to the floor in front of the bowl. "See? I won't fall now. You can let go."

I lifted my hand to make a shooing motion towards the doorway we'd just come through, then put it back down.

Miraculously, it seemed to have worked. Once my palm was back in place on the stone, the alien removed his hands from me. He did it so painfully slowly, lifting one finger from my body at a time, as if testing my strength with every centimetre he pulled back.

Finally, when he was satisfied I wasn't going to fall into a puddle of my own piss, he rose and moved away.

The sigh of relief was only halfway up my throat when he resettled himself directly in front of me.

He crouched, elbows on his knees, eye pinned to me.

"I said you can go," I cried. I was starting to shake with the effort it was taking just to hold myself on my knees. "Go! Like, out of the room!"

His eye narrowed, and he rose again, only to cross to the wall opposite me and lean back against it, his wings curling forward over his shoulders.

"That's not any better!" I snapped.

He said something in return, but the only thing I caught was my own name punctuating his alien sentence like an annoyed exclamation mark. Then he crossed his arms over his chest again and stared, the physical manifestation of *I'll wait.*

"I guess you don't understand what shy means," I muttered. The rest of that saying came pinging back to me in my sister's voice. *A brave man gets to eat the soup; a shy man can't even eat cabbage.*

Elvi wouldn't have made herself suffer kneeling on hard stone and tightening the muscles around her bladder like this. She would have peed, staring alien or not. Hell, she would have pissed right on him if it had suited her purposes.

"What's so great about soup, anyway?" I said sullenly.

Then, I squeezed my eyes shut, doing my best to pretend I was alone, and peed.

CHAPTER TWENTY-TWO
Skallagrim

Suvi finally gave up on her ridiculous notion of being left alone in her weakened state and urinated. She did it with her eyes shut and her chin tipped down towards the floor as if silently submitting to defeat. I didn't like seeing her like that, with her head lowered in hideous unhappiness.

But if she believed for one fleeting fraction of a heartbeat that I was going to leave her in a room alone when she couldn't even stand up on her own, then she didn't know me at all.

Perhaps fair, considering how little I knew myself these days.

I shook off the shadow of that thought as the stream of her urine came to a trickling end. Even though she'd now cracked her eyes open, the movements of her right hand were near-blind, feeling along the stone.

"The pull to rinse is behind you," I said, realizing even as the words left my mouth how pointless it was to try to speak to her. She couldn't understand me, and blabbering at her was useless. My wings flexed, pushing me bodily away from the wall as I strode around behind her, crouched, and pulled the lever.

Suvi gasped as the stream of water hit the flesh between her legs and simultaneously came down to rinse the bowl clean. Rather mercifully, my view of everything was obscured by the white fabric bunched around her hips. It had been hard enough not to ogle her when I'd righted her flimsy blanket covering back in the other room. Watching a glistening stream of water sluice over the pink skin of her cunt would be an intolerable and unmitigated distraction, and Suvi did not need a man distracted. She needed a man with half a brain left in his head to adequately take care of her. To take care of her the way she deserved.

To take care of her the way I'd failed to until now.

That set my fangs grinding and had my belly going sour, and any foolish lechery related to Suvi's fever-weakened body vanished.

I ignored the sluggish way she swatted at my hands as they gripped her waist and hauled her up. I was about to lift her entirely against my chest once more when she noticed the stone tub in the corner of the room and, in a voice stronger than I'd heard it in days, nearly feral in its enthusiasm, cried out, "*Bah-uth!*"

"What?" I grunted, making sure she was alright on her feet but not yet willing to let go. "The tub? You want to bathe?"

I supposed it made sense she'd want to cleanse herself. Jolakaia had wiped her flesh with cotton cloths at various intervals, but even I knew that was not comparable to the delicious swipe of flowing water over scales. Or skin, in her case.

Holding her to me, I leaned to the side, checking through the open door to confirm that the main medical room where the bed was remained empty. *Cursed Jolakaia.* The more Suvi's condition improved, the less time my relative spent here. Normally, I neither noticed nor particularly cared. As long as Suvi was sleeping as comfortably as possible it mattered little if Jolakaia was here or not.

But it mattered now. Because Suvi apparently wanted to bathe and I did not need to ask her, did not need to understand her words, to know that she would not want to do it in my presence.

"I can call to the guards outside and make them fetch Jolakaia," I grumbled, frowning at the empty room beyond us. I wasn't actually sure whether they'd listen to me or not – they only answered to Koltar – but perhaps being reminded of their broken-limbed comrades in their splints and casts could persuade them to do as I commanded.

Suvi didn't seem to hear me, or maybe it was that she just didn't understand me. Her floppy limbs nudged mine, as if through the sheer power of her might she could drag me over to the bath herself.

I thought about refusing her. I really did.

I couldn't.

Not after how much she'd suffered because of things I'd done and hadn't done, things I hadn't known or remembered. She'd been sick and in pain and confined to her bed for more than six days now. If she wanted a cursed bath then by the stars she'd get one.

"You realize I cannot leave you alone," I said as I picked her up and carried her over to the tub. Leaving her to kneel down and piss on her own was one thing (and already beyond anything I'd be willing to do), leaving her alone in water whose surface her small head could slip silently beneath was quite another.

Quite another, as in I would never in my infinite, blasted lifespan do it.

I reached the side of the high, smoothly carved river stone tub, then placed Suvi down at the bottom of it, white covering and all. She clutched the edges of it together in tight little fists, the grey and black points of her eyes darting around the room before settling on my arm as I reached for the tap.

Maybe she thought the tub was meant for something else, because when the water plummeted downwards into the tub she gasped and jerked her feet away from the liquid pooling in a rumbling froth at the bottom. I was about to turn it off to try to figure out where I'd gone wrong and what she really wanted when she sighed and slowly eased her feet back towards the water.

Only to yelp loudly and yank her feet away with much more energy this time. She crawled to the far end of the tub (it really was a rather massive thing for someone as small as her) and started flapping one hand at the water while using the other to hold her bedding around her like some sort of shield.

"What is it? What's wrong?" I asked, turning the water off. It certainly couldn't have burned her – I'd specifically made sure to keep the tap towards the cool water setting.

But therein lay my mistake. Her flat teeth chattered, and she held the bedding around herself not as a shield, I realized, but as its true intended purpose – a blanket to conserve heat.

"You only just recovered from your fever," I grunted, fighting to keep the scowl from my brow. "I'd have you covered in filth before I let your temperature rise simply so you can bathe."

Images from earlier days came back with haunting vengeance. Suvi burning up in bed, shaking and whimpering, screaming...

I jerked my snout and raked my claws through my hair as if I could dislodge those memories by simply tugging hard enough. But no. I was fairly certain that I could forget my mother's name, forget my own, but that nothing would make me forget the torment of watching Suvi in that sickroom.

Suvi was speaking to me, but even if I'd known her language I doubted I would have caught any of it. Her teeth slamming against each other marred any words I might have gleaned.

My fingers fell from my hair and drummed along the side of the tub as my gaze swivelled between my shivering little star at the bath's tap. Perhaps using heated water would not be too much of a problem. Letting her shiver and shake like she was certainly couldn't be good for her. And I remembered how she always wanted me to heat her water even before drinking it. Maybe she was far more sensitive to cold water than I was.

"Alright," I said, returning my claws rather hesitantly to the tap, "I'm going to turn this water back on. Warmer this time. But I am not going to let you overheat."

I would keep the temperature well within what would be safe for her.

What that temperature range actually was for her kind, I had no idea. But I figured that by watching her closely I could hopefully figure it out. The second she looked unwell, the hot water would be drained and replaced with cooler stuff no matter how much she might argue.

So slowly my arm nearly shook with the effort, I turned the gleaming stone handle of the tap until the water warmed. Suvi reached her slender fingers towards the falling stream, her smooth pale brow creased at first, but slowly relaxing every moment the water grew warmer. When she sighed, and all remaining tension drained from her face, I stopped turning the tap.

She exhaled again. She began to draw her knees up to her chest, and then, as if that simple movement was too much effort for her, gave up and leaned sideways against the tub, resting her chin on the ledge. As the tub filled, her blanket bloomed around her like a river flower, the soaked white cotton floating, tremulous petals.

She watched the rippling movements of the fabric.

And I watched her.

It was hard not to. I hadn't seen her this content since before she'd gotten ill. Even in sleep in her sickbed, she'd had a look of unhappiness, a look of pain. This was the first time in far too long her pretty face was unmarked by suffering.

Pretty...

It was a pretty face, I decided. She had always been beautiful to me, but in the way a celestial body could be beautiful. At the beginning, I'd barely registered her features in a solid, physical sense, focused solely on the light she emitted, the way she somehow beat back the darkness. And then, when she'd gotten sick, I'd been too busy combing over every crease in her features, searching for signs that she might be getting better, or skies forbid it, worse.

But now, as she adjusted herself, pressing the flesh of her cheek to the tub's stone edge until the supple skin got slightly squashed, I just saw her. She was not a star right now, nor was she sick. She was simply Suvi.

And Suvi was pretty.

I hadn't gotten a good look at any of the other people she'd been with on the other world.

I wondered if she was considered attractive among her own kind.

And I wondered, more foolishly than I'd imagined or hoped myself capable of being, if I could be considered attractive. Not necessarily among her kind in a general sense. But to her. Very specifically.

I grimaced at the memory of seeing my own face in the river days ago. One eye gouged out and replaced with knotted scar tissue. Hair in a tangled, matted disarray instead of oiled and braided the way I knew I'd once worn it, the way I knew was considered beautiful.

I tried not to think too much about it. If my face was not worth looking at, then I'd simply spend all my time and energy looking at Suvi's. Vanity served no purpose here because the only purpose I sought to serve now was her.

But even so... Even so...

Even so, I could not stop my claws from rising to my hair in an instinctive movement meant to smooth the strands.

The lift of my hand caught Suvi's shiny eyes. She started, gawking at me as if I'd just rather rudely appeared before her even though I'd been here the entire time. She huddled against the side of the tub, grabbed at the soaked, sinking fabric and pulled it back to her body the way a starving creature might snatch at scraps of food. Then she gestured with her chin, the way I might do with my snout, towards the door.

"Oh, no, little star. That is not happening," I muttered, crossing my arms and frowning down at her. I was as rooted to the spot as a tree, un-yielding as stone. She could set her flat mouth in that stubborn Suvi way of hers all she wanted, but I would not budge. "Do whatever you need to do, but I will remain beside you as you do it."

Based on the flare in her eyes that looked a lot like anger (anger I wel-comed, because anger meant strength and energy and recovery and *thank you, little star, thank you for your anger, pour it over me like water*) she ap-peared to get my meaning.

It poked at me, the way her blissfully relaxed expression had vanished now that she'd remembered I was there. Dug beneath my scales, made my tail and wings twitch.

She'd brought me more peace than I'd known in years. More peace than I'd known in entire mortal generations.

And all I'd done was carve away at hers.

The tips of my split tongue lashed against the roof of my mouth in irri-tation. I could not grant her the complete privacy she so obviously wanted.

But perhaps...

Perhaps I could take a few very small steps back.

Suvi watched me warily as I walked backwards away from her. I stopped when the backs of my legs hit a wooden chest against the wall. I sat upon its flat lid, then gestured roughly down at myself as if to say, *See? See how much space I give you? I am not such a brute as you might think.*

Never mind the fact that I'd been a brute to her before.

Never mind the fact that the moment the darkness came creeping back in, I'd become that brute again and crush the space and fledgeling sense of privacy between us like a flower in my fist.

But for now, there was no darkness. For now, everything was mostly alright. Suvi was mostly well and I was mostly myself and therefore I was halfway content to sit over here at the wall, unwanted as the Callabarra guards at the other door, and let her bathe in peace. Like this, I could see nothing of her but her head above the tub's ledge, and for now it was enough.

Sort of.

Not entirely, but...

Blast. Who was I fooling? It was not enough. It was never enough, not even when my hands were on her body and my snout pressed directly to her skin. Being away from her made pressure build against my chest until it felt like I – a male who could control water with a mere stroke of his mind's will! – was drowning. But she did not want me near her now, did not want me to see her or touch her the way my sanity's survival seemed so hinged upon doing, and because she did not want it I did not do it.

And what could that be if not some sort of progress?

What could that be if not something to be congratulated, something to be lauded as proof of my own worthiness?

But I did not congratulate myself.

Instead, I watched Suvi with the eye I had left and began to finger-comb my hair.

CHAPTER TWENTY-THREE

Suvi

It was obvious I wasn't going to lose the dragon dude anytime soon. I'd just have to deal with having him glued to my side like some kind of massive, muscled barnacle for now. I honestly wasn't sure if he was my captor or some sort of bodyguard/nurse combo now, but either way, he wasn't moving and I would just have to suck it up and accept it for the time being.

At least, from the angle and distance of where he sat now, he probably couldn't see much of me besides my head. Unless he had some kind of alien X-ray vision, which for all I knew, he probably did.

He didn't appear to be making an attempt to stare right through the stone of the tub, so that had to be a good sign, at least. His eye never left my face, watching with stern attention while he used his claws and thick fingers to slowly untangle his hair.

I turned off the tap, bath now full. Well, not exactly full, since it was built for someone much larger than me. But full enough that I was submerged up to my shoulders. Keeping the alien firmly in my sights, though doing my best not to make it obvious I watched him, I undid the sodden knot of the sheet and let it peel away from my skin to sink to the bottom of the tub.

There wasn't anything that looked like soap or shampoo around, and I soon gave up on that, the simple act of swivelling my head around on my shoulders feeling like a monumental task. Instead, I just leaned on the side of the tub again, pressing my cheek to the edge, marvelling at the tiny pleasure of the cool stone against my face contrasting with the warm water caressing my shaky body.

I watched the alien, no longer bothering to be subtle about it (that was too much work), and he watched me back in the un-subtle way he'd done the entire time. It was jarring seeing him dressed in those long white robes, so strange seeing him methodically comb his hair, grunting with annoyance whenever he hit a snag the way a human might. He'd been so incensed, so feral when he'd first found me. Even after that, he hadn't seemed to care at all about things like his nakedness in our time together. Obviously, he had language and intelligence and immense power – I knew that even before – but now...

Well, he still wasn't human. One look at his face confirmed that. But his face wasn't exactly just reptilian, either. He had a snout, yes, but it wasn't long and thin and jutting far out from his face the way a crocodile's did. It was shorter, more blunt, angling upward into cheekbones and eyes and a brow that, despite the scales, actually felt quite reminiscent of a human's. The sclera of his eye was black, though it was nearly invisible, most of the eye taken up with a gold iris that blazed so bright it was practically flame-white in the centre.

Not human. Not lizard. Not dragon...

Alien. It was the only word for him.

Even as he braided his detangled hair into one long plait exactly the way a human might. He tore a strip off the sleeve of his robe to tie the plait at the bottom, then let it hang. His hair was so long that even braided it hung to his waist.

I found myself bizarrely admiring the effect, thinking that the style suited him before I reminded myself firmly that he'd abducted me and brought me here against my will. I wasn't supposed to be thinking thoughts like *wow having his hair pulled back really draws attention to the elegant line of his jaw at the back of his snout.*

"So, what's your deal?" I croaked, the movement of my mouth making my face slide slightly against the tub. I was too tired to lift my head. "You took me away from the other humans and brought me here... for what? Just so you'd be stuck babysitting me? Don't you have better, alien things to do?"

His hair now dealt with and hands free, the alien leaned forward, placing his elbows on his splayed thighs and interlocking his fingers together, watching me but not answering. Despite the soft fit of his robes, the fabric strained across the bulk of his shoulders, and I thought I detected the tiny sound of fabric tearing, probably at one or both of the holes where his wings emerged. He either didn't notice or didn't care about the ripping, and I assumed it was probably the latter, because even with one eye I doubted much escaped his notice. Not that he would have seen the fabric tear, but surely he would have heard it with...

I blinked, realizing this was the first time I'd seen his ears. They were mostly flat to his head and positioned roughly where a human's would be, but instead of being rounded they stretched back and up with long, tapered tips, like an elf or a goblin or a Finnish haltija.

A haltija is supposed to be helpful, to protect you, I thought sourly. And then, more than sour this time, bitterly, unbidden words came echoing back.

He brought you to an alien hospital and helped you pee and drew you a bath, didn't he?

I sighed, putting a hold on the examination of my captor/guardian/whatever-he-was and observed the backs of my feet. I was too tired to lift up my legs and hunch over to inspect them, but with some gentle prodding and staring through the water I could tell the blisters that had festered back there were healing well. There was still some residual redness and tenderness, but it was nothing like the horrible, infected mess that had been there before. And the pain now was nothing like the fire I'd felt burning through my fever sleep.

That must have been some kind of medical procedure, I thought. That agonizing burn hadn't exactly felt like antiseptic being poured onto a wound, but then again I'd barely been conscious, so who really knew? In my delirious panic, I'd imagined that I was being tortured, but in reality it was clear now that my infected wounds were being treated somehow. The flesh was pink and healing. My fever was gone. I was weak, sure, but I'd probably recover my strength eventually.

I was going to be alright. Apart from the whole abducted-by-an-alien thing, anyway.

"Thank you," I said quietly. For the moment, I ignored the rising hackles, ignored the fact that the only reason I was here and had gotten sick was because of him. And honestly, maybe even that wasn't entirely fair. I could have removed my boots before the blisters got so bad. I definitely should have taken them off and not slept in them all night. He didn't force me to keep my alien microbe-soaked boots on open wounds all night. That was, honestly, on me.

Clearly, he had helped me. He hadn't let me die. And he very well could have. Because who was I to him, really?

We were strangers.

I was *no one*. A human he wouldn't even deign to tell his name.

Maybe the stress of illness had left me weepy, but that stung more than it should have.

"Will you tell me now?" I whispered, squeezing my eyes shut against stupid tears. I huffed a steadying breath then opened them again. "Your name?" I pointed at my own face. "Suvi. You understand that. I know you do because you call me by my name all the time. I'm Suvi. You are...?"

I didn't really expect him to answer, because he hadn't before so why should he have bothered now?

But his eye brightened with alertness and he suddenly straightened up, like a pupil in class who'd just realized with a surprised sort of pleasure that he actually knew the answer to the teacher's question. For the first time since we'd been outside, his snout pulled into that fang-toothed grin of his. He bumped a scaly fist against his chest and with his rumbling voice, he answered me.

"Skallagrim."

And just like that, he ceased to be *the alien* or *the dragon dude*.

He had a name, and he'd finally shared it with me.

Skallagrim...

It was something.

A start, at least.

CHAPTER TWENTY-FOUR
Suvi

I didn't let things start and end with learning Skallagrim's name. My next goal was to learn the alien language. There was only so long I could be hurt and angry about my situation and try to wall myself off from everyone. I was the only human here, and being able to communicate with the dominant species was becoming more and more pressing. That, and I honestly just needed something to occupy my time while I recovered in bed. There was no TV, no internet (as far as I knew anyway, though the room I was in did seem to be powered with something like electricity). There was no small indoor garden to tend to like I'd kept back in Helsinki, no books to read, no socks or scarves to knit. Nothing to do except try to wrap my human brain around the language I came to learn was called Bohnebregg.

At first, the task tired me quickly, even though all I did was listen and try to parse whatever Skallagrim said to me, or to understand what he said to the other alien, Jolakaia, who came each day bringing food and checking on my legs before leaving again. I'd sit up and watch the two of them and struggle along, my mind like sludge as it tried to catch a word here or there. Often, when Skallagrim and Jolakaia had had a particularly long conversation, I'd drop like a rock off a cliff into sleep immediately after. But even in sleep, I kept at it, Bohnebregg words ghosting through my head, echoing on the outskirts of my dreams.

It was something to focus on. A goal to propel me forward when, for the moment, I really had nothing else to look forward to or work on. And boy, was it something to work on. Learning Bohnebregg was no easy feat. Unlike Finnish, the alien language was very gendered. Nouns were gendered (masculine, feminine, and neuter/plural) which affected not only the way articles and adjectives interacted with them but also verb conjugation.

This was how I learned that Jolakaia was a Bohnebregg female. Luckily, I had some experience with gendered language constructs from the Swedish I was fluent in and the smattering of French and German I'd learned in school, but it was still tricky for my muddled brain to take on.

It was a lot, so I spent seven full days barely speaking, only listening. But there came a point where simply listening only got me so far.

So then I started asking questions. I'd point at the floor, at my bed, at my face, requesting that Skallagrim rattle off the Bohnebregg counterparts.

I mainly spoke to him in English, and I did this for two reasons.

The first reason was that my human mouth and throat struggled to form a huge portion of the Bohnebregg sounds and syllables. I couldn't force out the guttural hiss that accompanied male adjective endings or verb conjugations, nor did I have a split tongue to make words practically vibrate in my mouth in order to indicate something in the plural form. The first time I tried to say something in Bohnebregg, Skallagrim had tensed, concern swallowing his face like a storm, before walloping me on the back with his massive hand. I'd tried to speak to him in his own language and he'd apparently interpreted that as his frail little star choking to death on her own saliva. Which, to be fair, I may have actually done. Not to death, of course, but the attempted hiss had definitely created a bit of an awkward spit-in-the-windpipe situation.

The second reason I stuck with English was the more foolish of the two, but I couldn't shake it, no matter how ridiculous I knew it was. English was the common language spoken among the humans on the mission Skallagrim had taken me away from. Part of me still held onto the absurd hope that one day, Skallagrim would take me back to them. And if that happened, I wanted him to be able to understand what other people were saying.

So, English it was. I narrated nearly everything I did out loud in English – *I am sitting; I am walking; I am wearing a white robe like yours; I am drinking water; yes, I like the fish; no, I do not like it when you watch me pee. Pee! You know, urinate, pass water, piss... Oh for fuck's sake.*

Maybe Skallagrim was just as bored and needing stimulation as I was, because he threw himself into the process with gusto. He did just as bad a job trying to speak English as I did Bohnebregg, but he was an enthusiasatic participant nonetheless. When I'd mime something at him and say the words – *I close the door, I open the door* – he'd usually repeat the action himself and then translate it into Bohnebregg so I could become familiar with more and more sentence compositions. The result wasn't anywhere near perfect, but after three weeks of convalescence and intense, immersive language study, we'd managed to cobble together a somewhat decent understanding of each other.

But spending that much time in my room talking basically only to Skallagrim had the unintended consequence of making me feel a lot closer to him than I was comfortable with. I wasn't sure I wanted to be his friend the way it kind of seemed like I was now. I wanted to understand him, and anyone else here, so that I could survive and figure out my next steps, not so that I could let down my defences in front of the person who'd essentially abducted me.

But more and more, it felt impossible to keep him completely out. Despite the violent way we'd met, Skallagrim had otherwise proven himself trustworthy. Other than a slightly annoying propensity to pretend not to understand me in certain circumstances (I swear I reached for my toes and said, "I bend over," about a dozen times before I realized that he was messing with me, a grin stretching his snout, eye glittering with amusement) he didn't seem to want me for any nefarious sexual purposes. He didn't appear to need me as some kind of forced labour, either. All he did was make sure I ate and drank and didn't collapse on my way to the bathroom, all while asking Jolakaia pointed, borderline obsessive questions about my recovery.

Maybe I should have been less worried about accidentally becoming his friend and more worried about...

"Am I your pet?" I asked Skallagrim about four weeks after my arrival at the place called Callabarra (I still wasn't sure if Callabarra was the word for hospital or clinic or village or if it was just a name of some sort).

Skallagrim was seated, his massive body folded onto a stool that, even with its alien construction, seemed a little too small for his bulk. He lowered the bowl of fish stew he'd been trying to foist on me for the past five minutes. In trying to feed me, he had been reminding me of how I'd tried to coax my old, sick cat Viiru to eat before he'd died, and the question had just burst out.

He replied with a phrase that I still hadn't quite figured out but that I thought meant something noncommittal, like *it depends*. Then he said, "What is a pet?"

"It's... it's an animal you keep for... companionship. Like a little friend. You feed it and..." I faltered. These concepts weren't as easy to explain as lifting up a cup and clumsily stating *I have a cup!*

Skallagrim appeared to ponder my words before replying.

"An animal used for-" He ended off the sentence in a way I didn't understand.

"Didn't get that," I muttered, waving off the bowl he'd surreptitiously tried to pass me while talking.

With a grunt, he placed the bowl on a nearby wooden table.

"Some animals," he pointed a claw at the fish stew, "are caught. Some-" He said something else I didn't understand. Then he made an upward motion with his fingers that looked like a plant blooming. And when he added something about animals pushing the ground – ploughing? – I realized he was talking about agriculture.

"No, not farm animals. Not work animals. It's pretty obvious I'm not going to be able to pull a wagon or plough a field for you. A pet is just... just an animal you..."

I barely stopped myself from saying, "an animal you love." It felt weirdly embarrassing even though I was certain he'd have no idea what the English word "love" even meant.

"It's an animal you like," I finished lamely, cheeks flushing. "It lives in your house with you. You take care of it."

Skallagrim gently rubbed at the underside of his snout with his knuckles, something he often did when thinking or trying to grab onto some particularly complex English sentence structure. He no longer ran his claws through his hair like I'd seen him do before. Now, he retied it into a long, neat braid at the beginning of each day.

He curled his hand into a fist and let it drop from his snout. Then, he leaned forward and looked at me with so serious an expression that it was almost hilariously at odds with the absurdity of the following question.

"Do you want to be my pet?"

It was a quirk of Bohnebregg language to switch into the third person for emphasis or when asking an important question. Which meant that, instead of *Do you want to be my pet?* It actually sounded more like, *Does Suvi want to be my pet?*

Using my name like that made the question feel both uncomfortably intimate while also creating an odd distance – like a parent asking something of a child.

"No!" I said emphatically. "I can't be your pet!"

"Why not?" he asked, seeming sincere. "I feed you. I take care of you. If I had a house, you'd live in it." His scaly brow bunched slightly. "*When* I have a house, you'll live in it."

Oh, my. Deciding not to touch *that* little morsel of information with a two-metre pole, I retreated into just repeating, "I can't be your pet. A person isn't a pet!"

But he only frowned and asked, "Why?" again, throwing me back into the feeling of a parent-child dynamic but this time with the roles reversed. *Only a toddler or an alien would ask why a person can't be your pet...*

"Because! A pet is not... It's a part of your family but it's not your *equal*." I raised both my hands, indicating an equal amount of space with each by holding both index fingers a centimetre away from my thumbs. "Equal," I said. Then, I kept my left index finger and thumb a centimetre apart but stretched the distance between my right finger and thumb. "Not equal."

"A pet is not your equal," Skallagrim echoed thoughtfully. "A person is above their pet?"

I grimaced, wondering what Viiru would have thought of that if he'd been alive and able to understand what had just been said. He probably would have immediately puked somewhere inconvenient just to watch me clean it up and prove the concept wrong. But I was getting tired, and couldn't figure out a way to explain how cats in particular weren't equal to their owners because they were actually the supreme beings of the household.

So instead I just nodded weakly. "Pretty much."

"Hmm," he rumbled. "Then perhaps I am your pet."

I smacked my hand to my forehead. Clearly, I'd done a piss-poor job of explaining what a pet was. But at least now I knew that wasn't how Skallagrim thought of me – he seemed to have absolutely no concept of what owning a pet meant.

"No, Skallagrim, that's-"

But he cut me off.

"Little star," he said, cocking his head slightly so that the side of his face that still had an eye was closer to me, as if he could see me better that way, "you are so far above me that-"

The rest of the sentence rumbled right past me in a rush of unknown words I had no context for. I truly couldn't say if I just didn't recognize any of the words, or if exhaustion was starting to slow down my ability to translate. Skallagrim must have noticed my blank stare. He grabbed the bowl again and thrust it down onto my lap without waiting for me to take it from him.

"Your strength fades. Eat this," he muttered.

"I'm not hungry."

"Eat it anyway." He smirked. "It would make your pet very happy."

Good grief.

I stared down at the surface of the stew, not returning his expression of lighthearted mirth. I was done with the inane turn this conversation had taken. Goddamnit, I wanted something *real.*

"Why am I here, Skallagrim?"

"In Callabarra? You were-"

"No. Why am I *here*?"

I paused, unsure if I were brave enough to ask the next question.

The shy man can't even eat cabbage.

Fuck cabbage.

"*Why did you take me?*"

I flinched, almost as if someone else had asked the question. Then I forced myself to look up.

Skallagrim had turned his back on me. Now, *that* was unusual – normally he didn't dare take his eye off of me for more than about ten seconds. His wings rustled, muscle and tendon flexing over bone, and his fingers twitched where they hung at his sides. As I waited for a response, my eyes traced the intricate patterns of golden lights flickering along the deep green expanse of his wings, like a thousand tiny fires lighting the shadows between the boughs of some night-drenched forest.

"I took you because I had to," he said at length. "There was darkness and I..."

He stopped, and I waited for more of an explanation, but it didn't come. I couldn't even make sense of the little bit he'd offered me. Oh, I was pretty sure I'd gotten the literal meaning of the words. Jolakaia had showed Skallagrim a button on the wall that turned the lights in this room on and off, and he'd stood beside it for ages, pushing it over and over again with a grin on his snout while we'd called back, "On! Off! Darkness! Light!" to each other in our respective languages.

"One day I'm going to need a better answer than that," I said quietly when he didn't add anything else.

"One day," he replied, "you will get one."

"But not today."

"No."

"And probably not tomorrow."

"No."

"So when, then?" My voice cracked.

His wings tensed upward then drooped, as if his whole body were heaving a sigh, and for the first time, I wondered if he was even more tired than me. I truly wondered what he'd been through before he'd taken me from the other humans. Why he'd been naked and deranged, crashing into the planet with the force of a cataclysmic natural disaster. I wondered why he'd lost an eye. Why he had no house.

Why he spoke of darkness.

"When I have the words," he finally answered. "The words to name you."

"What do you mean? You have words to name me. Suvi, for one thing. And you're always calling me little star."

His next sentence went over my head. He said something else about naming me, or maybe about assigning me a word and then explaining the meaning of it. My temples ached, and I gave up on trying to figure it out.

It's odd, though, the way things can leap into your hand the moment you stop reaching for them. Because it was only after I finally ate my stew and put my head down, only on the very edge of sleep, that Skallagrim's sentence finally clicked.

When I have the words, he'd said. *The words to tell you what you mean to me.*

CHAPTER TWENTY-FIVE
Skallagrim

Nearly forty days after our arrival at Callabarra, Suvi turned to me and said, "I want to leave."

My own mind supplied the last word of that sentence: *I want to leave you*. With my heart squeezing, *squeezing* until every beat hurt somewhere deep inside, I hissed with furious fervour, "You *can't*."

Her soft brows crinkled inward, a sign of confusion. Or irritation.

"We have to stay in this room?"

We. She said **we**.

"You... you just want to leave the room," I clarified, feeling terribly off-balance. I tightened the muscles along my back and tail, thrusting my wings outward then back in to try to centre myself.

"Yes!" she replied. "I'm strong enough to walk. I've been doing my *drillz*."

I still wasn't entirely sure what her human *drillz* were. They seemed to be a set of exercises. But whenever she tried to explain the process to me, she said it was related to a human activity called *hawk-ee* and I did not know what *hawk-ee* was. Maybe some sort of military engagement. The *drillz* looked like they could be basic training for some sort of warrior, I supposed.

Though imagining Suvi as anything close to a soldier was... difficult. Not because I necessarily thought she was weak – at least, I assumed she wasn't any weaker than the other soft-fleshed people of her world – but because gentleness seemed to be bred into her very bones. She could be stubborn, and she had her moods, of course, but there was no denying the goodness in her, the shy sort of kindness at her core. I tried to picture her killing a man and it did not feel like anything near truth. I was not the only one who'd noticed – more than once, Jolakaia had quietly remarked to me that Suvi followed the way of cotton without even knowing what it was.

Besides, Suvi hadn't wanted or used the knife I'd given her back at the abandoned house. She hadn't even noticed that it had been taken away during her fever (Jolakaia told us that only the Mother's Claws could carry weapons in the temple). A missing weapon would have been one of the first things a warrior noticed upon waking.

So. She was not a soldier. But still she faithfully did her *drillz* to regain the muscle that had atrophied in bed. At first, it had started with a few walking laps around the room. Slowly, walking had become jogging. Then jogging had turned to short sprints back and forth, touching invisible points on the ground as she pivoted. (It was very hard not to stare at the bouncing of her breasts beneath her robe when she ran, but by the skies I was a strong male and I could do hard things if I set my mind to them and if I sometimes faltered, if I occasionally failed, then no one would be the wiser anyway.) She also did squatting movements and lunging movements and sometimes looked like she was pretending to grip something like a shovel or a spear.

Suvi stared at me with eyes so shiny with expectation that the grey centres of them practically looked silver. I could think of no good reason to stay in the room if she did not want to. I did not plan to remain in this room or even in Callabarra indefinitely—only until she had recovered—and that recovery largely seemed to be complete. There were still two guards stationed at the door outside in the hallway, and no one had specifically given us permission to wander, but it wasn't as if anyone could stop me. I made an internal vow not to break any more bones, then hastily added the stipulation, *but only if no fools get in my way.*

I could only be expected to endure so much.

"Fine," I said. "Let's go."

Her eyebrows crawled upwards in surprise.

"Wait, really? Now?"

"Yes, now." Her surprise at my words bothered me. It bothered me that she thought she could plainly tell me what she wanted and yet also assumed I would say no. She obviously did not understand that I would do everything in my immortal power to take care of her, to keep her happy, to do whatever it was that she wanted.

But then again, when I'd thought she'd been asking to leave me, I'd immediately refused her.

Well, acquiescing to that particular request is not within my power, I reasoned savagely with myself.

I briefly wondered, for the very first time, if there were no looming threat of darkness, would I be willing to let her go? If I did not need her as some sort of antidote, some sort of anchor, would I still want, *need*, to keep her like this? Would I still feel the same possessive, protective urges towards her – the desire to hold her, to hoard her?

If there were a way to return her to her people, could I do it?

Would it hurt?

Merely thinking about it hurt, so I stopped. I focused on things I could control and make sense of in this very moment. Right now, all Suvi wanted was to leave this room and, *blast me into the cursed stone sky*, I could at least make that happen for her without losing my mind philosophizing about what it might mean or how it might feel.

As if to demonstrate my devotion to her will, I used my power to snap open the door that led into the hallway with a resounding *thwack*. The two guards outside jumped to attention and peered inside at us.

"We are taking a tour of the temple," I told the two of them as I wrapped my arm around Suvi's narrow shoulders and led her through the doorway. Though my tone, and frankly the words themselves, left no room for opposition or complaint, the blasted Mother's Claws still found a way to try.

"But the Honoured Eye has not-"

"If Koltar has a problem with it, tell him he can seek me out directly to discuss it," I interrupted brusquely. I was merely irritated by the guards; I was not yet enraged. But the way Suvi was already cowering back towards the sickroom, as if afraid that she was doing something wrong— as if afraid that these cotton-headed idiots had some sort of authority over her and she was breaking their ludicrous rules—was rapidly bringing me to that point. I tightened my arm around her, not allowing her to retreat any further.

The two guards eyed each other, then both jerked their snouts up and to the right in approval.

As if I sought such a thing from ones such as these.

I cannot wait to get out of here. I was not sure where we would go or what we would do once we left Callabarra, but as long as I had Suvi at my side I supposed it did not really matter.

"I have seen very little of this place and I do not know the layout," I told her as we walked through the hallway. "We will be wandering."

Despite my ignorance about the temple, I knew more of it than Suvi did. Her eyes were round as river stones as she took in the high-ceilinged hallway with its many tubes of light. I did not need her to say it to know that she remembered none of this, even though we'd been in this hallway before. She'd been too sick to notice any of it.

My fingers twitched against her shoulder. I could not think of that night, think of Suvi suffering, *dying* in my arms, without the demented, flapping wings of panic rising hard against my ribs. My breathing felt oddly tight. I forced myself to stay present in this moment with her. Last time I may have carried her through this place, but now she walked with her own two tiny feet, strong and steady beneath the safeguarding sling of my arm.

Not knowing what other path to take, I simply retraced our steps from our arrival. This led us through the main, pavilion-style entrance into the temple. Two children carrying armfuls of what looked like bandages stopped and stared at us, Suvi especially, before being prodded back to their duties by a voice calling from an adjacent hallway.

Suvi came to a jerky stop before the swaying curtains that separated this large space from the outer courtyard.

"Daylight," she breathed.

I gave a growl of acknowledgement. A light, warm breeze shifted the curtains where they hung, letting in wedge-like shafts of sunlight so thick they almost appeared solid, like generous slices of Sionnachan butter on bread.

Sionnachan?

I could feel the exasperated tightening of my snout and jaw as I tried to remember what "Sionnachan" meant. It described a place, I was fairly certain. Apparently a place with butter.

When my mental toiling brought forth no new information on the subject, I gave up on trying to remember for now. Instead, I stood with Suvi and watched the wind sway white curtains, letting the light in. The curtain I'd torn down for my makeshift robe that first night had been replaced.

"Can we go outside?" Suvi asked.

I snorted. Of course we could. It was not as if a flimsy row of curtains could have locked us in. But for Suvi, it seemed like the curtains were a solid wall of stone. Like they represented a line she could not cross.

With a flick of my power licking outward like the breeze, I parted the curtains and led her through them.

Instantly she raised her hands in front of her face, scrunching her eyes shut against the sunlight.

"*Paska,*" she whispered. That was a word I heard from her somewhat regularly, but had not determined the literal meaning of yet. It often accompanied pain or annoyance.

Remembering how she'd needed shade before, I raised a hasty wing above her head, casting a cooling shadow over her. Once adequately shaded, she lowered her hands and then opened her eyes in stages. Fully shut to squinting, squinting to a narrowed very blinky sort of gaze, until they were finally open all the way.

"I *mist suhn* light."

I only caught the first and last words of her statement, but based on the wistful way she sighed I assumed it was something to do with not having been outside in many days. I did not realize that would bother her so much. She had not seemed to enjoy the outside in our first days together. She got too cold, got too hot, and the sun seemed too bright for her skin and her eyes. But there she was, stepping out from under the protective rooftop of my wing, tipping her face up to the sky just so she could feel the light come down upon it.

Eventually, she lowered her face again and looked around. I did the same, feeling rather like a dunce for not taking note of our surroundings earlier. No one here posed any real threat to Suvi while I stood beside her, but I still needed to know who and what was near to us at all times.

"This is *bue-tih-full,*" she said.

"What's that word? Courtyard? Yes, this is a courtyard."

I hadn't taken much note of the space before, but did so now. Sun gleamed on the river stone beneath our feet and drenched the massive natural pillars of the trees directly across from us. But there was more in the courtyard I had not seen before. Raised, curving garden beds interspersed with benches rimmed the rounded space. Greenery sprouted from the gardens, and Suvi wandered to the nearest one, bending down and resting her hands upon her knees.

There was nothing I could either imagine or remember that compared to the elegant curve of Suvi's body when she bent down like that. Her hair tumbled forward over her shoulders in a pale river whose colour defied definition. Not quite gold, nor silver, nor any variation of white, but some shifting combination of the three, gleaming like liquid metal. Her spine created a graceful curve leading into generously rounded hips, hips that would be perfect for grasping so I could ease her backward onto my –

I wrenched my gaze from her backside and stared at the bright sky, fangs on edge and groin throbbing. Now that Suvi was no longer so sick and weak, now that she'd regained her strength and energy, it was harder and harder to ignore the way I wanted her. Because that want ran very, very deep.

I brought my eyes slowly back to Suvi, this time keeping my attention fixed to her face in profile. Her expression was relaxed, maybe even happy, as her grey gaze roved over the various grasses and flowers in the garden bed. Perfect, innocent little star. Completely oblivious to the dark, demanding heat pooling in the belly of the male who stood behind her.

We might have stayed like that all day. Suvi studying the plants while I ruminated on the effort it took to contain my cocks in my slit these days.

We might have. If the sky had not started shifting overhead.

It darkened, though there wasn't a cloud in sight, before solidifying into a sheet of hard rock. *Sky door.*

It was how I'd brought Suvi here.

And now someone, someone potentially as powerful as I was, was doing the same thing.

"Get behind me!" I did not know why I even bothered saying it. I was already reaching for Suvi, grasping her by the arm and thrusting her behind my back. My wings slammed open as I gripped her wrist and walked her backwards, staring upwards the entire time.

Mother's Claws spilled from the temple, filling the courtyard, aiming weapons upward. But they did not seem overly afraid, just cautious.

"It is likely Aeshyr."

A voice from beside me made me snap my jaws and hiss, but it was merely Jolakaia who'd followed the Mother's Claws out here. My breath dragged in and out. Darkness clouded the edges of my vision, and my bones felt suddenly too large for my scales. Suvi was struggling at my back, trying to break from my hold, but I did not let her go.

"The other stone sky god I told you about," Jolakaia said slowly. "Remember, Skallagrim? He comes here to trade, that is all. He's never shown any violent inclinations towards anyone here. You need to get a hold of yourself!"

I shook my snout once, twice, like I was trying to dislodge an insect from my ear. I remembered her telling me about him. I even remembered wanting to speak with him, to ask him questions. But being faced with him here, now, as he cracked open the sky and descended into the courtyard while Suvi was right there at my back was another matter entirely.

Suvi was no longer fighting my hold. She'd noticed what was happening overhead, and when she saw the other stone sky god, the one called Aeshyr, she crowded closer to me instead of fighting to pull away. That change in her – from fighting me to huddling against my spine – made ferocious heat expand in my chest. She did not like to be captured by me, cornered by me. But when faced with a new danger, something frightening, something male, I was the one she hid behind willingly. I was the one she trusted. *Me*.

She knew that when it counted I'd protect her. And by the skies, as the other winged male touched down, I vowed I'd do it.

My starmap buzzed, my power primed to lash out and drive him back the moment I needed to – the moment I sensed the merest whiff of a threat from him.

"Skallagrim," Jolakaia murmured low but sharp, a warning. A warning not to fight, not to rage, not to destroy half the people in this courtyard and leave the other half limping and limbless. I ignored her, because above the heads of the Mother's Claws between us, Aeshyr's eyes met mine.

My first thought was *those are a dead male's eyes*. Hollowed out and life-less. His face seemed hollow, too. Pale skin stretched too-tight over hard bone. In places, it almost appeared as if bone jutted right out of his body. There were shiny, black, near-metallic-looking blades embedded in his skin along the sharp line of his cheekbones. His face was closer to Suvi's in struc-ture than mine – no snout. But Suvi's had life and colour and movement and his did not.

His hair was shorn very short, shorter than Jolakaia and the other ser-vants of the temple. What little ghostly buzz of hair was left told me the colour was pure white. His brows had hair, like Suvi's, but were almost in-visible. With thin lips and a nose that did nothing special to draw attention, all there was to look at on his emotionless face was the black slashes along his cheekbones and the haunting emptiness of those dark eyes.

He did not look angry and made no show of violence, but somehow his flat stare across the courtyard was more disconcerting than if he'd come through the sky door roaring and raging. I became aware of how tightly coiled every muscle in my body was, my breath rushing in and out as he ap-peared not to breathe at all.

And then he started to walk. It took me a moment longer than it should have to even realize that he'd begun to move. The first thing I no-ticed was the way the Mother's Claws had parted for him, and then the way he seemed to be larger, closer than before. I jerked and snorted when I fi-nally clued in that he was striding – rather, more like gliding – on long, lean legs towards me.

Now that the Mother's Claws had shifted, I could see the rest of him. Plain dark trousers, heavy-looking black boots (that somehow made not even the slightest whisper of sound on the stone) and a tattered-looking dark vest made up his form of dress. His starmap glowed moon-white on skin that was nearly as pale. The black, shiny protrusions were not just there on his cheekbones. Hard plates of it were visible beneath his vest at his shoulders, and along the lengths of his arms – one long spear of black from shoulder to elbow, then another from elbow to wrist. Even his knuckles had hard points of black poking out of white joints.

His wings were large, but starkly skeletal. A frame of black bone sup-porting the stretch of very thin, translucent flesh. It was only the spread of his glowing starmap across his wings that made the skin between bones visible at all, only the pulsing light that showed that these were real wings, living wings, not simply the wasted branches of bone.

Can a stone sky god die and yet keep walking?

He came to a stop before me. Those lifeless eyes gave me the impression that he was searching my face even though his gaze did not move at all. I kept my wings extended, shielding Suvi from view as she remained still at my back, like a warm, Suvi-shaped stone.

"Skallagrim," he said. His voice was like wind scraping over desolate plains. "I see you've found her."

"Found..."

And suddenly I'm not with Aeshyr but with another white-haired male. We're standing together in the river, and I know he loves me but he's worried for me, his familiar face grim.

"You know what will happen," he says, and it feels like an omen. "You know what will happen if you do not find her."

The collision of the memory with the present shook me, and I grunted with the force it took to remain here, remain standing, remain in Suvi's service. Aeshyr was somehow already gone, moving past me into the temple, and in a delayed, drunken movement, I turned to face him so that Suvi remained hidden. How a male who looked like barely more than a strung-together set of bones in boots could move that quickly defied all reason.

"He has come to trade. Nothing more," Jolakaia said, much as she had before.

But Jolakaia was wrong. This time, he would not merely trade and disappear.

This time he'd have questions to answer.

He knew me on sight. He knew my name.

I see you've found her.

Who else could he mean but my little star? He knew about Suvi without even seeing her at my back. How? In the blasted expanse of the stone skies, *how?*

I would speak with him. He had at least some answers for me, I was certain. Part of me wanted to chase him down right now, pin him to the stone, take that strange dead-eyed face between my claws and order him to speak.

But my first priority was Suvi. Seeing her safe mattered more than anything else. As Aeshyr disappeared into an unknown part of the temple, I took Suvi back to her room.

And then, despite her confused protestations and the unease unfurling in my guts at the thought of even momentary separation, I left her there.

CHAPTER TWENTY-SIX
Skallagrim

It did not take too long to find Aeshyr. Or, rather, it did not take too long for him to finish up his business inside the temple and come through the hallways to leave again. If I'd had to actually search him out, it would have been much longer. But as it was, while I stalked down unfamiliar hallways in the temple, he came as if to meet me, a wooden chest balanced on one black-plated shoulder. His limbs were deceiving in their length and leanness – but like this, one arm up and holding the chest – the hard lines of corded muscle were obvious in the golden light of the temple.

"Aeshyr! Halt. I have questions for you."

The blasted man did not halt. But he did make a raspy sound of acknowledgement, as if inviting me to ask my questions while we walked. I bristled, then forced down the irritation, falling into step beside him. I sensed that as soon as we reached the courtyard he'd be in a hurry to leave, so I wasted no time asking the question that burned at the forefront of my mind.

"How did you know about Suvi?"

"I don't know what a Suvi is."

I held the tips of my tongue in check and fought the urge to cuff him on the back of his shaved head.

"You know whom I speak of. When you first saw me you said, 'I see that you have found her.' How did you know I'd found Suvi?"

"Ah." That actually did make him halt. He watched me with those lifeless eyes. "You truly do not know what she is to you? How she's done what she's done?"

Every other thing that came out of Aeshyr's mouth seemed designed to give offense. This time, I tensed against the idea that he could know more of Suvi than I did, but the gut-deep curiosity was stronger than any anger I felt. As if starving and standing before a plate of food proffered by this strange stone sky god, I found myself saying, "Please." A pause. "She's my..."

My little star my human my friend my captive my sacred hope my only salvation my female, mine mine mine...

The words remained inside me. Out loud, I just said, "Tell me what you know."

I wondered if Aeshyr's face was capable of any emotion at all. He was entirely expressionless as he said the words that brought my entire universe down into a single point and then made it all explode.

"She is your true mate, Skallagrim. Your fated bride."

The hallway tilted. I snapped my wings to one side so that I did not go crashing into the wall. I regained my footing with immense focus and then, with a strangled voice I did not recognize and a lack of wit I did not wish to acknowledge, replied, "*What?*"

"Your mate. Your fated mate," Aeshyr repeated slowly, as if dealing with a dunce. Which I rather felt like at the moment. He hoisted his crate into a better position on his shoulder and resumed walking. I scrambled to keep up with him, once again surprised by his sudden movement that didn't really look like movement at all.

"You were mate mad, Skallagrim. For a very long time, even by our standards. I am not surprised it's obliterated so much of your mind and memory."

"Watch your words," I hissed reflexively, even though he was right.

He did not appear to register my testy comment. He just ploughed on with that low voice, his tone as emotionless as his face.

"You descended into violent darkness because you had not yet found your bride. That is what mate madness means. I was born long after you went mad. I never saw you before today, but I'd heard tell of the half-stone sky, half-Bohnebregg prince who left his world in a rage and had not returned."

His eyes remained forward, his steps ghosting over the stone.

"But now, you have returned. And clearly, you are no longer mate mad. The only prevention or cure for such a thing in a stone sky god is finding his true mate. When you mated Suvi and gave her your knot, you sealed your bond, tied your lifespan to her mortal one, and saved yourself from the madness."

I did not even attempt to hide the way my feet tangled together, making me stumble and nearly fall.

"I have not mated her!" I said loudly, too loudly, my voice bouncing off the walls. There was a defensiveness in my reply that made me wince. Like I needed to prove that, despite my lecherously wandering eye, I hadn't actually indulged in my wanting. "And I don't have a knot!"

Aeshyr made a sound in his throat that could have meant anything. Maybe surprise, maybe simple acknowledgement.

"If you haven't mated her then your current state of mind won't last. Just being near her will not sustain your sanity for the long-term. Eventually, she will starburn, you will starburn, and you'll grow a knot and give it to her. Or else you will fall into madness once again."

Two children passed us as he said that, but they didn't seem shocked by the talk of rutting and knots and madness. For the first time in the conversation, I realized that Aeshyr was not speaking the tongue of Bohnebregg, but I could fully understand him.

"Are you speaking the stone sky language?" The question was a good distraction from everything else he'd been saying. My head ached with the whirl of his words.

So did my cocks.

"No," he grunted. "Riverdark."

"Then how the blazes am I understanding you? It took days and days of endless talking and teaching to get to the most basic level of conversation with Suvi," I snapped, my frustration mounting. We reached the curtains, then passed through them to the courtyard. The sun beat down and made Aeshyr look even paler than before.

"I assume you have webbing, but it must not be fresh enough to have picked up your mate's language."

Webbing. That word tickled something inside my brain. A ripple in the river.

"Here." Aeshyr put down the Bohnebregg-constructed chest. Metal clinked inside it. His hands free, he pulled one side of his vest away from his pale, sinewy torso and dug inside an inner pocket. The pocket could not have been very large, but somehow his entire hand disappeared inside it and spent far longer rooting around in there than made any sort of sense. Finally, he pulled out something shimmery, crumpled in his fist.

He dropped it into my outstretched palm. Not it, *them* – two scraps of silken webbing with strands glinting in every colour imaginable. A name bubbled up, then burst without warning or context. *Ruhnwebbe.*

Instinct told me what I needed to do with the shimmering pieces.

"We... we need to put these in our ears," I said slowly, as if testing the words, testing my own memory.

"Correct." Aeshyr hoisted the chest up onto his shoulder again.

"Why do you even have these?" I eyed his vest with suspicion, wondering what else jangled in the impossibly large, unseen pockets.

"I never know when the mortal leadership here will die and I'll need to begin communicating with a new Mother's Eye. Besides, I'm a trader. I have all sorts of things on hand."

"But I have nothing to trade for this."

Not that I would consider giving the webbing back to him now. The thought of effortlessly communicating with Suvi made my insides feather with want. If he decided to take the webbing back now, he'd have to fight me first.

But Aeshyr made no move to swipe the bits from my hand.

"You can owe me."

I eyed him closely as I put the pieces of webbing in the pocket of my robe.

"How come they didn't make you wear a cotton robe to enter the temple?"

He plucked at the frayed edge of his vest with his free hand. "This is cotton. I always wear it when I come here."

"It looks worn. You need a new one."

"Works as well as any other."

I found myself grinning at him. I did not like the fact that I owed him for the webbing, and his flat stare still gave me the distinct discomfort of conversing with a corpse, but I could not deny the way I was warming to him, ever so slightly.

He did not return the expression.

"Do the Warlords of Riverdark smile?" I asked. If I'd ever met another from that world, I could not recall it.

"They do," Aeshyr answered. "I don't."

Without another word, he hurtled upward into the sky with more speed and force than those skeletal wings should have been capable of. The sky turned to stone, he opened his door with a vicious crack, and then he was gone.

Blast. I wouldn't have minded asking him a few more questions. But it seemed that Aeshyr was finished answering them.

I stared up at the fading remnants of his sky door, stone dissipating into bright blue clarity.

For a long moment, my mind was blank. The river motionless.

And then, the full force of his words crashed over me like a mighty wave.

Suvi was my mate. Mine in every conceivable way. She'd led me out of the darkness, and now she would share her life with me. And I would tie mine to hers.

The relief at that was thick. Palpable. And the relief was not about the fact that mating Suvi presented a permanent cure for the darkness. The mate madness.

The relief was that, even once permanently cured, I would not have to give her up. She was my mate and I would keep her. It was my right and it was the only thing that made sense. I no longer entertained questions about whether I'd be willing to let her go if I no longer needed her as an antidote.

I already knew I was not willing.

Now I understood why.

CHAPTER TWENTY-SEVEN
Suvi

S kallagrim couldn't have been gone for more than half an hour, but it was the longest he'd been away from me for... well, this entire time. I tried to appreciate how nice it was to have some alone time. True alone time (as long as you ignored the two guards outside the door, which was currently closed.) But after five minutes, then ten, then fifteen, anxiety started to gnaw at me. Everything I knew about Skallagrim had shown me that he was basically a tank in dragonish alien form. I doubted anything could hurt him out there. So I wasn't *worried*, exactly. But there was discomfort. Discomfort at not knowing where he'd gotten to. I couldn't tell whether it was some messed-up codependence I was forming, a toxic attachment based on the fact that he was the only one in this entire world who understood me when I spoke...

Or if I actually missed him.

I wasn't sure which option said worse things about the state of my mental health, to be honest.

But whatever it was, whatever the reason, the longer he was gone from the room, the more fidgety I got, until I was pacing, warming up for the body-burning, mind-numbing repetitiveness of doing hockey drills. I hadn't done hockey drills in years, but I fell into the old muscle memory like it was nothing at all. I'd started building up a little bit of muscle again, maybe even more muscle than I'd had before when I spent all day doing mandated research for the military on the ship. I'd regained some weight in my recovery, too, which I was grateful for. Getting back my strength and maintaining the familiar folds and curves of my body made me feel much more like myself. And being in an alien world, that was a precious thing.

I was so far from everyone I'd ever known.

But at least I could recognize myself.

I was just starting to work up a sweat doing some lunges when Skallagrim returned, the door opening then closing with a bang so loud I nearly jumped out of my skin.

Panting, half from the surprise and half from the exercise, I looked over at him.

Something seemed... off. He was different from before. We'd developed a somewhat easy (or perhaps not easy, but unavoidable due to proximity) intimacy being together nearly non-stop for more than a month. But that feeling suddenly went cold and vanished. It was as if his being out of the room for thirty minutes had erased weeks of contact between us. All those endless hours of conversation and bumbling language acquisition, awkwardness and even laughter, vanished.

Hell, the man had even seen me naked. More than once.

But now...

Now he looked at me as if for the very first time.

I fussed with my robe, unsure what to make of his almost ominous silence. And not just silence – distance. Usually, he was within arm's reach of me at all times, unless one of us was in the adjoining bathroom. But now, he remained where he was, all the way across the room, his back and his hands plastered to the door he'd just shut as if someone had glued him there. He was breathing heavily too, I suddenly noticed, his gleaming green and gold chest heaving beneath the white robe. His eye on me was brighter and more intense than I'd ever seen it, and yet, at the same time, his gaze was incredibly serious. Solemn.

My sweat became a cold one. Because something in his gaze, his expression, reminded me of when Elvi's doctor told me she wouldn't make it. A sobering sort of gravity that told me bad news was coming my way, and quickly.

"What happened?" I said, fighting for a steady voice.

Something had changed.

It scared me that I didn't know what it was.

Because in all the turmoil of recent days, Skallagrim had been my only constant. If something was going on with him, something that would change how things had been, how they were...

If he decided to leave...

No. You don't need him. You're a survivor and you will figure this out.

If he decided he didn't want to be around me anymore, if he had other things to do, if he left me here and never returned me to the ship... Maybe I could stay and find some way to be useful. I understood enough Bohnebregg to at least be able to do something around here. I'd scrub floors if I had to. Perhaps I could help in their gardens. Jolakaia was the only one I'd had much exposure to in this new place, but I liked her well enough. She seemed caring and gave me hope that maybe she would vouch for me even without Skallagrim.

In Skallagrim's silence, I built up a whole emergency plan about how I'd survive in this world without him. If I couldn't stay in this specific building, maybe I could find somewhere to go beyond it. When we'd been out in the courtyard area today, I'd seen the buildings beyond – what looked like an entire alien city.

Or I could go back to that abandoned house, if I could find it, anyway. Maybe, just *maybe* I could hack it on my own out there. Catch fish in the river. Start a small Bohnebregg veggie farm. I was a botanist for fuck's sake, and even if my training had been mostly restricted to Earth plants, surely I could figure out some way to feed myself without my big, scaly babysitter who currently stared at me like he'd never seen me before in his life.

When Skallagrim finally did answer, it took so long that I'd forgotten I'd even asked a question.

"I talked to Aeshyr."

I shivered. *Aeshyr.* That was what Jolakaia had called that other winged being who'd come from the sky. The creepy one. Despite the wings, the glowy bits of skin, and the ability to apparently travel between worlds the way Skallagrim did, Aeshyr looked completely different from Skallagrim.

Skallagrim was an alien like Aeshyr, sure, but he was also a sculpted marvel of power and vitality and, frankly, beauty. There truly was no way to deny Skallagrim's beauty – he was fucking drenched in it, like river water running endlessly down his scales. Even the rough scar of his lost eye didn't diminish the stark, almost arrogant appeal of his features.

In contrast, Aeshyr had looked like...

Like something mostly dead. Something that should have been relegated to the nightmares of folklore, like a vampire or a zombie or one of the shadowy ghouls of Tuonela, the Finnish land of the dead.

"OK..." I breathed out when Skallagrim didn't elaborate. "Is he... is he still here?"

"No."

Well, that was a bit of a relief. The dead-eyed Aeshyr was gone. But that still didn't explain Skallagrim's sudden weirdness around me.

"Then what is it? Why are you..." I couldn't think of a way to easily express my current whirl of thoughts in English, so instead I flapped an impatient hand at him and settled on saying, "Why are you just over there looking at me like that?"

Skallagrim cleared his throat in his odd, dragon-like way. It was a harsh, husky sound that honestly seemed like it should have been accompanied by a puff of smoke out of his snout. Then he reached into his robe's pocket and pulled out pieces of some kind of shiny, rainbow fabric.

"Put this in your ear."

It was a fairly simple sentence, but there was no way I'd translated it correctly. I was about to ask him to repeat himself, or to explain, when he reached up and shoved some of the rainbow stuff inside his own ear. I gaped, then grimaced when I saw just how far he shoved it in there. His snout tensed, and then he gave the side of his head a solid wallop with the butt of his hand before finally crossing the room and closing the distance between us. He held out a second piece of the fabric.

"Put this in your ear."

Alright, I guess I had translated that properly the first time.

I shook my head rapidly.

"No way. Why? And where the hell is the one you put in *your* ear?"

I cocked my head, staring suspiciously up at his ear. He'd shoved in a large enough scrap of the fabric that I should have been able to see the ends of it poking out, but I didn't. It was like it had melted into his ear canal and disappeared.

Well that's alarming.

"It will help us talk. Understand each other," he replied. He said something else, a word that shared the same base as the verb *to translate*.

"You mean to tell me," I said, "that a slip of fabric is... What? Some kind of alien translator?"

"Yes."

That made about zero sense. A translator would have to be some sort of machine, wouldn't it? Like a computer, with data and memory and a speaker to spit the translated words into your ear? It wouldn't be some shiny, silky thing that was ethereally pretty but ultimately as limp-looking and useless as a doily.

But he's already put one in his ear...

"Does it work already? Can you understand everything I'm saying better now?"

When he said yes, I didn't believe him.

So I decided to test him. I tried to think of saying something with words I'd never used around him before. Vocab we would have had no reason to cover until now.

Snow.

We'd never once talked about snow. We knew each other's words for air and sky and light, but not snow.

"We get a lot of snow in Finland."

His eye glittered knowingly.

"Sounds cold," he quipped back instantly.

I started, shocked, then frowned in denial. Maybe I had talked about snow once before after all...

"Vinland..." His snout struggled with the soft F sound. "This is your... Your..." He mimed shaping a sphere as if with invisible clay in the air.

"Not my world. It's a country. It's the place I was born on the planet I've come from."

He seemed to absorb and understand that perfectly, which was jarring, to say the very least.

Switching gears, I said something else, this time in my third language of Swedish, which I was sure I'd never once spoken around him.

"Salmiakki is a type of Finnish candy. I hated it as a kid but now I love it."

He practically smirked.

"Sounds good."

I switched to Finnish without even realizing I'd done so. I didn't even know what I was saying until my throat closed up with pain at the end of the sentence.

"My sister's name was Elvi and I miss her every day."

His look of smug triumph vanished. His head jerked back, and he looked so shocked and sad for me that I knew, I fucking knew, that he'd understood perfectly. There was no conceivable reason for him to be looking at me like that otherwise.

"Suvi..." He came closer, then stopped practically mid-stride when I crossed my arms over my chest and hunched away from him. He looked even more pained now, but he didn't come any closer now. All he did was hold out his hand and say for the third time, "Put this in your ear."

It wasn't a harsh demand. But neither was it a request. What would he do if I refused?

What would *I* do? Go on fighting to catch every alien word, while he understood me with ease no matter what language I spoke?

And if this thing worked, it seemed like I'd be able to understand other languages too. Not that I was exposed to any other ones besides the Bohnebregg tongue, but still. For some far-off, distantly dreamed-of future where I was no longer trapped here, it could come in handy.

I'm just being practical, I told myself sternly. *It's not just because I hate conflict and he could crush me like a pine nut if he wanted to.* I took the scrap of stuff from Skallagrim's hand. My fingertips scraped across his palm, and at the contact Skallagrim's arm spasmed, like I'd shocked him. I snapped my hand back, clutching the scrap, absurdly worried that I'd somehow burned him.

"Are you alright?" I asked, peering at him. Skallagrim flexed and loosened the fingers of his hand several times, then let it fall to his side, though his posture was anything but relaxed. When he answered, his voice sounded strained.

"There is much... Much to say. I need you to understand each word."

His eye fell meaningfully to my closed fist.

Even though I'd already decided to put the thing in my ear and hope it didn't short circuit some important bit of human biology in the process, I was suddenly afraid to. He looked too intense, some raw and unnamed emotion etching itself into the lines of his scaly face, and the instinct to hide from whatever he had to say was more clear and more ominous than any other I'd ever had in my life.

Elvi wouldn't have hidden from whatever it was. She would have shoved the translator right in and then would have demanded an explanation for all the heaviness in the air. She'd never shied away from hard questions and even harder answers. As a child, I'd been hotly embarrassed by that sort of behaviour from her. She was never afraid of offending anyone – neighbours, our landlord, my teachers – and I was doubly afraid of it for the both of us. But as I got older, I'd admired her for it. She wasn't rude, and she was an incredibly kind person, but she didn't let the quietness of courtesy smooth over the ugliness of the problems that still existed underneath. She didn't let things fester or go unsaid.

And neither would I.

I didn't even pause to take a deep breath. I just lifted the delicate, iridescent silk and shoved it into my ear canal.

Well that was a mistake.

That was my first thought. My second thought was, *How the hell did ten thousand bees get into my head and why are they all on fire?*

There were no thoughts after that. None with words, anyway. Just the acid, buzzing burn of pain unlike anything else I'd ever experienced. The closest sensation was the therapy done to my feet, but that had at least felt somewhat external. This was inside my skull and I *couldn't get it out.*

I wasn't aware of my legs collapsing until Skallagrim surged forward and caught me. I gasped and half-sobbed, unable to breathe past the agony. With a feral urge, I raised my hands, clawing at my ear, smacking at the side of my head.

Skallagrim lifted me onto the bed and scraped the hair back from my right ear. He roared something – *Jolakaia!* – but it was a distant crash of sound beyond the furious magma-hot vibration. I thought a door might have opened and closed, but I couldn't see it as I leaned forward and wrapped my arms around my about-to-explode head.

I wasn't sure if the buzzing began to dim, or if the words were growing louder and louder.

"What in the river have you done to her?"

"I gave her the webbing from Aeshyr! The one that translates. It didn't cause such a reaction in me! And Koltar has it too and obviously that self-righteous fool is just fine!"

"She is not our kind! I don't even know what her inner ear looks like and you've gone and shoved a foreign object in there. No! Don't argue, Skallagrim. You should have consulted me first. We could have done a more thorough examination and-"

The words were cut off as I made a strangled sound. This one wasn't a sound of pain. It was a sound of *Oh my fucking God I can understand every single word they're saying.*

Skallagrim was there in an instant, gripping the sides of my face with frantic hands, his single eye burning even harder than my head.

"Suvi. Little star. Stay with me, now. Stay with me!"

"I'm not going to die. I think," I groaned. Already, the pain was ebbing, flowing out of my head like pus from a boil, leaving behind a weakened throbbing. My entire brain felt bruised, but as far as I could tell it was still functioning.

Another hand pressed beneath my jaw.

"Her heart rate is very elevated," Jolakaia snapped. "Even more than when we administered the Mother's Light on her feet. You have put her body through immense stress and pain, Skallagrim."

If a green-scaled alien could have visibly paled, I was pretty sure Skallagrim would have. He looked stricken, like he'd been the one to get wrung out with agony instead of me.

I wanted to comfort him. To smooth this all over. *It's fine. I'm fine. Yes, I was hurting, but yes, I think I'll be OK. Probably. Eventually. I put it in my own ear. I did this to myself.*

It was like the translator could bring back the voices of the dead, because Elvi's voice was so suddenly, shockingly clear that I half-expected to see her standing in the very room.

*When other people make you bleed, you don't get down on your knees and bandage **them** up.*

She'd said that to me when I was being bullied and had wanted to placate my tormentors instead of fighting back. It was right before she'd put me in hockey.

So I didn't tell Skallagrim it was alright.

I didn't say anything at all for a moment. I waited to see if the ghost of my sister had anything else to say. I'd suck up everything – every word – even the ones where she was berating me. Because that echo of memory was all I had left.

But there wasn't anything more. At least, not from her. Jolakaia's fingers poked and prodded at me, and she shone a tube of light into my ear, making a hissing sound of disapproval that was unnerving.

"What?" Skallagrim said tightly. He didn't look at her when he said it, but at me.

"It looks like inflammation."

"Then by the blasted river, give her something!"

"I will," Jolakaia shot back. "Something I actually know won't harm her tissue, you moronic stone sky god. I would say that being immortal has made you careless with the lives of others, but even Aeshyr has a lick of sense about him when he deals with mortals!"

"Did she just say... immortal?" I breathed, my throat feeling like scraped-raw even though I couldn't remember screaming.

Skallagrim's snout was tense, his eye a burning ember.

"Yes. Though I will not be for much longer."

My heart seized up.

"Are you going to die? Is that what you needed to come in here and tell me?"

It's OK. It's OK. You'll be fine without him. Mostly fine. Sort of.

He's the only one you've got in this world but even if he's gone one day you'll find a way to... to...

To not fall apart.

"Not for a while yet, I trust," he said firmly. "Suvi, I do not want you to worry about me right now. I want you to rest."

"I'm not worried!"

I'm just... I'm just imagining being here without you. Living in this far-flung world without the only alien who's become familiar to me, and oh fuck, I really am worried and what the hell is that supposed to mean?

What am I supposed to do with this? This tangled bundle of resentment and worry and care that gets thorny with grief at the thought of not having him beside me anymore?

"Just lie down." That soothing voice was Jolakaia's, not Skallagrim's. Exhausted, my whole body drained of resistance, I did so. Jolakaia prodded my head to the side and put a few drops of liquid into my ear.

"Keep your head like that for a while," Jolakaia said. "Let it soak in. And try not to touch."

My hand had already been lifting to do it. It dropped with a thump on the bed.

"Is anything.... *in* there?" I asked.

When Jolakaia didn't answer, I remembered that she couldn't understand my human questions. Skallagrim shook himself, as if from a deep and terrible dream, and translated.

"No," Jolakaia replied. "The webbing has completely absorbed and there is nothing left of it to examine or remove."

I shivered and fought the urge to dig my finger inside my ear to check for myself. How could the stuff have just disappeared into my body like that? It had been completely solid! Did it melt based on body heat? But then there would be liquid left or *something*. And it hadn't melted in my hand!

Jolakaia said something about my heartrate normalizing. She reminded Skallagrim in a scolding tone that I needed to stay still, then after a few more checks on my ear, she left.

"How do you feel?" Skallagrim finally asked, planting himself on a stool beside the bed. He bent, placing his elbows on his knees, bending forward so that his face was in my line of sight with my head cranked to one side on the bed.

"Tired," I said honestly. "My head hurts."

He flinched, then raked his claws so viciously through his hair that his braid came undone. He didn't seem to notice. Or if he did, he didn't bother fixing it.

He hasn't done that in a while...

"Suvi... I cannot express the regret I..." He took in a ragged breath and dragged his golden gaze up from where it had fallen to the floor between us. "I did not know it would hurt you like that. I am so sorry."

An achy lump grew in my throat. He'd never apologized to me before. Or if he ever had, I'd never understood him.

It was something.

But it wasn't quite enough.

"Are you apologizing for the pain I just went through right now, or for everything you've done? Are you sorry for abducting me in the first place?"

He hesitated, and it wasn't a pause of uncertainty but rather of *Oh, she's not going to like my answer to that one.*

"I am sorry for your pain," he said slowly. Slowly, but so fucking surely. "But I am not sorry that I took you."

"Why not!" It was only the migraine building behind my eyes that kept me from shouting it at him. "Why is a few minutes of my pain worth an apology, but not that fact that you kidnapped me! You took me from my own people, Skallagrim!"

His eye narrowed, and though he didn't look happy, he certainly didn't look contrite.

"You need rest. I don't want to talk about this now."

"We *will* talk about this now!" I started to sit up, but Skallagrim was up in a flash, his hand splayed across my décolletage and anchoring me in place.

"You must remain lying down."

"I don't have to do anything you say! You won't even talk to me now that we can understand each other!" I tried in vain to sit up again, but the weight of his palm and fingers was a force I couldn't hope to budge.

One shift of his hand and he could crush your ribcage if he wanted to. Stop antagonizing him.

"Just tell me," I groaned. My head hurt. Everything hurt. I probably did need to rest. To just shut my eyes and go to sleep.

But I needed to hash this out even more.

"Tell me what is going on. You promised me, once. When I asked you why you took me. You said you needed the words to explain. Well, yippee!

Now you've got them. I understand you. So just tell me what this is! Tell me why you took me and why you don't even feel one bit of remorse about it!"

His hand, stone-heavy, slid upwards until he palmed the base of my throat. Against the solid alien weight of him, my human strength was barely a whisper. I felt puny. Fragile. Ephemeral and easily snuffed out.

His thumb stroked a slow line up and down the throbbing point of my pulse.

It seemed like he'd stand there staring down at me, caressing my throat in silence, forever. But finally, his hand stilled, and he spoke.

"I do not regret taking you because you are meant to be beside me. You are mine, Suvi. You are as much mine as my own scales and claws are. There is no force left in this universe but the one that tethers me to you. You can call it fate. Or destiny. Or the convergence of the brightest little star against the darkest span of sky. But there is only one word I need you to hear from me now and I bid you to listen well because it is the most important thing I'll ever say."

A hushed beat.

I didn't breathe. Maybe he didn't either, because when he finally said the word, it came out in a harsh, cathartic sort of sigh.

"*Mate.*"

I blinked in dumb confusion. His fingers twitched against my throat.

"You are my mate, Suvi. My fated bride. I have been clawing my way down a dark path towards you for a very, very long time, and at this point, little star, I could no more be without you than I could my own beating heart." His snout tugged into a slight smile, but it was more rueful than joyful. "So, no, Suvi, I am not sorry that I took you. And if faced with the choice again, I would still take you. Every single time."

"Every single time," I echoed, almost too shocked to be angry. At least, not angry yet.

"Regretting taking you would be like regretting something as inevitable and inescapable as sunrise."

And here came the anger. I tried to sit up again, and maybe the rage made me seem stronger, because this time he didn't try to stop me.

"Inevitable?" I said, disbelief at his audacity and lack of accountability fusing with fury. "*Inescapable?* No. You are the one who abducted me! You crashed into that planet and you saw me and you took me. *You* did, Skallagrim! No one else! You can't blame fate for something that was entirely based on your own actions! You could have left me alone. You could have left me there!"

His wings snapped outward then back in with a fearsome, leathery crack.

"No. I could not have." His single eye burned through a narrow slit and he gripped my chin with gentle but demanding claws. I thought he was going to say something else, but instead he just, on the bitter edge of a whisper, repeated it.

"I could not have."

CHAPTER TWENTY-EIGHT
Skallagrim

This was not going well. First, the unexpected amount of pain the webbing had caused Suvi, and now this. We could hear and speak to each other freely now, but understanding seemed a more distant prospect than ever. It was easier when we lacked the vocabulary for this – lacked the ability to brush up against the ugly and difficult things. It was far easier to speak on subjects like food and weather in stilted sentences than to speak of pain and longing and fate even with the swords of a hundred thousand words hacking away at the problem.

"I was mate mad, Suvi."

I said it bluntly, my fingers at her jaw, forcing her to keep looking at me. I needed her to understand. I barely understood and remembered all of this myself, but what I did know, I had to communicate to her properly.

"I was mate mad," I said again, my voice coming harsher. "It happens to my kind when we do not find our mates. We lose ourselves to darkness. And even now, I am still half-lost!"

Her round eyes widened.

"But you're right here!"

"Do you not remember how I found you?" I hissed. "Did you not notice the state I was in? I was a beast! I was nothing but anger and bloodlust and pain in the shape of what once could have been called a man! I could barely see out of my eye! I used to have two, you know. Now one is gone and I don't even know how I lost it! It's been generations. Do you understand that? Hundreds of years lost inside the fading cage of my own mind!"

Her face was pale under the green of my fingers. She no longer looked angry, but shaken to her little human core. Good. I'd tried to protect her from what I'd gone through. Even tried, in a way, to protect myself. But now it came rushing back, and I wanted her to hear it all. To understand what I'd been through. What I'd done.

And how she'd saved me and half the blasted universe in turn.

"Who knows how many worlds I've smashed through?" I growled. "Who knows how many I have killed? I certainly do not! I was... I was an *apocalypse*, Suvi! A harrowing force no one and nothing could stop, not even me. Until *you*."

Her breath snagged. Her eyes were very, very shiny. But she did not blink and she did not cry.

"Haven't you ever wondered why I call you little star? It's because you were the first light, the *only* light I could see! You were a beacon, blazing in that blackness. The first thing I was truly aware of in eons. The first thing I did not want to kill." My fingers slid backwards from her jaw into her hair. "And now I know why. You're my mate, Suvi. Only a stone sky god's fated mate can pull him out of that kind of madness. Only my destined bride could have been a light in that kind of vicious, drowning dark."

"You've... killed people."

I'd killed people even before the mate madness, but I decided now was not the best of times to let her know that. I merely gave a deep rumble in affirmation.

"And, what, if I'm not with you you'll go crazy and kill people again?" Her voice was rising higher and higher, as if every word was climbing up the back of her throat.

"Yes. I must remain with you." I paused, then charged forward, because if I did not tell her now then when? "And I must mate you."

Her face hardened.

"Just like that? I have no say in the matter? Doesn't matter if I want it, want *you* or not? I have to be with you to keep you from going on some fucking rampage across the cosmos? How the hell am I supposed to do anything with this, Skallagrim?"

I tried to ignore the jab of her words. The words about not wanting me.

But they hurt nonetheless. And I was not proud of how that pain shaped what I said next.

"You may not want me now, but you will," I seethed. "You will starburn for me, and I for you. And just as you were the only one who could keep me from the darkness, when you burn, I will be the only one who can help."

"Starburn? What the hell is that?"

I frowned, trying to claw back memories that Aeshyr's brief explanation had ignited.

"It's like heat. Unbearable heat. You will have the urge to mate. With *me*," I added with a hasty hiss, in case she got ideas about going to find some other male when she was wanting.

Not that I'd let another male get close. If they thought broken bones were bad when they would not let me past the gate...

"Heat. Oh, my God. I'm going to go into heat." She tried to shake her head, then knocked my fingers away from her face so she could complete the movement. My instincts told me to hold her again, touch her, do anything not to let the cold distance metastasize between us. But I had at least some shred of cleverness left in me and it told me to remain still. Remain standing beside her bed to show her I could control myself, could restrain myself, could respect her wishes.

Even if her wishes did not involve my hands on her.

"Remember when we were talking about pets? And you asked why I'm not your pet because you're taking care of me now? Well, shit, maybe I am nothing but a pet to you! Nothing but a dog. *Heat!*"

"I will experience the starburn, too," I pointed out rather archly. "I will be in just as much need."

"Great. Even better. So, we're both fucking dogs then. Or dogs fucking, I guess. Wow."

Tension throbbed between my wings and between my legs and between my eye and the place the other eye had been.

"I do not actually know what a dog is," I said when she added nothing else.

"It's an animal. Often kept as a pet by humans."

She stared at the floor, appearing to chew on the inside of her cheek. Then her head snapped up and something like hope, or maybe relief, was clear in the set of her mouth.

All I could think when she spoke next was that I should have seen this coming.

CHAPTER TWENTY-NINE
Suvi

"**B**ut you don't even have a penis!"

Skallagrim was very still for a moment before he jerked his snout in confirmation.

"You're right."

I seized on that, manic with relief. *See! See! How can I be your mate when we aren't even biologically –*

But then he said something that made my thoughts, and the walls of the world all around me, entirely fall away.

"I have two."

"No you don't." My reply was instant. A smack of denial quick as a slap across the face. Skallagrim didn't have two dicks any more than I did. It wasn't real. An impossibility confirmed by the lack of visible genitalia at the shining scales of his groin.

Lack of *visible* genitalia.

Oh...

Oh no.

"I can show you if you want."

"No! No thank you!" I stammered. How did we go from teaching each other verb conjugations to him offering to show me his dick?

His *two* dicks! His two *alien* dicks!

"You're going to rip me open!"

That was what came out of my mouth next. Not, "This will never happen," or "You are absolutely insane, maybe even more insane than when you first found me." Nope, somehow my practical, survival brain had skipped right forward to the actual act itself.

"I will not!" The ferocity of his reply, the biting boom of it, so much louder than he'd been speaking before, made me flinch and snap my mouth shut.

He began to pace, wings stretching inward and outward reflexively, like he wanted to fly right out of this room and only the constant movement of his feet on the ground prevented him.

"I am aware that this is all a shock to you. I am aware that perhaps I have not always been good to you. I could not help myself from taking you, but I accept that this has made you unhappy and I will have to work through the consequences of that. But *Suvi!*" He stopped his pacing, pinning me with a golden eye sharper than any blade. "I would never, *ever,* do anything to hurt you that way. I would die before that. No, do not scoff at me, Suvi!" He slammed a punishing hand against his chest. "I would *die.*"

His voice lowered somewhat, and he resumed his pacing.

"When your feet were injured, and they became infected, I thought I would, you know. I thought that if you died, this would all be over. Everything just... *over.* I have not felt a fear like that in my entire eternal life." The next words felt like they were meant more for him than me. "I should have known who you were to me then."

"How did you not know? How come you had to get Aeshyr to explain all this stuff to you?"

"The madness took from both my memory and my mind. My mind is largely restored. But my memory..." He heaved out a scraping sigh. "My memory is rather in pieces at the moment. Though I do suspect that when we mate, and the mate madness is permanently cured, my memory will probably come back."

"Oh, great. So, not only does your sanity and the protection of countless innocent people across the universe depend on me being with you, but your own memory does, too?" I rubbed my pounding temples. "And I still think you'd rip me open, by the way, no matter how much you say you'd never hurt me."

"When you starburn... I believe... That is, I have the vaguest sense of memory telling me that... Or maybe it's instinct..." He threw his clawed hands up in an apparently universal gesture of frustration. "I believe the starburn will physically change you. So that you can take my knot and not be injured."

I blinked at him and said nothing.

So. I was going to go into heat like an animal. I would apparently want to fuck Skallagrim's brains out. All so that Skallagrim didn't go back into an alien rage and kill a bunch more people?

This is fucked.

I eyed Skallagrim, and something suddenly occurred to me.

"How do *you* feel about all this?" I asked.

So far, I'd been stewing in my own reactions to this situation. But in a way, Skallagrim was even more trapped and powerless than I was. He, too, would go into some involuntary mating frenzy. And if we didn't do what was needed, his mind and memory would pay the price. He would lose himself again, maybe forever this time.

And he was immortal, at least for now, based on what he'd said.

So forever really would be forever.

Not to mention the danger he would pose. He might kill people he liked without even wanting to. He might kill Jolakaia.

He might kill me.

And just like fucking that, I knew I'd do it. At least once, at least enough to fix him. I'd mate him or whatever the hell it was that he needed if it meant saving him and everyone else.

"Why do you ask?" was his only reply. He seemed almost suspicious, like he needed to know my reasons before he came up with an answer.

"Because this is a lot! You're trapped in this situation, just like me. Neither of us chose this and that's only really sinking in for me now. So I wanted to know how you felt."

He jolted, spine going very straight. When he spoke, it was with a brutal, damning clarity.

"How do I feel? Grateful. Blessed. Hopeful for the first time in too long to remember. I feel *alive*. I feel like Skallagrim!"

He returned to the side of the bed, and I thought he'd touch me, but he didn't.

"I feel like I would crush the universe between my claws just to keep you safe. I'd kill for you. Die for you. End a thousand and one worlds for you. I feel... Obsessed. Half-bewildered by my own longing." He paused. Then, his voice going husky, added, "Aroused."

"*Aroused?*" Oh, why was my voice so squeaky? I cast my eyes up and down his robed figure, looking for signs of the heat he'd mentioned. "Are you already..."

"The starburn has not touched me yet," he responded tensely. "But that does not mean wanting hasn't. Even before I knew who you truly were to me, I'd vowed to keep you."

He wants you.

He wanted you even before all this mate stuff.

My stomach flipped and I couldn't come up with a reply to that. Apparently, I didn't need one, because he kept speaking.

"If I am trapped, as you say I am, then it is a trap I walk into willingly. Bind me, Suvi. Corner me. *Keep* me." He got down on his knees and then tipped back his snout. "I offer my throat to your blunt human teeth and bid you bite down as hard as you can."

CHAPTER THIRTY

Suvi

Awkward didn't even begin to cover how the next couple days felt after Skallagrim's announcement. The loose sort of friendship that had grown between us was gone, replaced by something hot and weird and heavy that clung to me even more than my robe did. Skallagrim, who until now had often been quick to grin and laugh, was subdued, quieter, more intense. Strangely, he also started refraining from things he'd done without thought and hesitation before.

Before, he'd had no issue grabbing me to help me out of bed or supporting me on the way to the bathroom. He'd force food into my hands when he thought I needed to eat and he'd pluck me off the floor and deposit me into the bed when he thought I needed rest.

He did none of that now.

He didn't touch me. Didn't speak to me much, either.

Kind of ironic. We both had the webbing. We had more language between us than ever before.

But the words had all dried up.

It occurred to me, more than once, that he was hurt and trying to hide it. He hadn't exactly given me a love confession, but he certainly felt differently than I did about this whole situation. He was extremely attached to me. He'd wanted me for a while. He was aroused by me, dear God.

He said he'd end a thousand and one worlds for me.

And all I'd done was... well, reject him. Not in so many words, and I already knew I'd sleep with him just to stave off the disaster that refusing him would apparently cause, but he had to know I wasn't happy about how this was all unfolding.

But could you blame me? Finding out I had to fuck an alien, even one I'd grown to like, was kind of a lot, even without the whole *I'll go insane and probably destroy entire galaxies without you* bit.

So, he kept his distance. I kept mine. And I tried not to notice how strange it felt, how bizarrely lonely it was, not to be touched by him.

I also tried not to freak out about the thought of going into heat. Every bit of sweat, every uncomfortably warm moment when I tossed blankets off in the night, created a writhing anxiety. I stopped doing my hockey drills, paranoid that the heat of the physical exertion would somehow bring it on before I was ready.

As if I'd ever be ready at all.

By the third day, I couldn't stand being in this room with Skallagrim any more. I needed space. To breathe air not shared in a closed chamber with him. If endless proximity in a small space was going to bring the star-burn on faster, then I had to get out.

I didn't ask him when I came to my decision, didn't speak to him at all. I just hopped off the bed, opened the door, and walked out. Two Bohne-bregg guards outside jerked their heads towards me. They looked like they might be about to try to stop me...

Until their eyes went, in fearful unison, to something above and behind my head.

"Let my mate pass."

The guards moved aside, but suddenly I couldn't take another step. Skallagrim's words had completely halted me. Frozen my feet to the floor. He'd told me I was his mate a few days ago. It was all I'd been able to think about since then.

But he'd never called me *his mate* to someone else before.

My breath shook as I felt the ghost of his bulk behind me. He wasn't touching me. Still never touching me. But he was there. I could feel him without actually physically feeling him. My skin tingled. So did my nipples. His very presence was a whisper of touch along the sensitive line of my spine.

And suddenly it wasn't enough. I almost tipped backwards. Just to feel him all the way.

I gasped, then stumbled into the hall and away from him.

Of course, he followed. I should have known he would.

"I should have made it clearer," I said as I walked down the hallway. "I want to be alone."

"If you think you will go anywhere without me then I, also, have not been clear enough."

I sighed. I could tell from his tone there was no arguing with him, so I didn't even bother. At least we were out of that little room. And he probably needed to stretch his legs just as much as I did.

I went by memory, and Skallagrim wordlessly followed, until we had emerged into the courtyard where we'd seen Aeshyr arrive.

Just like the last time we'd been out here, it was a hot and beautiful day. A few clouds, luscious as ice cream, drifted lazily across an otherwise brilliantly blue sky. I closed my eyes and tipped my head back, letting sunlight bathe my face even though I knew that I'd soon have to pull up my hood to protect my skin against it.

"Skallagrim! Suvi!"

I opened my eyes to see Jolakaia coming across the courtyard towards us. She gave me a long, penetrating look, then jerked her snout in satisfaction.

"You look well, Suvi."

I'd gotten so used to conversing freely with Skallagrim that I almost responded in Finnish or English, assuming she'd understand me. But she wouldn't. She didn't have the webbing in her ear. The Bohnebregg word for "thank you" was a gnarly one, but I managed to get it out with a bit of a smile.

"It is good to get some fresh air," Jolakaia said. "I myself was just on the way to the temple's gardens to gather some of the herbs we Mother's Hands use."

At the word garden, I must have made a sound, or else displayed some other kind of obvious reaction, because both Jolakaia and Skallagrim peered at me more closely.

"Would you like to accompany me?" Jolakaia asked. She said it rather tentatively, as if the thought I'd want to see the gardens had never occurred to her before. Her gaze very clearly went to Skallagrim then, as if seeking his permission, but I was the one who answered.

"Yes, please!" Good grief, my Bohnebregg accent was terrible.

I winced, then turned to Skallagrim, finding him already staring at me. I blushed, told myself it was just the warmth of sunshine on my cheeks, and said, "Could you please tell her that I used to study plants where I came from? I'm a botanist. I would love to see the gardens and learn about them, if she'd take some time to teach me."

Skallagrim mulled this over for a moment. I heard the distinct sound of a little bit of my heart cracking when I thought he was going to say no. How sad was it that so much of my happiness these days relied on a simple walk outside a windowless room to see some flowers?

But he did translate, and faithfully. I could understand every word, so I knew he'd relayed the message properly. Jolakaia looked taken aback and then she examined me with newly appreciative eyes.

"I did not know you had such expertise. Come, yes, I will show you."

We had to go back through the building, which I now knew was a temple, not simply an alien hospital, to get to the gardens. The gardens were at the back of the sprawling structure, and I let out a low exclamation when I saw them.

It looked like something from a painting. More like art than real life.

Directly ahead of us, currently shaded by the temple with the sun behind it, were dark squares of soil occupied by what looked like mushrooms. They grew in soft, round puffs, their flesh jewel-blue with saffron-yellow spots. Just beyond them, partially shaded, were twisting vines with huge, heavy red gourds growing, kind of like pumpkins, but shiny as apples.

There was a path through this shady part of the garden, and Jolakaia led the way, pointing dark claws at plants as we passed.

"Spotted sprouts. Red vinefruit. Both edible," she explained. We entered the sunny area of the garden, where things grew taller, with longer stalks and fluttering leaves. Jolakaia stopped and bent, slicing through the stalks of a plant with fluffy flowers that looked like they were made of bunches of feathers rather than petals. She held it up in the sunlight, letting the breeze ruffle the unusual and charming thing. It reminded me of a little chick.

"This is Mother's Breath. It is anti-bacterial and anti-inflammatory. When you were very ill from your infection, we administered this to you both internally and externally.

I looked at her, and the tiny bird of a flower she held, and nodded solemnly.

"Thank you," I said. Skallagrim may have been the one to have brought me here, but without Jolakaia's help and healing I might not have been standing now in that beautiful garden.

"Of course. The Mother of Cotton bids us to help those whom we are able."

"You talk about the Mother a lot," I said. "And a lot of things seem to be named after her. Mother's Breath. Mother's Hands, like you." I stopped, remembering the one-way language barrier, and cast a silently pleading look at Skallagrim, who thankfully translated without further prompting.

"Oh, yes. I suppose Skallagrim does not remember enough about it to explain."

She tucked the Mother's Breath flower into the pocket of her red robe. Then she pointed up at the sky. No, not just the sky. She was pointing at the sun.

"The sun represents Roakan. He is the Father of Metal and the god of war, glory, and bloodshed." She grew thoughtful. "Have you ever seen our sky at night?"

"Yes," I said. I'd been out there with Skallagrim.

"So you have seen the two moons. The large one and the smaller."

I nodded again, and she'd spent enough time with me to know that meant "yes."

"The larger moon represents Callanna. She is the Mother of Cotton, goddess of healing, protection, and peace. She has a daughter, Shara, the little moon who accompanies her across the sky each night."

Jolakaia bent to cut off more of the Mother's Breath flowers for her supply. She kept speaking as she worked. Skallagrim remained silent, but even without looking at him I could sense the possessive way he supervised our interactions with his gleaming eye.

"Roakan and Callanna are husband and wife. They are mates."

"Really?" I said, not expecting that. "Doesn't seem like cotton and metal mesh that well."

Skallagrim translated, and Jolakaia's snout tightened in a smile.

"No, they do not. The story goes that Roakan would not give up his warring, hoarding ways even after the birth of their daughter. He fought often and was always the victor. Which meant he killed often. Callanna could not bear to see so much pain, and when she could not convince him to follow the way of cotton, she took Shara away and she left."

Wanting to be useful, I tried to help Jolakaia collect some of the Mother's Breath, but the stalks were extremely tough and impossible to slice through without shears of some sort. Or claws. Without speaking, and without needing me to ask, Skallagrim came closer and his claws snipped through the stalk of the plant I'd been tugging at.

I moved my hands to give him better access, which meant that when the flower came away, he was the one in possession of it. He held it up between us – an obvious offering – but he didn't move to give it to me.

He wanted me to reach forward and take it.

Flushing and having no idea why, I did. I tried to erase the sudden awkwardness I felt by hurriedly passing the flower on to Jolakaia. Skallagrim's eye followed the flower until it disappeared into her pocket. Then he looked away.

"Ah, thank you," Jolakaia said, not appearing to have noticed the odd and tiny moment that had passed between Skallagrim and me. She continued speaking. "When Roakan realized his mate and child were gone, he entered a rage. Not just any rage. A Bohnebregg berserker's rage. He fought his way across the world trying to find them, spilling so much blood that it formed the mighty Bohnebregg river that flows today. And still, he fights and searches."

She raised a hand towards the sun.

"Every day, he tracks hotly across the sky, his anger so bright no one can look at it for long. And every night, Callanna and Shara loop back around behind him, following at a distance, healing those he's hurt."

Her hand lowered, and she looked suddenly weary.

"Roakan is so incensed that he does not even realize that the ones he searches for are right behind him, trying to undo the damage he's done. But that is the way of metal. It adheres more to the laws of anger and vengeance than it does good sense. Always fighting forward and never once stopping to look back."

Skallagrim chose that moment to say something, his voice cutting.

"Perhaps if Callanna and Shara would stop running and simply stay with Roakan then he would not rage the way he does. I believe that he must hurt more deeply than any other they would deign to heal."

Jolakaia stared hard at Skallagrim, and I glanced uneasily between them.

"You sound like my brother when you speak so," she said, and even though I had no idea who her brother was I got the feeling that was not a compliment. Her gaze fell on me, and her expression softened somewhat. "But perhaps there is hope for you yet."

How do I feel?

Hopeful for the first time in too long to remember.

I blinked away the memory of Skallagrim to focus on the real one before me.

The one who did not look happy but who also didn't seem to have anything else to say.

Jolakaia turned and led us swiftly onward, as if Skallagrim's mood wasn't going to get in the way of the efficiency of her work. She led us past more bursting blooms, giving greetings to a few others who wore green robes and were called the Mother's Seeds. The Mother's Seeds appeared to be responsible for taking care of the plants here.

Jolakaia continued naming and explaining the plants, and I committed everything I could to memory, longing for a pen and paper to take notes. As traumatic as it had been to be ripped away from Earth, and then ripped away again from the other humans on the mission with me, this was still the experience of a lifetime. I was getting to study honest-to-goodness otherworldly flowers! What other botanist would get a chance to do something like that?

On the outer edges of the walled temple garden were great glass domes, sparkling like dew drops. Jolakaia explained that these functioned as warm, dry zones during the planet's rainy season, and that that way they could prolong the growing season of many of the important plants and herbs here.

Growing tall near the far walls were plants I recognized – the fluffy-topped stalks I'd seen outside by the river.

"I've seen those before!" I said, excited to actually recognize something. "Can you tell me what they are?"

After Skallagrim translated, Jolakaia replied.

"These are Shara plants."

"Shara…"

"Yes, that Shara." She plucked one and let me look closer. "Cotton and metal intertwined. Elements from both her parents."

"So that really is metal growing out of a plant," I breathed in amazement. What I wouldn't give to be able to examine that in a lab!

"Yes," Jolakaia said, seeming a bit confused by my reaction. "Metal grows just as cotton does."

"Wow. Sorry. Where I come from, metal has to be mined. It's very limited and precious because of that. It's incredible you can just… Well, just grow it like this!"

"It is precious here, too," she said, rather grimly, after Skallagrim translated. "Those who follow the way of metal beyond these walls kill each other for it."

I frowned, not understanding her.

"But… Why? It obviously flourishes here. I saw tons of it out by the river! Why would people kill each other over it when there's so much of it and it's a renewable resource? Can't people just… grow more?"

Jolakaia breathed out, and it was a sound flinty with exhaustion.

"There is no glory for a Bohnebregg warrior in foraging or agriculture. The metal, and the weapons made from it, are precious to them precisely because they must be won in war from someone else."

She snorted.

"The look on your face is exactly why I left that life and came here. In Callabarra, we use metal for tools. To create new machines that can heal. And we do it all with what we've grown or collected ourselves in peace. That is the way of cotton. We follow those tenets faithfully, and we have grown and flourished. Although, we've only been able to grow Callabarra to its current size and state because of Aeshyr's protection."

I shivered at the mention of that corpse-like male.

"Do you know what he uses the metal for?" Skallagrim asked.

"I do not," Jolakaia said. "Perhaps Koltar does. Whatever it is for, he seems to require a great deal of it. He has been coming to this world much longer than I've even been alive to collect it. But as he's always come in peace, wrapped in cotton, we've had no reason to fear him. And he keeps us hidden from Bohnebregg warriors who would otherwise tear this city apart merely to lord themselves over the scraps."

I shivered again, harder this time, at the thought of people coming here and destroying everything just to fight over metal that already existed throughout the natural landscape. I risked a glance at Skallagrim to see what he thought of all this, but his stony face gave nothing away.

"And how about you?" I asked him, unable to hold the question back. "Do you remember enough about before to know where you stood in this sort of thing?"

"I remember little." He stared at me like nothing else existed. Not Jolakaia, not the gardens, not the burning rage of Roakan in the sky above. "But I know that I did not follow the way of cotton."

My heart fell, and I hated that it did. That I was disappointed in something I'd already sensed, already could have guessed.

"How did you even know to bring me here?"

"Aeshyr is younger than me. He only started hiding this village with his protective spells after I'd left the planet. But some hidden part of me remembered that there was a small collection of healers here once. Healers who eschewed hoarding metal and lived in peace. I do not believe I ever troubled myself with them before, but at some level I knew that they were here."

"And here we still are," Jolakaia said. "In much larger numbers, now. With the protection of Aeshyr's spell, it is actually safe for us to use, store, and create with metal. We have healed many. And we have invented things – amazing, powerful things, that do not exist outside these walls. The way of metal does not allow for much in the way of invention, unless you're inventing new forms of weaponry."

I didn't have any new questions for the moment, so Jolakaia continued the tour of the gardens, going slower now, bending to show me each plant individually and explaining their benefits and usages and quirks. Skallagrim said nothing else, and if it weren't for the annoying way my body seemed at-tuned to the very bulk of his presence, I could have forgotten he was there.

Could have.

Didn't.

Even with my robe's hood pulled up against the sun and blocking my peripheral vision, I could feel him.

Eventually, Jolakaia had to return to her temple duties. Her pockets now stuffed with supplies, she went back inside the temple, sending a promise over her shoulder that when she began preparing the plants I could watch and maybe even help. I was already looking forward to it. Something to do besides skittering awkwardly around Skallagrim all day. A job. A pur-pose here besides waiting for the starburn so I could fulfill some bizarre and unfair role laid out for me by biology and fate.

When Jolakaia disappeared into the temple, another figure came out. A Mother's Claw robed in black. He hobbled along with a wooden crutch at his side. When he saw Skallagrim and me, he visibly tensed.

"Why's he glaring at you like that?" I asked. While Jolakaia was the on-ly one who spoke to us in a friendly way, I hadn't noticed too much outright hostility from anyone else.

Skallagrim glanced over.

"Oh. Him? I broke his leg."

"You... you what?!"

I reared back from Skallagrim in shock. I couldn't tell if I was more sur-prised by what he'd just announced, or the blasé way he'd said it. *I broke his leg.* He said it like he'd done nothing but spill water on the other man's lap. No – he said it like it was even less than that! Most people would at least have the decency to look the tiniest bit embarrassed to spill something on someone else.

But I didn't see embarrassment in Skallagrim, or remorse, or really any care in the world at all for the man he'd injured so badly. It had been weeks, and the other male was still using a crutch and looked like he could barely walk!

He did say he didn't follow the way of cotton...

"Why?" I demanded. It had obviously happened recently, since we'd arrived here, so it wasn't like he could blame the mate madness. He would have had a clear mind at that point.

A storm of emotion, or maybe a memory, darkened his one eye.

"He refused me entry to Callabarra when you were injured. So I destroyed the gate into this city and while using my power I broke the bones of several Mother's Claws in the process."

"Several?! You mean you hurt more people?"

Every emotion Skallagrim didn't feel about the situation hit me double. I was absolutely mortified and nauseous with guilt that people – multiple people! – had been injured. And in a way, it was because of me.

"You look unhappy," Skallagrim noted, bending until his snout was level with my face.

I swatted it away.

"Of course I'm unhappy! I just found out that I wasn't brought here in a peaceful way, but that you battered your way in! I can't believe they even agreed to help us at all after that!"

"I can," he said without missing a beat, "because I promised to kill them all otherwise."

My blood went cold. I physically felt it – an icy pour through my veins.

"I don't know you at all," I whispered. Weeks on end of being with nobody but him – talking, eating together, even laughing – and I'd had no idea.

For the first time, Skallagrim sneered at me in a way that looked like contempt or disgust. It was such a disturbing shift from his usual grin that the feeling of him being a stranger became so intense I was nearly dizzy with it.

"Well, then I suppose we are even. Because I largely do not know myself these days. I could not even remember my own name until Jolakaia said it to me."

I crossed my arms, trying to will away the goosebumps gathered on my skin.

Skallagrim said nothing for a short while, then muttered, "Does it help at all that I did not precisely intend to break any bones? It just sort of... happened. In the heat of the moment."

I lifted my chin, looked him square in the eye, and said, "No."

Then I turned on my heel and strode over towards the Mother's Claw in the shadows.

"Suvi," Skallagrim growled. There were a thousand unspoken demands and desires beneath the sound of my name. A warning not to go any further. A question about what I had planned. And maybe even a thin note of pleading for forgiveness.

But it wasn't my forgiveness Skallagrim needed to earn.

The guard's glare faded pretty quickly once he realized I, closely followed by Skallagrim, approached. His eyes wheeled around in his head, as if trying to find exits from the situation.

"Hi! Hi, it's alright!" I came to a stop before the guard.

He stared at me in confusion. Of course, I'd spoken to him in Finnish like an idiot. I plastered what I hoped was a calm smile on my face and did my best to greet him in Bohnebregg. His scaly brows bunched in surprise – he'd clearly understood me. But he said nothing in return.

Kind of fair, considering the glowering giant behind me had literally broken his leg and then threatened to kill him and everyone here. *For fuck's sake.*

"Skallagrim," I said firmly. "I want you to translate. Please tell him I'm so sorry for what happened."

Skallagrim looked as if I'd just asked him to eat his own shit.

"Absolutely not," he hissed. "You could have died because of this fool and the other guards! If I had been a weaker male, if I had not been able to subdue them and bend them to my will so quickly, who knows what would have happened to you!"

"Jolakaia said that they're obliged to help those who ask! If you'd simply asked for help, they would have!"

"I did," he snapped, "and they took too long opening the gate. You were so sick, Suvi! You were dying and every moment counted! Forgive me for caring more about you than the snapping of a few inconsequential bones."

"Inconsequential?! Skallagrim, he can barely walk!"

This wasn't going well. The poor guard looked like he didn't know how to extricate himself from the situation without calling attention to himself. I'd wanted to come apologize to him, but now I was just holding him hostage to our bickering.

"Tell him," I said, suffusing my voice with as much of a commanding air as I could. I wouldn't back down on this. *Elvi would be proud.* "Tell him that I'm so sorry he was hurt and that if there's anything I can do to help, I will."

Skallagrim's eye roiled like magma. He looked over my head at the other male.

"Suvi regrets the circumstances of our arrival," he said in a huff. And then, with another sneer – how many times was he going to make that new, alarming expression today? – he added, "She hopes you heal just as quickly as one such as you deserves."

"OK. Enough out of you!" I rolled my eyes and stepped between the two males. Skallagrim obviously wasn't going to translate properly for me, so I'd have to get by with my garbage Bohnebregg. I made the sentences as short as I could to avoid pronunciation errors and managed to ask the guard for his name.

"My name is Nakib," he said cautiously, as if even telling me something as simple as his own name was going to get his other leg snapped.

"Nakib. My name is Suvi." I cringed my way through a poorly pronounced and nowhere near eloquent apology. It wasn't anywhere near enough, but maybe Nakib registered some kind of sincerity on my face, because he relaxed a little bit.

"Now I understand the talk about you. Jolakaia has told the other Mother's Hands, and so it has passed to us Claws, that you follow the way of cotton. I believe it now." Then, more quietly, leaning slightly forward, he added, "Once that other male moves on, you are welcome to stay."

A pair of huge hands settled on my shoulders and yanked me back so quickly I didn't even have time to suck in a gasp of surprise. Skallagrim's broad back was suddenly before me, muscles bunching beneath cotton and pulsing green wings filling my range of vision.

"I do not like the way you speak to *my mate,*" he growled. "Another word about keeping her here without me, and having her alone, and you'll end up with a broken neck instead of just a-"

"Skallagrim!"

He angled his head back over a tense shoulder so he could see me.

I stood, shaking, my words stopped up in my throat. Knowing that Skallagrim had hurt people, even killed people, before meeting me had felt real only in a blurry, distant sort of way. Like someone else had done those things instead of the man I thought I'd come to know. But now, here, faced with Nakib's broken body and listening to Skallagrim make actual death threats right in front of me, reality crystalized.

Then shattered outward with a stabbing vengeance.

I shook my head, swallowing tears, and walked past them both into the temple.

"Suvi!"

Skallagrim abandoned Nakib immediately, stalking behind me.

"I can't right now, Skallagrim. I just... I can't."

"Can't *what?* Suvi, look at me!"

The hall flew by me, like it was moving instead of my feet.

"I can't, Skallagrim! I can't look at you right now because I'm scared that all I'll see is a mask. All the times you've helped me, the kindness you've shown me, the care and gentleness – it all feels so fake now. So inconsequential. Like it wasn't even real at all. I'm learning who you are beyond the walls of our little room, who you *really* are, and I don't like-"

Skallagrim seized my wrist, halting my harried progress. He whirled me back around to face him, and for a moment he almost looked shocked that he'd done it. He stared blankly at my wrist held in his claws, like it was someone else who'd grabbed me.

And then his face hardened, darkening as if with some sudden decision. It was as if, since he was already touching me, he might as well keep going. The physical distance that had grown between us over the past little while collapsed like the last log turning to ash in a fire. His grip tightened, and he backed me up against the wall, his other hand going to my jaw, holding my chin firmly.

"Do not tell me what is real and what is not," he murmured. "How I am with you, how I care for you... Do not tell me those things are of little consequence. Do not tell me that the most vivid and important moments of my life are false."

"How can you say that when you don't even remember most of your own life?"

"I remember or have relearned enough. I was not raised to follow the way of cotton, Suvi. My father was a powerful stone sky god. My mother was a battle-hardened berserker princess. Once, I was a warlord prince of this land. And even now, my instincts make me want to fight and take and hoard. The need for bloody victory has been bred into my very bones."

His wings pulsed in and out, rhythmic as a heartbeat, punctuating each sentence. "I am proud. I am possessive. I am violent. I will not hide these things from you."

The way he caged me in and leaned down to me cast his face in shadow. But his eye was bright.

"I know myself well enough to say with clarity and conviction that no one would accuse me of being a soft male." His thumb stroked at the inside of my wrist, caressing tenderly, drawing sparks beneath my skin. "But I am soft with you, little star. *For* you. And it is truth. The greatest and most guiding truth I have ever known." Something buckled in the furrowed set of his brow. "Is that not enough?"

Something that felt a whole lot like loneliness ached in my chest until all I wanted to do was touch him back. I missed Skallagrim even though he was right in front of me.

I caught myself just before I nuzzled into the hand cupping my jaw, horrified by my own lack of control.

Was I that touch-starved?

Or was it because it was him that held me?

"I don't know."

It was my response to my own questions and to his. His eye searched my face for a long moment, his snout so close to my mouth we could have kissed. I almost thought we were about to. And disturbingly, I had no idea if I'd push him away, or...

But in the end, Skallagrim was the one who pulled away. Not too far. Just enough for me to push off the wall and stand properly. He released my wrist and jaw, and the absence of him felt suddenly wrong. Cold and strange. I rubbed at my own arms and started to walk, trying to shake off the feeling.

Skallagrim fell into silent step beside me.

But inside my head, there was no silence. Because someone – maybe the ghost of Elvi's voice, or maybe my own subconscious – was nagging at me.

He only broke Nakib's leg and hurt the others for your sake, you know.

Skallagrim watched me from the side. I could feel it.

That just makes it even worse! I shot back internally at the voice. *It's not like I asked him to do that!*

You couldn't ask him anything because you were unconscious, the voice pointed out blithely. And then, suddenly louder, pounding, gong-like and accusatory, *Would you rather have died than have somebody fight for you?*

This time, the answer wasn't "I don't know." The answer was as instant as instinct. I couldn't hide from it, couldn't shy away.

No.

I wanted to live.

I may not have liked his methods, but Skallagrim had fought for me, for my life. It was terrible, bloody over-kill (and thank goodness no one was actually killed) but it had saved me, *he* had saved me, and...

And he was afraid.

That voice sounded more like Skallagrim's than anything, which was very odd.

I supposed it didn't matter because I knew the voice was right.

CHAPTER THIRTY-ONE
Skallagrim

It was with relief that I realized things were not as dire between Suvi and me as I'd thought when she halted a few steps inside the medical room and said, "I don't want to stay here anymore."

Tension between my wings suddenly eased, and my first real smile in days stretched at my snout.

"Of course, Suvi," I said quickly, warmth blooming in my chest at the thought of creating a real home with her. "I will take you away from here. I will build you a house. A glorious palace on the river and we will-"

"No."

We had just walked into the room and she was ahead of me, looking towards the far wall. Now she turned to me, and her expression showed none of the hope and anticipation I felt. It was just as closed-off and weary as it had been before.

"I don't want to leave Callabarra," she clarified. "I just... I can't stay in this room anymore. I need windows. Sunlight. *Space.*"

There was a lingering emphasis on that last word, and I knew exactly what she meant. *Blast.*

"You mean space from me."

Her words did not confirm it. But her eyes did.

She will starburn soon. She will starburn and the bond will be sealed. I tried to soothe myself, to fight the mounting panic that told me she would never need me as I needed her, and, even worse than that, that she would never truly want me, either.

You're just as trapped as I am. That's what she had said.

I'd argued with her then, but by the stars in that moment I truly felt it. Trapped by fate, by circumstance, by my own inadequacy in the eyes of the only female who mattered.

I was losing her. Losing her and I'd barely even had her to begin with.

That made me very afraid. And being afraid made me very, very stupid, as evidenced by my next thoughtless words.

"Don't you think I'd want somebody willing?" I hissed, claws flexing. The hole of my right eye ached. "It is not as if I chose this. It is not as if I chose *you*."

The irony was that at that point, you could have lined up every female in the known universe, paraded them before me in a smiling, enthusiastic row, and I wouldn't have spared a single one of them a glance. They could all be naked, on their knees, writhing with pleasure and begging for me, telling me they loved me, telling me they'd mate me, ease my burdens and my madness and my mind, and it wouldn't even matter. Not one infinitesimal bit.

Because none of them were Suvi. My grey-eyed, luscious, kind, clever, gentle, generous, stubborn little Suvi.

My Suvi.

My little star.

How dark the night feels without you.

Suvi looked as if I'd slapped her. Her voice was very hard, but it was small, and it made me hate myself.

"I want to go back to my people. To the other humans."

"That is not an option."

The sooner she understood that, the better. Maybe once she stopped longing for something that could never be, she'd turn just a little of that longing onto me. Her mate, for the skies' sake!

"Why not?" she asked.

"Because I do not even know how to find them!" I retorted. "Maybe you did not notice, but they left the planet in their craft nearly the same moment we did. I have no way to discover where they are now." Something tugged at me as I said the words, made me think they might not be entirely true. There was something locked up in memory I could not access. Perhaps would never be able to access, even after Suvi starburned and we mated. But there *was* something...

Something that told me I could find a way to get her back to them, if I really wanted to.

Which I did not.

"You could take me back to my planet," she said evenly.

"I do not know how to find that, either," I growled. "I have never been there, and I do not know where it is on the starmap." Normally, I would hate feeling so incompetent, so ignorant about the universe, in front of her. But at least in that moment such ignorance served me. There was no way to take her somewhere if I could not find it.

She sighed, crossed her arms, and looked away.

"I shouldn't go back there, anyway," she whispered. "It probably isn't safe for me."

The world tilted.

"What isn't safe for you?"

"Going home. My people... I didn't want to be on that ship, on that planet where you found me. I, and other human women like me, were forced into service of our planet. To go to other worlds, study them, find resources or types of energy that could be of use to our governments."

Her voice shook and I wanted very badly to kill somebody for her. If only she would let me.

"I was pulled right out of my bed. Abducted in the dead of night, drugged, shoved onto a ship and sent off-world and then forced into service of the ship's mission."

Tension was a hot throb along my spine, making wings tighten and darkness dance at the edges of my vision.

"They forced you?" I could not stop myself from reaching for her, drawing my knuckles along her rounded cheek. "They hurt you?"

Maybe I would find her planet for her after all.

So I could burn it into nothing.

"It wasn't as bad as it could have been," she replied stiffly. She gave a bitter laugh. "I'm a people pleaser. I fall into line easily. I'm quiet. I have friends... Friends who often ended up with a black eye and a night spent in the ship's brig for fighting back. But never me."

That was some relief. But the next thought was not.

"And these are the ones you wish me to return you to?" I wondered aloud in disbelief. "These ones who've forced you into servitude and hurt your friends? Who might one day hurt *you*? You'd rather return to *them* than be with me?"

She appeared as if she wanted to be angry or offended by my question, but then her expression collapsed into confusion. Her smooth forehead wrinkled, her mouth opening and closing several times without sound before she finally said, "Well, it's not that simple!"

"Make it simple for me, then. Explain it to me." Perhaps, with my memory gone and madness still nipping at the edges, I needed things broken down into the smallest, simplest shapes possible. Because what she was saying did not make any sense.

She did not explain it. Not really. Perhaps it was too complicated, even for her, because all she said was, "I just... I don't know what I want."

"When the starburn comes, you will know exactly what you want," I countered. "And what you will want is me." It felt like a cruel thing to say to her in that moment, to remind her of what was coming for her, for us both, so I tempered the tone in which I said it. Made my voice a low rumble, nearly apologetic.

Nearly.

Not quite.

She veered away from the subject at claw with such speed and at so sharp an angle, that I found myself floundering to keep up.

"I don't want to stay in this room anymore."

Sunlight, she wanted.

Space.

And I was nothing if not devoted to her, because I did not argue, did not offer some meaningless placation like "I will see what I can do." I merely steered myself right back out the door and said, "If my mate so desires it, so will it be."

CHAPTER THIRTY-TWO

Suvi

Fortunately, Jolakaia and her wife Zev had a small second-floor apartment attached to the side of their home that they sometimes rented out to young citizens of Callabarra that currently stood empty.

Unfortunately, it had a single bedroom.

With only one bed.

It was a large bed, at least. A huge square with a wooden frame and a comfy-looking cotton-stuffed mattress, built for two Bohnebregg people (and I'd yet to see a Bohnebregg adult under six feet tall) to fit comfortably.

It also took up so much space in the bedroom that there was no room on the floor for a Bohnebregg adult (or a half-stone sky, half-Bohnebregg male as huge as Skallagrim) to sleep down there.

That's fine, I told myself as I surveyed the space. I'd had the only bed in the medical room up until now. I could sleep on the floor.

But when I told Skallagrim as much, he balked, as if I'd suggested something as absurd as sleeping in the fucking river.

"Absolutely not," he growled. "If anyone is to sleep on the floor, it will be me."

"You won't fit," I said with a sigh. I rubbed at my temples. I couldn't remember the last time Skallagrim and I had had a normal conversation. One unburdened by all the circumstances of our strange meeting and even stranger staying together. When was the last time we'd talked, even laughed, and hadn't argued? Hadn't hurt each other somehow?

"Then I can sleep in one of the other rooms. Or out there," he said.

"One of the other rooms" meant the small bathroom or the little strip of a cooking area with alien appliances I didn't recognize at all.

"Out there" meant the little balcony that opened outward beside the bed, separated from the room by a yellow-and-green tinted glass door.

I sighed again, feeling, to be honest, like a total bitch.

"I'm not going to make you sleep outside," I muttered. Even when we'd been outside together, before we'd come to Callabarra, Skallagrim had constructed a shelter for me, or had found a house with a roof to protect me. And even with all the soreness and tension between us, I wasn't about to make him sleep outside all by himself now.

"Then we are at an impasse," he said mildly, though a tightness in the muscles at the back of his snout's jaw betrayed him. "I will not allow you to sleep on the floor. And you will not allow the same. And before you even suggest it, I will not go sleep somewhere in Jolakaia's home. I refuse to be that far from you."

Jolakaia and Zev's house was a lot larger than this apartment; there would be room for him. And even though we both knew that, the possibility of him (or me) sleeping there hadn't even crossed my mind. I didn't want to examine just what the hell that meant. What it meant that I was more interested in stymieing myself over the tight pieces of our sleeping arrangement puzzle rather than present the obvious option – one of us not sleeping here at all.

I'd told him I'd wanted space. I was realizing quickly that even after leaving the small temple medical room, I wasn't really going to get it.

At least there are windows.

Beautiful ones, too. The door leading out to the balcony was one huge stained-glass window, its shapes and shades reminding me of sun-soaked stalks of grass. Large panes of glass continued along the entire outside wall, letting in warm, dappled beams of late afternoon light.

The light spilled onto the bed, illuminating the simple comfort to be had there.

"Then we'll both sleep in the bed," I said, without allowing myself to stop and think about it. But even if I had thought about it, what other options were there? If I tried to leave to sleep in Jolakaia's place, he'd no doubt just follow me and stare at me all night while I slept, sulking. And we'd already established he wouldn't go somewhere else.

So, that was that. We'd sleep together.

Not like that!

At least... not yet.

I shivered, and a heated yet guarded look entered Skallagrim's eye.

"Are you certain?"

"I don't see any other options. Do you?"

He puffed out a wistful breath.

"Being separated from you has not been an option for me since the very moment I found you."

I supposed that was true, since being with me was apparently the only thing tethering Skallagrim to sanity.

"We only have to do it once, right?" I blurted.

The sudden shift in conversation seemed to catch him off-guard.

"Sleep once in the bed?" he asked. "You mean to stay in Callabarra only one more night?"

"No." I flushed. "I mean... To cure you, or whatever. We only have to mate once, right?"

He stiffened so instantly, so thoroughly, it was as if someone had replaced every limb and muscle and scale with pure stone.

"I cannot say for certain." He paused, and the next words he spoke grated harshly, sounding rusty, like they'd been lodged in his throat for years and it was only with great effort that he could remove them at all. "But, yes, I believe that to be the case."

I nodded.

"Alright. We'll sleep here together, side-by-side, until this starburn thing happens. We'll do what we need to do." Oh God, my cheeks were on fire. "And then after that, we can figure out how to find the other humans again. Maybe your memory will come back and you'll remember some way you know of to track them down."

The man could cross the universe with a beat of his wings and a bang of his fist. It seemed insane that he wouldn't be able to use his skills and experience to find the ship. Or maybe he could go seek help from someone like Aeshyr...

Lost in my own thoughts, I didn't see the ragged span of hurt ripping its way across Skallagrim's face. Not at first. But when my eyes settled on him again, he quickly composed himself.

"How very kind of you," he murmured. His voice was strained, maybe even sarcastic, but I couldn't quite tell. "How very *generous*. To offer your body up at my convenience, as my one and only cure. Like I am one of the temple patients who merely needs a bandage and a condescending pat on the head before you send me on my merry way."

"Well, what else could you possibly want?" I cried, throwing my hands up in defeat and confusion. "What else can I say? Yes, Skallagrim, I'll fuck you and then I'll marry you and we'll live happily ever after, all hunky dory? That makes no sense! We barely even know each other and if I hadn't helped you get your mind back, you probably wouldn't have spared me a second glance before you killed me back on that other planet! I will do what you need. What we will apparently both need, for fuck's sake. And then? It will be done. So, I'll ask you again. *What else do you want from me?*"

"Everything!" He said it with such brutal force that it shook me like he'd bellowed the word, even though he hadn't. "I want everything you have to give! Everything that I have already lost to you, river help me!"

He advanced on me so quickly that I immediately stepped backwards, only for my legs to collide with the bed. I toppled, landing clumsily on my ass, my hands thrusting out beside and behind my hips to catch myself. Skallagrim towered above me, points of illumination glowing madly between his scales and along his flexing wings, the windows behind him turning him into a silhouetted god of shadow and light.

"I want your words and your vows and your bond in marriage. I want your human mouth smiling against my scales as I hold you. Want your voice screaming my name as I rut you. I want the willing, open greed of your cunt."

The way I'd fallen left my thighs splayed on the bed. He stepped insistently between them, widening them with the girth of his huge legs. Heat poured through me, squeezing me inside.

"I want your precious heart. Your today and all of your tomorrows. I want *everything*, Suvi. And I want it *forever*."

We were both still wearing our white temple robes. Skallagrim's belt had come loose, and the robe hung at his sides, open down the middle. My eye went straight to his groin, where there was an unmistakeable swelling behind the scales there.

Oh God. Now? Already?

Dread mingled with a hot stab of horrifying desire.

"Are you..."

"I am not starburning yet," he hissed out. A throb pulsed between his legs, and the scales split there slightly, like a seam opening. I should have looked away, but I couldn't. My eyes were fixated there, and I was breathless with the thought that those scales might part further.

"But I cannot imagine how the starburn could possibly make me want you more than I already do," he rasped.

He spoke through tight fangs, then let out a strangled groan of defeat as the split in those scales suddenly opened fully, without warning.

He really does have two cocks.

That was my first thought, when the stiff, heavy organs bobbed outwards and towards me. Not, *Oh my God he needs to put those away,* or *I should run now.*

Nope. It was a simple, dazed admission of his honesty. He did indeed have two cocks. Alrighty, then.

We stared down at them, both of us surprised, but Skallagrim more so. He glared downwards at his own body like it belonged to someone else, someone he didn't like very much. Someone he couldn't control.

My mouth went dry as I examined his genitalia. I tried to do it with a clinical mind, to tell myself I just needed to know what I was getting into. But the way my gaze roved over him was not with detached curiosity.

It was with heated fascination. *Paska.*

The two cocks glistened, slick with some kind of moisture already. They were a deep, beautiful green, much darker than the emerald of his scales. The kind of green that spoke of sunless, silent forests in winter, or seaweed swaying beneath the waves. They appeared to sprout together from some unseen base in Skallagrim's slit, forming a jutting, up-and-down V shape in the air between us. The lower one was the larger of the two, heavy and huge, ringed at its fat tip with little bulges. Those bulges continued along both shafts, I noticed, almost looking like a pattern of scales but much smoother. Even the smaller, higher cock was massive, larger than most human men could ever hope to come close to. The bottom one was like a club. Like a weapon you'd use to smash in someone's brains in battle.

For the first time in ages, Skallagrim's alienness came slamming down on me like a fist. Even with our recent disagreements and arguments, he had still been Skallagrim. Maybe I didn't feel like I really knew him lately, but it was in the way that I might not know a human man who'd hidden things from me or who'd done things I didn't like. I'd grown so used to him that I barely noticed the scales, the snout, the fangs or wings anymore. He was just... Skallagrim. The man I'd spent more than a month with. The man who'd taught me to speak, who'd fed me, cared for me.

Who would kill for me.

But here, now, faced with the swelling, weeping monstrosity of his cocks, the reality seared through me.

He isn't human.

You are going to mate with someone who isn't human.

Someone who wasn't human, I'd thought.

Not something.

Even like this, splayed and so terribly alien in his body's lust, he was a man to me.

A man who, against all sanity and reason, I was precariously close to reaching for.

A man with two big, green dicks.

God help me.

"You said," I croaked, "Something about a... a knot..."

"Yes," Skallagrim ground out. His hands were in fists at his sides. "I will develop a knot during the starburn." And then, as if anticipating where my mind would go next, he added, "I do not know which shaft it will be."

This wasn't even his final fucking form? His dicks were going to transform like a goddamn Pokemon and become even more dizzyingly large and intimidating than they already were?

Impossible.

But then again, I supposed I was going to evolve, too. The starburn would change me. Make me able to take him. Maybe even take both of them at the same time.

Panic bloomed alongside sudden arousal, the two forces smashing together inside me until it was a dizzying, drugging mix in my blood. I wanted to fling myself off the balcony in fear.

I wanted to touch him.

I couldn't decide which of those things was more insane, and I did neither. I simply sat there and gawked while veins swelled and throbbed beneath the scale-like ribbing on his cocks. I noticed in a distant, nearly giddy way, that he had a slit at the tip of each cock, and that both were wet, which meant he must have been able to come from both shafts. And that was a dangerous thought, because now I was picturing it, picturing Skallagrim taut and arching, his face slack with pleasure, shafts bursting in explosive unison, or maybe one after the other, sending a hot spray all over me, inside me.

I'd known he was male. I'd even known that we were supposed to be mates.

But this was the first time I'd truly imagined him in a sexual way that wasn't edged with resentment and dread. I let my thoughts creep outward, slowly at first, then much quicker, fantasizing about what it really, truly would be like to have sex with him. To let him fill me. To have his massive body heaving overtop of mine, his scales rasping along my sensitive skin.

He won't hurt me.

I didn't know where that thought came from, but I knew instantly that it was true. No matter how big he was, he wouldn't hurt me. He'd never hurt me. If anything, he'd probably try to please me, rocking inside me until he found just the right places. And then he'd take me harder, brutal in his own need, but by then it wouldn't matter because I'd already be coming and shaking and screaming for him and –

"What are you thinking?" Skallagrim panted. If he'd been human, I was pretty sure he would have been absolutely drenched in sweat right now. His entire form was fraught with a barely restrained, trembling tension.

I unstuck my tongue from the roof of my mouth. Before I could come up with a lie, I answered him honestly. "I'm thinking about having sex with you."

He stuttered out a rasping groan. His hips twitched forward involuntarily, a jerk of movement that brought the tip of his bigger cock into wet, unexpected collision with my mouth. He drew back his hips with a swift snap, but he didn't apologize. He simply stared down at my face, my lips, mute and shaking. I raised a hand to my mouth, smearing salty moisture.

"And," he heaved out after a long moment, "do I please you? At least in your deepest, secret imaginings? Do I at least please you there?"

Lie. Lie, right fucking now.

But I didn't.

I nodded shakily.

Skallagrim's reaction was so sudden there was no way I could have prepared myself for it. In a second – less than a second – I was shoved to my back on the bed and Skallagrim was on his knees on the floor between mine. He was so huge that even kneeling beside the bed like this, he could keep one massive hand pressing firmly down against my abdomen while the other whispered upwards to grasp my hip.

I had nothing beneath my robe. My pussy was bared to him as he gave a stilted moan and dragged the tip of his snout along the screaming skin of my inner knee.

"Whatever you've imagined, whatever you desire, Suvi, I can do it. *Be* it. I can be whatever you want me to be."

I gasped and bucked when fangs nipped at my inner thigh. My pulse came fast, beating like a drum inside my clit. My toes curled.

"Let me show you, little star. Let me taste you." His breath fanned over my slick skin, lighting me on fire. "*Let me in.*"

I fisted the cotton bedding, hips straining. My mind completely blank, a featureless white slate cleared of all reason by physical need. There was no thought, no words at all, only each heartbeat chasing down the one that had come before until my whole body pounded.

This was crazy – I wasn't even starburning yet! – but suddenly, undeniably, I wanted him.

I didn't open my legs any wider.

But I didn't close them, either.

And that was all the invitation Skallagrim needed. Or maybe he'd just come to the end of his fraying rope of control. Either way, whether it was in triumph or in battered defeat, he let go and surged inwards. The end of hist snout bumped against my clit with near-bruising force, and I cried out before he dragged the twin tips of his tongue over the swollen spot in a soothing swipe.

If at any moment I forgot that he was alien, the sound that clawed out of his throat reminded me with vicious clarity. It wasn't even close to a human sound. It was a feral snarl, reverberating across my shivering skin.

His hands closed like vises around my thighs. He spread them wide, wide as they would go, hitching my hips upwards as he inhaled unsteadily. Then, his tongue plunged back in.

This was no tender, exploratory touch. It wasn't a slow, gentle probing so he could learn all my sensitive places.

But despite the desperate savagery of his mouth, he was learning, alright. Every time the tips of his tongues swirled over my clit and I reacted, he'd do it again. And again. Until there was nothing, no sensation in the entire world, beyond the whirling vortex of his slippery tongues across that exquisitely burning bundle of nerves.

But it wasn't enough for him. He wanted more, knew there was more, and was searching with hunger so hard and panting it almost felt like panic. With one tip of his tongue still rubbing greedily at my clit, the other slipped down, down through the wetness, until...

We moaned in unison when half his tongue shoved inside me.

Two tongues... dear God.

Technically, it was one tongue, but the two segments moved completely separate from each other. One side laved wetly over my clit, stringing sensation in tight chords, while the other began to fuck me. There was no other way to describe it. He was truly fucking me with his tongue, thrusting it in and out with the urgency of a swollen cock.

I wasn't going to last much longer. Some part of me wanted to fight this. To fight how good it felt, to fight the impending orgasm. Coming on Skallagrim's tongue would change something irreparably, something even more than the inevitable starburning heat would. This was different than heat, because this was entirely my body reacting to him, all on its own.

It was me who wanted this. Only me. Not destiny or biology or even Skallagrim himself coaxing me into it.

It was me.

And it was me who came first. There was no hiding from it, no running from that tsunami of blinding sensation, building from some hidden place inside me and undulating outwards until it met with the ring of pleasure pulsing around the area of my clit. When those two points of pleasure – one internal, one external – came into shuddering sync, it almost felt like dying. Complete obliteration, everything vanishing except the wave bearing me up, up, up, to such a dizzying height I truly felt that I might fall and break apart on impact.

I became aware of hands moving on me – large hands, sliding up from my hips over the padding of my abdomen. Without thinking, I grabbed at those hands, seeking an anchor in the storm. Skallagrim's fingers twined with mine just as I crested that effervescent wave. His tongue guided me with new, lust-sharpened expertise over the blistering edge and into an ocean so bright it was as if every star had fallen from the sky.

I floated there for a long, long time, buoyed along by pulsing aftershocks in my core. Skallagrim lapped at me, tasting the moisture, something so arousing and embarrassing I couldn't decide whether to close my legs or watch him.

I didn't close my legs, and watching him was a total trip. Without the flatness of a human mouth, he basically held his jaws open, suspended in an unfinished bite around my pelvis. His fangs gleamed like knives, so fucking close to puncturing right through my skin. His eye was screwed shut so tight it almost looked like he was in pain.

But then that eye opened. And it burned a golden line, like a laser, between our hands, my breasts, and up to my face.

Holding fierce eye contact, he thrust his tongue deep inside once more, curling inward until I gasped and bucked my hips.

Then, still capturing me in that unblinking stare, he released my hands and stood.

I stared up at him, limbs weakened, skin flushed under his gaze as he positioned himself between my damp, splayed thighs. His cocks jutted out almost angrily from his body, and I found myself wondering how the hell he fit those things inside him, usually so well-hidden.

The smaller, upper cock oozed pearlescent fluid. It dripped onto the slickened tip of the cock below, mixing with the liquid there until it all stretched downwards in a continuous, glistening rope of seed.

"I want you."

I sucked in a breath at the harsh vulnerability of his admission. He'd already told me that – much more than that. But something about the staggering simplicity of the sentence touched deeper inside me than any words that had before.

I want you.

There was no fluff in a phrase like that. No room for interpretation. Not much poetry, either, except for the naked art of urgency. Stark and honest as a blade.

For a whirling moment, I thought he might take me right here, right now. Shove one of those cocks inside me, or both, waiting for the starburn be damned. Need was as plain and as dark on his face as storm clouds on the horizon of a hot, clear sky.

But he didn't bend down to fit the head of one of his thick cocks against my body. Instead, he raised both his hands, wrapping each straining cock in a massive, murderous fist. Then, he started fucking them.

His hips snapped back and then shunted forward. He didn't stroke his cocks. He kept his fists perfectly tight and still, and from the thrusting motion of his pelvis and the way he stared so hard at my cunt I knew, I fucking knew, that he was pretending to drive into me instead.

He's going to do that to you soon.

Fire licked at the base of my spine. I watched him through glazed, slitted eyes, panting on my back as he rutted into his makeshift proxy for my body. His breath sounded like stone grinding on metal, his muscles seemed to tear at his bones, threatening to erupt right out of his scales, as he urged himself closer to furious climax.

My hand lifted from the bed, and it was like watching someone else's hand. My fingers hovered, hesitating, until on Skalla's next rutting thrust I touched the slick head of his larger cock.

At the contact, he spasmed.

Then he detonated.

His cocks burst with sudden, shimmering jets, the shafts jerking in fractured, throbbing unison as he snarled. I didn't know if it was because he had two, if it was due to his excitement, or maybe it was just normal for him, but the fluid seemed endless. Spurting onto my abdomen, my breasts, dotting my throat and cheeks until I closed my eyes against the onslaught.

Without seeing, I could only lie there and feel it. Feel the heated evidence of Skallagrim's desire exploding onto my skin until I was slick and coated.

Because my eyes were closed, I had no warning for the scaly hand that bumped the side of my cheek, smearing moisture across my skin. Large fingertips traced a path down to my jaw before caressing the softest places where my heart beat at my throat.

I didn't open my eyes. I didn't flinch away. Even with claws that could end me a hair's breadth from my artery, I lay still and let him do it.

Because after everything, even knowing what I now knew – that Skallagrim was impatient and possessive and that he'd killed before me – I trusted him. At least, I trusted that he'd never hurt me. I had no idea whether I could control his violence when it came to other people, but I knew as deeply as I knew my sister's name that such violence would never be aimed at me. For me, maybe. But not at me.

So I lay there and breathed and felt his lust cooling on my skin as his fingers and thumb stroked at my throat. When he finally spoke, it was with a disbelieving laugh shaking underneath the words, as if he was amazed that this wasn't a dream.

"Little star, pretty mate, I have made a mess of you."

My eyes fluttered open. He didn't look like he much minded the mess. In fact, he was looking down at me like I was the most precious piece of art he'd ever seen. My skin glistened with his pale fluid, like smooth, moonlight-spangled snow on the hills and valley of my breasts, the curve of my stomach. I drew my hand between my heavy breasts, feeling the slide of him. Skallagrim clutched at his cocks and grunted at the sight.

"The bedding, too," I realized, feeling dampness on either side of me. I was still floating on a cloud of fluffy hormones and bone-jelly relaxation and I wasn't ready to let dismay or embarrassment touch me. Not yet.

There would be time enough for that eventually. When I regained my sanity.

With what looked like a monumental effort, Skallagrim pressed his cocks towards his groin, the muscles in his slit contracting to cover them. It was like a fucking magic trick. Making not just one, but two dicks disappear.

And then I remembered that he could do things that most people actually would consider magic. He could levitate water and wood, boil liquids in the very air, and I stared up at him in hushed wonder, trying to decipher just why the universe had decided to put the two of us together.

Had he ever wondered the same?

And had he ever been disappointed? Disappointed that he'd ended up with a weak, quiet, stubborn, squishy little human who almost died from something as simple as river water touching a wound on her feet? If he'd had a choice, would he instead have wanted a glittering Bohnebregg female, or maybe someone from another world entirely? A warrior to match his strength, or some powerful alien queen? Didn't he say he'd been a prince before?

Ouch. That thought hurt more than I wanted to admit. Like a pin to the side of a balloon, it deflated the relaxation surrounding me.

"I should get cleaned up," I said. "And wash the sheets."

Skallagrim growled in complaint, but ultimately grasped my wrists and helped me up. Together we stripped the bed, and my face flamed at the spots of wetness I saw there. Not just his, but mine too. Bundling it all up with my also-soiled robe, I hurried into the bathroom and closed the door.

CHAPTER THIRTY-THREE
Skallagrim

While Suvi cleaned herself, scrubbing the stain of my seed from her skin, I placed extra, clean bedding on the mattress then sat upon it. I stared at some blank point on the floorboards, but I saw nothing. My mind was entirely caught up in replaying everything that had just happened between Suvi and me in rapturous, torturous detail.

Blast me into the stone sky, I'd never imagined her to be so beautifully responsive to me already. Her vulnerable skin so sensitive, so aroused by every touch. She had not taken the news of being my mate well, and I hadn't wanted to pressure or rush her, but it now occurred to me that I did not have to wait for her to starburn. I could woo her, seduce her, wring cries of pleasure from her even now. Make her want me, make her need me, before she even went into heat at all.

And then, when she burned, I would be ready. I would know every intricacy of her form, every secret, shivering place. I'd already learned some of them today, like the delicious little pink pearl of flesh at the top of her cunt that made her whole body wind up then let go with delight.

My cocks throbbed, agonisingly tender from the stimulation but still needing more. I regretted letting her go so soon. I was wary that by the time she stepped back out of the bathing area, she would have shut back down again. That we would go back to the disconcerting distance that seemed only to grow between us lately.

No.

I would not let that happen. She'd enjoyed my touch, my tongue on her. At least some small part of her wanted me.

I could work with that.

I was a tenacious male, and though my memory was not clear on the matter I was fairly certain I had always been the sort of man who got what he wanted.

And all I wanted now was Suvi.

As if my very desire had conjured her, my mate appeared, stepping out of the bathing area in a waft of shifting steam. The billowing white of it behind her almost looked like a pair of wings. Her hair was a damp silver serpent along her elegant neck, and moisture beaded along the visible areas of her smooth skin. I already wanted to taste her again. Disappointingly, she was not nude, but dressed in Bohnebregg garments Jolakaia had left for her – a simple pair of cotton leg coverings and a sleeveless tunic that appeared to be sized for children. In front of her she carried the wet and freshly washed bedding and her robe.

She breezed past me without a word. Her cheeks were very pink, and I was not entirely sure what that meant. Something to do with the heat of the bath, perhaps.

I stood and followed close behind her, sensing where she was going and what she needed before she had to speak. When she reached the door leading out to the balcony, I was already there, reaching past her to open it. I had to lean in close to do it, and when my chest brushed against her back, her spine went rigid in the most delectable way.

Once the door was open, she practically bolted through it and set herself to draping the wet things over the railing so they could dry. Meanwhile, I set myself to watching her, slowly retying the belt of my loose robe, enjoying the languorous spill of warm sunshine on my scales as my mate bent and stretched at her task. Skies take me, she really was the most gorgeous creature. A body so lusciously curved it made my throat ache. Hair like finely spun metal, and eyes the colour of rain at dawn.

She turned those eyes on me now, no longer able to hide behind the busyness of the laundry. She had done all there was to do. And now I stood between her and the door.

I grinned, knowing that my fangs were showing. The toothy look of a predator.

But a predator who so dearly loves his prey.

"Well, we might as well go back in," Suvi finally said, shifting from foot to foot under my stare. Carrying the wet things out here had dampened the front of her clothing, which made the fabric cling delightfully to her body. Even a few paces from her, I could make out the swollen tips of her breasts. Remembering how flushed they'd been beneath me, how pretty they'd looked shining with my seed made my cocks tug behind my slit.

"There's a toll," I said.

"Oh, wow. There are tolls even on alien planets?"

I frowned slightly, trying to suss out where I'd learned the word. Were there tolls on Bohnebregg, or was that a concept I'd picked up from some other world I'd visited?

I decided it did not matter. Suvi knew what a toll was and that was what counted.

She sighed with resignation.

"What is it, then? A kiss or something?"

I had not yet actually determined the requested toll. Before I could respond, she'd crossed the balcony to be, grabbed the sides of my snout, and tugged. She was not actually strong enough to pull me down, but I was helpless against her, helpless against those little hands with their deft, clawless fingers.

I bent, and she pressed her pink mouth to the tip of my snout, right along the seam where it opened.

I did not have a mouth like hers, and I was not entirely sure how to react or what to do. But the gentle press of her lips there made my loins heat. I grasped her waist and hauled her against me, letting her feel the swollen parts of me.

Instantly, she drew back.

"There! I paid the toll! Let me in, now!"

"No," I growled. "The price of the toll has just doubled. You must pay it again."

"That doesn't seem very fair," she said, scowling at me.

"It also was not fair to kiss me and let me go so quickly. I was not prepared. Now I am."

"Not prepared? What do you mean?" She gasped. "Was that your first kiss?"

I cast my mind back over the roiling river in my brain. I knew I'd lain with other females. I was certain I'd used my tongues on them in various places on their bodies. But I was also just as certain I'd never been with one of Suvi's kind before. This press of mouth on mouth did not feel familiar in the slightest.

"I do not know. But it is very possible."

She groaned, and slapped her hands over her face. She looked... guilty. I could not fathom why.

"What is it?"

"I can't believe I just took your first kiss that way. Paying a toll. Ugh."

"Suvi," I murmured, entirely besotted by how adorable she was, "are you concerned that you have somehow stolen some of my innocence?"

She did not answer, but merely made a mewling sound of horror that charmed me beyond belief. Her face was red behind her pale fingers.

"I have had other partners," I said gently. "I have lived dozens of your lifetimes. I may not have put my mouth on another's in such a way before, but I will remind you that I just had my tongues in a place far more intimate mere moments ago."

She snatched her hands away from her face.

"Don't say that so loud!" she hissed. "And... And that's not the point! It's not the same! A first kiss is supposed to be special!"

"It was with you," I replied. "I can ask for nothing more than that. Although..." My grin returned, and she narrowed her gaze in suspicion. "If you wanted to do it over again, and make it even *more* special, I would surely not object."

"Will you let me through the door if I do?"

"Perhaps. Though those tolls do have a pesky way of rising when you least expect it."

"That's not the only pesky thing around here," she replied, but there was no bite to her words. Her gaze was soft now. Searching. My fingers tightened at her waist.

She pulled me down again, more slowly this time, the whole movement like a caress instead of an impatient tug. This time, when her mouth touched the seam of mine, it was not a firm, quick jab of a movement. It was tentative and tender, a gentle wave murmuring across my scales.

I could feel her like this, but not enough, and parted my jaws ever so slightly to let the tips of my tongue lance out between my fangs.

She stiffened, but did not pull away. And then, glory of glories, she did the same thing, her little pink tongue darting to meet with mine.

I groaned, tightened my hold on her, and let my tongue surge in.

It was so much like rutting her with my tongue that my cocks were once again straining at my slit, begging to complete that same motion. I'd gotten to taste the hot inside of her mouth and the sucking tightness of her cunt, and I knew I had not even explored one-tenth of the places I wanted to.

I wanted to lick at the hollowed shell of her ear, nip at the place where her ankles met her legs, drag my snout against each rib so I could count them, taste every single place her heart beat.

But first, her mouth. I had to properly worship that mouth. Suvi had given up on trying to meet the thrusts of my tongue with hers and was instead letting me cradle her jaw, holding her mouth open to me, pliant under my power in a deeply arousing way. I slicked along the smooth upper surface of her tongue, flicked along the sides, grazed those laughably small, pretty teeth.

The sweetness of the moment did not, could not, last. Some of Suvi's stubbornness returned, and she began to pull back, bit by bit, until I was reaching for her through the air with my tongue. I decided that such a pose was undignified, even for someone who wanted her as desperately as I did, so I pulled back too, and reined it in.

Suvi's hair had begun to dry, fine long waves of that extraordinary, indefinable colour. Her breaths came quick, and her cheeks once again displayed that heightened colour.

"What does this mean?" I asked, drawing a careful knuckle along her rounded cheekbone, noting with wonder the suppleness of it.

Wonder turned to worry when she replied, "It's blood."

"What do you mean, blood?" I shot back, focusing hard on her face. I'd thought it was simply a quirk of her human hide to shift in shade. I replayed everything I'd done with my tongue, suddenly terrified that I'd pressed too hard on the insides of her cheeks and made her bleed somehow inside.

"It's not bad. It's not a bruise or an injury. The blood vessels dilate for increased blood flow, and you can see that from the outside."

Well, that was more than mildly alarming. I knew her skin was delicate, vulnerable, requiring protection and care. But it was so thin that you could even see the blood through it?

How could any creature that soft survive so long?

I thought of how two tiny wounds on her feet had almost killed her and my guts clenched.

She'll survive now. Because now, she's got a male with claws and scales who will take on any hurt for her.

My face must have looked grim, because now she was saying, "It's fine. It's normal, especially for someone with a lighter skin tone. It happens during exercise or... or moments of heightened emotion."

"What kinds of emotion?" I asked sharply.

"Um... Embarrassment, for one thing."

I watched her with a keen eye, decided that embarrassment was a better reaction to my tongue in her mouth than something like revulsion, and finally moved aside to let her in.

CHAPTER THIRTY-FOUR
Suvi

There was some food already there for us in the little cooking area of the apartment. After bringing in the laundry we ate a simple dinner together on the floor, my eyes going to the single bed every other bite.

Then, I went to hide in the bathroom. I wasn't proud of it, but there it was.

But there was only so long I could reasonably spend in there. I'd already used the alien toilet and washed my hands, and I'd bathed earlier in the day. After scrubbing my teeth with a Bohnebregg toothbrush, which was composed of some sort of stiff plant matter adhered to a wooden handle, there was nothing left to do but go back out there.

I didn't.

I stood staring at the door like a dumbass.

Until I heard the boom of Skallagrim's voice through it.

"If you take much longer in there I will assume that something's happened and be forced to come in after you."

The teasing glide of his voice made it very clear that he knew nothing had happened to me but that the threat of barging in here was real either way.

I wanted to call back tartly that the door was locked, not that it would make any difference to someone as strong as him. He could just use his alien telekinesis and smash it open if he wanted to.

It was silly to be this nervous about something as simple as going to sleep beside him. I'd slept in the same room as him for weeks already. I'd literally spread my legs for him earlier this afternoon, as much as I was still grappling to figure out just how, exactly, that had happened.

It was only sleep.

And it was only Skallagrim.

Soup. Cabbage. Time to go.

I opened the door and went back into the bedroom.

Skallagrim was already seated on the bed, at the edge, thick thighs spread.

He'd also apparently lost his robe somewhere along the way.

"Jolakaia left new clothing for you, too, you know," I said, taking relieved note of the fact that nothing was currently, ahem, *visible*, between his legs.

"Yes, I saw the trousers." A lazy grin tugged at the sides of his snout. "But it has always been my custom to sleep without them."

"Since when?" I cried, fists flying to my hips. He'd pretty much always worn his robe in the temple room, even when sleeping, leaning back against the wall.

His grin widened, grew devious.

"Since I had my mate to share my bed with."

Oh boy.

I considered telling him he wouldn't have anybody to share the bed with at all unless he put some fucking clothes on. But we'd already gone through that whole rigamarole earlier, and I knew we wouldn't come to any new conclusions.

One bed.

Two people.

One of them naked. For fuck's sake.

"You are a menace," I grumbled, wearily accepting the situation. At least it wasn't like being nestled against a human man with his dick flopping around. And, to be fair, the first few days I'd spent with Skallagrim (which included sleeping beside him) he'd been naked, too. This wasn't exactly new for us.

But it felt new. So much had changed since those first strange, confusing moments with him in this world. We could talk to each other now.

We were mates now.

Somehow. Apparently.

"Do I have to pay another toll just to get access to the bed?" I asked.

His eye glinted with something far too close to mischief for my liking, but all he did was scoot his big green frame over and gesture towards the mattress in silent invitation. I hauled myself onto the bed and crawled towards the centre. Skallagrim watched me, snout still curled in a smirk, his gaze greedy and arrogant as a cat, a cat who'd already had a taste of cream and was not quite patiently waiting to receive another.

There were no pillows on the bed, just the large mattress and sets of sheets. The top sheet had been pulled open to one side, I noticed, so that I could collapse right into that spot. I thought about Skallagrim waiting for me, arranging the sheets just so for my arrival, and couldn't decipher whether it had been a generous, thoughtful gesture, or one that had been calculated to get me into bed all the faster, like some kind of subliminal messaging.

Hell. With Skallagrim, it was probably both.

I pulled the sheet back over myself, dragging it up to my chin as if I had to hide my naked body, even though I was still wearing the fresh cotton outfit Jolakaia had left for me. Skallagrim still just watched me with that golden cat-eye look, until the awkwardness broke me and I squeaked out, "Well, aren't you going to lie down?"

His answer was to throw his body down in a great *thwump!* beside me. He was so heavy that he bounced me right up off the mattress and back down again. Before I could come up with some scathing retort, haughty with indignation, I started to giggle.

And once I started, I couldn't stop.

Giddiness spread through my lungs like laughing gas. My heart ran like a rabbit, my stomach tightening pleasantly after the bouncy fall I'd just taken. Skallagrim watched me with the pleased surprise of a man who wanted to pretend he'd done that on purpose just to make me laugh even though he hadn't actually anticipated this outcome.

Abdominal muscles beginning to burn, I took several steadying breaths and relaxed back onto the mattress, cheeks still stretched with a smile. When was the last time I'd laughed that much? When was the last time I'd done something fun?

Elvi was always making me do stuff like that – stuff to get me out of my comfort zone and make my heart beat fast. Whether it was hockey or sledding or pushing me, terrified but breathlessly laughing, into Lake Saimaa in the summer, she'd always made things fun. Even though she'd been eight years older than me and had raised me since our mother died when I was twelve, she'd always felt more like a friend my own age than an older sibling. If anything, I was often the more prudent and mature one between us, even when I was a child. Sometimes, when I nagged her about something or began worrying too much, she'd poke me and say, "I may not have any grandmothers left living but at least I've still got you."

After leukemia had ravaged her beyond what even her indomitable strength and spirit could withstand, I'd kind of just... let go of all that. Let go of laughter, of pure, vicious, feral joy. From her death when I was twenty-one until now, I'd just put my head down and trudged through life. Six years of studying and working, putting more effort into my relationship with my cat (who also died, go fucking figure) than I did any other people.

Finland was often quoted as being one of the happiest nations on Earth. I wondered now if I'd somehow become one of the unhappiest people in it.

But I wasn't in Finland anymore.

And, startling as the admission was, I wasn't unhappy, either. At least, not entirely. Not in this moment. Not with my cheeks still bunched and aching, my limbs slack but tingling with delight.

"It is good to see you smile like that," came the deep voice from beside me.

I sighed, but for once it wasn't one of weariness or frustration.

"Feels good to do it," I said. I rolled my eyes at the ceiling with what I was about to admit, but I knew in my bones it was true. "As crazy as you are and how rocky the way we met was, I think my sister would have absolutely loved you."

I'd only had two serious boyfriends before she'd died, and she'd disapproved of both of them for the same reasons. "Too boring," she'd told me. "You need someone with some life in them! Someone who can make you laugh so hard you think you'll pee. Who loves you so much you can't think straight!"

"Boring is nice sometimes," I'd argued back at her defensively, even though a small part of me had kind of agreed with her. Neither of my serious relationships had ever created an *I can't think straight* intensity of sensation. I'd never been compelled to say *I love you*, either. "Maybe I'm boring, too."

"You," Elvi had gasped, staring me down with crackling eyes and drawing herself up to her full height of five-foot-two, "are *not* boring. And you deserve someone who would set the fucking sky on fire for you."

Or turn it into stone...

Well, how's this for not boring, Elvi? I'm currently in bed with an immortal berserker alien who looks more like a dragon than a man.

And despite it all...

He really makes me laugh.

When I didn't say anything else, Skallagrim replied with, "Well, I am exceedingly sorry not to get the chance to meet your sister. She was clearly a woman with exquisitely refined taste."

And now I was laughing all over again. The ego on this alien! He had that half-satisfied, half-hungry cat look to him again as he gazed down at me, his elbow pressing into the mattress, the bottom of his snout resting on his palm.

"That's one way of putting it," I snorted. The mirth died down and my eyes misted. "She was amazing, you know? And she was so young when our mom died. She'd only just turned twenty, but there was no question in her mind that she'd come home and look after me."

"She was not at your home already?"

I traced the lines of glowing tubing in the ceiling with my eyes and laced my fingers together on my stomach.

"No. She was an *anywhere-but-here* sort of girl. We had different fathers, and she never really clicked with my dad as her step-father. She was out of the house, and out of the country, just about as soon as she was able to go. She did all kinds of stuff. Travel blogging. Working on cruise ships. I didn't see her that much even after my dad died because she was always off in Asia or out on some boat in the Atlantic or whatever. And plus, with the age difference, we just weren't all that close. At least, not until our mom died."

My throat got too tight to speak for a minute. Skallagrim waited with far more patience than I would have expected him capable of. One heavy hand came down over both of mine and gently squeezed.

"As soon as she got the news, she dropped everything and came home. I still remember the first time I saw her again so vividly. It had been more than two years since the last time I'd seen her. And the first thing I thought was, *holy shit, her hair is green.* Like, deep, dark, I-just-dyed-this-and-it's-still-box-fresh green. My next thought was how beautiful it looked on her."

I didn't have to glance over at Skallagrim to be reminded that he, too, had green on him. I felt him shift slightly, as if his chest had swelled on his next inhale, and I hid a small smile at his preening.

"She stayed in Finland with me after that. Settled back in our hometown and raised me."

"What happened to her?"

"She got sick. A human disease called leukemia. She was a fighter, my Elvi. But eventually there wasn't anything anyone could do. And after everything she'd been through, she deserved to rest."

His hand stroked mine, then suddenly tightened as his whole form went stiff beside me.

"Could you become ill with the same thing someday?"

I let my head loll towards him on the bed. His smirking look was gone.

"Unlikely. It's not typically hereditary or anything like that." I smiled, but it felt a little sour. "Don't worry. I promise to do this whole mate thing with you and cure you before I go off and die."

Skallagrim shot upright in the bed, like my words had run along the mattress and electrocuted him on contact.

"That is not why I ask!" he snarled savagely. "That is not why I worry!" He swiped his claws through the air. "Let my memory all be torn asunder. Let the entire universe tremble under the weight of my maddened rage. Let there be no hope left for me, no hope left alive for anyone! I do not care a whit for it, *any of it*, if I do not have you!"

I hadn't fully started crying while talking about Elvi.

But I started crying now. My eyes filled and overflowed. Skallagrim's enraged expression turned to one of dismay.

"Little star, I am sorry. I-"

"No. I'm sorry," I choked out. What I'd just said to him was incredibly unkind, and it was only fully hitting me now. "I shouldn't have said that. It wasn't fair."

He lay back down on his side, looped a strong arm around me, and hoisted me across the bed until I was curled into his front. He rested the bottom of his snout on the top of my head as I dug my forehead against the scales on his chest and sobbed.

"I am sorry," he repeated quietly, "for the anger in my reaction." He sounded like he was in pain. "But I cannot... I cannot think of losing you. I cannot even think around it."

I sniffed hard, then took a weepy breath, trying to calm down.

"I get it," I said weakly. "When Elvi first got sick, I told myself every single morning that she wouldn't die. It became like a mantra. Because if I'd stopped to consider the other possibility, I never would have been able to get myself out of bed in the morning."

His hand caressed the rounded line of my spine, warmth penetrating through my tunic's fabric.

"Grief for loved ones lost is a stone around your neck in the middle of the river," he said quietly. "It will drag you right down to the bottom."

"Have you ever lost anyone?"

As soon as the sniffly question was out of my mouth I wanted to smack myself. Of course he'd lost people. You didn't live as long as he had without people around you dying.

"Yes. My parents I am certain of. My mother's name was Jolakaia – a family name you no doubt recognize. My father..." He quieted for a moment, and his hand stopped stroking my back. "I do not remember my father's name. Or his face."

That broke my little human heart. As much as I missed Elvi, and our mother and my father, I could at least think about them. Time had worn away some of the sharp corners, turned many of the memories dusty, more akin to dreams, but at least they were still there. Still real enough that I continued hearing my sister's voice, even now.

"I'm sorry," I said again. I wondered how many times we were going to apologize to each other tonight.

"Oh, Suvi, don't be," he murmured against my hair. "You have already brought me back to myself in a way I did not think possible. And soon-"

His words cut off, and I knew exactly why. He had been about to say something about how more of his memory might come back after we fully mated under the sway of the starburn.

I appreciated that he didn't want to put pressure on me right now, but for the very first time, I looked ahead at what was to come without guilt or fear or resignation. I thought about what a gift I would be giving Skallagrim. If mating did restore some of his memory, in a way I'd be giving him his life back. Giving him his parents back. It might not work, of course. But if there was even a chance...

I suddenly faced the impending heat, and our joining, not with dread, but a little bit of... hope? Maybe even excitement.

At the end of the day and against all odds, I cared about Skallagrim. I cared about his mind, his memory, his pain. If I could pull him up from the bottom of that river, then I knew that I would do it. And I'd actually be glad to.

"Do you remember anyone else from your past?" I asked. "Or has Jolakaia told you about anyone?"

"No. I do not believe I ever had a brother. Although..."

He grew quiet for so long I found myself wiggling in his grip to look up at him. He shook himself as if from sleep.

"There is a male that I remember more vividly than any other. A stone sky god, like my father and me. With black wings and white hair. I feel that I was close to him, somehow..."

His words died off as my brows drew together. White hair and black wings...

It sounded like the one I'd seen before. The one who'd killed half our ship's crew, and my good friend Torrance, on the first snowy planet we'd landed on.

Maybe he was mate mad, too...

The winged being had come to that planet in an all-consuming rage just like Skalla.

I tried not to dwell on it, tried not to think of Torrance buried under that alien's avalanche of fury back on the frozen planet. Maybe it wasn't the same stone sky god at all. Skallagrim couldn't even remember who the person he'd mentioned was, or what their relationship had been like, so there would be no way to confirm. Plus, Aeshyr also had what looked like white hair, though it was shorn right down to the scalp, and bony black lines of wings. Maybe white hair with black wings was a common combination for stone sky gods, and Skallagrim was the outlier with his dark hair and green and gold body.

But even so...

It didn't feel right not to mention it.

"I saw someone like that, once."

Skallagrim went very still.

"The planet where you found me wasn't the first world we visited in our ship. We were conducting research on another world when someone – a stone sky alien, I assume – came through the sky. He went on a rampage. He killed half the soldiers from our ship. And... and my friend."

I never saw it happen. Torrance had been out in the woods on her own when we'd been shoved back onto the ship in the chaos. I saw soldiers felled by literal tidal waves of snow, wrenched up from the ground by the white-haired, black-winged alien. But I never actually saw her die.

I shivered and hoped, as I'd done many times before, that whatever had befallen Torrance had been quick and as painless as possible.

Skallagrim looked troubled, then brushed his fingers over the hollow scarring of his lost eye before returning his hand to my back.

"Perhaps that male was mate mad as well. It is impossible to say if he is the one whom I remember."

"Yeah, I figured. I just felt weird about not mentioning it."

He grunted and then said, "I did not know one of my kind had killed your friend."

I didn't say anything else because I was worried that talking about Torrance more would have me sobbing on Skallagrim's scales all over again. I didn't want to cry any more tonight.

He seemed to sense it, so he didn't say anything else on the matter. We remained quiet, lost in our own thoughts while wrapped gently in each other's limbs.

Soon, even thought drifted away from me. The inside of my head, just like my swollen eyelids, felt heavy. I nuzzled closer to Skallagrim without meaning to, and he responded with a rumbling sound and the protective drape of his wing over my body, which made me feel impossibly cozy.

I wasn't supposed to feel cozy. Mere hours ago I'd been dreading climbing into this bed with him. But now...

Now, I couldn't imagine us sleeping any other way in this room. It was both disconcerting and oddly comforting, to be so at ease nestled against his bulk.

His *naked* bulk.

But even that didn't seem to matter right now. The awkwardness and embarrassment I'd felt had been completely stripped away, worn down to only what was raw and real. Talking about your dead sister and bawling your eyes out all over a man had a way of getting to the heart of what mattered, I supposed.

Skallagrim's claws played idly in my hair. He was warm. So much warmer than you'd expect someone covered in scales to be. There was no heating source in the room, but I didn't need one with him in the bed. And he was so *solid*. His body felt like sunshine made into stone, and I sighed against that enveloping warmth. His breath rocked against me until I wasn't even aware of my own anymore, only his.

Or maybe we were just breathing completely in time with each other, two bodies, one rhythm.

I didn't know.

Because I was already asleep.

CHAPTER THIRTY-FIVE
Skallagrim

It was gratifying in the extreme that Suvi fell asleep so quickly while tucked against me. I'd wondered if, even though we'd agreed to share the bed, I'd have to grab her little body and drag her into it. Or if, once there, she'd remain stubbornly clinging to the far edge, putting as much space between us as possible.

But here she was. Against my chest. Under my wing. Her tear-stained face smoothed of pain.

This was already going much better than I'd expected it would.

And wasn't that thought just a happy little hum under my scales?

I did not need to rush. Already, slowly as a spooked but curious animal, she was coming towards me now. Giving me sacred little tastes of her body. And sharing more about her past.

Sighing, I brushed a silvery strand away from her sleeping face. A stone sky god had killed not just one of her kind, but one of her friends. I had not known that, but that helped me understand her just a little more. Understand her fear when I took her. She wasn't just afraid because I'd ripped her away from that ship.

She was afraid because she'd watched someone like me kill someone like her. Someone she cared about.

I ruminated on this, wondering if the male she'd seen could possibly be the one I remembered. I had no other memories of him, at least not yet. I did not know which world he hailed from. I did not know his name.

He'd been important to me, once. Of that much I was certain.

But beyond that...

Nothing but the black depths of the river.

I put it out of my mind. Maybe I'd remember more once Suvi and I fully bonded.

Maybe I wouldn't.

I decided that, ultimately, it didn't really matter. What mattered was here, now. Her.

I wanted to build a life with the bricks I had before me even if it was far from the foundations of my past.

I gazed down at Suvi's sleeping face, desperate to touch her, draw my snout against her neck, feel the fluttery pulse of her heart. But not wanting to wake her, I didn't. I remained still, watching, wing covering her like half a blanket, half a shield. And though I could have remained like that forever, soon I, too, was asleep.

CHAPTER THIRTY-SIX

Suvi

When I woke up, I was warm.

A little too warm, actually. I groaned, wondering how the hell I'd fallen asleep against the metal wall of a furnace.

But that furnace apparently had an arm. And when I struggled, it locked hard around my waist, tugging my back tighter against it.

"Too hot," I moaned, slapping sweat-dampened hair away from my forehead and opening my eyes. Although opening them didn't allow me to see much. Disoriented, I blinked at a vast, leathery sky of dark green dotted with gold stars. It was such a beautiful sight that I almost didn't mind the confusion. So I just stared blankly at that weirdly opaque sky until I realized in the hazy way of just waking up that it was Skallagrim's wing tossed over me.

No wonder it's so hot. Not only was his wing producing heat, it was trapping it, creating a starry tarp of insulation over top of me.

"Skallagrimmmmm," I moaned. But the arm at my waist held fast. Scowling, I started poking at the wing, which thankfully withdrew even though the bulky arm didn't. Sunshine flooded in. I gave another wiggly attempt at escape, then froze when the unmistakable ridge of a bulge behind Skallagrim's slit nudged at my ass.

"Skallagrim!" I hissed. "Are you..."

I had been about to say, *Are you getting hard?* but at the last second I faltered. "Are you asleep?"

He gave a smoky-sounding grunt that could have been an answer either way.

"I have to pee!"

He grunted again, this time more awake-sounding and more growly, but ultimately snaked his arm out from around my waist. I scooted forward, worried he'd change his mind, then got clumsily out of the bed and headed for the bathroom. After getting all sweaty in sleep, I decided to fill the tub with some water, washing first my body and then the clothes before hanging them, wet, along the edge of the tub. My robe was in here, clean from last night, and I put it on before heading back out into the main room.

Though I was the one who'd taken the time to get ready in the bathroom, Skallagrim was somehow the one who actually looked more put-together. Last night his hair had come loose, and one look at him as I'd fled the bed this morning had shown me a sleep-tangled dark mane surrounding the body of a half-asleep alien behemoth.

But he was no longer half-asleep, nor was he in the bed at all. He was standing, his hair tied back in a lustrous braid. And he was wearing clothes! He wasn't naked, or wearing the temple robe. He was wearing honest-to-goodness trousers, something I'd never seen on him before.

I... I kind of liked it.

His chest was bare, his posture excellent, his wings in a relaxed tuck behind him. My eyes scraped down the muscled planes of his torso, tracing the hard V shape that I now knew led down to the place in his scales that split open to let out his two cocks.

But I couldn't see that area now, because he was wearing trousers. And he looked damn good in them.

They were obviously a Bohnebregg garment, though Skallagrim was bigger than any other Bohnebregg male I'd seen so far. This resulted in the fabric being rather snug across his trunk-like thighs, and the pant-legs looked a couple of centimetres shorter than I would have expected, but on the whole, the look suited him.

"You look nice," I said, feeling heat tickle at my cheeks.

His posture got even better if that was possible, spine straightening and shoulders pulling back.

"You should know," he said, "that I intend to woo you." He said it casually, breezily. Like he'd just announced that he planned to take a walk this morning instead of lobbing some life-altering declaration at me.

"You... What?!"

"Woo you," he repeated. He cocked his head a little. "Perhaps you have no word for that in your language. I plan to court you." His eye darkened to deep amber. "Seduce you."

He was moving, now. Moving on those long, strong, trouser-clad legs towards me.

"Uh, is that really necessary?" I said, stumbling backwards.

"It is," he purred, advancing.

My back hit a very poorly-placed wall, trapping me.

"But you already... we already..."

We already came all over each other and fell asleep wrapped around one another last night.

Oh God.

"You do not yet want me as I want you." His tone was light. Too light. Like it was masking something, trying not to fracture under the weight of hidden hurt. "I have decided to change that."

"You can't just change it!" I stammered.

"I can if I woo you."

He said it in such a matter-of-fact way. Never mind the various layers of resentment and awkwardness built up between us. Never mind that he probably had no idea how human courting rituals even worked. Never mind that we were two entirely different species.

He was Skallagrim, stone sky god and Bohnebregg prince, a juggernaut of alien determination, and everything about his stance and words and tone told me that he would figure it the fuck out no matter what it took.

"But... you don't have to. The starburn..."

"I want you to want me without that," he said with quiet force. "To set your heart on me without heat forcing the way."

One of his hands grazed down my throat, gently sliding between the parted flaps of my robe until he palmed the place between my breasts. He wasn't even touching them, but my nipples hardened anyway. Warmed honey pooled at the base of my spine, oozing towards the place between my legs.

"That heart I've set my sights on is beating very quickly now, little star," Skallagrim murmured, bending to drag his snout along my jaw. His great thigh nudged between mine, exploding sensation through my core. "And your cheeks are red again. Are you embarrassed?"

I could hear the smirk in his next words, damn him. "And if you are, is it because you're embarrassed by my intentions, or by your own reaction to them?"

I was saved from answering (though not from further embarrassment, lucky me) by a loud, insistent growl from my stomach.

Skallagrim had been with me long enough to know exactly what that sound meant. He chuckled against my throat, the sound like melting chocolate dripping onto my skin, and then withdrew. I'd been annoyed at the wall a few minutes ago, but now I was frantically grateful for it, because I was fairly certain it was the only thing holding me upright now that the delicious hardness of Skallagrim's thigh wasn't nestled below my pussy.

"First part of wooing a human," Skallagrim said, as if he were an expert on the subject already, like he had a fucking PhD, "is to feed her."

Hungry, horny, and unable to argue with him, I nodded. And when he offered me his hand, I took it.

There wasn't much left to eat in the apartment, so we ventured outside. As soon as Skallagrim opened the glass door, the pleasant sounds of morning life floated in. Jolakaia and Zev's home wasn't in the more crowded heart of Callabarra near the temple. Instead, they lived nearer the edge, allowing a little more space around their home for a garden at the back and a few animals called *bikri* that were knee-high and generally shaped like crabs but with scales instead of shells. Apparently, they produced eggs, and I could see them from up here on the balcony, scuttling along at the sunny edges of the garden behind the house, like spidery alien chickens.

In front of the house was the street. Nothing fancy – not like the shiny embedded river stone in the temple's courtyard. Here, it was hard, packed dirt, worn into trails in places by the wheels of the vehicles that the Callabarra people used to traverse the city. They were kind of like bicycles, I supposed. They had two wheels, but required no peddling, and the seat was different. Instead of sitting on a small seat and having your legs hang down towards pedals or footrests, the seat was a wider, lower bench, bringing Bohnebregg knees towards chests almost in a sort of squat, with a steering apparatus propped up between the legs instead of high handlebars at the front. Apart from a small metal cylinder attached to the main frame, I could see no other engine or power source, but the vehicles did indeed seem to move all on their own at the pull of a lever.

If I wanted an up-close look at one of the vehicles, I only had to descend the staircase from the balcony, which Skallagrim and I did now. Because below the balcony was Zev's outdoor workshop, where she both built and repaired them.

"Oh, you're up!" called Zev, straightening from where she'd been bent over working on a Bohnebregg bike. Her hair was not as short as Jolakaia's, but was cut in a blunt sweep at her shoulders. She tossed down the tool she'd been using and pushed a pair of protective goggles up onto the top of her head like a headband. Her blue scales were dusty with dirt kicked up from the road, and I wondered how long she'd already been working out here while we'd been sleeping.

"Good morning," I said in choppy Bohnebregg. It looked like it took her a minute to figure out what I'd tried to say, then she flashed her long fangs in a smile.

"Kaia's got food for you somewhere in there," she said, wiping her clawed hands on a leather apron then jerking her snout towards an open window. Then she went to it and called inside. "Queen Kaia! They're up!"

"Queen Kaia?" I repeated slowly, casting first Zev, then Skallagrim a questioning look.

"Jolakaia," Zev clarified. "Queen of this house, my heart, and therefore the entire world as I know it."

Zev's beloved queen emerged a few seconds later, wearing the robes of a Mother's Hand instead of those of a monarch. In her hands she carried a tray laden with food. Zev gave a low cheer, then tried to grab something off the tray, but Jolakaia turned with a surprising grace, spinning until the tray was out of reach.

Jolakaia made a distinctly reptilian *tsk* sound.

"You've already had a double portion!" she said. "And you know you have to clean your claws and wipe your scales after you've been working with the metal before you eat! I don't want to have to get the blood-cleansers out because you've ingested too much of the dust again!"

Zev gave a lazy grin, hopped right over the bike she'd been working on, bumped her snout lovingly to the side of Jolakaia's head, and then headed around the side of the house towards the door at the front. Jolakaia watched her go with a look of long-suffering affection, as if she were wondering how she'd gotten so lucky and, simultaneously, how she was going to survive the woman who'd just gone inside the house.

Once satisfied that Zev wasn't going to give herself metal poisoning, she turned back towards us with the food – beautiful, big, fat pastries.

"They're stuffed with fish and egg. And those little mollusks that glue themselves to river rock. Did you encounter any of those when you were out there? They're rare around here these days, but very good."

I accepted a pastry gratefully and bit into it. The outer dough wasn't at all the texture I was expecting – it was much firmer, almost cracker-like – but still delicious.

"I did not notice them," Skallagrim responded. He watched me eat for a moment, his eye lingering on my mouth, then took a pastry for himself. He popped the thing into his snout whole, like it was nothing but a puff of popcorn.

"You and Zev eat the same way, Skalla," Jolakaia said, giving a resigned sort of smirk.

"I didn't know your name could be shortened to Skalla," I said, feeling a frown pucker the spot between my brows.

Skallagrim tossed his snout, his version of a shrug.

"You may call me that, if you wish." He did his snout-shrug thing again. "You may call me whatever you like."

I realized I was still frowning. I wasn't exactly jealous, per se. Jolakaia had been an amazing friend to both of us, not to mention the fact that she was related by blood to Skallagrim and was very happily married to someone else. But still, something about it irked me. It didn't bother me that she had a nickname for Skallagrim.

It bothered me that I didn't. There was a less formal, more intimate way of addressing him, and I'd had no idea. A casual friend would have known something like that, let alone the person who was supposed to be his mate.

"Skalla," I said slowly. Then, with a small smile, "I like it."

"I like hearing you say it." A huskiness had entered his voice. Jolakaia, who could only follow half the conversation, backed subtly away to give us some privacy. But I didn't want her to feel awkward. She'd housed us, given us clothes, and brought us the most amazing breakfast.

"Thank you so much for the food," I said to her in Bohnebregg. As I spoke, Zev careened around the side of the house, claws already outstretched for a pastry from the tray.

"Was that Bohnebregg?" Zev quipped. Jolakaia snatched the tray away until she'd given her wife a good, long look. Zev's apron was gone, and her hands and scales looked freshly washed. Zev was finally awarded a pastry. She popped it into her snout the exact same way Skalla had, swallowed, then looked at me. "Sorry, but you're going to have to get old Skalla here to translate for you. I didn't understand a single word that came out of that strange little mouth."

"Old?" Skalla said. I caught the warning in his voice, but Zev didn't. She snagged another pastry.

"Yes. Aren't you? Old, that is? Kaia said you've been around for hundreds of strides of the Mother." After swallowing her next pastry, she grinned. "Do not worry. Your scales have held up quite well for your age! Not as good-looking as your lovely Suvi, especially with the whole eye situation." She gestured at Skalla's scars, and Jolakaia looked like she wanted to slam her tray into her own face in embarrassment.

"I am sure Skalla is well aware of both his appearance and his age," she said, sounding pained.

Skalla's brow was drawn so low over his eye it looked like his scales might crack under the force of his expression. I patted his arm with gentle sympathy while trying not to laugh. There was truly no one, except perhaps Zev, who could look at him and see anything but a magnificent male specimen. But him getting all worked over the matter up was both funny and endearing.

"Don't worry. I still think you look nice," I whispered. Luckily, since I'd already said the same thing this morning, he had to be inclined to believe me instead of assuming I was trying to placate him now. Slowly, the look on his face morphed into something mostly neutral. Zev, completely unperturbed, reached for the tray once more only to find it empty.

"There are more inside," Jolakaia said with a sighing laugh, already anticipating her wife's question.

Zev took the empty tray and bounded away once more.

"And what will you two do today?" Jolakaia said. "I will be leaving for the temple soon. You are welcome to stay here, of course, either upstairs or down here with Zev. I'm sure she would appreciate the company. Though I will warn you, she will either talk your brains right out of your skull without stopping for breath, or she will become so hyper-fixated on her work that she will ignore you completely. There is no in between."

I snorted when I saw Skalla's reaction to that. He didn't say anything, but he didn't need to. His face did all the talking for him. He looked like he wanted to stay here and listen to more of Zev's quips about how sort of OK-looking he was (for his age of course) like he wanted a spray of acid in his remaining eye.

"Skalla can do whatever he likes," I said with a low chuckle, "but I was actually hoping to come with you to the temple, if that's alright."

Skalla looked surprised by that, and so did Jolakaia once he'd translated. I flushed under their questioning gazes.

"I just... I think I can help you," I said quickly, feeling oddly defensive. "I know a lot of people got hurt when we... um... arrived here. I'd like to contribute to the temple in some way to at least try to make up for it. To atone. I'm good with plants, and I've worked in labs. I'm sure I could assist with mixing up the medications."

"You need atone for nothing," Skalla snapped, wings and tail twitching in annoyance. "I've already told you that."

"Please, Skalla. Just translate," I replied wearily, not wanting to have this argument again.

He glared at Jolakaia and did so, though not entirely faithfully. I noticed he left out anything about me wanting to atone and simply told her I wished to help out at the temple. I rolled my eyes but decided that was good enough, because Jolakaia was already agreeing.

"That will work well. It will be a busy mixing day for me. My patient rounds have been reduced now that you are well and all the Mother's Claws' bones are mending."

I cringed, knowing exactly who had broken those bones and why. There was nothing I could do about what had happened now, but at least I could help out in some small way. Give something back, as paltry as the penance may be.

"If you've had enough to eat, then we shall go," Jolakaia said. "You can ride with me on my two-wheel if you like, Suvi."

"She will ride with me," Skalla corrected.

"We do have a second one... But do you even know how to ride?"

Skalla looked irritated by the question even though it was a good one. Who knew if they'd had vehicles like these on the planet back when he'd been here last?

Skalla slung one powerful leg over the two-wheel Zev had been working on and got himself into position with ease that had to have come from muscle memory. If he hadn't driven this precise sort of vehicle, he'd definitely been on something similar. He gripped the rounded steering mechanism in a way that looked very natural, then gave an affirming, sideways jerk of his snout.

"I remember. At least, my body does."

"Alright, then. Just don't go too fast. Children often dart out into the streets, and there are wagons that move more slowly. Plus, if you topple, Suvi's skin will not hold up against the fall as well as scales would."

Skalla scoffed, as if the very idea of me falling were ridiculous to him. And he kind of had a point with that – the guy literally had wings. He could just grab me and hop right up into the air to avoid the ground if needed.

It was decided. We would take the two-wheel and follow Jolakaia. Skalla got off the vehicle that still needed more work done on it and sat himself upon the newer one Jolakaia offered.

"I'm not sure I'm going to fit," I said, looking at the thin strip of seat left after Skalla had settled himself. He shifted backwards as far as he could and spread his thighs wider, but I still had my doubts. I loved my body, but there was no mistaking it – I did not have a small ass.

Not waiting for me to make up my mind, Skalla seized on me with his claws, lifting me and plopping me down between his legs. I was instantly overcome by the nearness of him, the wall of muscle at my back and the massive legs closing in both of mine.

It turned out there was enough room left on the seat – sort of. I perched on the front edge with the pole holding up the half-circle steering apparatus alarmingly close to my crotch. It wasn't like it was rubbing against me, though, so I figured this was alright for now. It would be almost as uncomfortably squishy a ride on Jolakaia's two-wheel, because her seat was a little smaller than this one.

After a quick verbal lesson from Jolakaia on the ignition (a simple button) and steering (a very intuitive mechanism, much like a cross between handlebars and a tractor's steering wheel) we were ready to be off. Skalla looped one arm around my waist, holding me fast, like a living seatbelt.

"You're only going to steer with one hand?" I asked him.

"Technically, I could just use my power to steer it. I don't need a hand on it at all."

He moved his steering hand to my knee. His thumb drew a shivery circle on a bit of exposed skin as he demonstrated moving the steering mechanism this way and that without laying a single finger on it.

"Noted," I choked out, trying and failing to ignore the trembling tingles working their way up my inner thigh from the gentle scrape of his thumb.

Unfortunately, ignoring the sensations turned out to be impossible. Because I discovered very quickly into the ride that the steering column did not just twist in a rotation, but it also moved backwards towards the seat and forwards to either decrease or increase speed.

Every time Skalla shifted the pole between my legs to slow down, it bumped against my clit. And then, when in that position and swivelled to turn the vehicle, it ground hard against me. Skalla kept his hand half on my knee, half draping onto my inner thigh, the other curled possessively around my ribcage in the perfect position for my heavy breasts to rest on him, my sensitive nipples rubbing against his scales through the robe. I was entirely frozen, jammed between the ferocious bulk of Skalla's body and the rod of the steering apparatus, unable to wiggle away from the mounting, involuntary pleasure.

I barely registered most of the ride. Callabarra with its alleys and buildings and chatter swam past me in a watery blur as I tried extremely fucking hard not to come. I was successful – barely. As soon as we stopped outside the temple, I leaped out of the seat as if it had burned me. Skalla gave me an odd look as I crossed my arms over my chest, stiff and flushed.

"Are you alright?" he asked, swinging his leg back over the seat and coming towards me, concern bending his brow.

I bit down on my tongue, focusing on the pain. As pathetic as it felt to admit, watching Skalla dismount the two-wheel and stalk shirtless towards me had me clenching in a dangerous way. *Paska*, one swipe of is tongue against me, no, a single whisper of breath on my throbbing flesh, and I would be coming. *Instantly.*

"I'm fine," I squeaked out.

He looked like he was about to say something, or maybe even touch me. With rubbery limbs, I hustled out of his reach, following Jolakaia into the courtyard and then the temple beyond.

CHAPTER THIRTY-SEVEN
Skallagrim

Even with the one-sided language barrier, Suvi and Jolakaia were becoming fast friends. They walked ahead of me together, leaving me to feel rather like some useless barnacle stuck to the back of their boat. I felt, as they smiled and chatted over various flowers and fungus, that I was intruding on some secret female social interaction. I was not only unneeded for their tasks, but also probably not wanted, and more than once Jolakaia, or Suvi, or both of them in tandem, scolded me for casting a shadow on whatever it was that they were examining. But I persevered, because being with Suvi, even if it meant following her in silence and staring at the sway of her back with a longing that practically turned me inside out, was worth it.

As Jolakaia gave Suvi a longer, much more detailed tour of the temple gardens than last time, I let my gaze track over the sun-drenched plants. Since our arrival, three Mother's Claws had positioned themselves in the gardens, and my mood soured further.

I should probably consider myself lucky that Koltar didn't insist on guards stationed at Jolakaia's home to watch us.

Then I snorted at myself. Because if anyone was lucky, it was the guards themselves. If they had tried to follow us from the temple to take up permanent stations at the door to the apartment, then they would have quickly found themselves with that very same door ripped from its hinges and shoved right up their –

"Are you coming?"

Suvi's voice distracted me from the amusing violence of my thoughts.

Her little arms were filled with flowers, soft colour pressed to her chest, her hair like liquid in the sun, her cheeks pink and eyes aglow. For a breathless moment I could not speak, could not even attempt to recall what she'd just said to me, so sharply had her loveliness seized upon me, like talons beneath my scales.

"We're going in now," she said. "Are you coming?"

"Coming... with you?"

Blast. I never knew a brain as half-decent as the one I'd always imagined I'd had in my head could be so thoroughly bludgeoned by nothing more than the sight of my pretty mate with flowers in her arms and sunshine on her hair.

"Of course," I said gruffly, trying to regain my footing among this sudden attack of stupidity. I'd never seen Suvi go stupid when she looked at me, and I wondered if this was solely a male phenomenon, or something unfortunately specific to me. I wasn't sure which option was less comforting.

What was comforting, though, was her little smile upon my answer. She was actually glad I was going with her, thank the cursed stars, because I was not entirely sure how I would have recovered if she'd looked unhappy instead.

I reached my hands for the load in her arms.

"Let me carry that for-"

My question was cut off by Jolakaia immediately depositing a massive, unwieldy bundle of flowers, leaves, and stalks into my upward-facing palms.

"Since you were obliging enough to offer," my cousin-niece said brightly.

"I was making the offer to my *mate*," I said archly. But both females were already walking back into the temple with their own bundles of collected plants, thoroughly ignoring me. Fighting to keep the many bits and bobs of plant-matter together in my hands (*skies above, why are so many of these blasted petals falling off!*) I followed.

CHAPTER THIRTY-EIGHT
Suvi

The room where Jolakaia and the other Mother's Hands mixed their medications was probably the nicest lab I'd ever seen. It was advanced, with alien machinery and glass beakers lined up along the walls, but it was also beautiful. Huge windows let in flowing sunlight, illuminating the wooden benches and copper-coloured metal worktops.

There was only one other Mother's Hand in the room when we arrived – an old Bohnebregg woman with dull, pond-green scales and short black hair that was interspersed with rust-red. It seemed that, when Bohnebregg people aged, instead of their hair going grey or white, it faded to something more reddish. Nutmeg and pepper instead of salt and pepper. Jolakaia introduced her as the oldest Mother's Hand in the temple. Her name was Koraba, and she gave us a gummy smile, several of her largest fangs missing, before returning to her work bent over what looked very much like the Bohnebregg version of a microscope.

Jolakaia led us to a clean, bare metal table, and we dumped down the cuttings taken from the garden. Skalla followed suit, his pile largest of all.

"I will give you a short tour before we begin," Jolakaia said. She took us around the room, demonstrating the various machines used for things like purification, distillation, heating, or cooling. As we went along, one question grew and grew until I finally had to turn to Skalla to ask him to translate it.

"What's the power source?"

It was something that had already been niggling at me. For example, the two-wheel vehicles seemed to have a small, tubular battery on them rather than a combustion engine, but I'd never seen any evidence of such things being charged. Likewise, I'd never noticed any wiring in the apartment, nor attached to any of these machines here.

"I do not understand," Jolakaia said.

"Where I come from we use energy, like electricity for example," I explained. "Metal can conduct it to power up appliances like these. But they're usually plugged into an outlet."

Skalla translated, but Jolakaia did not look any less confused than before.

"The power source is within the object itself," she said, tapping a claw on the metal side of a machine used to disinfect tools and beakers. "It is not simply conducted by the metal; it comes from the metal. Or, more precisely, from the Shara plant."

Now it was my turn to be confused. Jolakaia rolled her robe's sleeves up to the elbows, as if gearing up to teach me a complex lesson.

"Here. Regard the Shara plant." She held up one of the cottony, metal-lined flowers. "As the plant grows and thrives, it takes in sunlight, water, nutrients, heat."

I nodded. That much, at least, I could understand. I was a botanist, after all.

"The metal," her claw twanged against a bright thread, like she was plucking a guitar string, "conducts the plant's energy up and down its length. But it also acts as energy storage. This stored energy then powers the objects created from the metal. Even more than this, the metal retains an echo of its life in the plant – a memory of sorts – and it can continue to collect and distribute energy from sunlight long after it has been stripped out of the living plant."

"Are you telling me," I said, disbelief catching in my throat, "that you are essentially growing your very own self-sustaining, solar-powered batteries? In a garden?!"

After Skalla translated, Jolakaia jerked her snout in confirmation.

"Is it not so on your world?"

"Definitely not," I said, shaking my head and staring at the simple, brain-bendingly extraordinary plant Jolakaia held. No natural gas, no nuclear fusion, no hydro. All the Bohnebregg people had to do was to let these plants grow in their native environment, soaking up sun and energy, and in turn they could power entire cities with the stuff.

Instantly, I started thinking of all the ways such a plant could benefit Earth. We could eliminate pollution, shut down mines, save forests and oceans and people! So many people!

My excitement had a bucket of cold water dumped on it when I realized that this was exactly the sort of thing our mission had been sent out into the universe to do. The whole reason I was abducted from Earth was to find, no, to *steal* alien technology and resources that could sustain Earth into the future.

But no human ships had come to this world. At least, not yet. The Shara plant would remain here, untouched and safe.

And so would the people of Bohnebregg.

After my brief and mind-blowing lesson on Bohnebregg energy production (or cultivation, I supposed) and a few more demonstrations of the lab's machinery, we got to work. I learned how to use the feathery yellow Mother's Breath to prepare an antibiotic tincture, and how to extract Mother's Tears (a viscous clear sap) from the stems of plants of the same name. I peeled threads of metal from Shara plants, sliced stalks open, boiled and bottled, all the while peppering Jolakaia with questions translated by Skalla.

She didn't appear to mind at all. In fact, she seemed happy to have such an enthusiastic student. I was happy, too. I was so engrossed, so glad to be immersed in work like this, that at one point Jolakaia stopped, looked at me, and said with a laugh, "You were born to be a Mother's Hand!"

"I do like this sort of thing," I admitted, blushing at her compliment. "Back on Earth, I used my botany skills mostly for survey work. I'd go over project sites for utility companies and make sure they weren't harming any endangered species. Stuff like that. But..."

I gave my freshly collected Mother's Tears a stir with a metal rod.

"But I always had a passion for this kind of work. My sister got very sick and the chemotherapy – the human treatment for her illness – caused her a lot of problems with her skin. I used to create skincare products and salves for her in our kitchen using different natural ingredients."

No matter how tired or sick she'd felt, she'd always exclaim over a new batch of anything I came up with. "You should sell this stuff," she'd told me. "Seriously! Go on one of those American shows, get a bunch of start-up money, open a factory!"

When she'd said it, it almost seemed like it could have been real.

But then she'd died. I finished school, got a boring job, and to top it all off, got abducted twice, first by humans, then by Skalla.

Things really aren't turning out the way we thought they would, Elvi.

After Skalla finished translating what I'd said, Jolakaia put down the Shara plant she'd been working on and bumped her knuckles gently against my nose.

"I am sorry to hear of your sister. I, too, have lost a sibling. My brother still lives, but..." She stared at the metal table for a long moment, then said, "but I know I will never see him again. Nor do I wish to. But it is still a wound."

A wound. One that wouldn't heal no matter how many soothing plants you piled on top of it.

Tentatively, I bumped my knuckles against the tip of her snout, and when she smiled I knew I'd done the gesture correctly. We looked at each other for a long moment, and for the first time I noticed something odd gleaming on her chest where her robe gaped slightly.

"What is that?" I asked. It was a simple enough sentence, so I said it in Bohnebregg.

The thing I'd asked about looked to be a hunk of shiny metal embedded in the flesh of her chest. It was vaguely triangular in shape, roughly the size of my thumb with its narrow end pointing down like an arrow. If it was a cultural thing, like a piercing, I hadn't noticed it on anyone else.

"Ah," she said, glancing down at the metal hunk adorning her front. "That was a gift from the very brother I just mentioned."

Her voice was flat, which made me think it had been no gift at all.

"My brother Joleb is a vicious raider warlord," Jolakaia said, putting down the beaker she'd been holding. "He is very cruel, very wealthy, and very good at what he does. Many men have pledged allegiance to him. His army is the largest and most powerful on this side of the river. His hoard is the stuff of legend, built upon what was hoarded from the generations who came before."

Generations before...

I followed her gaze to Skalla, who stood directly behind me. Other than a twitchy pulse of his wings, he had no other reaction to her words.

"As his younger sister, I was expected to assist on raids," Jolakaia continued. "I did so, just as I'd always done for our father, until..."

She paused, appeared to gather her thoughts, then said the rest in a very mechanical sort of voice, like if she let any emotion into the words, she wouldn't be able to speak at all.

"Until we raided a village with no army and very little metal. I watched my brother slaughter innocents in their homes, pulling children from their beds, searching for any glinting scrap he could hoard. He would not let me tend to the wounds of any of them. I entered a berserker rage, but it was a rage against him, not those we fought. Of course, it accomplished nothing. I was beaten down by him and subdued by his loyal army. When my rage faded, and I became fully aware of myself again, I was bound by chains in our home."

She touched the metal stud on her chest.

"Joleb pulled out the scale above my heart with his own claws for my betrayal. Then he embedded this metal in my flesh. A reminder of whom I was meant to be loyal to."

She began to rub at the metal, like it was aching.

"I know it must have been very painful, but I was so angry that I do not really remember feeling it. I feigned repentance for long enough that I was eventually unbound. I escaped after that, wandered alone for days, until I came to Callabarra and vowed to follow the way of cotton."

Her hand fell away from her chest.

"I thought about taking it out. But ultimately, I've decided to keep it. It is a reminder, just as my brother intended it to be, I suppose. But instead of reminding me whom I serve, it reminds me of who I want to be, who I choose to be, every day that I am here instead of there."

I had absolutely no idea what to say to that. I silently bumped my elbow against hers on the table, knowing it wasn't enough.

"It is done," Jolakaia said simply. "It is done, and now we shall work."

But the look on her face told me it wasn't done for her. Not really.

Not while her brother was still out there. I remembered the abandoned house Skalla and I had stayed at for one night, and wondered if Joleb had been the one to drive the occupants out.

Or kill them.

CHAPTER THIRTY-NINE
Suvi

The rest of the day passed pleasantly. Jolakaia and I fell into a comfortable rhythm, working well together, while Skalla acted as our surly supervisor. He glowered from the corner of the lab as if he had no real interest in joining in the work but was feeling miffed he hadn't been invited to participate, anyway.

I found it cute. Alarmingly so.

Skalla had been beautiful to me before, no doubt about that, but cute was a whole other level. Cute implied affection beyond mere attraction.

Cute meant that I maybe, sort of, probably liked him. *Liked him*, liked him. More than thinking about him as the friend he'd become to me.

But then again, what kind of friend would eat you out with his split tongue and then promise, with absolute sincerity, to woo you?

But a part of me shrank back and couldn't accept it. I thought of Jolakaia's story about her brother's raiding, and knew that Skalla had probably participated in similar things. Hopefully not the slaughtering innocents part...

I glanced over at him. Of course, his eye was already on me. Our gazes met, then I wrenched mine away.

I tried to picture Skalla pulling children out of their beds and I couldn't. I really, truly couldn't. Maybe he had few memories, but the internal core of him had to be the same, right? And the Skalla I knew wouldn't hurt a child.

And if he'd hurt adults before, well...

People can change.

I remembered poor Nakib with his crutch, followed by Skalla's uncaring statement of, "I broke his leg," and sighed.

Skalla was at my side in an instant.

"She is tired. You are working my mate too hard," he said. He laid protective hands on my shoulders, which I was about to shrug off to show that I could keep going, when he started rubbing his thumbs in the most exquisite circles on either side of my upper spine.

The sound that came out of me was entirely undignified. And I didn't even care. I leaned into his touch, not realizing until that moment how long I'd been hunched over the table.

"We have accomplished much," Jolakaia said. "Thank you, Suvi. Let us return and see what my wife has scrounged up for us to eat tonight."

"That sounds perfect to me." I was already looking forward to being back at their place, surrounded by the scent of the dirt road and the herbs and flowers blooming by their house, listening to Zev chatter on. My eyes slipped closed, picturing the scene, as Skalla's massage on my shoulders deepened.

I felt warm thinking about how I could do this every day. I'd help in the lab, and maybe assist the Mother's Seeds in the gardens, too. Then we'd go home to the apartment, share a meal with Zev and Jolakaia, then Skalla and I would sleep side-by-side, just as we had last night.

I thought of all these things.

And I was...

Happy.

My eyes flew open.

Happy? How could I be *happy*?

Happy without Elvi?

Happy when I'd never see another human again and my friends were still stuck on the ship?

How could I possibly feel this way when I'd never even chosen to be here in the first place?

Guilty confusion burned in my stomach. I shied away from Skalla's hands and stood. Jolakaia and I began to clear the table, and Skala joined in, his eye never tearing itself from my face as we finished tidying up. Kobara had long since vacated her place. It was only us left in the room.

Which made the tall Bohnebregg figure watching us from the doorway all the more jarring when I turned around.

"Honoured Eye," Jolakaia said with quiet respect.

Much louder, and with none of the respect, Skalla growled, "What do you want?"

"Skalla!" I scolded him, shooting him a sharp look. Koltar had never done anything to earn our ire. He'd watched Skalla hurt his temple's guards and then he'd helped us anyway. He'd allowed us in, gave us his resources so I could be healed, and all of it under the threat of Skalla's rage.

"It was a perfectly legitimate question. I am simply inquiring what he wants," Skalla grumbled. "Surely you cannot find fault in me for that."

"Sometimes it's not what a person says but how they say it," I countered crisply, rolling my eyes. I turned back to the male in his saffron-yellow robes. "Hello, Koltar."

When it became very clear that Skalla had no interest in facilitating the conversation and I'd get none of his translating skills, I switched, with the stiffness of an unused muscle, to Bohnebregg. *The webbing in my ear has made it too easy to talk to Skalla in human languages.... I need to practise more...*

"Is there a thing we can make with you?" I said stiltedly. Crap. That wasn't right. I tried again. "Is there a thing we can help with you... You with?"

Close enough. Koltar smiled, obviously understanding the question, or at least the sincerity of it.

Skalla hissed out a dramatic sigh, as if it physically pained him that I was paying any mind to one of the most important people in the entire fucking city. He rubbed viciously at his snout, glaring at the Mother's Eye.

"I am come merely to see how you fare, Suvi, and to congratulate you. I did not get a chance before you left for your new accommodations."

"Congratulate..." I pursed my lips in confusion. "Why?"

"Why, for your bonding, of course!"

"My... what?"

Koltar's gaze went to Skalla.

"I have heard the good news. That you and Skallagrim are mated. I confess I am not well-versed in the matter. I am going on legends around the ancient princess Jolakaia and her mate – Skallagrim's parents – and the bits

I've picked up from Aeshyr. But from what I've gathered, the bond between a stone sky god and his mate is powerful indeed."

He was staring intently at me now, as if trying to see right inside my brain, and all at once it hit me.

He's congratulating me on sealing the mate bond by taking Skallagrim's knot.

My cheeks flamed, and Skalla made a rough noise before stepping in front of me, blocking me from view.

"You have bonded," Koltar said to the wall of Skalla's body, "have you not?"

Skalla's wings flexed with restrained fury, and I was glad it wasn't just me who found that question to be extremely invasive. Even Jolakaia looked awkward about the whole thing, turning to fiddle with the knob on a nearby machine.

"How about I bond my fist to the inside of your skull?" Skalla seethed, knuckles cracking with tension at his sides.

"Skalla," I said, scolding him yet again but much more quietly this time. I placed a calming hand on his back, and watched the muscles of his wings and shoulders jump in response to my touch. As strange as I found Koltar's question, I wasn't about to let Skalla actually hurt him because of it. To Koltar, I was an alien, and so was Skalla to an extent. It wasn't surprising for Koltar to be curious about these things, even if it did make me immensely uncomfortable.

Skalla exhaled roughly and forced his posture to relax.

Koltar said nothing for a moment, as if still expecting one of us to actually answer. I supposed he was used to people jumping to obey him and giving him whatever information he wanted whenever he asked for it. But there was absolutely no way I was going to answer him, and it was obvious that Skalla wouldn't either. I cringed at what Skalla would even say. *Yes, she is my fated mate, but alas, I have not yet been fortunate enough to get a single one of my cocks into her!*

Jesus Christ.

"Best wishes to you both," Koltar said at length. Jolakaia mumbled a respectful goodbye at his back as he walked out of the lab.

"I do not like that male," Skalla hissed vehemently at the now-empty doorway.

"Do you like *any* male?" I prodded.

"If I did, it would have been in my past," he said testily. "All the males among my current acquaintance are decidedly obnoxious and it would not grieve me to see their spines ripped out."

"Yeah, well, I'm sure they feel the same way about you," I replied with a chuckle and a pat on his tense back.

Skalla was possibly the most dramatic male, alien or human, in the entire span of the universe. But I was slowly learning how to deal with him. I trusted more and more each day that he'd listen to me when it really counted. He wouldn't hurt someone if I didn't want him to. At least... I was pretty sure he wouldn't. As long as I was conscious and able to tell him not to, that is, previous bone-breaking incidents aside.

"Come on," I said, patting him once more. "Let's go eat."

I almost said *let's go home*.

CHAPTER FORTY
Suvi

I configured myself into a new position on the two-wheel that was less comfortable but also far less prone to edging me into a near-painful state. I probably looked a bit silly – I was essentially sitting side saddle with my legs pressed together and thrown across Skalla's lap – but it worked. And this time, I could actually relax a little bit and enjoy the ride.

I wasn't much one for speed, and that was alright, because the Callabarra streets had just as many pedestrians and slow-rolling wagons as it did two-wheel vehicles. The drive was relaxed, the sun warming me gently as it dipped behind the tall wood-framed buildings at the city's centre. The further we got from the temple, the more the houses were spaced out, with gardens and small fields and even ponds dotting the properties. One house was even built on stilts above one such pond, and a group of about a dozen Bohnebregg children were playing a game there that involved a flat-looking rock and sticks. *Hockey* sticks.

"Skalla! Can we stop?" I said, twisting to keep the kids in my sight as we passed them. Skalla yanked back on the steering pole, the rod of it mercifully bumping against my hip instead of my clit this time, and brought us to a stop at the side of the wide, dirt road.

"What is it?" he asked with some tension as I hopped off of his lap.

"I just want to see what those kids are doing. It almost looks like they're playing hockey!"

Skalla turned his eye back towards the children we'd passed with renewed interest. I'd mentioned hockey to him before, I didn't think I'd done a great job explaining it.

"Come on," I said excitedly, grabbing his hand and tugging. "Let's go see."

It wasn't hockey, of course, but there were elements that made it similar enough to slap a sky-wide grin on my face.

There appeared to be two teams, each with six squealing Bohnebregg children. One team stood on one side of the pond, the other opposite them. There were three large hoops on each side of the pond, for a total of six, flat circles on the ground about a metre in diameter each and moving progressively further from the water's edge. The children took turns, one from the first team, then one from the other, on and on, each of them slapping the flat rock with their long-handled sticks as hard as possible. The goal, it appeared, was to make the rock skip across the pond's surface and land in one of the hoops on the other side. There must have been some kind of points system, because when one child got the rock into the hoop furthest away on that other side of the pond, their team erupted into cheers and the opposing side howled.

"It's not exactly like hockey," I told Skalla, unable to look away from the childhood goodness of the game. "But it's close enough." And even though the rules were different, the visceral joy, the thrills and the pain of the game, were instantly recognizable as ones shared in equal measure by human children. *All the way across the universe, and here we are, alien children playing the same kinds of games I did.*

"Let her have a turn."

I jumped, realizing Skalla was speaking directly to the children.

"Oh, no, that's alright," I said hurriedly, not wanting to encroach on their game. Just watching had been good enough.

But the children were already hopping excitedly at the prospect and rushing to offer me their sticks.

"Yes, yes! Let that pale, ugly boy try it!"

"She's female, you dolt!"

"Wait... Really?"

"Let the ugly female have a go!"

Skalla bared his fangs and looked like he was about to smack the ones who'd called me ugly. I snorted, barely holding back my laughter, and waved him off.

"Thank you," I said to them in Bohnebregg, grinning and taking the closest stick offered to me. It was different from a hockey stick. It reminded me more of a lacrosse stick, but with a curved wooden paddle instead of netting at the end. "Alright. Here goes nothing."

The wide-eyed children stood back and urged each other into breath-less silence, as if I was doing some magic trick that required immense con-centration instead of simply attempting to hit a rock with a stick. Trying not to lose my nerve under the weight of all those expectant little eyes, I nudged the flat rock into the correct spot and took a deep breath. Then I gripped the stick's handle and executed the movement with a resounding *smack*!

The rock skipped over the pond in great, bouncy arches, zooming right past the furthest hoop on the other side. I was fairly certain that going past the hoop wasn't ideal, but the children lost their minds anyway, jumping and screeching, both sides demanding my points be added to their score.

Skalla watched me from over the children's heads, giving me a look that made my chest constrict.

He was looking at me like he was proud of me.

He was looking at me like he loved me.

"I guess that was pretty good," I called to Skalla with a laugh, trying to lighten the moment. "Although I'm way more used to playing on ice."

Without moving his eye from my face, he lifted his hand out to the side, jabbed a single finger towards the water...

And the surface of the pond instantly solidified.

If I thought the kids had been excited seeing the "ugly female" hit the rock across the pond, they went absolutely ballistic after this new develop-ment. Whooping and hollering, they moved as one big, writhing mass onto the ice, instantly sliding and falling onto their sticks in giggling waves. They had absolutely no idea how to move on the slippery surface of the ice, but they also didn't seem to care much, and they revelled as much in the tum-bling down as they did the clumsy gliding around. *It probably doesn't get cold enough here to see ice like this normally...*

"Like this," I called, easing out onto the ice, marvelling at the perfect surface, like it had been freshly polished by the Zamboni. "Watch me!"

Jolakaia had lent me a pair of child-sized boots, and while they certain-ly weren't as effective as skates, I could at least try to demonstrate how to push forward across the ice correctly. The kids delighted in this lesson and took to the new motion as quickly as only children can do, little lizard-like feet propelling them forward. Soon, they were all more or less stable, and they naturally fell into a circular pattern of movement around the edge of the pond follow-the-leader style.

I slid into the centre of the pond, standing still there and letting the children with their hissing alien laughter swirl around me. Skalla was still watching me, and that look hadn't left his face. If anything, it had intensified. It was a look that asked for as much as it promised. A look that said, *I see you, Suvi. Do you see me?*

And suddenly, I was sobbing, standing on ice that felt so familiar. Skalla's eye darkened. He didn't even attempt to cut his way through the turbulent children. He merely opened his wings with a crack and vaulted right over their heads until he had landed directly in front of me.

"I'm not sad," I told him quickly, sniffing as he gently cupped my face and dragged his thumbs through the tracks of my tears. "I'm just..."

Nostalgic. Homesick. Hopeful.

Happy even though I shouldn't be.

Cracked open by the way you look at me.

"Thank you, Skalla," I said, my heart hurting in a way that almost felt good. Like a muscle getting sore only because it's becoming stronger.

Because it's been used.

He didn't answer me. He merely tipped his snout down to meet my mouth and tenderly drew my tongue against his. I wrapped my arms around his neck and kissed him.

The children didn't notice us, didn't have any reaction to our kiss at all as they skidded and screamed. They remained gleefully caught up in their own exuberance while Skalla and I were caught only by each other.

CHAPTER FORTY-ONE
Skallagrim

All that playing at the pond meant that we were late for the meal at Jo-lakaia and Zev's. There was food left, though, and the four of us ate outside as the stars came out. As the two moons – Shara and her mother – began their nightly healing trek across the sky, Suvi excused herself to the apartment, claiming fatigue. My instincts, my heart, and my loins (these days those three things seemed to be one and the same) urged me to follow her, but I held back a little, watching her perfectly rounded backside disappear up the stairs before speaking to Zev and Jolakaia.

"I would... seek your advice," I said, the words feeling unnatural on my tongue.

Zev and Jolakaia looked at me, as shocked as I was. No doubt they knew I was not the sort of male to ask for help. But in this case, I felt it was warranted.

"I want to... I've promised to woo Suvi. I was wondering if you two had any ideas."

Blasted river, just saying it made me want to peel my own scales off in vicious humiliation. I should know how to please my own mate, curse it all!

But, other than a beginner's knowledge of the places on her body that made her writhe and squeal, I hadn't gotten very far otherwise. I wanted to do more than just please her physically. When I'd seen how happy she was with those children at the pond today, when I'd watched her bloom on the ice I'd created, right before my very eyes, it had made me greedy to the point of pain. I wanted more of that. More of her joy. And I wanted to be the one to provide it.

Only problem was I had no idea how.

"Do you... Do you have any knowledge of human courting customs?" Jolakaia began. She spoke slowly, carefully, as if testing every word for how much it might offend me before moving on to the next.

"None," I admitted with thorny reluctance. "I assume that, in time, I could learn enough about it. But the heat could be coming any day now, and I want to win her love before that happens. I figured since you are both female, you must know what females like.

"We are female, but we are from Bohnebregg," Jolakaia said. "And even so, even among Bohnebregg females, there is much variance in taste and desire. I am not so sure what we can offer you..."

She looked stymied, maybe even discouraged.

"Do not give me those moping eyes," I snapped. "You look like you do not believe that I can do it."

"It is not that I don't believe you can," she muttered. "I just do not know what advice to give you."

I knew this was a bad idea.

"What about you, Zev?" I demanded. "Your wife is entirely useless on this matter. What say you?"

"You should show her your tools," Zev said, serious and earnest. "And your fishing gear. That's what worked for me."

"That is most certainly *not* what worked for you!" Jolakaia sputtered.

"Yes, it is." Zev said resolutely. "Do not listen to her, Skalla. I swear, my queen was all polite prudishness until she saw my workshop."

"Excuse me!"

Zev ignored her wife's indignant interjection. A sly look entered her eye.

"Getting her on my two-wheel was even better."

"Hmm." I considered that idea, then laid it aside. "Suvi seemed a little tense after the first two-wheel drive. I am not so sure about that idea."

Zev jerked her snout up and to the right.

"Alright. Definitely just the tools and fishing gear, then."

"I have fished for her," I replied, drumming my fingers against the underside of my snout. "And she did seem suitably impressed by that. But I do not actually have any tools or gear."

"I can lend you some," Zev replied helpfully. "Just make sure you give them back. And don't get any *fluids* on them."

"Stop, stop! Both of you!" Jolakaia cried. "This conversation is too absurd to be allowed to continue! Zev, I did not begin to love you because of your hoard of tools! But rather, when you first showed them all to me, you explained every piece with such purity of passion that I could not help but be moved! It was the same with the two-wheel! You were showing me your life's work with pride, and I found that immensely appealing. It had nothing to do with the objects themselves."

She swivelled her eyes onto me with regal haughtiness, and I suddenly understood Zev's nickname for her. That was my maternal side's commanding bloodline in her veins, alright.

"What excites you, Skalla? What is your passion?"

"Suvi," I said instantly.

Jolakaia cast her eyes skyward, and I could practically hear her unspoken prayer. *Mother help me, for I find myself surrounded by fools.*

When she returned her gaze to me, it was sober with conviction.

"You must offer her your true self, Skallagrim. The core of your being. Let her see it. Let your true nature draw her in."

I stared at her flatly, biting back the retort that it was my true nature, my authentic core, that I thought Suvi was most likely to reject.

I told her rather snippily that I liked Zev's idea better and then began to mount the stairs.

Just as I opened the balcony door that would lead me to Suvi, I heard Zev's whisper from below.

"He's in trouble, isn't he?"

And curse that Jolakaia – my own kin who should have spoken only in support of me! – for she answered, "I rather fear he is."

I did not mean to, but I pulled the door shut so hard behind me that the glass rattled like angry bones.

CHAPTER FORTY-TWO
Suvi

I didn't think I'd fall asleep before Skalla came up to the room. But after a busy day of working, then playing, all topped off with a solid dinner of grilled fish and riverweed salad, I found myself dozing off on the bed in the darkened room alone. I slipped deeper and deeper into sleep until a rattling bang jolted me awake. Head swimming, heart racing, I sat bolt upright in the bed, grasping at the bedding, my eyes going to the door.

Relief bloomed in my throat.

Just Skalla.

He didn't make his way any further into the room. He just stood there, a hulking silhouette made velvety by night. Moonlight spilled in behind and around him, making some scales at his edges jump into cutting silver clarity while the rest of him was solid shadow painted by points of glowing gold.

"I'm awake," I said softly, feeling rather silly for announcing it considering I was sitting up and staring at him.

"I know." A pause, then something that sounded like the click of fangs against each other. "I am sorry for the noise."

"That's OK. I didn't think I'd actually fall asleep like that! Are you tired?"

"Not particularly."

"Oh."

I wasn't tired now, either. My heart was jumping around in my chest like that rock skipping across the pond's surface. At first, my increased pulse was from being jarred awake.

But now...

Now, it was from being alone with Skalla in the darkness. I squeezed my thighs together.

"Skalla…"

"Do you have any interest in fishing?" he asked out of nowhere. "Or the tools used to procure the fish?"

"Uh…"

Well, that was a random turn for the conversation to take.

"Not really? I think I went fishing a couple of times as a kid. But it isn't something I'm specifically interested in." A small smile touched my lips. I wondered if he could see it. "Besides, I don't really need a fishing rod or anything if I have you with me, right? Since you can just wave your hand and lift them right out of the water."

He made a gruff sound I didn't have time to interpret, because he'd suddenly decided to move, and he was moving *quick*. In the time it took me to inhale, he'd crossed to the bed and pulled apart my robe. He palmed the rapid pulsing of my throat with one hand, the other sliding greedily down my abdomen until his fingers found the already-swollen point of need that was my clit.

"Wet," he gritted out.

"I…"

I couldn't deny it. Just this simple touch, just the shadowy scrape of his scales against my throat and his huge hand between my legs had my stomach swooping, my insides curling. It didn't even occur to me to close my robe. Or my legs. I sat there, moon-drenched, panting as Skalla's fingers worked firm, nimble circles over my clit.

"You're so blasted *soft*," he said, voice tight with longing. "But I like when this part of you gets hard." He lowered his snout, flicking the tips of his tongues over first one nipple, then the other, making them pucker until I was arching towards him for more. His fangs grazed my skin, sending bright bolts of sensation, almost painful and entirely erotic, down my spine. As he worked his forked tongue across my chest, I heard him shuck himself out of his trousers, the fabric hitting the floor with finality.

He shifted his hand, and my entire body twanged, tautly shuddering, when he dipped one thick finger inside me. He ground against my clit with the hard part of his palm, finger plunging in and out, filling the room with slick sucking sounds that grew louder as he moved quicker. His fangs were at my throat, now, his breath a hot, ragged roll down my neck, fanning over my saliva-dampened nipples. The robe slid down my arms, even the fabric's fall feeling like a caress, and goosebumps quickly followed.

"Oh. *Oh...*" I moaned, trembling violently under the sway of the cool air and the exhilaration of Skalla's hands on me. I reached blindly for him, clutching at his shoulders, running my fingernails down the scales of his chest. I sucked in a needy breath, my hips rocking urgently when I found the hot, hard shafts of him, already fully extended, engorged and slippery.

Skalla went rigid under my clumsy touch. I stroked him with both hands, trying to find my rhythm, unused to handling two cocks at the same time. But I must have been doing alright, because Skalla's entire frame spasmed, and a ragged moan tore from his throat as I dragged my fists up and down the silk-wrapped ridges of him.

"Little star," he groaned, driving his hips hard against my hands, "I... I am supposed to be the one seducing you."

I tightened my grip, a thrill biting at me when his cocks jumped against my fingers. He'd stopped thrusting his finger inside me, as if he was no longer capable of movement – of anything – while I stroked him.

That aroused me more than I would have thought possible. That I'd brought this massive beast of a man, a powerful alien, an immortal, to his literal knees just by touching him. Breathless with that rush of power and pussy aching for release, I started grinding myself against his hand, slowly at first, and then with a feral, frenzied abandon. His finger was still inside me, so large it was like a cock all on its own, and I rolled myself on him, riding him. Even in the dark, I could see the desperate burn of his eye watching the place his finger disappeared into my body.

"*Paska.* Shit, Skalla, I'm close," I whimpered.

Without warning, Skalla wrenched his hand away from me and shoved me onto my back. He captured my wrists, pinning my hands above my head, crushed his chest to mine, and fitted his pelvis between my spread legs. My heart gave one long, agonized throb, pulsing in every point of my body, as I anticipated the furious shove of one of his cocks inside me.

But he didn't penetrate me. He shunted his hips against mine, grinding, until his cocks became separated by my body. His smaller, upper cock was trapped between our pelvises, rolling maddeningly over my clit, while the large cock was forced downwards, its shaft settling snugly along the cleft of my ass. Skalla tossed his head back, his neck corded with tension, and I wondered if forcing his cocks so wide apart like this was hurting him. His breath sounded like drops of rain falling onto scalding metal – hiss after hiss after hiss – as he began to ride my body.

He wasn't even inside me, and already I was overwhelmed by him. I was entirely lost to everything except the swollen, brutal spread of his cocks, the two shafts tense as a set of jaws held open across my pussy and ass, throbbing to snap shut and bite. His cocks were trying to drive back towards each other to achieve a more comfortable angle, each one compressing against my flesh, the pressure made even harder by the crushing, urgent roll of Skallagrim's hips against mine. Though I was mostly pinned, I tried to meet his movements. There was so little give in the position that all I managed were ecstatic little twitches against his onslaught.

There was no elegant word to describe the way Skalla mounted me. It was humping, pure and simple. Primal and needy and so fierce that the mattress was shoved back and forth and the bedframe smacked up against the wall, a rapid drumbeat of wood on wood. And behind that drumbeat was the sound of slick flesh on flesh, my whimpering, and Skalla's hissing groans.

And then, the sound of tearing, and the sudden sensation of give beneath my ass. It took me a whoozy moment to realize it wasn't part of my body that had given way, but the bedding beneath. Skalla's frenetic pounding had forced the head of his lower cock down with such force that it had punctured the fabric.

He was literally fucking me into the mattress. His lower cock sank deeper and deeper into the fresh hole he'd created beneath me. I thought I felt that shaft gearing up to ejaculate first, swelling and pulsing against my ass as the torn-open mattress admitted his ridged head.

I gasped in triumph to find out I was right. Skalla's breath hitched, the muscles on his chest turned to stone against my nipples, and then his lower cock exploded, driving downwards and drenching.

It was as if the orgasm was contagious, like it could jump from person to person. Because as soon as that cock began spewing, the viscous heat of my own insides convulsed, then constricted, in shattering climax. But the virulent pleasure wasn't finished yet, because then it rolled from my pussy up to Skalla's other cock. Skalla snapped his jaws soundlessly, fangs bared, wings thrust outwards in ecstasy, as his other cock ejected hot semen all over both of us, sealing our bellies together.

I clung to Skalla with rubbery arms, barely able to do anything besides breathe as I tightened and released, over and over, drifting in that blinding orgasm's wake. I wouldn't drift too far, though. Because Skalla was here, solid as a boulder, something to anchor myself to and-

And he ripped himself away from me.

His arms wheeled, wings tilting, as he heaved himself off of the bed. Stumbling like a drunkard, he disappeared into the bathroom, closed the door...

And locked it.

I stared at the shut door in disbelief, the heat rushing out of me. Skalla's ejaculate cooled on my skin, and I wiped it off the best I could with my discarded robe, feeling suddenly cold.

"Skalla?" I called uneasily. There was no reply except the sudden creak of pipes and the rush of water into the bathroom's tub.

I sat on the ripped bed, cum-soaked robe scrunched in my hands, totally dumbfounded by what had just happened. That had been one of the most intense sexual experiences of my life, and as soon as it was over he was just... done?

"What the hell is happening?"

To keep myself from thinking about it, because thinking about it would lead to inevitable hurt that I wasn't ready for, I gingerly got to my feet, flicked on the ceiling lights, and surveyed the damage.

The mattress was fucked. *Literally and figuratively*, I thought ruefully. In the centre was a narrow but deep gash with cotton stuffing spilling out like entrails.

I had absolutely no idea how I was going to explain this to Jolakaia and Zev. Humiliation plagued me just imagining how that might go.

No way. If anyone has to explain it to them, it's going to be Skallagrim. It's not like it was my giant alien dick that ruined their bed.

Needing something to keep busy with while Skalla did whatever the hell was apparently so important in the bathroom, I stripped the bedding. Then, I set myself to pulling any soiled cotton out of the mattress. Fucking hell, he'd really let go in there. The mattress had an obvious, saggy dip once I was done disposing of all the Skalla-soaked bits inside. I did my best to re-distribute the rest of the clean stuffing, but it still didn't look right.

I glared at the closed bathroom door and muttered, "Next time, if there even is a next time, we are doing that on the floor. Punch a hole through the floorboards and get a splinter in your dick, see if I care."

I washed my hands in the cooking area, then scoured the small amount of storage, relieved to find what I needed – a small sewing kit. I repaired the tear in the mattress, then did the same to the bedding.

But even though the whole project took a while, when I was done it felt too soon. Now I had nothing to distract me from the hole Skalla's absence had created. And this was a hole that I couldn't sew up.

I chewed my lip, wondering if I should go check on him. But then I heard the sound of the tap turning, and the water's sluice coming to a stop. He was obviously conscious in there, and able-bodied enough to turn off the water.

He wasn't sick. He wasn't injured.

He was just... choosing not to be around me right now.

Well, that was just fine. After all, we barely spent any time apart. This was as good a time as any to get some space... when I was still quivering and wet from what we'd just done.

Yup. Perfectly fine. Just peachy.

I slammed the lights off. I didn't bother replacing the bedding yet because it would need to be washed. My robe needed washing now as well, and I didn't want to put on any other clean clothing until I'd had a bath.

Naked and angry – angry so that I wouldn't fall down a nasty hole of hurt – I flopped on the bed, curled onto my side, and fell into a tense, dreamless sleep.

CHAPTER FORTY-THREE
Skallagrim

I *always thought I'd have more time.*

The phrase felt oddly familiar as my chattering mind threw it against the dome of my skull.

I always thought I'd have more time.

More time before I starburned.

More time to make Suvi love me.

Well, there was no blasted time left now. The starburn had already begun. A hot magma creep along my spine that had made me feel like if I just rutted against my mate hardenough then I could spew that venomous heat right out of me.

It hadn't worked. Of course it hadn't.

I hurled myself into the bathtub, claws shaking as I wrenched the tap to the side. Frigid water poured into the tub, and I got onto my weakened knees, angling myself so that the icy torrent flowed directly over my viciously engorged cocks.

I hissed haltingly, screwing my eye shut as the water sluiced, liquid torture. But it was better than that heat. The heat that even now felt like it was stretching my very cells until they split.

Water pooled around my knees, then rose to my thighs, until my hips were submerged in the freezing stuff. The tub would overflow soon. Gritting my fangs, I turned off the water. Then I waited.

Waited... For what, I was not sure. The agony to end, I supposed.

But it couldn't. Wouldn't. Not until Suvi starburned and accepted me into her sucking depths.

Skies take me, I couldn't stop picturing it. It was as if some cruel artist had painted it on the back of my eyelid, so that even when I closed my eye, chasing escape, all I saw was Suvi ripe and glistening, splayed beneath me, begging for my knot.

The image was so close to the reality I'd just experienced in the bed with her. She'd been so perfect, wet and wanting beneath me, that I'd had to get away from her. Had to put space between us – not just space, but a door. Though the river knew how flimsy a thing a wooden door would be under the hammer blows of my lust.

Groaning, I let my hips twitch forward. Even the cold motion of water along my cocks was too much to bear. My larger, lower cock seemed to be more effected than the other, and when I cautiously probed the fiery shaft, I jolted in shock at the foreign shape I felt there.

I stood, sending water rushing against the sides of the bath. Fingers clenched at my sides, my lungs bellowing with breath, I stared down at myself.

My smaller upper cock looked much as it ever did, though more painfully engorged than usual. But my larger one...

My larger one looked like someone had shoved their fist inside it.

Halfway down the ridged green shaft was a bulbous, pulsing mass. When I grazed my claws over the bulge, my spine nearly snapped itself in half. I couldn't think of any sensation to compare it to. The closest thing, perhaps, was that it felt like touching the exposed nerve on a broken fang, at least in terms of how sensitive the flesh was. But though it was painful, pain wasn't the only, or even the most important feeling.

Because chasing the pain was furious, feral need. Need like fire, like acid, like...

Like the hungry heat of a star.

Now I know why they call it starburning.

I collapsed back into the cold water, misery clawing its way through my veins. There would be no relief from this until Suvi could take my knot. And she wouldn't be able to do that until she starburned.

But perhaps there was some hope. Maybe Suvi was already going into heat as well, her body spurred on by the pleasure we'd just shared. I stilled myself, holding my breath and straining my ears.

But I heard nothing besides the soft padding of Suvi's feet across the floor, then the sound of her getting into bed. Nothing to indicate she star-burned on the other side of that door.

Blast!

I let out my breath in a raging snarl, leaning back against the tub and gripping its sides so hard the metal warped under my fingers. No, she was certainly not in heat. If she were, I would hear her. Hear her panting, moaning. Hear her dragging herself to the door. She'd collapse against it, the musk of her heat penetrating through the wood. She'd place her little hand against that barrier and whimper for me. She would weep my name. *Skalla. Skalla. Skalla!*

I could practically hear it, her voice strained by the starburn. She would beg for me and only me.

And oh, how I would soothe her. How I would care for my little burning mate as only I could. I'd rut her, slow, and then *fast*, fast and ferocious. Maybe from behind, letting my upper cock slide against her sensitive nub while my other speared her. And then, when neither of us could stand it anymore, when we were both coming, coming, coming completely undone, I'd knot her. Sink my new, hot bulge so deep that she would forget what it was like to breathe without me in her.

And then, the moment she was ready, I would do it all over again.

I fisted my knot, shuddering at that ragged sensitivity, but I didn't let go. I couldn't. I needed *something*. I stroked and squeezed, knowing that my fingers would be nothing compared to Suvi's cunt but also knowing I had no other options at the moment. The knot throbbed under my touch. There was no sensual pleasure in this. This was merely a terrible necessity, the clutching motion of my hand mindless and mechanical as I hunched over myself.

When I came, it was not from the cock I squeezed. It was my smaller, upper cock that spewed. My knot throbbed, that entire lower shaft straining with a new rush of blood. But there was no relief. No eruption of seed. No easing of the knot.

The starburn will not last forever.

The knot would remain after this, but it would not always hurt so.

But for now, while the starburn was upon me, I grimly resigned myself to the fact that I would not be able to come from this cock until it was inside Suvi.

How long would it take for her to descend into this torment with me? For her to submit to the fated heat that would bind us? Stone of the skies, I hoped it would be soon.

I hated myself for wanting to bring about anything that might make her suffer. It was a selfish thing, to long for the moment when she'd burn, too.

But in my agony, I was weak.

And so, weak male that I was, I remained alone in the frigid water, tugging my knot again and again. Even though I knew it would not do a single, wretched thing to help.

CHAPTER FORTY-FOUR

Suvi

I woke up to morning sunlight falling over me in such blissfully thick waves that I thought Skalla was beside me, his body heat accounting for at least some of that warmth.

My first sleepy reaction was happiness that he was there. Comfort. Relief. I had the slight tickle of a feeling that I should be annoyed, and with my eyes still luxuriously closed, I thought back to last night and remembered why.

So, I suppose he decided to come to bed after all. After I fixed it all by myself, that is.

I opened my eyes, fully expecting to see the broad, starry expanse of his wing tossed over me and his face still in sleep, hair mussed.

But he wasn't there.

The languid comfort I'd been basking in vanished. I sat up, confusion turning to concern when I didn't see Skalla anywhere.

The bathroom door was still closed.

I bolted out of the bed.

I should have checked on him last night! I was too annoyed, too hurt, and let my pride get in the way. What if something's happened to him?

I pounded on the door.

There was no answer.

Knowing it was locked, I tried the handle anyway. It did not give.

"Skalla!" My voice was choked through a throat tight with fear. I rattled the handle again, then started hitting the door. That is truly what I did. I wasn't knocking. I was hitting it, slamming the side of my fist into the wood.

Still nothing.

I know he said something about not being immortal forever before but... *He still is. Right?* **Right?**

He'd been alive for hundreds of years. Surely he wasn't going to just... expire in there. Alone in a fucking bathroom.

Horrified, I wondered if I'd somehow done something to him. He'd careened away from me last night and I'd gotten all butthurt about it, but what if he now actually was violently ill with something? Could immortal aliens capable of crossing the universe and manipulating matter with nothing but their minds get that sick just from humping a human?

My fingers scraped against my scalp, tugging backwards on my hair as my palms dug hard into my forehead. It was an unconscious movement, one I only became aware of when my scalp started to hurt. I hadn't done it since Elvi was sick. Back then, I'd given myself a literal bald spot. *Traction alopecia*, my doctor had called it. How comforting that there was a nice, clean, clinical name for ripping out your own hair in anxious agony.

I am not going through that again.

I refused to sit here doing nothing but tearing out my own hair while someone I cared about suffered.

And like it or not, I cared about Skalla. Maybe even...

Maybe could even love him if I wasn't well on my way to that already.

But I'd never get the chance to find out if he died alone on a goddamn alien toilet.

"I'll be right back," I shouted through the wood. "And when I am, I am going to break down this fucking door!"

I hadn't exactly figured out just how I was going to do that. My hockey drills had gotten my strength and cardio systems back on track, but that wood was solid and thick, and it wasn't like I had an axe or a hammer or anything that could break down a door.

But I knew someone who did.

And since she and her wife technically owned that door, it would probably be a good idea to inform them of my plan, anyway.

I ran to the balcony door, and only as I yanked it open remembered I was completely nude. Groaning in frustration, I went back for my robe, ignoring the crustiness of it, and put it on, belting it furiously as I hurtled outside.

"Zev! Jolakaia!" I shouted, careening down the stairs like a madwoman, robe flapping wildly. Zev was already outside in her workshop. She gaped at me, shock clear in her eyes. They probably knew me as a pretty calm, serene human. Quiet.

Not quiet now.

"I need help! Something's wrong with Skalla and I can't open the door. I need a hammer... Or an axe... Or a chainsaw!"

Zev was squinting at me, as if trying to see me through dense fog, and I realized that in my panic I'd resorted to speaking in my native tongue, Finnish words spilling from my mouth. My brain worked and got nowhere, my mouth opening and closing soundlessly. I couldn't remember a single word of Bohnebregg. It was like the entire language, at least what I'd learned of it, had been erased from my brain. Distraught, I felt my fingers crawling back up to my hairline. I made fists and forced my hands down. I could feel hysteria rising inside me, about to sweep everything away and leave behind only a blubbering sort of uselessness. I couldn't let that happen.

"What's going on?" Jolakaia called from inside the house.

"No idea," Zev said. "Maybe she needs to eat something."

"No!" I cried, and by some miracle, it came out in Bohnebregg. Saying that one word unlocked the trove of language in my head. Not paying even the slightest attention to grammar, I told her what I could in bits and garbled pieces. When I'd finished speaking, Jolakaia emerged with a tray of food.

"Sorry. She is not actually hungry after all," Zev said. "She says that Skalla's sick or hurt. He has locked himself in the privy and will neither speak nor open the door."

I nodded, though it was more like the frantic vibration of a shaken bobblehead doll than a normal human gesture.

"Yes!" I said. "I need..." I gestured at the wooden worktable beside the house, shaded by the balcony above and covered in tools. "Tool. To break... door. Something..."

Zev was on it, crossing to the table with one long stride and returning with what looked to be a massive sledgehammer.

Gratitude made tears prick in my eyes. She was going to break down the door in her house to help me. Absolutely no hesitation. I could have kissed her.

Zev had already gotten her foot onto the bottom step, the gigantic hammer balanced on her scaly shoulder, when Jolakaia stopped her.

"Beloved," Jolakaia said, both affection and exasperation warming her gaze. "You forget we have a key."

"Oh!" Zev said. "Right." She looked at her hammer as if slightly disappointed she wouldn't get to use it. "I had better bring this, though. As back up. Just in case."

Jolakaia put down the tray and hurried into the house. I bounced anxiously on the balls of my feet, calves burning, wondering if we should just forget the stupid key and break the door down anyway.

But then Jolakaia was back, a metal shape gleaming in her claws, and the three of us sprinted up the stairs. Their legs were longer than mine, so they got up to the apartment a second before I did. Ever-efficient and no doubt wanting to get a look at the patient, Jolakaia didn't bother knocking or calling Skalla's name. She merely fitted the key to the groove of the door handle. Once unlocked, I thrust open the door.

I felt an instant spike of relief to see that Skalla wasn't unconscious on the floor. But when my eyes did land on him in the bathtub, he didn't look a whole lot better. He was lying with his shoulders and back against the side of the tub, his arms draped along its edges, his wings hanging behind him down towards the floor. His head was thrown back so all I could see of his head was the underside of his snout and his throat. His hair was a sodden, tangled mess, which was never a good sign for his state of mind. His glittering chest, daubed with water, rose and fell, so he was breathing, at least. And I doubted he could maintain that sort-of upright position if he were truly unconscious.

But any comfort I might have felt at the fact that, physically, he seemed mostly alright, was diminished by a whole new set of worries. A sense of wrongness twisted dark tentacles in my belly. Because Skalla, my Skalla, wouldn't stay voluntarily locked in a room away from me all night. He barely ever let me out of his sight. He wouldn't ignore my voice through the door.

It made the male before me feel like a stranger. The air was thick with something ominous, a warning not to get any closer to the sleeping monster in the water. The others must have felt it too, because even Jolakaia, the only one with any medical training, held back, peering uneasily into the room. Zev's grip on her hammer tightened.

"Skalla?" I called tentatively from the doorway, reedy fear clear in my voice.

He didn't move.

I took a step. Just one single step into the room, still gripping the door handle.

And it was as if that one hesitant step had electrocuted him.

His entire body spasmed, his scales rippling with the force of his muscles bunching and rolling beneath them. He groaned, and it was an ancient, terrible sound, the sound of a boulder being dragged from the stony place it had occupied for the last ten thousand years. That grinding sound emanating from his throat went on and on, finally petering out into two words I could recognize.

"Get. Out."

"What?"

That was my eloquent reply. But it was all I could manage. I couldn't make sense of this, any of this. I was completely bewildered faced with this new Skalla. This Skalla who, for some reason, didn't want me with him.

The door I clung to suddenly began to move on its own, pushing itself back towards a closed position. And like a crumb being swept along by the bristles of a broom, I was pushed with it. Instinct didn't serve me very well in that moment, because my body's instant reaction was to push back against the door. I wasted precious seconds with that futile motion, not having the presence of mind to realize that if I'd just let go of the door and taken a quick step to the side, I could have remained in the room. But that didn't occur to me until the door had shoved me all the way back out of the room and had closed itself firmly in my face.

"What's wrong with him?" It was a broken sort of question, one of pain and not aimed at anyone in particular, but Jolakaia answered.

"He's in heat."

I jolted, spinning around to find her no longer at the bathroom door, but at the foot of the bed. She gazed at the place on the mattress I'd repaired, then took note of the soiled bedding heaped on the floor. I was too worried about Skalla to feel embarrassed now.

"I believe this is the stone sky mating heat. I do not know much about it... But surely he warned you of it?"

"He did, but..."

But I didn't expect it to be like *this*. I thought it would just be some extra arousal thrown into the mix. But he looked like he was suffering. Badly. And there didn't seem to be anything I could do about it. I'd kind of assumed the starburn would happen to me first, for some reason. But I felt the same as before, while Skalla was falling apart.

I didn't have enough Bohnebregg words to say any of that in a coherent way. Plus, Jolakaia had already admitted she didn't know very much about this part of things. This wasn't a Bohnebregg phenomenon she could advise me on. I was going in blind, completely alone.

"What do I do?" I whispered. My voice sounded pathetic and weak. I straightened up and steeled myself. Skalla wasn't doing well and I could put my big girl panties on and deal with it. He'd taken care of me up until now.

It was time to return the favour.

"I do not know," Jolakaia said honestly. "I assume you will enter your own heat soon enough, but for now..." She wiggled her snout in a Bohnebregg shrug. "I say, just let him be. He's hardly a relaxed, easy-going male at the best of times, and it is clear he is not in the mood to be trifled with."

That comment kind of made me want to cry. If she only knew, if they all only knew, what he could really be like. What he was like when it was just the two of us. How he smiled. How he made *me* smile.

I am soft for you, little star, and it is truth.

But then again, even I wasn't seeing his soft side today. He hadn't even looked at me when he'd told me to get out of the bathroom.

"Alright," I replied. I had precisely zero intention of actually following Jolakaia's advice and leaving him to stew in that bath all day, but I knew if I said so now I'd only be met with opposition.

"I will leave this." Jolakaia held up the key and put it on the narrow table in the cooking area. "I highly doubt it will be of any use to you, since he can keep the door closed with his mind. But just in case you want to open it, perhaps to put some food in there later."

"And I will leave this," Zev said, leaning her sledgehammer against a wall. "Also just in case."

I wasn't entirely sure what I'd accomplish with the hammer because it was designed for brawny Bohnebregg arms and I didn't think I could even lift it above my head. But I thanked her anyway.

"I am due at the temple today," said Jolakaia. "If you'd like to come-"

"No," I said instantly, shaking my head. "No. I won't leave him."

Jolakaia gave me a kind, knowing look.

"I thought as much."

"Well, I'll be here all day," Zev said. "I cannot promise that my cooking is anything near as good as Queen Kaia's, but come down whenever you get hungry. And do not hesitate to fetch me if you decide you want to bash that door in after all. He can hardly hold it closed against you if it is in splinters."

I thanked them again, and smiled faintly as their words drifted to me from the stairs outside.

"That's a fine door," Jolakaia was saying. "We do not need to break it apart unless this becomes a true emergency."

"But I haven't gotten to smash anything to bits in *ages*!"

Soon, the sounds of their voices and footsteps had receded entirely. The balcony and wall of windows looked out over the side of the house, and not long afterwards I watched Jolakaia drive away on her two-wheel, heading for the temple.

Zev was still somewhere below, but for all intents and purposes, I was on my own now.

But I wasn't truly alone. Because Skalla was there, just on the other side of the door.

I went back to the door, drawn by an inexplicable and inescapable force. At the last second, I decided to grab the hammer and drag it over, too, laying it at my feet as I put my fingers on the door handle.

I fully expected it to be locked again. But it wasn't. And there was no resistance when I pushed it inwards. Skalla hadn't moved, apart from maybe slouching down a little further into the water. I didn't know if he'd fallen asleep, or if he knew I was there but was just too exhausted to maintain his hold on the door.

"Skalla," I whisper-shouted into the humid room.

His breathing hitched slightly.

Not asleep.

And then, that dragged-boulder voice again, working its way up from the depths of his body.

"Not one. More. Step."

He didn't use the door to push me out this time, but he did give the wood a warning rattle. I snatched my hand off the handle but refused to move away.

"You've always taken care of me. Now, I'm going to take care of you," I said, much more sternly than the bleating of my heart would have had me believing myself capable of. "Just tell me what to do."

"What to..." His voice broke off in a splintery laugh. With what looked like monumental effort, he raised his head from where it was tipped back, looking at me for the first time since last night.

Skalla had looked at me with intensity before. He'd looked at me with affection, with longing, with lust. He'd even looked at me in the crazed clutches of his madness when we'd first met.

But none of those looks were anything to this one.

His gaze had become a living, breathing, throbbing thing. As if his eye had its own heartbeat. His stare pulsed through the air to me, tasted my body the way a tongue might. Clawed over my skin, licked downwards with a near-physical touch – and a demanding touch at that – to the place between my legs. And there it remained, fixed and starving.

Not hungry. Not ravenous.

Starving. As if to death.

"I will tell you what to do," he rasped. "Leave. Now."

"There has to be something!"

His eye alighted on the hammer at my feet. A mirthless smirk touched his snout.

"You could smash me over the head with that. Might provide a little relief."

"Skalla!"

"Suvi!" he thundered back at me, his fingers crunching the edges of the tub until the metal there was even more twisted than before. "There is nothing to be done until you starburn!"

He breathed out hard, steadied his voice, then added more quietly, "When the heat hits, I will come to you. Crawl to you if I have to. But not until then. *Only* then." He tipped his head back once more. He spoke up to the ceiling instead of me. "Do you understand?"

"I... I guess so. But I don't like this! I wish I could do something for you."

"You can leave," he muttered.

Hurt bloomed, an ugly flower.

"I-"

"Please, Suvi. It is very, very difficult to sit here smelling you." He exhaled roughly, and it was like his whole magnificent body sagged, collapsing into itself. "Do not make me beg."

I couldn't even imagine someone as powerful and proud as Skallagrim begging. I wouldn't put him through that on top of everything else.

"Alright," I murmured, blinking to keep the hot prick of tears at bay. "But I will be back with food later. I guess just... try to rest for now."

He gave a scraping grunt in reply, as if he'd expended too much energy talking to me already and couldn't have cobbled together another sentence now even if he'd wanted to.

I saved him from having to use any more of his power and pulled the door closed myself.

CHAPTER FORTY-FIVE
Suvi

One day became two. Became three. Became four. Skalla did not emerge, though he did eat at least some of the food I brought him. We were both eating less than usual – him because of what he was going through, and me because I was so worried about him. He didn't seem to get any better, but nor did he get worse, as far as I could tell, so at least that was something. He spoke very little, and sometimes the only clue I had that he was in there was the periodic draining and refilling of the bathtub.

I didn't accompany Jolakaia to the temple again. I couldn't bear the thought of leaving Skalla up there alone. But neither could I pace back and forth in our room all day. So, I made myself at least somewhat useful. I learned which plants were weeds, and pulled them by the root out of the house's garden. I collected the spider-chicken *bikri* eggs, blue as polished sapphires, and tried my hand at cooking a few dishes that got Zev's enthusiastic approval. Sometimes, I watched her work on two-wheel machines and other appliances in her workshop, but I couldn't focus well enough on the alien tech to actually learn much there. My mind and gaze were constantly slinking upstairs to the suffering behemoth in the bathroom. Luckily, Jolakaia and Zev were kind enough to let me use their facilities for bathing and washing clothes and things like that. I was pretty sure that if I walked into the currently-occupied upstairs bathroom, undressed in front of Skalla and then opened my legs to pee, he very well may have had a fucking stroke.

And through it all, I didn't feel even a whisper of heat. Not a twinge, not a flicker of sensation. No fever, no extra arousal, no sense that anything had changed in me at all.

Before, I'd had so much dread surrounding the starburn.

Now I was filled with dread that it wouldn't come.

Why is it not happening yet? How long is it supposed to take?

Maybe there was something I could do to hurry it along. I fell asleep chewing on that problem, and on the morning of the fifth day I had a startling thought that sent me racing from the bed the second I woke up.

I slammed open the bathroom door.

Skalla wasn't leaning back against the tub, but rather forward over its edge, the way someone might do if they thought they were going to throw up but didn't want to do it in the water. His hair, ropy with tangles and moisture, dragged along the stone ground. His wings were slack, broken-looking, hanging downwards.

"Not hungry," he said haggardly.

I had no food to offer him.

But I had something else.

If I'm wrong about this...

I pushed that thought away and marched into the room. The humidity kissed along my bare skin.

He grew stiffer and stiffer on my approach, limp exhaustion replaced with torque and tension.

"Skalla, look at me."

Slowly, like a thousand invisible kilograms pushed down on the back of his neck, he raised his head.

His nostrils flared, and all the lethargy in him evaporated.

"What are you doing?" he snarled. He threw himself backwards and away from me. When I took a step closer towards the bathtub, he leaped right out of it, kneeling on the stony floor with the tub between us like a shield. "Why are you *naked*?"

"I have a hypothesis," I said, slowly walking around the tub towards his side.

He hissed and started moving sideways on his knees to get away from me. My cheeks burned, but I kept my chin held high.

"I think I might need to be near you to trigger the starburn."

That stopped him dead in his tracks. Or rather, his knee-slides. His eye bugged.

"What did you just say?"

"I think... I think I have to be near you. *Physically*."

He tensed, like he thought I was about to pounce on him or something. "No."

"What do you mean, 'no?!'" I cried. "It's already been five days! We have to at least try something!"

"Five days?" he asked with what looked like horror. "*That's it?*"

He groaned, long and low, and I took his moment of despairing distraction to hustle around the tub towards him. But his reflexes were still damn good, and in a flash he was up on his feet, stumbling backwards and away from me until his wings hit the wall.

He stood there panting, digging his claws backwards into the wood planks of the wall behind him, as if to anchor himself there when the rest of him wanted to rip away and come straight to me.

And for the first time in five days, I saw all of him. I saw what the starburn was doing to him. This entire time, I'd kept my distance, and most of his body had been hidden by the metal walls of the tub.

But not anymore.

His cocks were out. Already huge in normal circumstances, they now looked painfully engorged. The bigger, bottom one had changed since I'd last seen it. It now had a thick swelling in the middle of the shaft, bruising, pushing outward like a tumour. The blood drained from my face when I realized that was the knot. That massive, bulging thing would have to fit *inside me*.

"Oh, Skalla," I whispered, wanting to cry at the state of him. "Has it been like this the entire time?"

"That is none of your concern," he heaved out raggedly. "I do not need your pity, Suvi. I need you to get out of here. *Now*."

His eye was wild with panic. Panic at my proximity. Panic at what he might do if I got any closer.

I took a step towards him.

"Suvi," he growled. He looked like he wanted to say more but couldn't. His throat worked uselessly as I approached, the muscles of his chest and abdomen hard as carved stone. His jaws unlocked, apparently against his own will, and his tongue tasted the air. At the same instant, a hot spurt of seed erupted spastically from the upper cock, soaking the lower one. His claws sank deeper into the wall as he shoved himself backwards.

It was like he wanted to escape from me. It was a bizarre reversal of our roles – him, the original captor, now wanting to flee from the one he'd abducted. But I couldn't even laugh at the absurdity of it. He was suffering so much. He almost looked afraid. And if I were completely honest with myself, I hadn't wanted to escape from him for a long, long time.

"Just... Just let me try," I breathed, coming to a stop before him. Skalla's head strained back, but his hips bucked forward mutinously, trying to unleash themselves from his deteriorating control. I was close enough to him that his cocks made contact, bumping then sliding against my bare abdomen.

His upper cock ejaculated instantly, hot and slick on my skin. Skalla gave a tortured moan, his voice disintegrating into something choking and convulsive when I brushed my fingers along his distended knot. I gasped in horrified fascination at the heat emanating from him. It was like the knot itself was inflamed. *No wonder he's been soaking in cold baths this whole time...*

"Oh, Skalla," I said again, hating how much he was hurting. Even though I knew it wasn't my fault, I felt guilty. If I'd joined him in this heat earlier, he could have gotten some relief. We both could have. We could have sought that soothing touch in each other.

But that was why I was here, wasn't it? To get closer to him, see if I could trigger the starburn in myself. Grinding and coming against me had seemed to help it along in Skalla that night.

Maybe...

Maybe physical proximity wasn't enough.

Maybe I needed to fuck him. Get him inside me, let his fluids join with mine.

I had no clue if it would work, but it was just about the only idea I had left apart from dancing naked under the moon and begging gods both alien and human to please, for the love of all that was good, help us.

"Skalla, sit down," I said hurriedly. "I have an idea."

I didn't know if his orgasm had provided him with a tiny bit of relief, or if he'd just run out of will to argue with me. But either way, he sank down to the ground, his claws dragging jagged, ripped lines through the wall as he did so. He stared furiously at his genitals, as if they'd somehow betrayed him.

I stared at them too, chewing on my lip. There was absolutely no way I could take the bigger cock with the knot. Even without the knot, I probably couldn't have gotten that one in me. The upper one, though...

The upper one, I could work with. It was still big. *Very* big. But it wasn't a heavy club with a baseball-sized swelling in the middle of it like the other one was.

The smaller cock was still stone-hard after coming. Shimmering moisture beaded at its tip, as if it knew exactly what I planned to do.

Without warning, without giving Skalla a chance to run away, I got onto my knees and sucked the head of the smaller cock into my mouth.

Skalla gave a tight yelp. He jerked in my mouth, letting out another shuddering, salty jet. There was too much for me to even attempt to swallow. I let it dribble out of my mouth and over my chin, then kept working at him, sucking slowly, getting used to the girth of him in my jaws. Up until this moment, I'd been too preoccupied with Skalla's pain to feel any sort of arousal. But I felt it now, a small lick of heat under the damp, suffocating weight of worry.

I braced myself, laying my hands on Skalla's inner thighs as I slid up and down his length. I marvelled at the coiled muscle there. I wondered how any living creature could be so hard and so still.

It was almost eerie. Like someone had cast a spell on him, cursed him with a body of stone. The only sign I had that he was still alive and not constricted by rigor-mortis was the trembling, enthusiastic pulses of his cock in my mouth. Otherwise, though, he did not move and made no sound.

I need to hurry, I thought. I could feel his control fraying inside that miserable, hard shell, and for the first time I realized that he might actually hurt me. Not intentionally, of course. But there was a reason he'd told me to stay away from him and this was why.

I sucked and licked and examined that possibility within the confines of my own head. I analysed it coolly, distantly, like I was considering the possibility of Skalla harming a blonde, Suvi-shaped ragdoll instead of me. Despite the danger, I wasn't afraid.

But I still didn't want to waste any time. I stroked my clit frantically, then, when pleasure began to unfurl its warm feathers, I pressed two, then three fingers inside, trying to stretch myself in preparation for him. All the while, I kept sloppily sucking at him.

It was not my best blow job effort, I had to say. I hadn't given head in ages, and never to someone this big. I was out of practice and flustered, trying to coordinate my hand between my legs and the jerking motion of my head. But if Skalla had any complaints, he didn't voice them. Instead, he came again in my mouth, silent and straining.

There was never any eruption from his other cock, though, which was odd. Previously, both of his cocks had ejaculated, but not now. It probably had something to do with the new knot, and I cringed at the thought that Skalla hadn't been able to get any relief from the harrowing engorgement of that organ.

Unbelievably, Skalla was still hard, his head swollen behind my teeth. I was wet now, my fingers sliding, and I was probably as ready as I'd ever be without something like the starburn.

I lifted my mouth from him and shimmied forward on my knees. I slung one leg over his, then the other, until I was straddling his hips, my palms flat and firm on his broad, rigid chest.

Skalla's eye was screwed shut, his body still completely immobile apart from the twitchy vibrations of his extended cocks behind and below me. But when I wiggled back and pressed my wet pussy against the slick tip of his upper cock, his eye flew open.

He gawked at me straddling him, as if he'd had no idea I'd gotten into this position. It was like I'd done everything up until now without him while he'd retreated into some sort of feverish dreamscape. A flurry of emotions crashed over his face in rapid succession – shocked confusion; dismayed shame; blazing, animal lust; then sheer fucking panic.

I pressed down. Just a little. His cock nudged desperately inside without him even moving his hips.

His fingers flew to my waist, gripping hard, and for a second I thought he meant to pull me off. Maybe even throw me entirely out of the room.

But instead, he let out a groan, grim with resignation and torturous need, and slammed his hips upward in one furious thrust, spearing all the way inside me.

I threw my head back, staring blindly at the ceiling as my body stretched to its limits to accommodate his ardent bulk.

I'd thought I could maybe start slowly, inch my way down onto him, ride him while he held still the way he had a few seconds ago.

I was a fucking idiot.

I think I broke him.

Or at least, I'd broken something inside him. Where before there'd been only vicious stillness, now there was a roiling chaos of motion. He was frenzied, bucking wildly, gripping me tightly to his chest. Even though I was on top, any control I'd had over the situation was gone. My body wanted to tighten up, to fight, to flee. But this was Skalla, my Skalla. And my Skalla needed me.

Maybe some part of me needed this, too, because behind my clenching defense against his girth, beyond the unfathomable, crashing ache of his body in mine, something sweeter beckoned. Like a candle in the dark. A mere flicker of pleasure, wind-whipped at first. Hard to hold onto.

But getting stronger with every pummeling thrust.

I collapsed onto Skalla, my breasts crushed to his chest. I wrapped my arms around his neck as his hips pistoned, engines of rapid, relentless motion. He snapped and snarled, grinding his knot against my ass. I knew that agonized part of his body was screaming for entrance, that every fibre and nerve of him was begging him to shove that cock in somewhere – *anywhere* – so that his knot could get some wet, squeezing relief. To my profound relief (and to the dismay of some suicidally aroused part of me) he didn't even try. He just kept jack-hammering his hips in the current position, rolling the ridges of his shaft over stretched, sensitive places inside until I was keening, limply writhing, already at my limit but somehow wanting more.

I whined his name, throat feeling raw, and he gave a blistering moan in return. He drove into me so hard and fast that I was no longer aware of individual movements. He was one unending tremor of stimulation inside me, rapid, unyielding, never giving me even a moment to breathe. To let go.

I hovered on the edge of sudden, breathless orgasm, trapped there. Trapped by the burning slam of him, trapped by a rhythm so frenzied it was nearly hysterical.

I was nearly hysterical. I bucked uselessly in Skalla's iron grip, trying to throw myself over that aching edge, trying to find release that never came. Pressure grew and grew inside, white-hot, scalding in its ecstasy. I cried – sobbed – against Skalla's scales, clinging to him, driving myself closer both to him and the climax that hovered just out of tantalizing reach.

It wasn't out of reach for Skalla, though. His manic motions stuttered without warning. A roar ripped from his throat, he thrusted again, and again, then once more, a hard, slow jam upwards. His cock pulsed and then spewed inside me, spurting liquid heat.

That did it. Finally, my orgasm came for me, crested then crashed down, rolling over my body like a riptide, dragging and drowning, until I could barely breathe. Skalla was so big I could barely even clench around him. My pussy milked him spastically while I wept, the muscles fluttering weakly, struggling for purchase, before my body finally slammed down around him so hard he gave another feral bellow and he came all over again.

Finally, Skalla actually began to soften a little after spewing. Only the cock inside me, though. The large cock was still as rigid as ever with its turgid knot.

But he wasn't soft for long. He ground himself against me, giving little panting growls above my head, and was quickly back to full hardness inside my still-spasming core. I went entirely slack, giving myself over to him completely, my muscles spent and limp. It felt like the only thing holding my body together now was Skalla's hands, Skalla's arms, Skalla's shaft.

Another orgasm. Another roar of what could have passed for pain. And then, this time, Skalla really did pull me off of him. One second he was gripping my hips tightly, holding me in place while he bucked up into my body. The next, I was plucked right off of him.

Skalla set me down on my ass on the floor – there was no way I'd be able to stand yet – and stared fiercely away from me.

"Not enough," he growled, palming the underside of his knot and then hissing like someone had stuck a knife between his ribs. "It will not be enough until-"

He gave up on finishing his sentence, instead shoving to his feet, taking a few limping steps, and then plunging back into the tub again. He fell in so heavily that water crashed upwards and over the sides. A small wave of it soaked my legs, puddling around my hips. The water felt good. It cooled my skin and soothed the tender places between my legs.

"Please go, Suvi," Skalla said, and it was barely above a whisper. "Go. And do not come again until it's time."

This time, when he asked, I went. And I didn't argue.

CHAPTER FORTY-SIX
Suvi

The next morning, I was starting to think that my hypothesis was bunk. I'd thought (and, frankly, hoped) that introducing some of Skalla's biological matter into my system would have triggered an immediate reaction.

But it didn't.

Other than a lingering ache between my legs, I didn't feel any different from before. At least, not physically.

Mentally, though? Emotionally? That was a whole different story.

I felt both closer and further from Skalla than ever. We'd had sex – he'd come inside me again and again – but now I couldn't even touch him with a single finger. And it hurt.

I wanted to hug him, to tuck him into bed and take care of him, to tell him that everything was going to be alright. I wanted to run cool water over his scales, clean him off, rub him down, gently stroke the painful places. I wanted to feed him riisipuuro – traditional Finnish rice porridge – topped with bilberries. That was always the way Elvi would make it when I was sick, and I was irrationally sad that I couldn't do the same thing for Skalla now.

It was strange. Strange that being separated from Skalla was now what brought on my most intense feelings of homesickness.

I still brought him food – nudged along the floor into the room from the doorway – and he picked away at it, eating the bare minimum to keep his extraordinary body alive, but that was the extent of our contact.

Sometimes I just sat in the bedroom without him and stared at the bathroom door.

Sometimes I pressed my hand and my forehead to the wood, straining to hear any sound from him. Occasionally, I'd catch a sigh, a grunt, or a groan, but otherwise it was silence punctuated twice daily by the draining and refilling of the tub.

By the morning of the seventh day, I was distraught. Miserable at my inability to help him. I'd once looked at the starburn like some sort of betrayal, like my own body would turn against me and make me want what I wouldn't ordinarily want.

Now, it felt like a betrayal that it was taking so damn long.

I stood outside the bathroom door, angry and hurting and quietly acknowledging the fact that Skalla might have gotten what he'd wanted after all.

He'd never gotten the chance to woo me the way he'd desired, the way he'd promised.

But, more and more, it seemed as if he'd somehow, some way, against all reason and logic and against even my own human defence mechanisms, gotten me to love him anyway.

I was sick with worry for him, and it went far beyond the care I'd feel for an acquaintance or even a good friend. His suffering turned me inside out. His absence was a physical sense of soreness. I missed him desperately. Missed his voice, his touch, the hulking stature of him always so reliably close behind or beside me. I missed his grins, his warm golden gaze.

I missed him most at night, when I couldn't try to distract myself by cooking, gardening, or helping Zev with other various chores. The bed that I'd once been so nervous about sharing with him was wide and cold and empty. Lying in the darkened quiet, I couldn't back away from the special kind of loneliness that came from missing someone who was very near but terribly, impossibly far away at the same time. All the way on the other side of something as insurmountable as an unlocked door.

Yep. There was no denying it.

I was anguished because I loved him.

It was as simple and as messy as that.

But acknowledging that fact didn't do a single thing to help. In fact, it felt bitter. Because what was the point of loving someone this way? Of loving them when you couldn't do a single fucking thing to help them?

I remembered asking that distressing question back when Elvi had been at her worst. On the verge of breaking down entirely and trying to soothe myself with ridiculous, child-like superstitions, I'd made her healing bilberry-topped riisipuuri like she'd always done for me. But of course, it wasn't enough. She couldn't even force herself to eat it, anyway.

I felt like that again now. Like I was holding a bowl of rice pudding and it was rotting in my hands because ultimately it meant nothing at all.

He's not sick, I reminded myself unsteadily and without conviction on the seventh night. *He's suffering, but he's not sick. He's not going to...*

I tore from the bed, scrambling to the bathroom and opening the door. It was completely dark in there apart from the glow cast by the constellations of golden light all over Skalla's body. He raised his heavy, dripping head.

"Don't die," I said, squeezing the doorhandle so hard my knuckles cracked. "Don't die. Because..."

My heart raced. I felt like I was about to fall through the floor.

"Because..."

The brave man gets to eat soup.

"Because I love you!"

I slammed the door shut and threw myself back into the bed without waiting for a reply or even waiting to register his reaction on his face. I curled up tightly in a ball, wrapping my forearms around my own knees, my fingers tingling with anxiety. I'd never said "I love you" to a man besides my own father before. I hadn't said it to anyone at all in years. A nervous laugh bubbled up out of my throat, but there was relief in it, too.

At least he knew now. He might be stuck in there without me, both of us wondering why I wasn't starburning yet, but he could at least hold onto that much.

When I eventually fell asleep, I dreamed of Elvi. She was beautiful, healthy, and smiling, her shiny green hair falling all around her shoulders. In her hands was a bowl of soup. She held it out to me with pride and triumph clear on her face, like she was giving me an award.

"Thank you," I said, taking the bowl from her, not once questioning how or why she was here. In the murky, tilting way of dreams, this felt totally natural. I wasn't surprised to see her in the least. I wasn't dragging her into a hug or telling her I missed her because this was a dream and of course in a dream she wasn't dead. Maybe, in dreams, she never had been.

But neither was I specifically aware that I was dreaming. I just.... was there. With Elvi.

And the soup.

"Eat it," she told me, still looking so proud of me. "You've earned it."

There was no spoon, so I raised the bowl to my mouth and took a sip. It wasn't like any sort of soup I'd ever had in Finland. It was Bohnebregg fish and riverweed stew. But once again, cloaked in the bizarre normalcy of the dream, I didn't once question why my dead sister was bringing me soup from an alien world instead of from home.

I also didn't question why the soup was so fucking *hot*.

The sip was molten, and yet somehow it didn't burn me. It didn't cause pain to the surfaces of skin it touched, it just heated me from the inside out, raising my core temperature as it went down my throat into my stomach. It was like I was back in a Finnish sauna, but somehow the sauna was inside me.

Though it didn't hurt, it disturbed me. Maybe it disturbed me precisely *because* it didn't hurt but should have. My stomach churned, like that one single sip had turned all my insides to soup. The places between my legs and around my womb felt hot and liquid and strange.

I tried to drop the bowl, but the bowl was already gone.

Elvi was gone.

Everything was gone but that oozing heat, the burn that did not properly burn because it sluiced instead of scorched.

Fluid fever, it melted my mind until, of all the entirety of language I'd collected over my lifetime, only one single word remained.

Skallagrim.

In the heated dreamscape, the word was entirely devoid of literal definition, but I knew that it meant something to me. Something vitally important.

When I was strong enough, I would take that single word inside my throat...

Then scream it.

CHAPTER FORTY-SEVEN
Skallagrim

My little star called me forth from the darkness.

Like a soldier beckoned to battle, I rose in the night and I went.

Water dripped down my scales with every harrowing step. My scales bristled like hairs, fangs tight, cocks jutting ahead of me and wings flexing behind as I came upon my mate.

Suvi was naked. Splayed and writhing. Her spine arched in pulsing motions, making her breasts and abdomen shake. The moonlight through the coloured glass was like liquid on her, as if she were as wet as I was. Her hair was a fanned-out river, her cheeks darkened with need, her eyes shut. The air was thick with the cock-swelling scent of her. One needy roll of her hips revealed the seam of her cunt, and it was drenched, spilling moisture onto her inner thighs.

"Skalla," she said again, a mere whimper. It seemed as if she meant to scream it, but did not have the breath to do it.

Starburning.

The word came to me as if from a great distance.

There was no moment of clarity, no sudden realization. I'd known without concrete thought, without words, without anything but bone-deep feeling, what she'd needed when she called me.

For the first time in days, I thought nothing of my knot. The arousal, my need, got locked into some cage inside myself, imprisoned by a drive much more powerful than any other I had ever known.

The instinct to take care of my mate.

"I am here, Suvi," I rasped.

Her eyes opened, landed on me, glassy and feverish. For a moment, I wondered if she could even see me at all.

But then she mewled in pain, a sound that fanned the primal flame of that need to protect her, and she reached a little hand for me. She did not retreat or hide. She did not race past me into the cold clutches of the bathtub. Stricken and suffering, she sought no other comfort. She sought only me.

Because she loves me.

"Suvi," I murmured. My voice sounded deeper than it usually did. An authoritative growl. "Lie back and spread your legs."

She whined. With dismay, I saw the tears streaked across her cheeks.

"Suvi," I said again, coming to the edge of the bed then dropping to my knees on the mattress above her. I gripped her thighs, massaging with my thumbs, and she keened. "Spread your legs. *Right now.* Let me take care of you."

She gave a hitching breath and then, like the perfect little mate that she was, she obeyed. Her heated musk, already thick in the air, crashed over me with the weight of a mountain. Normally, with some effort, I could have withstood such a thing. But under the mighty influence of her tiny body's gravity, I fell the way a dying man might fall.

And I drank from her the way a dying man might drink. Desperately, hungrily, wanting to bathe myself in her, fill myself with the sweet slick of her heat.

Her flesh was hot and swollen. When I plunged both tips of my tongues inside her and stretched, her shuddering passage gave way more easily than it would have before. Her silken canal was deeper, wetter, more pliable now. Ready for my knot. My upper cock spasmed, completely untouched, a jet of seed spewing forth.

Suvi ground herself eagerly against me, her fingers instantly digging themselves in my wet hair and dragging me closer. It was as if she wanted me to bury my entire snout inside her, and if there were some way to do that and still breathe, by the river, I would have tried. Blast, maybe I did not even need to breathe. Seemed as good a way as any for an immortal to expire.

But she told me not to die. Because she loves me...

That had my upper cock spurting again – remembering the terrified yet determined look upon her little face. And that beautiful, human voice I loved so well, trembling but fused with the kind of authority only she could wield against me, commanding me to live.

Suvi rocked, her hips frenzied, her arms quivering as she held me. I hated that she suffered in the starburn, but the force of her reactions aroused me desperately. Usually, there was some shyness, some hesitation in my human mate. Now, there was only need.

And in that need, both her bane and antidote, I was there.

She came to climax quickly, shouting and shaking, sweet fluid pouring out of her. Even as she clenched and bucked, she still yanked me hard against her body, as if it wasn't enough, would never be enough.

"Skalla, I need... Not that, please." She sobbed when I withdrew my tongue. "*I'm afraid.*"

I jolted, then raised my head to look at her. Really look at her. Her eyes met mine, slits of hazed silver.

"Of me?"

"No!" She cried instantly. Her gaze, made innocent and honest by pain, widened, and I knew she did not lie.

"Then what?" I growled, pulling her by the thighs until she slid towards me, her hair folding and then stretching along the mattress above her head.

Her face twisted, human tears spilling like stars.

"I'm afraid of how empty I feel without you!"

With the force of a universe ending, her words blasted all rational thought from my skull. My brain was no longer a brain but a coiling, writhing mass of activated instincts. Ancient. Darkly urgent. Entirely unstoppable.

Logic and will died that night. Died under the roiling realization that my mate was scared, that she was empty, that only my knot could fill her.

I lined up my large cock, losing what was left of my shredded mind at the feeling of her wetness coating my agonized tip.

Then I pushed inside.

The molten silk of Suvi's body was beyond comprehension. A blistering miracle against me, around me. I moved, stroking powerfully inside her, my knot licking greedily against her folds, seeking entrance with each thrust.

Suvi's mouth stretched in a soundless scream, her back bowing right off the bed. My knot was not inside her, not yet, but already she was coming again, her orgasming channel sucking at me, body begging.

There was no way to make this last. To draw it out. To be gentle or thorough or slow. The starburn needed what it needed and it took what it took.

From both of us.

As Suvi moaned and clenched, I pressed my knot against her, *hard*. There was some resistance – the knot was so much thicker than the rest of my shaft – but now she was begging, little pants of *please, please, please,* and the black ball of tentacles that was my brain told me to knot my mate so I did.

Swallowing a roar and bracing my hands on the mattress on either side of my mate's heaving chest, I shoved against the resistance, every nerve fraying with the spine-bending sensation of having my knot almost, almost, *almost* inside her.

For a long, miserable moment, it seemed as if she would not admit me.

But then, all at once, with the wet popping sound of a stone being sucked into a mouth, Suvi took me. *All of me.*

My upper cock ejaculated instantly, its shaft jerking against her soft thatch of hair, spraying jets of fluid all over her abdomen and breasts. My knot swelled further inside the constricting tunnel of her cunt, something I had not known was possible. It surged with hot agony, twitching and pulsing like a creature of its own, some wretched, living thing I had neglected to feed until now.

Suvi didn't make a single sound. She merely squeezed my braced forearms and stared at me, her eyes as round as moons and fixed on my face.

I did not ask her if it hurt. I was not even capable of that. And even if I had been, there was no way I could have ripped myself away now. Suvi clenched, dragging my roiling knot one tiny notch forward. Then her body clamped down so hard that she locked me entirely into place – a place deep inside that felt as if it had been moulded just for me.

She threw her head back, white throat bared, and came for a third time. Seeing her so lost to me, lost while I was inside her, sent my upper cock shooting yet more fluid across her skin. My claws sank into the mattress as I stared down at the sublime waves and valleys of my mate's luscious body, a body soaked with my seed and stretching around my knot so perfectly that it was like a dream, a dream so vivid that someone could peel it right out of me. Pin it like a tapestry to a wall with a knife.

I had her now.

I loved her and I wanted her and I needed her and finally, *finally*, thank the cursed river, I had her. I had her beneath me, coming on my knot, commanding me and submissive to me all at once, so beautiful she broke my stone sky heart.

How absurdly and undeservedly lucky I was.

To have a little star like that fall down upon me.

To have her love me.

I could not move anymore, my knot as clutched by Suvi's depths as it was. But I did not need to grind and rut her now. Release was coming. I could feel it, beginning with a throbbing warmth at the base of my tail, spreading into my groin, turning to prickling embers. My upper cock spasmed again, or maybe it had never stopped. Without warning my lower cock felt suddenly hotter. My knot gave one great, bruising throb, then burst.

Suvi gasped, digging her blunt claws against my scales, as I soaked the deepest parts of her over and over again.

It felt like I was bleeding out inside her. Like the very core of my being had liquified and was now surging entirely into my mate.

I was giving her everything.

I was coming *home*.

I could no longer tell what was her body and what was mine. The sensation was beyond pleasure, beyond climax, beyond anything I'd ever known, and it ripped me apart, broke me down, shattered me until the only thing holding me together was Suvi's cunt tight on my cock and her hands upon my scales.

Time flowed around us like a river but we did not flow with it. The moment was endless. My *seed* was endless. My knot eternally swollen and seeming permanently fixed inside my mate, I came and came, spilled myself into her for hundreds of heartbeats until it truly felt as if my heart would beat no more. And that would be alright, I decided. Everything would be alright so long as I was with her.

But my heart kept on beating. My cocks kept on spewing, but more slowly now. Bit by bit, I became aware of things other than the life-ending ecstasy of Suvi locked around my knot. I noted the way I breathed so hard it scraped my throat raw. I felt the shaking tension in my arms as I kept myself from giving into the dangerous, physical urge to crush my heavy body down on top of hers. I felt the trembling caress of her fingers along my arms, heard her sated moans. Saw the fresh tears on her face.

Something must have blackened in my expression, because she drowsily shook her head.

"It doesn't hurt," she whispered, and oh, how those words were like a balm upon my scales. Despite her lack of pain, though, she began to cry more intensely, her body shuddering with the force of it, making her tug and vibrate around my cock. I eased onto my elbows, sending the tips of my tongue along her cheeks, her jaw, tasting the tears and wiping them away. Soon, she'd calmed. She wrapped her little arms around my neck, nuzzling into me.

"It doesn't hurt," she said again, sounding sedated. "I'm yours. And it doesn't hurt one bit."

She shifted her hips against mine, humming serenely at the feeling of my knot still in her.

Then she yawned against my throat and fell fast asleep.

CHAPTER FORTY-EIGHT

Suvi

I woke to the feeling of something very important being pulled gently from within my body. I moaned in groggy complaint at the sudden emptiness, and a resonant voice that I recognized rumbled soothingly. Something cool and damp began stroking at my face, and after it passed down to my neck I cracked open my eyes to find Skalla on his knees on the floor beside the bed. He was stroking me with a damp cloth, periodically pausing to dip it into a small basin of water before resuming again.

I didn't need to remember the heat, the starburn. I was still in it. When Skalla passed the cloth over my breasts, making my nipples harden, the fever peaked once more inside me. Instantly, I spread my legs and moaned again, a wordless plea, and I grabbed his arm and pulled him roughly towards me. Before now, I would have been horrified to act so wanton, to need someone else that much.

But there was no self-consciousness, no humiliation now. I didn't know if it was because of whatever surging starburn hormones were currently at work within me, or if it was simply because this was Skalla. My Skalla. I knew he would take care of me with such confidence that I didn't even need to ask.

And I was right.

With a heated stare, he abandoned his rag to the basin and then rose over me, towering and beautiful. Desire flared, then turned devastating, like I would die if he didn't fuck me. He could see it, and no doubt felt the same. His cocks were already jutting and hot, and I whimpered with need at the sight of his knot.

"Little star, I have you," he ground out, lining himself up to my quaking entrance. "I will take care of you."

I was already wet. Or maybe still wet. How long had it been since the last time? It could have been minutes or days and I would have had no idea.

Skalla penetrated me with his largest cock, stretching and filling me, and then stopped when his knot brushed tantalizingly against my skin. I bucked wildly against him, desperate for him, as if drugged with the need to feel his knot swell into place inside me. My movements made my clit bump against the underside of his smaller cock, and my entire body spasmed violently. Skalla splayed a huge hand against my burning abdomen to steady me, made another deep, soothing sound. Then, with a single, potent thrust, he was in me.

This was it. This was what I'd needed. This was every good thing I could have possibly imagined experiencing. This was hunger and satiation, hurting and healing. It was completion. Like I'd never been truly whole until this moment.

I'd never believed in souls in a literal sense, but I did now. Because with Skalla swelling into place deeper in my body than I would have thought possible and his eye speaking plainly to me without uttering a single word, I knew that we were meeting on a plane beyond the physical. Our spirits; our souls; the raw, core kernels of our beings collided.

I knew him. He knew me.

His heart was like my own.

His wings smashed outward as ecstasy gripped him, but he never closed his eye, never turned it from me. It was then, staring at me and so deeply knowing me, that Skalla came, his knot expanding and then his cocks releasing. It was almost laughable that he'd just cleaned me off. Because here I was covered once again in the ardent viscosity pumping from the narrower cock that now jerked against my pubis.

Feeling Skalla erupt on me, in me, was pure fucking magic. I came with shattering intensity, my body coiling so tightly around his knot that he went rigid and gave a broken groan.

"My mate," he gritted out, fangs flashing, wings flexing. "Mine, Suvi. *You are mine.*"

"I'm yours," I mewled, and it felt like an echo, like something I had said before.

Or maybe it just felt so familiar because I knew it was the truth.

———————— ✝✝✝\\✝✝✝ ————————

THUS BEGAN THE PERIOD I began to affectionately refer to as The Week of Fucking.

For days, it felt like all Skalla and I did was have sex and sleep in short bursts. We ate, too, but only because Skalla often stopped to make me. He was especially concerned about me drinking enough water. One newfangled feature of my starburn-transformed biology was that I got gushingly wet in preparation for taking Skalla's knot, and my mate's brow was often furrowed with worries about dehydration.

Sometimes, the sex was deliciously slow, almost languid. It was lovemaking. Skalla would stroke into me with the first half of his large shaft, the thrusts deep and controlled while he pressed the underside of his upper cock against my clit with delirious results. And only after making me come what felt like a dozen times that way would he finally knot me.

Other times, it was rutting, feral and frenzied, the carnal actions of animals in heat. Which, to be fair, we kind of were.

But perhaps even more miraculous than the sheer amount of time two creatures could spend grinding at each other without keeling over dead was that the more we did it, the more of Skalla's memory returned.

It still wasn't much, but it was coming back. Murky flashes that I saw him furiously trying to piece together when he thought I was asleep. After one particularly intense round of sex, as Skalla pulled his spent cock with its deflated knot from my core, he suddenly stiffened. His eye went cloudy, fixed somewhere very far away.

Then he said a word that, even with my translation abilities, I didn't understand.

"*Wylfrael.*"

"Skalla?" I frowned, gently patting his chest. "What's Wylfrael?"

"That was his name. The white-haired male." He sat heavily down on the mattress beside me. "I think... I think I loved him." He brushed his claws along the place where his snout met scarring. "I think he took my eye."

He turned his remaining eye solemnly on me.

"And I think I might have killed him."

I took one of his hands in both of mine, running my gaze over the scales, the claws, the strength of it. It was a hand that I'd grown to know almost as well as my own. A hand that fed me, caressed me, protected me, loved me.

And it was a hand that had killed. Over and over again.

I held that hand and I squeezed it hard, accepting the good and the bad in silence. Because, at least for the moment, there was nothing else to say.

CHAPTER FORTY-NINE
Suvi

By the end of The Week of Fucking the effects of the starburn had begun to wear off. I no longer felt like I had a limb-weakening fever, and Skalla was able to go longer and longer periods with his cocks flaccid and tucked inside his slit (though the shape of the larger one was permanently altered by the development of his knot).

When the temporary, physical symptoms of the starburn dissipated, they did not go without leaving scars. But they were nice scars, I decided. The kind that turned beautiful and silver and didn't cause any pain.

Once the intense heat had passed, I was left feeling closer to Skalla than I'd ever been to any other living being – even Elvi. I was intensely aware of him at all times, like he was the gravity anchoring my feet to the world. I had loved him before. But it had been a messy and fearful sort of love. The starburn had gathered up the jagged pieces of it and melded them together in its forge until it was strong and smooth and whole, like metal.

Like the fire lily, I'd survived the blaze. And now, I bloomed.

I still desired Skalla physically. I craved him. Even after the starburn had entirely passed, I welcomed his knot at least once a day. But now, I wanted him simply because he was Skalla and he was mine. I wanted him because *I wanted him*. Not because heat made me feel like my body would combust without his knot inside it.

We fell into a comfortable rhythm. We began to accompany Jolakaia to the temple again during the day, and I revelled in putting my hands and skills to work in the gardens and lab. In the evenings, we'd eat with Zev and Jolakaia. Skalla stroked trembling orgasms from my body and knotted me as the sun went down, and we'd fall asleep tangled in each other's limbs.

One week passed. Then another. Our rhythm became something more solid. It was a life that we were building. The things I'd left behind – Earth, my human friends on the ship – felt further from me than ever, but slowly, the pain of that loss grew just a little bit duller. It wasn't that being with Skalla this way now made everything alright. The grief hadn't gone away. But, much like my body had changed to accommodate Skalla's knot, it felt as it my heart had changed too. It had grown so that it could hold onto loss and joy in equal measure.

The two feelings didn't negate each other or compete with each other. Neither one made the other less true. I still missed Elvi, and Torrance, and my living human friends terribly, but I knew that I could move forward into something that felt a whole lot like happiness if I only let myself.

So I did.

And with that choice, I accepted that I'd never get to see my human friends again.

Until one night, about three weeks after we'd finished starburning, when Skalla sat bolt upright in bed and murmured madly into the darkness, "I remember. *I remember how to find them.*"

"Find who?" I groaned, rubbing blearily at my eyes. We'd both been sound asleep. I rolled onto my back and squinted up at Skalla's glowing frame. He was hunched over, gripping the bedding tightly in his lap, his wings vibrating with tension against his back.

He didn't answer for a long moment, and I was almost back to sleep when he replied, "Your human friends."

Well, now I was fucking awake. I snapped upright into a seated position, then scrambled on my hands and knees until I was in front of him. I needed to see his face for this.

"What? What do you mean? What did you remember?"

I'd gotten used to him suddenly remembering and remarking upon things from his past out of the blue. But I'd never expected this possibility. The ship had left the world we'd been on. Even if Skalla began to remember more about that event, there was no way for him to know where that ship had fled to.

Right?

"Heofonraed," Skalla said. He spoke hurriedly, as if worried that the words, the memories, would disappear if he didn't speak them into the air this instant. "Heofonraed. It's the... the meeting... The Council! The Council of the Gods!"

"What's the council?" I prodded when he suddenly lapsed into tense silence.

"It's... I do not entirely remember. But I know there is a group of stone sky gods with powers beyond my own at a place called Heofonraed. I do not remember ever asking them for help before, but I can picture the gates so clearly now. It's as if I was just there..." He paused, touched the scarring on his face, then shook his snout like he needed to clear his head, to find a path through overwhelming memories.

He gazed at me steadily, conviction firm in his voice. "I can go there. I can petition them to use their resources to find the machine that took your friends away."

A tingling buzz made my hands shake against my legs. Skalla swept my fingers into his, steady where I wasn't.

"I can picture the world clearly enough to open a sky door there," he said, figuring out the steps of his plan and explaining them to me all in one go. "I will petition the council for assistance. Once I know the location of the humans, I will travel there. I will destroy the vessel, kill the men who took them. And then," he looped his fingers through mine, his eye boring fiercely into me, "I will bring every last one of your friends safely back here to you."

CHAPTER FIFTY
Suvi

Neither of us went back to sleep that night. After it was decided he would go, things happened very quickly. By the time the sun had begun to rise, plans were fully in place.

"Say it again," I urged him, excitement and nerves fluttering so hard in my stomach I was nauseous. "I want to make sure they'll understand you."

Skalla did his growly, dragonish throat-clearing thing. Then, in fangy, hissy English, he said, "Suvi is in a safe place. She sent me here to save you. I am her friend and you can trust me."

Skalla had scowled and objected to being merely called my friend, but I figured that in the chaos that was sure to accompany his arrival, letting my friends know he was my mate, that he'd fucked me, was probably a bad idea to get them to trust and actually go with him. *We'll deal with that little issue when they're all here. Safe...*

I felt light-headed at the thought. The women I'd missed so much, whom I thought I'd never be reunited with again, were suddenly within reach. They'd been flung somewhere across the universe and it was like I could reach out and grab them. And it was all because of Skalla.

"Thank you," I said quietly, tipping forward and laying my cheek against Skalla's chest. His arms and wings folded around me in a protective embrace. I nuzzled closer, then sighed. "I know you won't be gone that long, but I'm going to miss you."

His chest swelled beneath me.

"And so you should miss a mate as grand as I am," he scoffed. I laughed, then leaned back and swatted at him teasingly. He caught my face between gentle claws and bumped his snout to my ear. Softly, and much more seriously, he murmured, "I love you, little star."

"I love you, too. Don't take too long, alright?"

"I will not. I do not believe it will take more than a day of conversing with the council before I have access to the humans' location. From there, things should be quick. I do not imagine it will take long to destroy the machine and disable the crew running it." I felt his grin against my skin. "Knowing what I know of human females, I expect the most challenging part will be getting a group of stubborn, untrusting women to actually come with me."

"You have to take them all," I said, feeling worried and knowing that he was right. "Even if someone doesn't want to come, just..." God, I couldn't believe I was saying this. "Just take them. Once they're here, and safe, it'll all be worth it."

"I will not leave a single one behind," he vowed. "And I promise not to break anyone's bones in the process."

I gave a queasy laugh, then swallowed, my throat feeling very dry. My head was hurting. Probably because of the lack of sleep. I leaned forward to hug him again, my face turned to the side. I watched the Bohnebregg sun rise and warm the world, thinking about all the new humans who would soon be in it, and smiled.

After a quick breakfast for Skalla – I didn't eat anything, too nervous – we went outside and down the stairs to inform Zev and Jolakaia of the plan.

"They can stay here, at least at first. We'll make room," Zev said firmly.

"Koltar will have to be persuaded," Jolakaia warned.

My stomach plunged in worry at the thought that my friends, after everything, might not be let in. But Skalla merely snorted in derision, and his confidence helped mine get steadier.

"I will persuade him with my fists, then," he said with a nonchalant toss of his snout. Then, more thoughtfully, he added, "I can take care of the women outside of Callabarra if need be. I can build a new home for them on the river. And if one should become injured, or fall ill, I can fetch you to examine them, Jolakaia."

I gazed at Skalla, my insides turning to goo at the male who was volunteering to house and feed and care for about twenty other humans he had no real need for. But he did it without thought, without hesitation. And I adored him for it.

I hugged him again, squeezing hard. And then, there was nothing else to do or say. No time left to waste. Skalla didn't bother leaving the city by foot – he simply vaulted up into the air right from the very place we'd been standing outside of Zev and Jolakaia's house. A few shouts from nearby neighbours rang out like applause for the arc of his powerful body through the air. Children, maybe some of the same ones who'd played at the pond with us that day, ran into the street, gawking and shouting. Some of them jumped, as if hoping that they'd sprout wings midair.

I shaded my eyes with my hand, watching Skalla become smaller, wings pounding and urging him ever upward. Then, once he was so high he looked more like a little toy figurine than the room-filling Skalla I knew, he stopped. The sky hardened in a great sheet before him, opaque as if darkened by a gathering storm. I knew what was coming next, but the sound of Skalla's fist cracking the stone of the sky still made me jump and gasp anyway. The children dispersed at the great crack, scurrying back to houses and the arms of parents. I barely noticed them, my eyes entirely fixed on Skalla as he darted into that black chasm...

And disappeared.

I wasn't prepared for the wave of dizziness that came over me at the sudden loss of him. I was in an alien world without him.

I was alone.

I lowered my gaze and saw Zev and Jolakaia with me, and I smiled.

Not alone.

I smelled the remains of the breakfast Jolakaia had prepared, heard the sound of two-wheel vehicles in the road, watched the glint of sun on Zev's metal tools, and my smile widened.

No, I was definitely not alone. And this world wasn't quite so alien anymore, either.

CHAPTER FIFTY-ONE
Suvi

I never would have expected myself to be able to sleep in the nail-biting nervousness of waiting for Skalla to return with my friends, but I did. By mid-morning, some of the adrenaline had ebbed out of my system, and I was struck down with exhaustion I hadn't experienced since I'd been recovering from my infection in the temple. I said a quick word to Zev, whom I'd been sitting with most of the morning after Jolakaia had left for the day, and mounted the stairs. My body felt heavier than before, and by the time I reached the top I was sweating profusely. I forced myself to drink a little water before collapsing onto the bed.

When I woke up, the sun was setting, turning the Bohnebregg buildings and roads the colour of warm rust, which was then made greenish by the stained glass. For a long moment, I couldn't orient myself without Skalla in the bed beside me. I frowned at the empty stretch of mattress, my brain feeling foggy, before I remembered where he'd gone.

I sat up quickly in the bed and instantly regretted it. My head swam, nausea rose, and I had to fight very, very hard not to puke my guts out. *This bed has taken enough abuse,* I told myself, cold and sweating and gritting my teeth, *I can at least spare it that much.*

Ugh. This was my own fault. I now remembered I hadn't eaten any breakfast, and I'd obviously slept through lunch. I'd barely had anything to drink, either. Strangely, even though I was probably a bit dehydrated, I had to pee badly. I eased myself out of the bed, going slowly, like I was ninety years old, then hobbled over to the bathroom to do my business and wash up.

Then I drank some water, slowly. The water didn't sit well, and once again I thought I was pretty close to barfing. I eyed the floor and thought with resignation that it would be easier to clean than the bed if needed.

Luckily, I didn't puke, though I had an instinct that I'd feel better if I just did it and got it over with. I set down my cup and sank to the floor, rubbing my temples.

Maybe I'm in Skalla withdrawal, I joked bitterly to myself.

Whatever it was, it was piss-poor fucking timing. What would my friends think if they came back to find me in the throes of some alien stomach bug? *Hey, girls, so glad you made it! It's totally safe here and you, too, can come down with Bohnebregg flu if you stay here long enough!*

I grimaced, then noticed how dark it had gotten outside. Jolakaia would probably be home from the temple by now, barring any medical emergencies that had shown up for her to deal with. Maybe she'd have something to settle my stomach. Keeping her image fixed in my mind, I hauled myself up and made my granny-like way down the stairs.

She and Zev were both outside together. A tray of what looked like cooked fish was between them on the table. Oh, God, it definitely smelled like fish. The scent, one I normally didn't have a problem with, nearly toppled me. I groaned and bent over on the last step of the staircase.

Jolakaia hurried over, laying a hand on my back.

"I think I'm sick," I belched out.

"I am sorry, Suvi, but I do not understand you."

Paska. I'd slipped back into Finnish. Stumbling over Bohnebregg words, I managed to relay the message. Jolakaia and Zev helped me over to a bench at the table where I promptly folded over at the waist and put my head between my knees. Jolakaia poked and prodded at a few places – my arm, the side of my neck – then stood back.

"You are not as hot as you were when you were ill. No fever. Though your heartrate is faster than usual."

"No fever. Good," I muttered. It took everything I had not to clap my hand over my mouth and nose at the stink of that fish. It was only my deeply ingrained need not to offend that kept me still, panting through my mouth.

"Which human conditions cause these symptoms?"

"Bacteria," I replied. It took me a minute to remember that word. I couldn't recall if I'd ever learned the Bohnebregg word for virus. That's what it felt like. That or a migraine, maybe. The lack of fever had to be a good sign, at least.

"Hmm. Nothing in the food or water has changed," Jolakaia said thoughtfully as I stared down at my feet. "I do not believe you've been exposed to any new plants or herbs at the temple, either. It could be some kind of delayed onset of a reaction to something..."

"Maybe," I grunted. It didn't feel like I was having an allergic reaction to anything. And this wasn't how I felt when I got my period, either.

My period.

My head got even lighter. I pushed it further down between my knees.

I'd been here more than two and a half months and I'd never had a period.

That's alright, I told myself quickly. My cycle had always been a bit irregular, which is why I hadn't really noticed that it hadn't come yet.

It didn't necessarily mean anything.

Or maybe it fucking did. Because no period on its own was one thing.

No period while the scent of fish was like a punch to the gut was another.

"Jolakaia," I said shakily, "Could I be..."

Fucking hell, I didn't know the Bohnebregg word for pregnant! Trying to urge some other related word out of my brain felt like I was pounding the inside of my head with a meat tenderizer.

"Could I have... Small person... Child..."

Thank God Jolakaia was clever enough to catch on without me needing to mumble through more broken Bohnebregg.

"Pregnancy? Of course it is possible. You..." A careful pause. "You do know how pregnancy occurs, do you not? I've examined your physiology and I assume it is similar for your kind as it is for Bohnebregg females."

"Yes," I confirmed.

Yeah, I knew how women got pregnant. I just didn't exactly clue into the fact that I could actually become pregnant with a fucking alien, that's all. We were completely different species! From entirely different worlds! He was immortal, for fuck's sake!

But the more I thought about it, the more I realized I was an idiot for not acknowledging this possibility before. How many studies had I read, experiments had I run, that showed cross-breeding different species of plants was possible, often in very surprising circumstances? Even Skalla's own parents had been from different worlds, and they'd obviously produced him!

Where there was a will, there was a way, and the biological forces of reproduction apparently had more than enough will to make up for my lack. Not that I never wanted children, or anything... I just wasn't expecting it be happening right fucking now with an alien male for the father.

Dread hardened in my guts. I placed my hand over my lower abdomen, knowing deep inside that I wasn't sick, that this wasn't a virus or an allergy.

This was a little baby Skallagrim fucking up my insides.

Despite the shock and nausea, I found myself grinning down at the ground at that image. It wasn't some terrible, phantom thing happening to me. It was something Skalla and I had created together. I couldn't yet picture what a baby like ours might look like, but I could picture Skalla's face when I told him the news upon his return.

I knew Skalla. And I knew he'd be happy.

I took a deep breath, raised my head a little, and showed Zev and Jolakaia my smile.

"I'm pregnant," I said firmly, knowing it was true and also knowing that everything would turn out alright. I sighed, feeling like a weight had been lifted off of my shoulders.

Then I promptly puked between my feet.

Zev ran to get water, and Jolakaia helped me move away from the vomit. Just like I'd thought I might, I felt a little better now.

"I do not like your symptoms," Jolakaia said uneasily. "Pregnancy should not cause vomiting."

I snorted.

"It does for humans," I told her. As far as I knew, this was textbook morning sickness (despite the fact that it wasn't actually morning). Zev returned with the water. I rinsed my mouth and took a few cautious sips. Jolakaia insisted I eat something, but when she saw me turn green at the thought of going anywhere near that fish, she instead brought me the

Bohnebregg version of a smoothie – a cold slurry of mixed fruit. The tart sweetness was refreshing, and I felt immensely relieved at the fact there was at least one thing around here that was remotely appealing to eat. It might not have had much protein, but at least I could swallow some of it.

It took a while, but I finished it all, and Jolakaia seemed satisfied enough with that. She helped me back to bed with firm instructions to call for her if I needed anything, and to not let myself get dehydrated. I thanked her sincerely, beyond grateful that I had her, and Zev, to rely on until Skalla returned. As Jolakaia headed to the door after watching me lie down, she suddenly stopped as if she'd forgotten something and turned back.

"Congratulations to you and Skalla both," she said softly. "A child is a great blessing. May this new life be wrapped in cotton."

My throat got too tight and hot for me to thank her for her words. I blinked away tears as she left and closed the door. But they weren't sad tears. They weren't simply happy tears, either. They were tears of shock, hope, confusion, and a new sort of love so sharp it almost felt like pain. *May this new life be wrapped in cotton.* I imagined a baby – soft and small, maybe with a little set of wings – wrapped in a cotton swaddle, and my heart hurt. But in the best possible way.

I can't wait to tell Skalla.

I was so focused on the thought of him that I dreamed of him. And when a broad-shouldered figure came through the door in the middle of the night, it was like he'd walked right out of my mind and into the room. Groggy, I reached for him, whispering his name.

But when he got closer, and I realized his scales didn't glow, that his face was entirely dark with shadow, I knew that it wasn't Skalla at all. It wasn't Zev or Jolakaia, either. I inhaled roughly, fear spiking in my lungs.

"Do not scream," said the figure. And when he spoke it was with Koltar's voice.

CHAPTER FIFTY-TWO
Skallagrim

There must have been something else I did not remember, something I was doing wrong, because I stood before the gates of Heofonraed and they did not open.

I called out to the council, I pounded my fists against the smooth polish of the stone, I flew up and down, looking for another way in. But nothing happened. For a grim moment, I wondered if I'd killed them all, but I did not see how I could have found my blasted way in even in my mate-mad berserker rage. These gates were not like mortal gates, not like the one at Callabarra I could topple with the merest wave of my hand. And the Eafor-swynne were still here – the two great guardians of the gate – and I did not see how I could have gotten past those two towering swine with their rolling red eyes and lethal horns without a fight.

No, I was fairly certain I had not killed the council. If anything, they would have been the ones with the power to restrain me in my rage. I paced back and forth along pearlescent stone, my eye falling upon a crack by my feet that seemed wholly out of place and yet entirely familiar. As if I had watched it form.

As if I had put it there.

I stayed much longer than I intended, not willing to go back to Suvi and see disappointment in her eyes. She had been excited. Hopeful. Happy. She deserved what I had promised her and not a single thing less.

But if the gates would not open...

No. I would stay a little longer. Try to find another way.

So at the very least I would be able to tell her that I'd done everything I could.

CHAPTER FIFTY-THREE
Suvi

While no one else on Bohnebregg came anywhere near Skalla's immortal strength, they were all still much larger and stronger than humans. When Koltar wrapped a firm hand around my upper arm, I knew immediately there would be no escaping that grip as he pulled me up and out of the bed.

I still tried anyway, tugging hard, a fleeting animal reaction to run, to pull away from the teeth of a trap even if it tore flesh. In a cerebral sense, I had no idea what Koltar was doing here. But instinct told me it couldn't be good. Especially if he didn't want me to scream and let anyone else know he was here.

He's almost always at the temple... He's never come here before.

It could be no coincidence that the first time he came to this apartment it was when Skalla wasn't here. I was alone. Protectionless. *Pregnant.*

Nausea swept through me, and I thought now might be a great time to hurl, especially if I could aim it down the front of his robe. Might give me a second of distraction to pull away and figure out what the fuck was going on.

"What do you want?" I whispered shakily.

"Come with me."

No. My whole body reacted to that command. There was no good reason, alien or human, for a man to come take a woman from her bed in the night like this. The last time I'd been pulled from my bed I'd been drugged and abducted, forced into off-world service. Somehow, this felt even more malevolent, despite the lack of violence.

I dug my heels in – literally – planting them as hard as I could against the floor, but when he pulled me I stumbled forward. He led me out the door to the balcony and down the stairs.

Halfway down the steps, I decided to scream after all. I needed allies. I had no idea where he was taking me, or why, and I sure as shit did not want to find out. *He follows the way of cotton, right? He's not going to hurt someone else if I get their attention!*

I sucked in a choked lungful of air.

"Zev! Jolakaia! *Help me!*"

Koltar sighed, like I was a child who'd disappointed him. He stopped on the bottom step and stared at me, irritated but calm, as the house came to clattering life.

Jolakaia, followed closely by Zev, stumbled out of the house. Confusion washed over their features when they saw what was happening and who was holding me.

"All is well," Koltar said, his voice smooth with authority. "This is temple business that does not concern you."

For a heart-breaking moment, I thought they'd both take him at his word and let me disappear off into whatever dark place he planned to put me. He was both the religious and political leader of the city. The Honoured Mother's Eye. I'd never seen anyone disobey him.

Zev and Jolakaia exchanged a look.

A sob of relief strangled my throat when both their expressions hardened, resolute.

"She is our guest," Jolakaia said. "And she is... *ill*. Surely this business can wait until morning?"

Koltar's fingers got slightly tighter on my arm. Because no doubt he expected that by morning, Skalla would be back. I frantically searched the sky for any sign of my mate but I saw nothing.

"No," was all Koltar said. "I will be taking her now."

"Where?" All three of us said the word at the same time.

Apparently Koltar was finished answering questions. He stepped down to the ground, pulling me with him.

But Jolakaia planted herself in front of him.

There really wasn't any discernable difference in strength or size between Bohnebregg males and females. In all honesty, I'd kind of forgotten
how big Jolakaia was. She was so calm, so kind, that it made her less impos-
ing. Plus, she was smaller than my Skalla with his stone sky blood, so my
perception of her scale had been warped. But now, standing tall in front of
Koltar, she cut an impressive figure, especially flanked by Zev.

He'll never get through both of them, I thought, giddy with light-head-
edness. *And then Skalla will be back and we'll take the other women and get
the hell out of here.*

But Koltar didn't admit defeat. He didn't seem worried at all. He just
had that same disappointed parent vibe going on.

"You defy the Mother's Eye?" Koltar said quietly. Jolakaia flinched a little, but otherwise held firm before him.

"In this matter, yes, I do," she said evenly. "I cannot see why you must
take our guest from our home in the middle of the night like this."

"And that is why I am the Honoured Eye and you are not," Koltar
said, not necessarily unkindly, but with a condescension that made my skin
crawl. "The way of metal is still strong within you and unworthiness clings
to you like weeds from the river. The Mother shows me a path you cannot
see. I merely follow it."

Oh, boy. Koltar sounded positively human the way he was using spir-
ituality to justify whatever fucked-up plan he had for me. Thankfully, despite her faithfulness, Jolakaia didn't seem to be falling for it. Maybe it was
because she'd spent so much time outside of Callabarra, or maybe it was because the instinct telling her that something was very wrong here overpow-
ered her devoutness. Or maybe it was just because she cared about me.

Whatever it was, she didn't budge.

Koltar stepped forward, no doubt expecting her to step back in response. She didn't. Their chests collided.

And then Jolakaia shoved him back with a snarl.

Koltar looked briefly startled, his claws flexing against my arm. Then,
as Zev reached a hand for a heavy tool on her workbench, hoisting it like a
club behind Jolakaia, he gave another one of those *I'm-so-disappointed-in-
you* sighs. He slipped his free hand into his robe and pulled out a small metal tube.

With a click of his claw against an unseen button, its end began to glow, and I realized with horror it was a weapon – the same kind I'd seen various Mother's Claws toting around.

"No!" I gasped, stretching to try to knock it from his hand. But he simply held onto me while pushing me away at the same time, keeping me arm's length from his body.

Jolakaia's claws swiped through the air, but Koltar was faster, his small tube aimed, then activated, sending a burst of bright energy at her. She crumpled instantly without a sound,

Zev did the same not even a moment later.

At the sight of their limp bodies on the ground, I retched, then vomited. Koltar didn't let go of my arm, but he did lean slightly away from me in disgust. When I was finished, he hauled me upright once more. But all the strength had gone out of me. I sagged, sobbing, reaching for Zev and Jolakaia's motionless bodies.

"Stand up and walk properly or I will carry you," Koltar said flatly.

"I won't leave them!"

I'd seen too many people I cared about die. My parents. Elvi. Torrance. Now Zev and Jolakaia, the kindest friends I could have asked for in this world. Killed simply because they'd been protecting me.

I should have never called them for help. I should have just gone with him quietly!

Guilt and grief turned to rage, and suddenly I was filled with strength I didn't know I had. I yanked against his grip so hard his claws made my upper arm bleed, and used my other hand to punch, smack, and scratch at Koltar's face and chest. But my human fist did nothing to his scales. He grew tired of my onslaught quickly and shoved the glowing end of his weapon against my stomach.

I stilled instantly, heart turning to ice, because it wasn't just my stomach anymore, was it? It was no longer just a tightly-coiled collection of human guts and organs taking up that space. There was a whole little life taking root in there, the beginnings of a baby that belonged to Skalla and me, and the sensation of the weapon so close to it made me nearly senseless with fear.

"Please," I whispered.

I would beg for my child even if I'd never considered begging for myself.

Koltar didn't withdraw the weapon, but he did turn me, his claws now wet with my blood. He bumped the weapon against my lower back, and, as if he'd cranked a lever there, twisting it like a wind-up toy, I snapped into wobbly forward motion.

Koltar frog-marched me through the quiet darkness. Out here, away from the centre of the city, there were few lights at night. Everyone was sleeping and all was still. Peaceful.

We didn't encounter anyone except the odd animal in a yard gazing dopily at us. I wondered if it would do any good if someone saw us, anyway. No one but Zev and Jolakaia would think twice about stopping Koltar. Any other neighbour would probably just buy his "temple business" line. That, or they'd get shot down just like my two friends were.

Bitterness, or maybe literal bile, rose in my throat. I swallowed the acid of it, stumbling along as Koltar pushed me from behind.

We were very close to the outer edge of the city, heading for the wall instead of going deeper into Callabarra towards the temple. We clomped through fields of food stuffs and Shara plants, the metal-lined cotton puffs swaying in the cool night breeze. It was too perfect a scene. Too serene. I'd always been shocked and disturbed by that. The way things kept on being beautiful when it felt like everything was falling apart. The morning Elvi died had been one of the most gorgeous sun-drenched days imaginable. Reeling with grief, I remembered that loveliness feeling like a betrayal.

We passed through a door and reached the ring of the city's main outer wall. There was a small gate back here, but no one seemed to be manning it. *Of course not. Koltar commands the Mother's Claws and if he didn't want anyone at this post tonight, he'd make it so.*

Koltar opened the small gate, shoved me through, then closed it again like we'd never been there at all.

I hadn't been out of the city for months and I was disoriented by the wide, rolling landscape ahead. Needing to ground myself, I turned my head back to catch a glimpse of the city, to soak in the sight of the last place I'd been with Skalla, the place where our friends had died.

But, as if wanting to drive the knife of this night a little deeper between my ribs, the city was *gone*.

My knees buckled, and I would have fallen if Koltar hadn't been holding me. Rationally, I'd heard about Aeshyr's protection of this place. The way it became somehow cloaked to outsiders. But I'd never actually witnessed the phenomenon since I'd been unconscious when we'd first arrived here.

"No," I choked out, desperation thick in my voice. The city was gone. Vanished. Not even a dot on a foreign, unknowable horizon. I would never be able to find my way back here even if I had the chance. It was as if the city had never even stood at all. In its place was grass and Shara and then the gleaming river beyond.

The river was where Koltar led me, taking a wide berth around the invisible bulk of Callabarra. A small boat waited for us.

Do not get in that fucking boat.

I reeled backwards, knowing that this was my last chance, because if I got in that boat and went wherever he wanted me to go I knew I'd never find my way back. I also knew I wouldn't even be alive to try.

But Koltar merely lifted me and plonked me down in the vessel. He hopped in smoothly behind me, starting up the boat and steering it out into deep water before I could even think about jumping back out. I hadn't gone swimming in a while, but I'd always been pretty good at it. I could still try jumping, but...

But we were already well out into the centre of the river. And this wasn't some little creek. The Bohnebregg river was a monster of a body of water. Wide as a lake with surging currents in the deep areas that I knew I couldn't win against. Sitting in the bottom of the metal boat, my hands cradled my abdomen, and I knew that I wouldn't jump. Jumping out here would mean drowning, and I had to squeeze every second out of my life that I could in case a chance for escape came.

Either that, or Skalla returned.

My eyes scanned the sky, my pulse leaping every time a dark stretch between stars made me think it could be the stone of Skalla's door. But he wasn't here.

Not yet. But he will be...

I stopped my fruitless search of the sky and watched Koltar instead. He steered the boat but did not turn on its light.

"Where are you taking me?" I asked. I didn't actually expect him to answer, but he did, bluntly and without emotion.

"I am taking you to people who will kill you."

OK. Wow. I knew this night was headed in a bad direction, but it was kind of wild to hear him just announce it like that.

My fingers dug into my stomach.

"Why take me all the way out here? Why not..." I didn't know the Bohnebregg word for shoot, and I struggled with the sentence construction before I remembered that Koltar had some of that webbing so that he could talk to Aeshyr. I switched to Finnish. "Why not just kill me the way you did my friends?"

He gave a hissy, sneering sound. "They are not dead," he muttered, his eyes fixed on the river ahead. "I will deal with them upon my return, but they are alive. We do not kill in Callabarra."

Oh, thank God. I blinked away new tears, these ones of relief. I swiped at my face.

"So you don't kill people in Callabarra," I said, "but you take them to someone else to do your dirty work for you? You kidnap people instead?"

He snorted, then gave me a cold look.

"Ah. But you are not one of my people."

"I suppose I can't argue with that. But still... What did I do?" I was more angry than plaintive. "What is this punishment for? I haven't done anything to deserve this!"

"It really has very little to do with you," he said. His eyes were ahead again, like he was watching for landmarks. "But Skallagrim is a threat to my city that I will no longer tolerate."

"Are you insane?" I cried. "It has very little to do with me, but I'm the one getting killed over whatever this is? And you have to know that when Skalla comes back and finds me gone he's going to go absolutely berserk!"

Berserk in the literal sense. He would smash the city into a million pulverized pieces. How could Koltar not see that?

But when he glanced back at me again, he looked at me with a furrowed brow as if I were the ignorant one. The one who truly didn't understand what was happening here.

"You don't know, do you?" he finally asked.

"Know what?!"

"That when you fully mate with a stone sky god, he loses his immortality. His lifespan becomes bound to his mortal mate's. It does not matter how strong he is. It does not matter where he is or what he is doing. The moment his mate dies, so does he."

I blinked uncomprehendingly at Koltar's back as he continued to steer the boat down the river.

"It is the only way to eliminate a stone sky god," he continued. "The only way for a mortal, that is. Skallagrim is made of metal, through and through. Not only is he powerful and unpredictable but he knows where Callabarra is."

"He would never do anything to betray the city!" I shot back. "Especially now that we're together. He listens to me!"

"He has already toppled the main gate of our city and injured several of the Mother's Claws," he pointed out icily. "Not to mention the fact that before he left this world generations ago, he was a raider prince who killed and hoarded with the best of them. A natural enemy of our cause. And now he knows how to bypass the city's protections. He knows where we are, how many we are. How defenceless we would be against him. All of this, and he has never once stopped to seek forgiveness or repent."

"He's changed since then!" I said. "He only wants me to be happy. He's not going to start raiding for metal again like he did hundreds of years ago!"

Koltar gave a mirthless hiss of a laugh.

"Men made of metal, like your mate, do not change. Their blades merely get sharper over time. Impossible to wrap in cotton."

"What about Jolakaia! She changed! You allowed her into the city!"

"She is not an all-powerful immortal who can obliterate us with a wave of her hand," he countered. "Or, formerly immortal, I suppose, since Skallagrim no longer qualifies. Jolakaia was committed to follow the Mother before I even found her. When I first saw her, I knew she could be wrapped in cotton if only given the correct guidance." He sneered. "Although, since she was the one to expose us to Skallagrim, bringing him directly to our gates without seeking permission, I would say she is not the best example for your case."

My mind whirled, trying to figure out how to get out of this now that I knew what Koltar's motivations were.

"Well, we aren't even fully bonded yet!" I bluffed. "So it won't even work anyway!"

"Ah, yes, that is why you looked so horrified when I told you he would die when you did," he said sarcastically. "And even without that expressive face of yours, you are absolutely drenched in the scent of him. Much more so than before. No, I am certain you are bonded now. Lying will not do you any good."

Fuck.

"What if we leave?" I asked. "As soon as Skalla gets back, I'll make him take me somewhere else. Anywhere else! You'll never see us again. I swear."

"I am afraid that is not enough. Skallagrim cannot continue to live with the knowledge he has gleaned about us."

"But... but you let Aeshyr come and go! He's a stone sky god too!"

"As far as I know, Aeshyr has no mate to make him mortal. And as he made his trade bargains with a previous Honoured Eye, long before my time, I had very little say in the matter. We have come to rely on him to shield our city. Shield it from the likes of your mate."

"I already told you, he's changed!" I knew it was pointless to reiterate that point, but I couldn't stop myself. This all felt so unfair. Yes, Skalla had done damage, before my time and even during it. But shouldn't he have at least been given a chance to prove himself worthy of trust?

But then again, why would we want to prove ourselves to someone like this?

"So then you're just going to kill me. An innocent person."

I almost told him I was pregnant then, hoping to make him feel guilty enough that it would change his mind, but at the last second I decided not to. I didn't know if it could be used against me somehow. And besides, the next person I was going to tell about the baby was Skalla.

"*I* am not going to kill you," he reminded me.

"No, just relying on somebody else to hold the blade," I spat. "I'm sure the Mother would be proud to see that her Honoured Eye has become a fucking despot."

He made no response to that, perhaps no longer interested in trying to justify his fucked-up logic to me. And that was just fine, because I was done hearing it. I stared mutely out at the passing landscape, startling when I recognized an abandoned house up on a hill. Suddenly wanting to weep, I wondered if my boots were still there, abandoned among the dust and the ghosts.

I didn't know how much time had passed, but it felt like maybe an hour or two at fairly high speeds before another building came flickering into view. It was massive – palatial – all high wooden beams and open pavilion rooms, perched above the river and nestled in shivering grass. Despite the late hour, light spilled out of it. So did raucous Bohnebregg voices.

A boat came instantly towards us from the darkened shore, as if someone had been anticipating our arrival, or maybe some scouts from the property had seen us. Something whistled through the air, and I yelped in shock as a heavy metal hook landed in our boat, its chain pulling tight as it snagged on the side. The sound of something grinding across the water echoed, and I became aware of our boat being forcibly pulled towards the other. Koltar killed the power and let it happen.

Maybe I should try jumping now...

We'd been heading towards the building, and the water wasn't as deep here. I could probably swim to shore...

But then what? I'd just be pursued by the other boat and maybe even killed all the faster. And now I knew it wouldn't just end my life, and the new one inside it. It would kill Skalla, too. Skalla would be back soon – he had to be. I just had to get him enough time.

"I spoke with Prince Joleb this morning," Koltar said to the two massive Bohnebregg warriors manning the other boat as ours got near.

I know that name. Jolakaia's brother!

"Here is the creature I promised him," Koltar continued.

Creature?! What the hell had Koltar told them about me? That I was some kind of exotic hog they could roast over a fire?

Koltar gestured towards me, as if showing off the merchandise, and in that moment it was as if everything in my vision had pulled inward into a single point. *There it was.* The stun weapon he'd used on Zev and Jolakaia, tucked into the inside of his robe. Like an angry cat, I leaped for it, surprising him just long enough to snatch it and aim it directly at his chest. Swearing, I pressed my fingers uselessly along its length, searching for some kind of trigger or on-switch.

I was too slow. A clawed hand seized on the side of our small boat, dragging it over the last bit of the way until the two boats collided, rocking each other violently in the water. I lost my balance, stomach flipping, and probably would have fallen if that same hand hadn't lifted from the side of the boat and grabbed my wrist in a powerful grip.

"What is this?" hissed the Bohnebregg male who'd grabbed me, staring down at the metal tube. He squeezed me hard enough to bruise, and I cried out, dropping the tube involuntarily. He caught it with his other hand.

"Merely a torch to light our way," Koltar said smoothly, though I thought I could sense some nervousness beneath his polished demeanour.

"Doesn't look like a torch," the male said.

His companion grunted in agreement. "Looks like a weapon. But not like any design I'm familiar with."

The first one's finger must have found the hidden notch or button, because suddenly the end began to glow.

"Ah, look, Bracka," he said, grinning dangerously. "Shall we test it?"

My mouth went dry.

It doesn't kill. It doesn't kill...

Well, it didn't kill broad-boned, scaly, Bohnebregg people. Who knew what the hell it could do to a squishy, soft-skinned, pregnant human?

But it wasn't me the warrior aimed the tube at.

It was Koltar.

"This was not the agreement," Koltar said sternly, as if he could use his authority to frighten these two. But these men were not his devoted Mother's Claws. "I was to deliver the god Skallagrim's mate and then leave."

"Our Prince never planned to let you leave," said the one holding the weapon. "A man seemingly from nowhere coming down the river in a boat as nice as any of ours? A man no one knows, whom none of us have ever seen before, with no allegiance and no warlord? And now, you come with a weapon unlike any I have ever encountered? No, we were always going to take you, too. It was only the promise of killing this strange creature and her god that kept us from imprisoning you when you came to us this morning."

The weight of Koltar's miscalculations seemed to hit him all at once. He spun and crouched, looking like he was going to dive right into the water the way I'd thought about doing so many times already. But the male holding me just laughed, the sound vibrating right down into my tender arm. Then he aimed the weapon at Koltar's back and fired.

Koltar instantly collapsed into the bottom of the boat.

"River drown me," swore the one who'd fired. "He dead?"

"You'd better hope not, Tarak," said the one called Bracka. "You know Prince Joleb wanted to interrogate him. Find out which army he's spying for."

"But he did actually bring us..." Tarak frowned down at me, lifting my hand to inspect it with a half-fascinated, half-repulsed look. "This thing. It seems he did speak true about bringing us the foreign creature. Perhaps he is no spy."

"Then where did he get this boat from?" Bracka said. "Do you know how much good, forged metal went into this thing? There are no nearby villages with hoards like that these days – we have conquered them all. And look at the design. It is very unusual. And his weapon! What, did he just pull that fully-formed out of the river? Prince Joleb is right to think him a spy. The only question is for whom. I know of no army with boats or weapons like this one."

"Hmm. You speak true. So. Is he dead?"

Bracka jumped into our boat and nudged Koltar with his foot.

"Still breathing."

Relief sighed out of me, not because I was glad Koltar was OK, but because it meant he'd told the truth about Zev and Jolakaia not being dead. They were alright back in Callabarra. And they'd be able to tell Skalla what had happened, assuming he and I both lived that long.

"Alright," said Tarak. "Let's tow it all back, then."

I thought maybe I'd get left in the boat to be towed, but it turned out only the lump of Koltar remained there. Bracka returned to their vessel, and

Tarak lifted me into their boat, too. They began to steer towards shore and the great house. Their boat seemed a little slower, a little louder, than the one from Callabarra, as if their tech was less advanced.

It was strong enough to make decent speed, though, even while pulling along the other boat. Soon, Bracka was mooring both vessels at a wooden dock while Tarak dragged me out viciously by the arm.

"Let's go. Do not keep our Prince waiting."

I bowed my head and kept my mouth shut for now, trying to keep my wits about me as I let Tarak haul me along by the wrist. He and Bracka both wore some kind of leather trousers, studded with metal, huge blades strapped to their hips. Thin metal chains were draped over their chests and woven into the hair they wore long and braided the way Skalla did. Bracka hoisted Koltar's limp body and pulled up the rear, which meant I was basically sandwiched between the two hostile warriors. My bare feet padded over the wood of the dock, then the sandy shore, then up a path through the grass and reeds to the house. The stars and moons no longer cast down their silvery veils, having retreated behind clouds as if they couldn't bear to watch what was about to happen to me. Ahead, the house provided the only light.

For a disorienting moment, it reminded me of the temple at Callabarra, because it had similar white cotton curtains hanging to act as a wispy barrier between the outside and the inside. But the temple was always peaceful, lush with quiet. The air here was discordant with alien shouting and booming laughter.

I hoped the laughter was a good sign. It sounded like there was a feast going on, or some kind of party. Maybe everyone would be in good enough spirits not to want to hurt me, at least for a little while...

And by then Skalla would come.

Tarak shoved the curtains aside and pulled me in. I squinted against the light. It wasn't all that bright in here, but it was certainly brighter than outside, and it took me a second to adjust.

"Prince Joleb," Bracka said as I squinted and blinked. "We have the god-mate and the spy."

By the time my eyes had adjusted and I could open them fully, I found myself staring at the brawny chest of the largest pure-blood Bohnebregg male I'd ever seen. He was almost as big as Skalla, towering and broad-shouldered, his scales gleaming in shades of dull green and bright copper.

Wait, no.

Those weren't scales. Much like Jolakaia with her single metal stud, Joleb appeared to have done the same thing to himself but with a much larger design. Scales all along his chest had been ripped out and replaced with metal studs. The glints of metal continued along his throat, leading my gaze up to a face that made me gasp and get dizzy all at once.

It was the face of a Bohnebregg male I'd never seen before. And for a horribly confusing moment, I thought it was Skalla's. Because his eye was so much like my mate's, golden and piercing.

And because he only had the one. Like my mate, somewhere in the thorny path of his past, he'd lost the other. But where Skalla had an un-adorned knot of scar tissue, Joleb had instead shoved a perfectly smooth metal marble in the empty socket. Similar to a glass eye, but without any ef-fort to actually make it look like an eye besides the spherical shape. His hair was long and black and braided, his snout so achingly familiar I had to hold myself back from reaching out and touching it.

"So, you are the god-mate," Joleb said, his voice powerful and deep. "Fated bride of my ancient kin, Skallagrim, who apparently has returned to this world. Or so that one tells us." He jerked his snout at Koltar's uncon-scious form. "Is it so?"

I shook in silence, not knowing what to say, or if I should even speak at all. If I confirmed who I was, would he kill me instantly? If I kept him wait-ing, would he kill me instead for my insolence?

"Perhaps it does not understand our language. It doesn't even have a snout!" said a voice from somewhere behind the Prince, and for the first time I became aware of more people – *many* more – warriors standing and lounging and sitting at benches throughout what seemed to be a feast hall. But no matter where they were in the room or what they were doing, they all had blades at their belts and their eyes fixed on me.

"Hmm," Joleb growled thoughtfully. His eye narrowed. "Don't look down."

I only barely stopped myself from looking down. But I did react – a stuttering sort of blink that gave me away.

"She understands," Joleb said.

Paska. He's clever. I'd have to be very careful. But he hadn't killed me yet and I was hoping that things might still work out in my favour. That I could stretch this out a little longer.

Please, Skalla, get here soon!

I thought of him, maybe fighting human forces right this very moment, trying to free my friends, but didn't let myself despair. Not yet.

"You know my words," Joleb said, dragging me back to the present. "Now answer them." In a flash, his claws were wrapped around my throat, squeezing. There was silken malice in his voice when he leaned in and muttered, "Answer me before I rip your tongue out and you never speak again."

He released me without warning, leaving me to stumble and choke, grasping at my neck.

"I am... Skallagrim's," I said, fighting through panic for Bohnebregg words to use.

"And where is your mate now?"

"He is..."

Fuck. What should I tell him? Should I lie?

I settled on mumbling, "He is not here."

That earned me a vicious backhand across the face, so forceful it made lights dance in my eyes as I twisted and fell painfully onto my hands and knees. My head buzzed, the right side of my face feeling like it had been stung by a thousand angry bees. When I swallowed, I tasted blood.

"Do not take me for a fool, female. You think I do not see that your mate is not here? I did not ask you where he is not." He crouched down then grabbed me by the hair, pulling me up so I was forced to look at him. "I asked you *where he is.*"

Koltar chose that moment to rouse himself slightly. He groaned from where he'd been dumped on the floor. As much as I hated the Honoured Eye, I was grateful to him then because he'd distracted Joleb. The Prince released my hair, letting me sink back down to the ground.

But Joleb wasn't done with me yet. Because even though he'd stalked over to Koltar, it was me he addressed.

"Who is he?"

"He is... A man. I do not know. He took me."

It was hard to talk. My lips felt like they'd already ballooned to twice their natural size, making my normally terrible Bohnebregg accent even worse. Joleb glowered down at Koltar, and he looked so much like Skalla I thought I might throw up. Even the studs of metal between his scales reminded me of the lights that glowed on my mate. Joleb had no wings, of course, but otherwise the resemblance was uncanny in the extreme. It was like I was glimpsing some kind of alternate universe version of the man I loved.

Or like I was seeing who he might have been if he had never found me.

"Put him over there until he wakes fully," Joleb said, speaking to no one in particular, though several men jumped to obey his order, putting Koltar behind a bench in the corner.

Koltar apparently decided he'd made enough noise for now and lay still, which was just fucking dandy, because now Joleb was focused entirely on me again.

"They say," he said slowly, like he was savouring each word, "that if you kill a stone sky god's mate, you kill him, too."

"They say... many things," I hedged, hoping I wouldn't get another slap. But, surprisingly, that made Joleb grin fiercely.

"That they do, female. That they do. But family history also tells me it is so. The great Princess Jolakaia died in battle, did you know that? And her stone sky mate Faerwyrth dropped like a rock to the bottom of the river at the exact same moment, though no weapon ever touched him."

Faerwyrth. That was Skalla's father's name. A name he hadn't been able to recall yet on his own.

I have to remember that. So I can tell him when I see him.

Yet another reason to get through this and survive. So I could tell the man I loved the name of his forgotten father.

Joleb came to crouch before me once more, sliding a razor-sharp claw beneath my chin. "I could be a god-killer, too. A legend among men."

"You could," I said, swallowing more blood and remembering something Jolakaia had once said about her brother and men like him. "But... no glory."

Anger flared in his eye, and I winced, ready for another slap, but it didn't come. He didn't ask me to go on, but he was clearly waiting for me to explain myself. Hoping I wasn't making the biggest mistake of my life, I raised my chin and held his gaze.

"No glory in that," I said.

I cursed myself for relying so much on the webbing and not taking more time to learn more Bohnebregg so I could speak it better. But there was nothing I could do about it now. With the limited words I had, I pieced together what I hoped would be a net to snare Joleb and save myself all at the same time.

"I am weak and soft," I said. "No claws." I held up my hands to show him. "No knife. No scales. No fight. Just a soft female."

The anger was gone from his eye now, replaced with something I wasn't sure I liked, something that seemed to grow when I'd said *soft female*. I ignored it and forged on, praying that this Prince's pride would doom him and be my ticket out of here.

"I am easy to kill. No battle, no glory. Yes, Skallagrim dies. But you do not really kill him." One of my eyes was swelling, but I fought to hold Joleb's gaze, speaking slowly and as clearly as I could. "You cannot be a god-killer if you do not kill the god."

The room had already grown quiet since our arrival, but now it was hushed with thick dread, as if everyone knew I'd lobbed some grave insult at their leader's head and they were waiting for him to explode. Which, to be fair, was kind of the whole point of what I'd just said. I wanted to insult his manhood, his prowess as a warrior, and give Skalla a chance to come back and get me before Joleb gutted me like a fish.

And thank my lucky fucking stars, it actually seemed to be working.

"Perhaps you are right," Joleb said, and then everyone in the room, including me, seemed to let out their breath at the same time. His snout took on a nasty smirk. "Perhaps I will keep you. After I become the god-killer and rip out every one of Skallagrim's scales in front of you, perhaps I will let you live." His gaze grew greedy, and he buried his claws in my hair once more, but more gently this time, letting the strands run through his fingers like water. "I've never seen hair like this," he murmured. "The colour of moonlight on metal. Yes, I think I will keep you after all." He cocked his head. "I know Skallagrim will die when you do. But does it work the other way around? If he dies, will you perish, too?"

"I don't know," I said, and it was the honest truth because I really had no fucking idea.

His grip on my hair tightened possessively, making my scalp burn with pain.

"I suppose it does not matter if you die when I kill your mate," he purred darkly. "You will be mine either way. And whether you are dead or alive, your hair will gleam just as prettily all the same."

CHAPTER FIFTY-FOUR
Skallagrim

After spending far longer than I'd intended to at the gates of Heofonraed, I had to admit defeat. There was no way in. And for all intents and purposes, it seemed there was no one even there to answer. Perhaps things had changed since I'd been mate mad. Perhaps, even if I did not kill them, they all had died and for some reason had not been replaced. The Eaforswynne were still here, guarding who in the stone sky knew what, but no council answered my calls.

This was disconcerting, but even worse was the fact that it meant I would not be able to find Suvi's friends. At least, not quickly. I supposed I could start opening sky doors at random, searching the universe one little corner at a time for the group of them, but who knew how long such a task would take? Theirs was one miniscule machine in the entire scope of a sprawling starscape. It would be worse than trying to find one specific grain of sand in the churn of the Bohnebregg River. For Suvi, I would at least attempt it, but I felt physical pain at the idea of being away from her for so long while searching in such a fruitless, inefficient way.

It was with a foul mood that I hurled myself back up into the sky above Heofonraed. It was as if I was beating the sky itself with my wings, trying to alleviate my frustration. River help me, I could already anticipate Suvi's hurt disappointment. I hated that this would not be the reunion I had promised her. Instead of returning victorious with all her friends, I'd be coming back empty-clawed, and I did not feel worthy of her.

Some small, fearful part of me even went so far as to worry that Suvi might no longer love me if I failed her in this. Which was absurd, because Suvi loved me before I'd even remembered Heofonraed. She loved me without ever knowing there was a possibility I could track down her friends. So it was foolish to think that her love would be rescinded over such a thing now.

But perhaps I was a fool. A great, blundering, fine-scaled fool.

Because that foolish thought scraped at me. It dug in with claws, got between my scales, and it hurt because it felt far too much like truth.

Going from angry to furious, I smashed the sky open with my fist.

The sky door opened directly above Callabarra on Bohnebregg, but I could not see the city due to Aeshyr's protection spell. I had to say the word to reveal Callabarra, and for a gut-gripping moment I panicked, thinking I'd forgotten it as I'd forgotten so many important things already. But then, like a single drop of water, it was flung from the river in my mind.

"Falreth!"

The landscape below wavered, then drifted away, revealing Callabarra. From up here, it looked very different. Maybe even a little wrong. Dark. Though it was night so of course it would be dark, and there were a few lights here and there, so what was I doing thinking it odd that the city was dark? But all the same, something about it felt... Not right. I glanced back at the sky. The sky door had faded, but everything still looked strangely opaque. There were no stars.

Cloud cover. The first I'd seen so thick like this since my return, and the river inside sloshed and churned and suddenly spat out the words *rainy season*.

Without being able to see the moons and stars, I couldn't tell how long it had been night here. But still, I knew I'd spent far longer at the gates of Heofonraed than I'd meant to, hoping to avoid having to come back here defeated like this. But there was nothing left to do about it for the moment, and as much as I hated going to Suvi and seeing her hurt little face, I desperately wanted to be with her after being gone all day.

I flew downwards, alighting on the balcony outside the small apartment. But the eerie sense of wrongness intensified, got hard and twisty, because the apartment door was open. And my Suvi *was not in the bed*.

My heart spasmed, my scales leaping along my limbs in a great, anxious ripple. I forced myself to remain calm, because Suvi was probably just downstairs with Zev and Jolakaia. She must have gotten lonely without me, and the last thing she needed to see was me insane and enraged like I'd been the first time we met. If I smashed into the main house, she'd probably be terrified that our bonding hadn't fully taken hold, which I knew it had. If my long time at the gates of Heofonraed had taught me anything, it was that the mate madness had been entirely cleansed from my blood and body and brain. I needed to be at her side again because I loved her and I missed her, not because my entire being was suspended on the edge of a blade balanced above the abyss.

Though I wasn't so sure, now, because when I looked into that dark, empty apartment, where her scent was already stale, abyss was what it felt like.

Taking the stairs by foot was too slow. I snapped open my wings and sliced down through the air to the ground. But the abyss grew all around me, because the door to the main house hung open, too. I could smell Zev and Jolakaia much nearer and fresher than Suvi. A sound behind me had me spinning, and there I saw them.

Zev was lying prone, seemingly unconscious. Jolakaia was on the ground, too, but she was not down there to heal her mate but because she also appeared to be injured. She groaned, rolling stiffly onto her side and attempting to rock onto her hands and knees.

In a cracking flash of an instant, I'd wrenched her up. I sat her heavily on the workbench and held her by the shoulders so she would not topple.

"*Where is Suvi?*"

The time it took for Jolakaia to open her eyes and focus them on me was an eternity of agony. I could feel black smoke gathering all around me, lining the edges of my vision, and it was not the darkness of mate madness but the pulsing tunnel vision of a berserker rage barely held back. Suvi's scent, especially out here, was faint and fading, and there was another scent, too, one I thought I recognized but couldn't immediately place as my control grew taut and nearly snapped.

Jolakaia had been good to me and especially to Suvi. I did not want to hurt her. But if she did not wake up to tell me what had transpired, then hurting people would no longer be a mere possibility, but the inevitable outcome of fury that was becoming near-delirious with fear.

I shook her aggressively by the shoulders. She gave a crackly, pained-sounding exhale, trying once again to focus her gaze on me.

It didn't work. Her eyelids slid shut even as I shook her again. Zev looked like she would be no help – she was even worse off than her wife, still lying unmoving, though I could see that she was breathing.

"Blast it all into the stone sky, Jolakaia, *wake up*!" I roared directly into her face. Her eyelids flickered...

Then she slumped back into total unconsciousness.

My knuckles cracked with tension as I gripped her shoulders, my body urging me to sink my claws in and slash. Growling in frustration, I let her go, leaving her on the bench and stalking out into the street.

This far from the city's centre, and without the moons and stars, the street was bare and black, the buildings shadows. There was space out here – gardens and farmland. The neighbours were far enough away in their homes that none of them seemed to have been woken by me. Yet.

Well, they would awaken now. They would help me, tell me what I needed to know, or curse them all I'd –

"I saw her."

Rage had been enfolding me so completely, drawing me into the terrible comfort of its smoke, that I hadn't seen the child in the street. A tiny one, young but clear-eyed. I recognized him, I realized, from that day at the pond. That day with Suvi, my beautiful mate, the little star I could not see.

But he had.

Berserker violence nearly blinded me for a moment, told me to wring the information out of him even if I had to twist the bones from his sockets. I shook my snout, trying to right myself. I reminded myself that he was the only one out here with any information on where my mate might have ended up, and if I hurt him too badly or killed him, he'd never be of any help to me.

I probably should have been more concerned about not killing him because he was an innocent child rather than the fact that he might know where Suvi was, but just then I did not have the capacity to feel that way. In that terrible, Suvi-less moment in the night-drenched street, he only mattered because he'd seen her. I'd just have to stop and feel some shame about that later because right now there was no time or space inside me for anything but fear and fury and finding my mate.

"Where?" I hissed, slamming down onto my knees so I could better look the child in the eye. He wore comfortable cotton clothing, rumpled by sleep, but he did not seem like he'd only just woken.

"I saw her. That kind, ugly female. She left that house." He pointed behind me to Zev and Jolakaia's.

I swear to the stone sky if one more water-brained fool of a creature calls her ugly...

"Where did she go?"

"I do not know not know where he took her."

"He?"

A man. A *male*. A putrid creature with cocks had come for my Suvi. Took my soft little star from her bed in the night when I was not there to protect her and now I was going to raze this entire city to the ground, kill every male who lived here if I had to, until I found the one responsible. I bellowed, ground-shaking, feral, and now neighbours spilled into the street from properties down the way, sleepy and confused. Many of them, upon seeing me, retreated immediately back into their abodes. A set of adult hands snatched away the child I'd been speaking to. The child wriggled in his mother's arms, trying to maintain eye contact with my rapidly disintegrating gaze.

Somewhere in my blistering brain, the scent I'd caught on the balcony and stairs suddenly registered. Recognition snapped into place at the same moment the child called out from above the shoulder of the mother who carted him swiftly inside. As if sensing a door was about to slam closed between us, he didn't bother forming a long sentence. He simply shouted a single word, a name, tossing into the air like a rock skipping 'cross a pond, a toy that I was meant to catch.

"Koltar!"

The door closed. Violence bubbling like acid behind every scale, I launched into the air and aimed my body for the temple.

CHAPTER FIFTY-FIVE
Skallagrim

The only reason I did not smash my body through the roof of the temple, entirely collapsing it, was because of the chance that Suvi might have been inside. Instead, I landed in the courtyard, my body hurling down so hard that the river stone there cracked outwards from the impact. I rose to my full height, claws flexing and wings beating in time with my rabid heart.

"KOLTAR! Come out here and face me!"

Koltar did not emerge, but Mother's Claws did, hurrying in their black robes with their odious, impotent little metal tubes aimed at me.

I grabbed the nearest one, wrapping my hand 'round his throat. It wasn't until a wooden crutch clattered to the ground that I realized it was Nakib.

Oh, good. I've been waiting for an excuse to finally kill him.

"Where are they?" I hissed, reminding myself with only some effectualness not to squeeze too hard or he'd suffocate and not answer me. "Where has your foul leader taken my mate?"

"What... are you talking about...?" he choked out, grasping at my fingers.

It took everything I had not to crush his blasted throat. And I could do it, too. With my stone sky blood I was already stronger than any man here. On the edge of a berserker rage, I could squeeze this neck like it was made of soft fruit instead of flesh.

But I didn't. Not yet. I held on to a glimmering silver thread of sanity named Suvi because if I entirely let go I'd lose my wits and I could not afford that now.

"He took Suvi!" I roared. "And do not think for a second I will believe a lie, so tell me once and tell me true, *where have they gone?*"

More people were in the courtyard now. Mother's Seeds and Mother's Hands, standing behind the Mother's Claws, the temple and city light warming their red and green robes. Though I was mostly focused on Nakib, I could sense confusion in the crowd. Like what I was saying made no sense to them. Nakib coughed and gagged, and when he gave me no more information I threw him down so hard I might have broken his other cursed leg. The Mother's Claws looked about, as if waiting for orders. But Koltar was not there and in his absence, one of them decided to take his chances and blast his weapon at me.

I'd give him something – I did at least feel it a bit. A buffet of wind against my front that knocked me back a half a step.

As if encouraged by the first one, the others, more than a dozen of them, let loose a volley of shots from their weapons, energy blasts pinging off of me in rapid succession.

I should have known that questioning any of them was pointless. They were loyal, alright, but they were loyal to Koltar above all else.

Fine. I would pummel my way through the temple, room by room, hall by hall until I found Koltar and my mate and if anyone wanted to get in my way then he could pay the price of that foolishness with blood.

Snarling, I lifted my claws, and with an outward lick of my power I wrenched every weapon from every set of hands and smashed the tubes to metallic dust. My vision smoking over with bloodlust, reason receding into the storm inside me, I raised my hands higher to demolish the body of every Mother's Claw who stood before me. Thunder clapped, a resounding, quaking smack of sound, and I half thought that I'd produced it.

Just before I brought death down upon the Mother's Claws' heads, a voice I recognized spoke, confusing me just long enough to halt me.

"He is not in the temple."

It was Koraba, oldest Mother's Hand and someone I'd spent a great deal of time with in the temple at Suvi's side.

"Get back, Koraba! Do not approach him!" growled a nearby Mother's Claw, but Koraba waved her off.

"What you seek is not here, Skallagrim," Koraba said. There was no fear in her face or her voice as she approached me. "If Suvi is missing, we will help you find her. But you cannot come and cause violence here in our most sacred place."

"You have not yet seen violence," I seethed. "And since it was your Mother's Eye who took my mate, I cannot trust any of you to help me!"

More confusion. More murmurs among the crowd. And suddenly, there was doubt inside me. Doubt that any of these ones knew where Koltar was, or that he'd even taken my mate in the first place.

"Our Mother's Eye would not cause harm to one such as her," Nakib piped up from the ground. "If he did take her, do you not think perhaps it was because he was helping her? She probably wanted to flee from you, and Koltar led her away from your monstrous nature and into sanctuary."

Clearly, I had not squeezed Nakib's throat hard enough if he could still spout filth like that. I glared down at him, realizing that I hadn't actually injured him badly when I'd thrown him down, because he was already standing up with the help of his crutch. Furious, practically foaming at the mouth with hatred of him, of anyone who stood between Suvi and me, I blasted power at him, snapping the femur of his good leg just to shut him up. He collapsed in pain-stricken silence while several Mother's Hands gasped and hurried forward to examine him.

"Why do you think Koltar has taken her?" Koraba said. The Mother's Claws had drawn rank around her. They were weaponless, now, but I could tell that several of them were on the edge of a berserker rage, just like I was. The way of cotton meant not giving into those violent urges, but I supposed I had created exceptional circumstances that allowed them to veer from their peaceful ways. That, or some of those bristling Mother's Claws would have some serious praying to do when this was all done.

"Because I *smelled him!*" I bellowed at her. "And he was *seen! There are witnesses!*"

"He is telling the truth!" I twisted back, chest heaving, to see Jolakaia roll up and dismount weakly from her two-wheel. She wobbled, tried to take a step, then appeared to decide it would be better to stay holding onto her two-wheel for support.

"He is telling the truth," she said again, more quietly this time, panting like just speaking was taking a great effort. "He took her from her bed in the night when Skalla was gone. And he used weapons on my wife Zev and I when we questioned him."

The confusion that had been simmering came to a sudden, riotous boil. Shouts and questions rang out on all sides. Many accused Jolakaia of lying, hissing at her, throwing her history back in her face. She took it all with a steady gaze, remaining still but strong under the insults, until suddenly the words buzzing through the air like weapons blasts took on a different tone, became centred on Koltar.

"Why would the Honoured Eye take her?"

"I still do not think he did it!"

"Where is he now, then? He always spends the night in the temple and yet he is not here!"

"He must have had good reason. He is the Mother's Eye and he sees the path she lays before us."

"Nakib was right. He must have saved her."

"Why would he steal her to save her? Why would he not tell any of us?"

"Who manned the front gate earlier tonight?"

"I did! And no one passed!"

"But did Koltar not take Padra off duty at the back gate tonight?" That question was louder than any other, silencing the voices. It came from Koraba. Her aged voice was like a blade, every word a damning blow. "*Who manned the back gate?*"

The Mother's Claws looked around at each other, then at Koraba, then at me.

"None of us."

"There's another way out of Callabarra besides the front gate? And Koltar made sure no one was at that post tonight?" I asked.

Koraba jerked her snout *yes*.

So he'd taken her right out of the city, then. That seemed to make sense as much as it filled me with dread, because if he took her away from here it would be to make sure no one saw whatever he planned to do.

"I do not think that he will harm her. At least, not directly," Jolakaia called from her two-wheel. "Whatever his motivations, he is still the Honoured Eye. He follows the way of cotton. He will not kill her."

"Curse the way of cotton!" I shouted. "If I never hear of it again it will be far too soon!" I pointed an accusing finger at my cousin-niece. "He blasted you and your wife with weapons and took my mate. Is that the way of cotton?"

"But the weapons do not kill," Jolakaia said. "They stun and weaken, but they are not lethal. We use them when circumstances are dire, otherwise the Mother's Claws would not be allowed to carry them at all. But he will not kill her, Skalla. I am sure of it. Taking life is the worst offense before the Mother. No matter what Koltar's plans or motivations, killing her with his own hands is not among them." She paused, then her eyes grew huge with horror. "*With his own hands.*"

My heart seemed to stop within my very chest.

He wanted her dead and so he'd get someone else to do it.

It all fell into place now. As my memory had returned in Suvi's arms, I'd recalled more and more about the mate bond. Aeshyr had even mentioned it – that my life would be bonded to Suvi's.

When Suvi died, so would I.

And as killing my sweet little star was a whole lot easier than killing me, that was who Koltar had taken. The most vicious sort of coward, he'd waited until the shield of my love was withdrawn and he'd struck like poison.

I'd always hated Koltar and I should have trusted my instincts. Should have crushed his pathetic skull back when I'd had the chance! But I'd tempered myself, restrained myself from hurting, from killing, so that Suvi would not hate me.

But I'd rather have her living, breathing hate than have her dead.

"Joleb," Jolakaia breathed. "Skalla, he is the only warlord left with an army in this territory. If Koltar has taken her somewhere, then-"

"Where?" I cut her off savagely. I yet stood, which meant that somewhere out there Suvi still breathed. But who knew for how long? I certainly did not, and the not knowing made terror like nothing I had ever experienced yawn open in front of me, a chasm so deep and wide that even with my wings I was not sure that I could cross it.

"It's your old home!" she said quickly, her words slurring slightly as she tried to speak faster than her weakened state would let her. "The house you grew up in. Follow the river away from where the sun will rise. You will know it when you see it."

I could recall what it looked like. Even before my memory had started coming back more strongly, I'd glimpsed it in that fractured vision of Wylfrael in the river.

I didn't waste any more time. I was up in the air, spearing out of the city, following the river and finally giving into the seductive darkness of the berserker rage. My body stretched and swelled as I flew, scales flaring outward with the force of my fury.

If you hate killing, Mother of Cotton, then you'd best turn your eyes from Bohnebregg tonight.

That was my last conscious thought.

But soon after that, there was no thought.

No words. No logic.

Even my own name disappeared, just as it had before.

But this time, hers remained.

I would not forget it. *Could not* forget it. I could go mad for a thousand lifetimes and still her name would be there, more recognizably a part of me than my own heartbeat. Even now, that organ did not pulse in service to me, but rather called for her, a brutal chant, repeating the same two syllables over and over again.

Su-vi. Su-vi. Su-vi.

CHAPTER FIFTY-SIX
Suvi

The room I'd been left in looked like something out of a fairytale picture book. Those images of dragon hoards under mountains that were basically just massive piles of gold coins and goblets and jewels? Yeah, they had nothing on Joleb's hoard. Metal filled every bit of the floor, every corner, was piled up high against the walls, undulating down like a wave before rising high in a big shiny crest in the centre of the room. There were metal coins and goblets, just like those illustrations I'd seen as a child, but also weapons. *Tons* of weapons. Blades and axes and hammers and chains, all entangled together and balanced in their precarious piles. Not long after my arrival, Joleb had led me here and plopped me down, since apparently I was a part of his hoard now, too. Koltar was nearby, not actually inside this room, but chained by one of his hands to a wall in the hallway beyond. I could see him from here, and he was awake now, but he didn't say or do anything besides sit there. I didn't say anything to him, either, even though I had some choice fucking words for that pious idiot. I kept my eye on him whenever I wasn't watching the huge mounds of metal all around me, paranoid that all that weight would come crashing down on top of me if I weren't careful.

This was, as far as I could tell, the largest room of the palatial house. I guess it had to be, to store all this freaking stuff. It was at the back of the house, open pavilion-style and looking out over a courtyard with a fountain surrounded by tall grass and reeds instead of looking out over the river. Unlike Koltar, I wasn't chained. I guessed nobody was worried about the little human trying to escape or using one of the many massive weapons left within my reach. Probably because there was nowhere to even escape to. If I fled deeper into the house, I'd just get lost and trap myself before being discovered. And I couldn't run outside, because most of Joleb's army was right there in front of me. They'd made their way out of the feasting area and were patrolling the courtyard and area beyond in small groups, occasionally talking and laughing and looking my way before casting their eyes up to the sky.

I cast my eyes up, too, but the sky was so heavy and dark with clouds I had no way of knowing if it had turned to stone the way I'd seen it do before. There had been a terrible smashing noise from up there, like Skalla's fist cracking open the door, but before I could get too hopeful the sound had happened again, that time preceded by a flash of lightning in the distance. The warriors had begun grumbling about storms and the rainy season, and I told myself to wait just a little while longer.

I wasn't the only one waiting.

Joleb walked past Koltar and into the hoard room, threading carefully through wobbling piles until he stood right behind the place where I sat. I hugged my knees to my chest and forced myself to keep staring forward, outside.

"Alas, I am not a patient male," Joleb said on a sigh. I was aware of him bending into a crouch. Each of his knees jutted out on either side of me. I crunched my body inwards, making myself as small as I could so that I didn't touch his inner thighs.

"I did not think I would have to wait so long for Skallagrim."

He pinched a few strands of my hair between his finger and thumb, then tugged. It hurt, but by that point everything hurt. Half my face was like a furnace, my shoulder had stopped bleeding but throbbed venomously, and the nausea had returned with a vengeance. The only thing more overpowering than all these pains was my exhaustion. I didn't know if it was a pregnancy thing, or if it was just a result of all the stress hormones that had been unleashed in my body tonight, but my bones felt like they weighed double what they normally did. If I weren't in such a dangerous situation and desperately watching for any sign of Skalla, there was no way I could have stayed awake.

Joleb tugged again, harder, then let go. He let his hands come to rest on his knees, perfectly balanced, his chest a hair's breadth from my back.

He lowered his snout to my ear, his breath stirring the hair he'd just been pulling.

"Maybe he will not come at all."

"He'll come." I kept my voice very neutral, not betraying any of the fear or longing or disgust I felt. I tightened up my body even more, wrapping my arms protectively around my abdomen.

"Hmm. Let us watch for him together, then." Without warning, he grabbed my shoulders and hauled me to my feet. I cried out in pain when he gripped the place Koltar's claws had cut me. Fresh blood began coursing down my arm, but Joleb didn't let go. He merely marched me forward, holding my shoulders firmly and standing far too close behind me as we both stared at the sky outside.

At the sight of their Prince, the warriors became quieter and more alert. They stopped chatting and joking with each other, turning their own snouts upward to stare at the starless night.

But there was nothing. No sign of Skalla, none I could see or hear, at least. And, minute after minute, Joleb's fingers got harder on me, until I was on the verge of tears, and it was as if he blamed me for Skalla's absence.

"He'll come," I said again, the words barely above a sob, and I wasn't sure if I was saying it more to Joleb or myself. Joleb's huge fingers slanted inwards, spanning my collarbones, claws prodding at the tender artery of my throat.

He'll come.

That time, I only said it inside my own head.

But no matter how quiet the words had been, it was as if that silent vow had fucking conjured him.

Because *there he was.*

I didn't actually see him at first. Nobody did. He was too far away, too high up. But when lightning suddenly blistered the sky, illuminating everything, bright as daylight, it illuminated him, too. Just for a second. Not even a second. A fractional glimpse of a spearing shadow with a wingspan that made me dizzy. And then, in the dark that followed, he sped like an arrow, now close enough for me to see the miniscule glowing points among his scales.

Thunder boomed so frightfully loudly I would have slammed my hands over my ears had Joleb not been holding onto me. The murderous explosion of it went on and on and on, only now it wasn't thunder, it was *Skalla*, and he was roaring like he'd brought down the very storm himself. The skies opened at that exact moment, rain pouring down in sheets of pure black, obscuring Skalla's golden, glimmering form until he hit the ground with the force of something that could end the fucking world.

The quake he created slammed all the way into the house, shaking the walls. Directly behind Joleb and me, the great piles of weapons shivered, then fell with a lethal clatter, a landslide that would no doubt have killed me if I'd still been in the room.

Skalla rose in the rain, terrible and terrifying, an avenging alien angel with stars strewn across his wings and murder in his eye. Joleb's warriors bellowed. They tossed their snouts, stamped their feet, and drew blades. Maybe it was some trick of the rain splattering off of them, but they seemed to get bigger. Like every cell in their bodies was growing, stretching their scales along limbs newly swollen with power for battle.

"Ah. My loyal berserkers. See how they rage for me?" Joleb said. "But Skallagrim rages, too. Let us see what your man can do."

He was right. Skalla was not anything like himself. He looked the way I'd seen him in his mate madness, like every nerve in his body stood on painful end and wouldn't lie flat again until it was bathed in blood. He howled. The sound was inhuman, and yes, he'd never technically been human, but this was the ripped-throat call of a monster.

"He cuts through them like a blade through water," Joleb breathed in amazement, and he was right. There had to be more than fifty men launching themselves at my mate, but one after the other, they fell and fell and fell before the molten weapon of his rage. I watched him kill and kill again, but I couldn't fear him. He was Skalla. My Skalla.

He'd come for me. He was killing for me.

And I was not afraid.

"I suppose it is time that I go and join the fray," Joleb said. "Earn my new title of god-killer."

He finally released me, and it was very hard not to show him how much of a physical relief that was. He stepped in front of me and took two blades from his belt. He must have activated something on their handles, because the edges of the blades began to glow white-hot.

"Stay in here, female," Joleb called back at me as he stalked out into the storm. "If you die when I kill your mate, I don't want to have to drag your corpse through the mud and make all that shiny hair dull."

I didn't get a chance to answer him, or even really process what he'd said, because a moment later something flew by me, smashing into a nearby wall and creating a massive hole. Turned out that *something* was an entire, gigantic adult male, dead now, his body tossed by Skalla like it was nothing but a pebble.

Now that Joleb wasn't holding me in place, I scrambled back into the hoard room, not wanting the next flung corpse to land on my head. It was much harder to get through the room now – there was no longer a path through the mountainous piles. All the treasure had toppled together into one huge mess of metal. I went slowly, sometimes crawling, sometimes wading, careful not to slice anything open on the swords and knives and scimitars strewn this way and that.

The metal had spilled all the way out into the hallway and, losing my balance slightly, I slid down the incline until I'd landed on my butt right in front of Koltar.

He was on his feet in an instant. At the same time, our eyes fell on the axe on the floor between us. Choking in a gasp, I lunged for it, but Koltar's arms were longer. His claws seized it and then swung. I braced for the blow that I knew I wouldn't be able to dodge in time.

The blow landed with a metallic clang, and I had a second to think that was very odd before the burst of pain came.

But it didn't come.

I opened my eyes just as a second clang split the air. Koltar was bringing the axe down in sharp movements against the chain that bound his other hand.

"He should have killed you when he had the chance," Koltar hissed between blows. The chain began to weaken and warp. "Then we would all be safe."

"Oh, please. You don't think Joleb would have killed you, too? He's got you chained to a fucking wall!"

"Not for long," Koltar said. "And even if he had decided to kill me, I do not fear death. It just means I will be carried in cotton to the Mother's fields all the sooner."

"Yeah, right, like she'd want you in her fields after everything you've done," I spat. God, talking this much was making my head pound with hot misery.

With a hard yank, Koltar wrenched the chain apart. His hand came away from the wall, the metal cuff still locked around it.

I assumed he'd drop the axe then.

But, alarmingly, he didn't.

He straightened, his grip tightening on the handle. My heart crawled all the way up to my throat when he turned to face me with that weapon in his hand. I stumbled back into the mess of the hoard room and grabbed the first sharp thing I could find – a short, pointed sword. As Koltar advanced on me, I knew with chilling certainty that if I had to kill him I would do it.

"The Mother knows that all I do, I do for her," Koltar said, his voice hard and rising, like he was delivering a sermon. "If I have to kill one to preserve her path, surely she will not turn from me for that."

He raised the axe. I tightened my hold on my blade.

The brave man gets his soup and the brave woman gets to see her mate again.

She gets to live to tell him his father's name. And to tell him that he's a father now, too.

I would never be willing to give up that moment with Skalla. I screamed and swung the blade.

Without actually knowing I'd done it, I activated the same white light on the sword that I'd seen on Joleb's blades. Maybe it was heat or electricity or some other alien form of energy, but whatever it was, it sliced through Koltar's wrist like the man was made of butter. There was no way, even with a sharp sword, I'd normally be strong enough to drive it right through his scales like that. But there I was, severing his hand like it was nothing at all. The hand and the axe both fell to the floor with a sick thump. Blood spewed from the stump, and even as I held my sword aloft between us, ready to strike again, I found myself stammering out a frantic, "Sorry!"

Why the fuck are you apologizing? He was going to kill you!

I wasn't sure if that was Elvi's voice or mine, but whoever's it was, it was right.

"Never mind," I panted, jabbing the sword shakily towards him. "I take that back."

Koltar moved as if in a fugue, apparently not noticing or caring about his missing hand or fallen axe. He reached his remaining claws for me, aiming for the throat.

But before I had to lift my sword higher to defend myself, he halted so sharply and suddenly it was like someone had shoved against his chest. And the next moment was very confusing, because there actually *was* a hand at his chest, only it wasn't attached to a person. I thought that somehow it was Koltar's own severed hand, only, *no*, this one had dark yellow-ish scales instead of Koltar's blue ones. The yellow-scaled fingers were still clutched in death around the handle of a... *something*. I couldn't actually tell what the weapon was because it had been buried hilt-deep in Koltar's chest.

There was no question who'd done it. I doubted Skalla had even seen me in here yet, and even so, he was still saving me. Doing it in perhaps the most gruesome way possible, by literally ripping another man apart and hurling the entire severed hand and weapon like a fucking dart, but still.

Koltar stared blankly down at the fist jutting out from his chest. He lifted his bleeding stump of a wrist, remembered dazedly that his hand was gone, then used his other one to peel the yellow-scaled fingers from the weapon's handle. He dropped the lifeless limb, then looked as if he was going to try to pull out the weapon sunk into his chest, but he didn't get that far. He collapsed down onto his knees, then fell forward onto his face without another sound. He didn't pray. He didn't beg for forgiveness. He didn't breathe.

He was dead.

Now that he was no longer an immediate threat I had to fight, horror rose in my throat at the scene before me. I vomited violently, my body heaving and fighting to spew up whatever was left inside me, even though there wasn't much. The act of retching made my head spin. I kept the sword in one hand, plastering my other against my forehead as if that would somehow ease the pressure inside my skull.

I have to find Skalla.

But in the end, he found me. Not exactly intentionally. He burst through an outer wall into the hallway, his limbs locked around Joleb as the two of them wrestled, frothing with berserker power. Joleb still had a handle on one of his blades, and he wrenched it up, slicing through the thinner skin of one of Skalla's wings, driving the white glow of the blade upwards until it hit bone. Silver blood poured from the wound, and I screamed.

It was my scream, more than any pain he could have felt, that sent Skalla spiralling into an even more virulent state. His entire frame spasmed and pulsed, his scales jutting outward like spikes on horrifying angles as he locked his fingers around Joleb's throat and lifted him high into the air with only one powerful hand.

I dropped my sword and smacked my hands over my mouth, sobbing against my sweaty skin, needing so badly to call out to him but not wanting to distract him now. Joleb bucked and swung his blade down onto Skalla's snout, but thank fuck it didn't seem to have much of an effect on his scales the way it had on his wing. He was made of stronger stuff than a regular Bohnebregg male – my own experience with Koltar had shown me that a white blade like that should have cut right through his scales.

But it didn't. The blade bounced off, like a skate not finding purchase against ice, and with a shouted curse, Joleb locked eyes with me.

And then he hurled it.

My hands fell away from my face and it was like they moved through thick honey, because everything seemed to have slowed. The blade rotated end over end, handle over blade. I knew, rationally, that it must have been moving fast, because it looked like a glowing ring and it whistled through the air as it came for me, but still, it didn't *feel* fast. Skalla's maddened eye rolled in his head. He saw me. Saw the blade.

Saw that he'd never make it in time.

There was no time even though that blade moved *so fucking slow*.

Even my breathing was slow. A calm, deep in-and-out as death hurtled white-hot towards me.

Skalla dropped Joleb and then the slowness winked away and everything happened fucking fast. Like he was punting a hockey puck across the rink, Skalla used his power to send Joleb skidding bullet-quick along the floor. Just when the massive, sliding warrior would have taken me out at the knees, Skalla drove his fist high in the air from the other end of the hallway, and Joleb jerked upwards with a rough movement, his body levitating in the air before me. The unmistakable sound of many bones crunching at the same time rattled my teeth, and then, before I could take another breath, was the jarring *thunk* of impact. A bright white point appeared at Joleb's back, right at the level of my eyes. The blade he'd hurled with his own hand was now buried in his guts.

I assumed it would be done then – no one would survive that, except maybe Skalla – but my mate didn't seem to be done yet. With Joleb limp and hovering in front of me, I couldn't see Skalla, but I could hear him, his breath tearing from his throat, his steps like the thunder that still boomed outside. More bones snapped, ribs, I was pretty sure, and I wondered if Skalla would break every single one. If he'd keep going even when there was nothing left in Joleb's limbs but dust. Even when I begged him to stop.

But then Joleb was flung aside. His corpse crashed through yet another wall, and all I could see now was Skalla.

"You came," I whispered. "I told them that you would."

I laid my hand against his chest. I could barely see the green or the glow of him now, so slick was he with blood – blackish from the warriors and the silver of his own. But I felt his heart surge beneath my hand, and it was the heart I knew.

Blood-soaked and berserk, with a single burning eye and only one working wing, dragging the deaths of more than fifty men behind him, he was still my Skalla.

I wrapped my arms around the man who'd become my home, closed my eyes, and wept.

CHAPTER FIFTY-SEVEN
Suvi

Skalla didn't hug me back. Not at first. His breath stuttered hoarsely in and out of him, and he trembled, as if restraining himself because he couldn't quite trust himself not to crush me. It reminded me with bittersweet nostalgia of when he'd gone into heat before me. He'd been scared to touch me then, too.

"Hold me, Skalla. Please," I sobbed.

And then, with a great groan of release, he did, his arms closing around me like iron. But even so, I could still tell he was being careful. His hands roamed my back gingerly but frantically, his snout burrowing against my throat, sliding down to my shoulder. I flinched when his scales touched the wound there. He froze, then withdrew, and it made me sad to see that he now had red blood on him too.

His eye looked a little clearer, now. His scales pulsed in shimmering waves down his body, like he was trying to get them to lie smooth again. But when his gaze registered the swelling on one side of my face, the cracked lip, the bruised eye socket, his gaze smoked over and his scales puffed right back out.

"Who," he rasped, sounding vengeful and haunted all at once, "did this to you?"

"Joleb," I whispered. "But you've already killed him."

He snarled low in his throat, then tugged at the torn, blood-soaked sleeve of my tunic.

"And this?"

"Koltar. But you've already killed him, too."

We both looked at Koltar's body. Skalla was still for a long moment. Then, with a furious shout, he sliced his hand through the air. He hurled

Koltar's corpse into the hoard room, where it crashed into heaps of fallen metal. Skalla was enraged all over again, and for a second I thought he was actually going to go drag Koltar's body out of the hoard room simply so he could start pummeling it. I grabbed his bloody wrist with both of mine.

"Please, Skalla. I need you with me. It's done. Just... Just stay with me. *Please.*"

His scales flattened instantly. When he turned his eye to look at me, his gaze was sombre.

"Suvi," he said, voice raw with pain, "it breaks my heart to even hear you ask me that." His arms went around me once more, the bottom of his snout settling against the top of my head. "I am here now, little star. I am here, and here I plan to stay."

And stay with me, he did. Not at the house, though. As soon as the storm subsided, I was desperate to be out of here, away from the calamity and death. Though he assured me that he would heal quickly, Skalla didn't trust himself to carry me in flight with his torn wing, so we took the boat from Callabarra and steered it back towards the city. As we moved over the water, Skalla filled me in on what had happened while he'd been gone. Apparently, the council he'd visited to ask for help had not opened their gates, and he hadn't been able to locate the human ship. The disappointment of that stung, but after the trauma of tonight and the gratitude I had that Skalla and I were both alright, I pushed it aside for now. We were alive and we were together. We would figure everything else out in time.

I didn't see the city, but Skalla knew where to stop the boat. This was the first time I'd been conscious on the approach to Callabarra, and I marvelled at how completely the city was made invisible. From here, standing on the banks of the river, there was nothing ahead but gentle slopes of rain-bejewelled grass and plant life.

But Skalla knew where to go. He cut a straight, confident line towards nothing, carrying me when I began to shiver from the moisture on the plants soaking my clothes. Heat poured off of him, comforting me, warming me to my core, like I was in a sauna back home. I sagged against his chest, too tired to care about how much blood was getting on me now.

"Falreth," Skalla intoned into empty air. I recognized that the word was not a Bohnebregg one, but all the same understood the meaning with the webbing in my ear. It meant cotton.

The landscape got kind of wiggly, like it was a projection and something had gone wrong with the slide. Then, Callabarra was there, the front wall and gate of the city so close I could reach out and touch the wood and stone.

"That's incredible. Can all stone sky gods do that? Hide things like that?"

"Aeshyr is a warlord of Riverdark," Skalla explained. "He comes from a world of mages with powers outside the scope of a typical stone sky god. They are one of the few other races who can travel between worlds."

"*Few* other? You mean there are more alien species that have achieved space travel?"

He grunted in confirmation. I didn't know why I was so surprised. Us humans had figured it out and there was no way we were the smartest ones out there.

I turned my attention back to the gate as Skalla lifted one of his arms from me and pounded on it. I winced when I saw the parts that had obviously been newly rebuilt after Skalla had damaged the structure last time. Luckily, a Mother's Claw opened the gate instantly, though she almost looked like she wished she hadn't when she saw the state of us.

Twisting in Skalla's arms, I looked down at him, and then myself.

Skalla's scales were almost entirely black with blood, apart from the silver dripping from his own wing and the places on his lower legs wiped somewhat clean by the wet reeds and grass. His face and hands in particular looked like they'd been dipped in tar. His hair was unbraided, tangled, and caked with fluids, and at some point in the battle, or maybe when he'd swelled up in his berserker rage, he'd lost his trousers. He was a magnificent, terrifying, naked god of gore carrying his injured mate into the midst of Callabarra.

There was no one in the streets, and when we got to the temple I understood why. Because it seemed as if everyone in the entire city was awake and standing there. The courtyard was packed with Bohnebregg bodies all crushed together, and many more citizens had spilled out into the main road outside. Loud, confused-sounding chatter spiked and rolled through the crowd like radio static, but it fell silent, incrementally at first, then all at once, when people began to turn and see us.

In a solemn hush, the crowd parted before us, creating a path through the courtyard. At the end of that path, in front of the main entrance into the temple, I could see Zev and Jolakaia with the other Mother's Hands. I allowed myself a few sloppy tears of relief seeing them, then gave a great big sniffle and sucked it up because we had important shit to sort out now, and nobody needed human tears getting in the way.

Zev and Jolakaia were up and running – kind of clumsily, like their legs were weak – the moment they saw us.

"She needs healing," Skalla said urgently, lifting me slightly away from his chest to show Jolakaia my shoulder.

"Oh, Suvi," Jolakaia said softly, examining my shoulder and then my face. She called out some instructions to a nearby Mother's Hand who then sprinted into the temple to fetch supplies. "No sign of infection like last time," she said. "We will likely need to suture the wound, though. Your flesh tears so easily and these claw marks are deep." She sighed, cast her eyes up to the sky, then down again. "The Mother was truly protecting you tonight if this is all my brother did to you."

"Actually, this wound was from Koltar," I said in Bohnebregg. "And if he'd had his way it would have been much worse."

The silence didn't budge, but tension bloomed inside it like fungi. As if every single person present had suddenly gone rigid. It almost made me feel guilty, like I was the bearer of bad news. I knew how much the Mother's Eye was respected. Koltar had been both the religious and political leader of this entire city. The devotion and respect he'd been shown was monumental, and to hear that he'd been involved in something like this, that he wasn't who people had thought, was no doubt devastating to the citizens of Callabarra.

But this was the truth. And it needed to be heard.

"Where is Koltar?" Koraba came forward from the others. "He must be held to account."

"He is dead," Skalla snapped. "As is every other foul creature I found at that house."

Jolakaia flinched slightly, then breathed out, as if in relief but the kind of relief that hurts a little bit. Zev pressed her snout to the side of Jolakaia's, a silent comfort.

"I'm sorry," I said to Jolakaia. I wasn't sorry that Joleb was dead. But I was sorry for her, because he'd been her brother and no matter how you looked at this situation, shit was weird and layered and really fucking hard.

But when Jolakaia met my gaze, she didn't look sad or angry. She looked very calm. Like a violent storm had passed through her and all that remained now was quiet. Peace.

The crowd, though, was not as peaceful. They didn't seem too worried about the local murderous warlord dying, but Koltar's death was another story. Some citizens of the city fell to their knees. Others clutched at each other in shock. Some gazed furiously upwards, as if wanting to drag the Callanna moon down so she could explain just how her Eye could have gone so astray. But the moons were hidden still. And Koltar was too dead to explain anything to anyone.

"A new Mother's Eye must be made to see," Koraba said. She spoke firmly, with authority. As she was the oldest Mother's Hand, I supposed she was probably the highest-ranking person around without Koltar.

"I nominate you, Koraba! Wisest of the Mother's Hands!" called someone from the crowd.

"Ha! I am too old for such a position," Koraba shot back.

"You cannot defy the nomination. The Mother will decide," Jolakaia said, and Koraba jerked her snout to the right.

"Yes, young one. I know. Fine! But being in the running does not prevent me from choosing my own candidate. I nominate Jolakaia!"

Zev grinned and puffed up with pride at the exact moment that Jolakaia shrank back. The reason for Jolakaia's awkwardness became clear very quickly when complaints and jeers began to spew like vomit from the gathered citizens.

"She comes from metal!"

"Same foul blood as Joleb!"

"Bah! A stain on the Eye!"

"We are going from one murderer to another!"

"It should be Koraba!"

Koraba raised her hand high then closed it in a fist. Slowly, though un-happily, the others quieted.

"The Mother will decide!" she called out sharply, echoing Jolakaia's words. "But my nomination stands!"

She raked her eyes mercilessly over the people watching, snout raised high.

"Who among us is more worthy than one who has been on the path of metal and has turned from it? Where is the wisdom in following the path of cotton when you were born on its smooth road and you know no other way? Jolakaia has walked in the world, has tasted the bloody glories of met-al, and still, she chooses Callabarra. Still, she chooses cotton. She has been relentless in her service to our city because her true spirit is that of a healer. That is the way of the Mother! Let any citizen who disagrees with me prove that they have cared for more of our sick or injured than Jolakaia has!"

No one spoke.

"It is as I thought. None can make such a claim." Koraba turned her stern eyes onto Jolakaia, who was still slouching shyly. "Stand tall, young one," she commanded, and Jolakaia straightened, as if disobeying Koraba was far worse than any of her current feelings of embarrassment. "You are as worthy as any other. The Mother will decide."

In the end, one other person was nominated, a male named Porat whom I vaguely recognized in his green robes as one of the Mother's Seeds I'd seen working in the temple gardens.

"Now what happens?" I whispered to Zev as the three candidates as-sembled in the centre of the crowded courtyard.

"Now, the Mother of Cotton will decide," Zev said. At that moment, two Mother's Hands came out of the temple. One carried the medical sup-plies Jolakaia had sent her for, and she made a beeline to me. The other went towards the candidates carrying what appeared to be a pile of folded cotton rags.

Skalla held me close as the young Mother's Hand began cleaning my shoulder. It stung badly, but soon she'd applied some kind of numbing cream for the sutures, allowing me to focus on what was happening ahead as she closed up the wound.

The three candidates removed their robes and then lay flat on their backs on the ground. Koraba, old and stiff-jointed, took a while to get down into the position, but she shooed away anyone who offered assistance. Once all three were lying flat, the Mother's Hand went along the row of them, laying a square cloth of white cotton on each of their bellies.

"They must remain lying there," Zev explained. "Wind will come and tug at the cotton, but that cotton will hold fast on the body of the Mother's chosen eye."

"What if no wind comes?" I asked.

"It is the beginning of the rainy season. There will be wind."

As if on cue, a breeze whispered through the courtyard, making the cotton on the candidates' bellies flutter. Porat's was raised a little higher than the others, and after a moment of butterfly-like hovering, his cotton square drifted onto the ground beside him. He rose and left the row, leaving only Koraba and Jolakaia.

The Mother's Hand working on my shoulder finished up her neat sutures, applied bandages, then dabbed ointments around my eye and onto my cracked lips. I could sense the tension in Skalla, letting someone else get that close to me when I was injured, but he kept his possessive growls to himself, though I felt the restrained rumble of them in his chest as he held me.

"Thank you," I whispered, and she nodded at me before heading to join the other Mother's Hands. I returned my attention to Jolakaia and Koraba lying on the blue river and gold stone ahead. I frowned, noting cracks in the stone beneath their bodies. Had those cracks always been there?

I didn't have time to dwell on it, because another wind was blowing, now. This one stronger, humid, insistent. It tousled my damp hair, skimming my skin like a physical caress. The crowd was so quiet that the sound of my own heartbeat, and that of Skalla's, flooded my head. I realized I was holding my breath without even meaning to as the wind reached Koraba and Jolakaia.

It wasn't an aggressive gust of wind. It wasn't grabby or greedy or pushy. But it was strong, and like the hand of a firm but fair mother, it did not yield until the job that needed to be done was complete.

The cotton on both women's bellies fluttered.

I gasped along with the crowd. What did it mean if they both lost their cotton squares? Would they have to repeat the whole process with new candidates? I chewed nervously on my lip, then swore internally when I remembered my injuries there.

Suspense throbbed.

The wind was like breath.

Koraba's cloth floated away.

At the same moment that Koraba's cloth hit the ground, Jolakaia's also lifted right off her scales. I strained to sit up in Skalla's arms and see better, as if the gravity of my gaze could somehow hold her cloth in place. But it was pointless. The cloth was already lifting higher, skimming away from Jolakaia's belly towards her chest where it would surely blow away, except...

Except, like someone had pinched it right out of the air from below, it suddenly stopped.

And it stayed.

In that place above Jolakaia's heart, where her brother had ripped out her scale and shoved in a cruel hunk of metal, the cotton square had snagged.

All at once, like someone stopping breathing, the wind was gone. A shivery, sacred sort of stillness settled in its wake. Oddly, I felt my eyes fill with tears as I stared at the perfect white square caught on that piece of metal pain.

I'd never contemplated destiny in any serious way before; I'd always considered myself too pragmatic for that. But now, it was as if I could see every moment of Jolakaia's life that had pulled her, magnet-strong, to this exact point in time. *I thought about taking it out*, she'd said about that metal piece on her chest. But she hadn't.

Then, I turned my teary gaze up to Skalla's bloodied face. *Fated mates*, he'd called us. And suddenly I couldn't stop thinking about how every single thing that had ever happened to me, every choice I'd ever made, even the ones that had been made for me, had brought me directly to him. A universe apart, he and I had been moving towards each other without even knowing it.

If I hadn't studied botany, I might never have been taken from Earth. If I hadn't been put on that specific ship and been on that specific planet at the exact right time, Skalla never would have found me. If I hadn't had the brave sister I'd had, I might never have been bold enough to find my way towards loving him. It actually scared me how any infinite number of things in the tiniest variations could have made our paths diverge, could have led us away from each other.

And yet, here we were.

Here we fucking were.

"The Mother sees us and has chosen!" Koraba called fiercely. "Jolakaia, rise! Rise as her Honoured Eye!"

Zev and I cried out at the exact same moment, her with loving pride, me with some twisty, awe-filled emotion I couldn't quite name. The rest of the citizens of Callabarra, unable to deny the obvious choice of their goddess, shrugged off their doubts like old robes and cheered, a mighty chorus of sound rolling over the temple.

In the centre of it all, Jolakaia rose. Then, and only then, did the cotton finally let go and fall.

CHAPTER FIFTY-EIGHT
Suvi

Jolakaia's first act as the Honoured Eye of Callabarra was to send the Mother's Shrouds – grey-robed temple workers whose duties were to deal with the dead – to Joleb's house to clean up the corpses. I felt bad about that, as if Skalla and I should have been helping too, but Jolakaia rebuffed my weak complaints with a snort. She probably knew I wouldn't be able to take two steps into that mess without hurling my guts out, but she was kind enough not to say so. Instead, she just laid her hand on my shoulder and said, "He was my brother and I will take responsibility for him."

She went with the Mother's Shrouds as night turned to morning, and Zev tagged along to support her wife. In the end, Koltar's body was not returned to Callabarra to be swathed in cotton as was the custom. He was floated down the river on a burning death pyre, his body among Joleb and the others.

As for Skalla and I, we remained at the temple that night. I was too nauseous and exhausted to even consider a two-wheel trek back to Zev and Jolakaia's apartment, and we ended up right back in that same little medical room we'd once occupied together. It felt oddly nostalgic, like I was back in a university dorm or something, and it was strangely comforting. Especially now that Skalla was back with me.

As soon as we were inside with the door closed, Skalla collapsed to his knees and dragged me into his arms. My knees buckled instantly, but I didn't fall, *of course* I didn't fall, because Skalla was here and he would never let that happen. He cradled me gingerly against him, caressing my hair, my back, the uninjured side of my face with a passion that was almost frantic.

"Suvi," he rasped.

I realized his hands were trembling. Skalla, my great, magnificent mate, trembling.

"Shh. It's alright," I murmured.

"It is not alright! You do not know... You do not..." His arms tightened fiercely around me. "My little star. You do not know how dark the night can get without you." His breathing stuttered slightly before he quietly added, "I have never been so afraid."

I nodded, throat squeezing. I waited until I was sure I wasn't going to start bawling before I answered.

"I know. I was afraid, too. But I wasn't nearly as afraid as I could have been. I never lost hope. Do you know why?"

He didn't answer. I smiled softly against his bloody scales.

"It's because I knew that you would be there, Skalla. I never had a single doubt. I just had to hold on, because I knew that my mate was coming for me."

"I was," he hissed. "But I curse myself for spending so blasted long at those unmoving gates!"

"You were doing that for me. I'm really glad you tried even if it didn't work," I replied softly. "You came back in time. It's alright. Well... mostly. We're together, at least. We're both alive..." I sat up a little straighter in his arms. "Hey, how come you never told me about this whole *I-die-when-you-die* thing?"

His golden eye met mine with surprise.

"I did not think it mattered much," he said with a nonchalant jerk of his snout. "It is not as if you will have to prepare for my death one day. It will happen in tandem with yours. Just as I would wish."

"I guess I'd better be careful, then. I'm a lot easier to kill than you are!"

"Not with me by your side, you're not."

"Does it work the other way, too? Will I die if you..."

"No," Skalla said, and he sounded certain. "I remember hearing of mortal females who've outlived their stone sky mates. It is very rare, though, because even while mortal, stone sky gods are still exceptionally hard to kill."

"I wonder why it doesn't go both ways," I mused. "It doesn't really seem fair."

"Things do not require fairness to be. I went mate mad from your absence long before you were even born. I could not have prevented it if I'd even tried, because no matter how I searched, you would not have yet existed to be found."

"You're right. That is messed up." I sighed, looking down. "I just wish I'd known about the fact that bonding with you meant I'd basically cause your death one day. I doubt it would have changed anything but... But I just can't help but feel like I've taken away your future."

Skalla stiffened, then placed a very firm hand under my chin, forcing my head back to meet his raw but steady gaze.

"Let me make this abundantly clear to you, Suvi," he said, as solemnly as if he spoke a prayer. "There is nothing worth having now that you have not bestowed upon me." His grip tightened, his gaze bright and gold and sure. "You have given me my future, Suvi. And you have given me back my past."

My eyes filled, but I blinked and wiped them away. I didn't want to cry anymore tonight. I just sighed into Skalla's embrace, and let him hold me in the room's quiet.

"Oh. Speaking of your past," I said after a moment, suddenly remembering, "I learned your father's name. He was called Faerwyrth."

Skalla's chest muscles leapt with the tension of shocked recognition.

"Faerwyrth," he said slowly. "Faerwyrth... Yes. *Yes.* That was him." He stroked a tender knuckle across my cheekbone. "Thank you, Suvi."

"You're welcome." I was glad I'd remembered to tell him. But then I felt uneasy. Like there was supposed to be something else...

A sudden churn of queasiness reminded me exactly what it was.

My heart buzzed with nervous energy as I thought about telling him. I wondered if I should wait, if I should try to plan some kind of surprise for him. It wasn't exactly like I could leave a positive pregnancy test out somewhere for him to find. But still, maybe I could try to make it a little more special than this.

But as I looked at my Skalla – bloodied, battle-weary, and holding my injured body in an embrace as possessive and protective as it was gentle – I knew there was no better time than this. This was real. This was us. Tattered at the edges by violence, but holding onto something pure at the very centre.

Messy. Flawed. And utterly perfect.

"That's not the only thing you're going to learn about fathers tonight," I said, my voice shaking slightly. I rearranged myself so that I was on my knees, facing him head-on. Tears spilled down my cheeks, and I didn't bother trying to stop them this time because I knew it was pointless. But I smiled through them so hard it hurt. "Skallagrim of the stone sky and Bohnebregg, you are going to be a father. I'm pregnant."

Skalla didn't answer for a long moment. He just stared and stared, watching me with devoted awe, like I was the first sunrise he'd ever witnessed. Then, he smiled, a slow, poignant pull, and now I was the one watching the sunrise, because seeing Skalla smile at me like that was a thing of fucking beauty.

He brushed away my tears, being very careful on the swollen side, then pressed his snout to my temple.

"I cannot think of how to be worthy of all you have given me."

"You already are," I said sincerely, wrapping my arms around his neck. "Just keep loving me. Stay with me. Build a home and a life with me. That's all I ask."

"I will," he vowed savagely.

A tremulous laugh bubbled out of my throat.

"And maybe try not to kill or injure anybody else if you can help it. At least for a little while."

"I will not promise that," he said, and then he added with a tone so bitter and begrudging that it made me laugh all over again, "But for you, I will at least promise to *try*."

CHAPTER FIFTY-NINE
Suvi

After that night in the temple, we spent the next two weeks back at the apartment attached to Zev and Jolakaia's. We both needed time to recover from our injuries, not to mention a home base to ride out the worst of the early pregnancy fatigue and nausea. We didn't see much of Jolakaia – she was incredibly busy in her new role at the temple, and Zev was often gone helping her – but that was alright with us. We needed that time alone together.

Though it wasn't exactly a calm, quiet time with just the two of us. Skalla, it turned out, was a rather frantic father-to-be. Every time I complained of a headache, or ran to the bathroom to throw up, or became overcome with exhaustion, he'd exhibit an odd, antsy energy I hadn't seen since I'd been recovering from my infection back at the temple.

"Water!" he'd say, pressing cups into my clammy hands. "Eat!" he'd command me, shoving food under my sensitive nose. "Lie down!" he'd bark anxiously, pacing back and forth with a distinctly dragonish impatience until I listened. He fussed over me constantly, glaring pissily out the window at the thunder clouds when I complained of heat or humidity, and wrapping his body gingerly around me whenever I was cold.

But even with Skalla and his incessant care-taking, I couldn't be comfortable in that apartment for much longer. Pregnancy seemed to make my dreams much more vivid than before, and when I dreamed of claws reaching for me, I literally felt their cold touch, digging into my now-healed shoulder and re-opening the wounds. Often, I'd wake with a start and think that I saw Koltar, or Joleb, or sometimes even a human soldier, standing in the doorway. Worst of all, though, were the dreams where our baby was here, swaddled and safe in my arms, only to be ripped away by someone I couldn't see. I woke from those dreams crying so hard I threw up.

Skalla was also impatient to leave, not just this apartment but the city itself. With Jolakaia in charge, it probably would have been safe to stay in the city, but even so, Skalla brooded on the possibility that there might be someone out there who would follow in Koltar's footsteps and try to harm him through me.

So it was decided, once we were both healed and ready, that we would go. The question was where. Skalla didn't think it was a good idea to take me through a sky door while pregnant, and I agreed, because who the hell knew what kind of radiation or whatever that kind of event would douse me in? It would have to be on Bohnebregg. Even if we weren't going to live in Callabarra, I wanted to be nearby so that we could visit Zev and Jolakaia, plus Skalla wanted the Mother's Hands close enough that they could assist with the birth.

"I could build you a house," Skalla told me. "A new house on the river."

"That will take a long time, though, won't it? Especially if you're doing it on your own." I didn't feel right about asking people from Callabarra to leave their usual duties to come help us build a new house, especially during the rainy season when storms roared through the skies, drenching the land and whoever was unlucky enough to work upon it. I also didn't want to wait weeks sitting by myself while Skalla toiled away in the rain, because I already knew he wouldn't hear of me helping him in my current state.

"There is always..." He stopped, leaning against the wall of windows in the apartment, crossing his arms and snapping his snout shut.

"What is it? There's always what?"

He hesitated, then said, "There is always my old family home."

"You mean... You mean Joleb's house."

"I grew up there with my parents and lived there long after their deaths, so I do not think of it that way, but yes."

I chewed on that. My first instinct was to say *hell fucking no*. That was where I'd been kidnapped to. I'd watched multiple people die there. I didn't think anything could erase the trauma of those memories.

But it was also Skalla's childhood home. And my bad experiences in that house were mostly limited to the hoard room and the hall. I hadn't even gotten a chance to see the rest of the building.

And then I thought about our son (because apparently stone sky gods only produced boys) being born the same place Skalla had been. I thought about him swimming in the same spots Skalla had as a little boy, sleeping in the same room Skalla had once put his own bed, and suddenly my feelings on the matter didn't seem so black and white.

"Let me see it first," I said tentatively. "In the daylight."

Sunshine broke through the clouds the next morning, and after so many storms it felt like a good omen. I didn't want to go to the house by boat – I wasn't sure I could handle any rocking without barfing, plus that just made me think of Koltar – so Skalla borrowed a two-wheel from Zev and we went over land. The world looked extra green, vibrant and lush, after all the rain. I knew this wet season wasn't over yet, wouldn't be for weeks, but this little slice of sunshine illuminating the living landscape was enough for now.

When the house came into view, we saw it mostly from the side. Skalla slowed the two-wheel, and I told myself to give the building a fair chance. I knew Skalla would support whatever I wanted to do, and if I said no, that would be the end of it. But I would be fair. I owed Skalla that.

It really was a beautiful building. All smooth wood posts and a high, angled roof. So many of the outer rooms were open to the elements, the rustling curtains damp but fresh from the rain, and the entire thing looked out over the river with the most glorious view I ever could have imagined. It reminded me more of a resort on a tropical island than a house. And there was so much land! Stretching and verdant, undisturbed for kilometres. The gardens I could plant here! It could be a whole farm if I wanted!

Skalla took my hand and led me with a gentle tug towards the back of the house. My stomach went sour, and I almost pulled away, because the back was where everything bad had happened.

But when we got there, there was no darkness or thunder. No blood, no bodies. It was just a house. A house that had been damaged, no doubt, as huge sections of the walls back here were entirely destroyed. But it was still just a house. I stared at the now-cracked fountain in the courtyard, the broken beams, but no matter what I did, with the sun shining down so sweetly and everything looking so cleansed by the rain, I just couldn't drag up the ghosts of what had happened here.

In a way, the house was similar to Skalla and me. Like us, it had been through some awful shit. It had been beaten down and broken and witness to unspeakable things. But it was still standing. Emptied out of evil and waiting for something new. Something good.

We could give it something good.

I was aware of Skalla watching me intently from the side even though I didn't look at him. I nodded once, firm and sure, more at the house than at him, and simply said, "I'll want a sauna." Then I walked into the house, our *home,* for what I considered to be the very first time.

CHAPTER SIXTY
Skalla

Suvi had always had a lush stomach, and it only grew more generously round as we settled into the house and I began to rebuild. She seemed to think that she was growing rather quickly in her mid-section for the beginnings of her pregnancy, but as it did not seem to be doing her any harm, I did not allow myself too much worry over that. If anything, her health seemed to improve daily. By the time the rainy season dissipated, so too did her exhaustion and stomach ailments.

Sun reigned, and Suvi became lively again. Her appetite returned, and not just for food. While I'd cursed the first part of her pregnancy for making her so unwell, I now prostrated myself before it in thanks because it was almost as if she were in heat again. Morning, noon, night – it did not matter. She'd hoist her swelling body atop me, or press her backside against me, drawing my cocks from their slits with nothing but an arch and a sigh against my scales.

It was a time of bliss unlike any I had ever known. There was peace in this house, joy in my heart, and my bride in my arms. No thing. Mortal or otherwise, could hurt me now.

When I told this to Suvi, she pulled back to look at me.

"Your bride. You've called me that before. But we never got married."

"We are married in every way that counts," I told her huskily, heat spreading through my loins as I flicked the tips of my tongues against her throat. She shivered and sagged, allowing me to spin her so that her back was pressed to my front. I hoisted her cotton tunic up, groaning at the fragrant wetness already soaking her upper thighs.

"Do you want my knot inside you, wife?"

She moaned, grinding her head in an up-and-down *yes* motion against my chest. Desire sluicing through my bloodstream, I lined my sensitive head up against her entrance. But I paused when she spoke again.

"And maybe... Maybe the other one..." She gave a wiggle of her hips until her puckered back entrance twitched against the tip of my smaller, upper cock.

I nearly spilled right there, and through gritted teeth I hissed, "Are you certain?" We'd never done that before, though the river knew I'd fantasized about it.

"Yes," she breathed. "God, yes. I want to try. I feel like soon I'll be too big to try anything too new or crazy." She rocked back against me once more, and it was so dizzyingly erotic I, too, felt suddenly too big, like my cocks were more flush with blood and seed than they'd ever been.

"Bend over," I whispered. She whimpered and did so, placing pillows under her on the bed for comfort, her little feet flat on the new floor. The pillows were also new, as was the bed. Besides the structure of the house itself, nothing from Joleb's time remained here. Even the hoard had been cleared out, the metal donated to the Callabarra temple. The hot-edged weapons had been converted into various surgical and cauterizing tools, the other things melted down and repurposed. No, this was our bed. In our house.

And this was my mate bending down so sweetly over it, waiting for my cocks.

I fell to my knees in worship of what I saw before me. Sun spilled over Suvi so thick it was like milk or silk or some other liquid-like, luxurious thing that made her skin and hair shine. Her backside was gorgeous, her hips delicious in their pregnancy-thickened state.

Gripping her thighs, I eased them apart, forcing her feet to move outwards and away from each other in cute little bouncy movements. Then I dipped my snout between her legs and licked.

Pregnancy seemed to make Suvi far more sensitive. She was slick and delectably swollen, and it only took a few swirling flicks across her little pearl of pleasure to send her quaking in sun-soaked climax. I eased my forked tongue back and away from the places I knew would be throbbing hard now, but I didn't pull back entirely, instead using my tongue to drag slippery wetness back up the crease to her other tight entrance. She lurched and bucked when I licked her there, then gave a deep, raw groan when I lubricated my finger with her juices and slowly nudged it inside.

Tight. Even tighter than her cunt. My body rocked, cocks jerking forward at the thought of that tightness taking me.

But she couldn't be too tight. And she felt nowhere near ready for me yet. With painstaking slowness, I eased my finger in further, up to the thickened knuckle, and growled in satisfaction when she cried out with elation.

"Oh my God, Skalla," she panted, fisting the bedding with her tiny, clawless hands. "I feel like I'm *melting.*"

With how wet she was, she almost looked like she was melting, too. I dragged my tongue greedily down to her cunt, sliding back up with more slickened moisture. I used both tips of my tongue to lick at the tight ring around my finger, and with a flare of arousal I watched it give a fluttering clench and then relax.

After a few more thrusts and licks, I added another finger.

And then, when she was grinding and sweating and shaking, a third.

Suvi became nearly incoherent with pleasure when I stood, keeping my fingers in her and then sliding my larger cock into her cunt, stopping just before the knot.

"More, *fuck.* Please, Skalla, I can't!"

"Can't take me?" I growled, driving my fingers and cock into her in a simultaneous, claiming thrust.

"Can't wait!"

And who was I to make my perfect mate wait for anything she wanted?

I eased my slick fingers out of her, watching in lurid fascination as that dark pink ring stretched and clenched. Gathering more of her wetness, I stroked my upper cock, getting it good and soaked.

Then, I nudged the tip inside.

Suvi and I moaned in unison. I tried to go slow, but my mate was nearly feral, weeping and bucking and begging. I angled my hips slightly, so that I could have greater control over the upper cock's movements instead of driving the lower cock harder, and I slid it further and further inside.

Her insides shivered, milking me from root to tip. Her cunt clenched needily, and my knot swelled to the point of pain in response.

"Not yet," I whispered heatedly, splaying my hand across the heart-breakingly perfect sway of her lower back. "I want you like this for a while."

Thinking I would last "a while" turned out to be a pathetically arrogant sort of optimism. The reality was that once I started thrusting into her, slow, measured, shallow, my control disintegrated extremely quickly. And when Suvi squirmed, all her words evading her except one which became a desperately chanted command, "*knot, knot, knot!*" I could no longer wait.

With a groan that felt as if it split my very spine, I thrust as deep as I could go, jamming forward until my mate's wet body swallowed my aching knot and both shafts were hotly buried to the hilt.

Suvi's cunt around my knot had always been a mind-splintering experience. Having her squeeze my knot and take my other cock at the same time was something I was not entirely sure I would actually survive. The world-ending pleasure of it burst over me, burst over everything, like the destructive crash of a blazing star. Everything brightened, my vision going spastically white, as Suvi shuddered and screamed through her climax.

I came so hard that I almost didn't feel it begin. My whole body beat like a swollen heart, every nerve split and singing, each cell and scale trembling in tandem. I felt like I was entirely inside Suvi, as if even the parts that did not touch her were in her, caressed and milked by her, soaked in her sweetness. When my climax crested, it crested *everywhere,* turning every part of me, from wing to tail, into a spasming erotic organ, every limb twitching tight pleasure, my spine coiling, until with a rush it all moved *down*. Down, into the star-smashed pressure of my groin, where it swelled into my cocks and then burst forth from both at once.

I roared, and Suvi came again, crying out beneath me. Her skin was so soft beneath my hand, her insides silken and tight around me, all of her beautiful and so powerful she stole all thought from my head, all breath from my lungs. I was so overwhelmed by her, by the cataclysm of our joining, that I did not even know that I was speaking to her at first, grinding out words between the bellowed bouts of pleasure.

"I love you, Suvi. I will love you until every other star has fallen and you are the only one left to light the dark. And I want to marry you. Truly. Mark you as my wife before the world and, and, and..."

And then the words were gone, obliterated by a shattering second round of exquisite release that left me reeling, *reeling*, until I thought that, no, I did not reel at all, because I was *anchored here*. I was anchored by Suvi, by her body, by her love, and if I only held fast to her I knew that I could never be lost.

And so I held her and I locked my knot tight inside her like I'd never let her go.

Because I did not intend to.

CHAPTER SIXTY-ONE
Suvi

It was too hot today to wear even the thinnest cotton. I stretched out on my chaise longue in the back courtyard – one Skalla had crafted for me from river rushes and a soft, leather cushion – and I sighed dreamily in the sunshine. I wouldn't be able to lie out here much longer without burning, but for now, like a lazy, happy cat, I had absolutely no interest in moving. I listened to the sound of the cracked-but-mostly-repaired fountain, water bubbling over its stone, luxuriating in the honey-like sweetness of the afternoon. Behind me in the house, Skalla was puttering away on some project or another. All the damaged parts of the house had been completely rebuilt, but there was always something that man wanted to work on when he wasn't busy feeding or massaging or fucking me, often in that order but not always.

Lately, all his projects had been baby-related, carving cradles and designing ingenious little toys, and if I'd thought I couldn't love him any more than I did before, it turned out I'd been dead wrong. Because when I'd first stumbled across the baby items he'd been working on in his quiet secrecy for the nursery, I'd burst into tears and then immediately jumped his big berserker bones.

Maybe it was just the hormones. Or maybe I'd just gotten my human hands on the best damn husband in the universe.

Lying in the courtyard, I wondered if it would be this hot for our wedding. It was only two days away now, and I couldn't very well go as naked to our ceremony as I was right now. Although, technically, I supposed I was wearing something. It was a long, glimmering, looped chain of metal, hanging from my neck over my chest. It was jewellery that Skalla had created himself from the Shara plant threads. I cracked my eyes open, smiling at the sight of the sparkles against my heavy breasts, darkened nipples, and round stomach, then closed them again. I tossed one hand over my eyes to shade them, and started nodding off...

Only to be woken by the sound of my name. Except it was my name spoken in a deep, male voice I did not recognize.

I ripped my hand away from my face, hoping I'd heard wrong and that I'd find Skalla standing before me.

But it wasn't him.

And oh, *oh my fucking God*, I knew this creature. I recognized the snow-white sheet of his hair. I'd seen those black, bat-like wings, with those lights like blue flames flung across them.

It was him. The one who'd crashed into the world of our first mission. The one who'd killed half the crew and my friend Torrance, too.

Panic gripping me in a vise so cruel I couldn't breathe, I tried to scramble up into a seated position, but my stomach got in the way. Realizing that fleeing was stupid, because this guy was obviously faster than me, I instead gasped and then let out a blood-curdling scream.

"SKALLA!"

Skalla burst out of the house like a bomb going off. He arched through the air, colliding with the other male with the force of an entire planet's gravity. I got shakily to my feet and ran as fast as I could into the house. I knew I should retreat further, to hide – I had our baby to think about even more than myself – but I couldn't bring myself to let Skalla out of my sight as he grappled with the other male on the ground. I hid behind a wooden beam, chest on fire with fear.

Frankly, I expected to see another person get completely torn apart by Skalla right before my very eyes again. But strangely, the violence went out of my mate's hulking body all at once, like a plug in a drain had suddenly been pulled from somewhere inside him. And then he spoke, sounding stunned.

"Wylfrael?"

That was Wylfrael?! That was Skalla's cousin? He'd remembered more of the man over recent weeks, telling me stories about the two of them spending time together as boys, both on Wylfrael's world Sionnach and here. Their fathers had been brothers. Sometimes, I'd find Skalla sitting up in the middle of the night, staring one-eyed at the wall, and I always knew he was contemplating the fact that he'd probably killed his cousin. There was never anything I could say or do for him in those moments. He couldn't go to Wylfrael's world Sionnach to check if the man still lived because he wouldn't bring me through a sky door and he also wouldn't leave me here alone.

But it looked like Wylfrael was just fucking fine. He'd survived Skalla only to go on and kill my friend. I dug my fingers hard against the wood of the beam and listened.

"It's me, cousin," Wylfrael was saying, like he thought Skalla might not recognize him. "It's me."

Skalla got off of Wylfrael and stood, pulling the other man up with him. They both turned towards the house, but they didn't appear to see me behind the beam.

"I'm sorry I scared her," Wylfrael said. "It was not my intention."

I scoffed bitterly at that. He'd killed Torrance without a thought but now he didn't want to scare me? I glared, hating the look of this man. Where Skalla was warm and raw and vital, this alien male seemed... Cold. His eyes roiled like blue fire, and he held himself upright with a certain alert stiffness, like a fucking duke from a novel.

"What is your intention, Wylfrael?" Skalla asked slowly, staring hard at his cousin. "Why are you here?"

"I am here because my own human mate demands that I make sure her friend is alive," Wylfrael replied.

I blinked in shock. He had a human mate, too? Obviously someone who knew me if they'd sent him specifically to check on me. Which meant...

It was *someone from the ship.*

I waited with bated breath, but he didn't say anything more about who his mate was. Instead he narrowed his shockingly blue gaze.

"You are one to speak of my intentions," he hissed, "when you yourself crashed into Sionnach and almost destroyed everything. You almost killed me twice."

Skalla's thick, scaly tail swept over the stone, his snout tightening with what I could tell was regret.

"I barely remember that," my mate said with a harsh sigh. "I remember when the madness started, and with my last bits of reason, I went to Sionnach, because I trusted that you would do whatever it took to keep others safe from me."

"I tried," Wylfrael replied. "We fought over many worlds. I nearly died, and spent eons recuperating in some foreign desert, under red mountains. Then, you crashed into that world, too. I took you to Heofonraed, but they would not help me."

"They would not help you either?" Skalla asked, sounding surprised. "Not long after I found Suvi and rationality returned to me, I went to them. Suvi wanted to find out what happened to the other women. But they would not open their gates or hear my petition for information."

"There is much that I must tell you," Wylfrael said darkly. I shivered in the heat as he began to unfold the strangest tale. He spoke of a fake marriage bargain with a human he'd captured. Apparently, only mated males could be a part of the council, so he needed to present a false bride at Heofonraed so they'd accept him. And when he gave the name of the woman who'd agreed to this bizarre bargain, I nearly lost my grip on the beam and toppled right over.

Because it was *Torrance.*

She's alive!

At least, she had been at one point. But that hope began to dwindle as Wylfrael kept on talking.

"We, neither of us, had starburned," Wylfrael said, his hands folded tightly together behind a tense back, as if even just telling this story disturbed him. "I had no reason to think she was my true mate, even though by that time I had married her, and the marriage had become one of love, not falsehoods. So I took her to Heofonraed. Skalla, it was *chaos.*"

He paused, staring furiously at the cracked fountain, before continuing.

"They did not hold the customary vote but instead put me through a trial. They used some sort of deception, made me fight a great, foul creature. But when my blade pierced its heart, the illusion faded and my sword was buried in Torrance's chest."

He kept his tone icily neutral except for a sudden break of emotion on Torrance's name. I smacked my hand to my mouth to keep from sobbing.

"But we had not starburned. We had not bonded. She died in my arms. And I remained."

I'd assumed Torrance was dead this entire time, but somehow, this was far worse than the grief I'd already gone through. Because she'd been there, dangled in front of me, so close I could practically reach out and grab her. Save her. But now she was well and truly fucking gone.

"Wylfrael," Skalla said, his eye burning with pain for his cousin. "I-"

Wylfrael cut him off with an impatient twitch of his fluffy, fox-like tail. "I require no sympathy. She yet lives."

OK. Sorry. What?

Surely, I had heard that wrong.

But Wylfrael went on as if what he was saying actually made sense instead of sounding completely impossible.

"I took her to Sceadulyr. He got his shadows inside her and they did their work. He brought her back, though afterwards he dragged me half across the known universe in service to my debt to him."

Skalla angled his head my way, searching the house, and I could tell he was wanting to confirm I was there and that I was alright. Clearly, hearing about Wylfrael almost losing his mate had rattled him. Meanwhile, I was still over here fucking flabbergasted that my friend had actually died, just not the way I'd thought, and now she'd apparently been brought back to life.

"Ill tidings," Skalla muttered, turning back to Wylfrael. "Clearly, the council thought you'd die. It's an easy way to kill a stone sky god, to target his mortal mate that way. Cowardly." His voice hardened, fangs flashing, and I knew he was thinking of Koltar. "*Pathetic.* What is their purpose?"

"I don't know," Wylfrael replied. "But I've warned every stone sky god Sceadulyr and I have come across in our travels about what happened; told them not to take their mates there or try to join."

Skalla ran his hand down his braid and hissed a sigh.

"This can mean nothing good. This is something we will have to address, and soon." His gaze softened, and my insides softened right along with it. "Right now, I have little room in my head or heart for anything but Suvi and the babe."

"I understand," Wylfrael said, and it really sounded like he meant it. Like he, too, couldn't do anything but love Torrance, and for the first time I thought that maybe he might just be the tiniest bit alright in my books. "Congratulations, by the way. I couldn't help but notice."

I frowned in confusion, then it hit me. *Couldn't help but notice my belly.*

Skalla grunted.

"I am going to ignore the fact that you saw so much of my mate's body just now. Otherwise I'd have to kill you."

"You already almost did. *Twice.*"

"I am sorry for that, Wylfrael," my mate said, and I knew how painfully sincere he was. I knew how what he'd done in his madness still gnawed at him with venom that went just a little deeper every day.

"I am endlessly thankful that I was not successful," Skalla added. "I would have come to Sionnach, to see what became of you, but I have not been able to tear myself away from Suvi, especially now that she carries my babe in her belly."

"I am just glad you and I are both alive," Wylfrael replied. "And Suvi, too. I admit, I feared I'd find something very different here today."

There was taut silence, both males likely imagining the same horror that I was – the horror of what would have happened to me if my touch hadn't soothed Skalla's madness right away.

If he'd accidentally killed me.

"Torrance will be glad to hear the news," Wylfrael said, breaking that ugly silence. "All the women will be. They are together, safe on Sionnach."

Skalla grinned, and I smiled so widely that my cheeks pinched. They were alright! Wylfrael had obviously somehow managed to do what Skalla couldn't. He'd freed them from the ship. *We knew where they were!*

"And that news will make Suvi happy," Skalla said.

Ha! That was putting it mildly. I was fucking thrilled!

"I would take her for a visit to Sionnach," he continued, "but I find myself concerned about bringing her through a sky door while pregnant."

"Perhaps I could bring some of the other women here to see her?" Wylfrael suggested.

OK. Yup. This guy was definitely getting the Suvi stamp of approval now.

"Yes. Bring them any time. Suvi is healthy, but even with me here, I fear that she grows lonely. Being around her own kind, especially as the birth nears, would do her good."

"Then it is done," Wylfrael promised. "I will bring them as soon as they wish to visit."

"We will look forward to it," Skalla rumbled. "Will you stay and take a meal with us, or will you return to Sionnach now?"

"I will go now," he said. "I want to get back to Torrance."

Skalla had already turned from his cousin, striding towards the house, towards me.

"It is good to see you, Wylfrael," he called as he stepped into the shade of the pavilion. "Until we meet again."

Wylfrael took off with a leathery snap of his blue and black wings. A moment later, he'd opened a sky door and disappeared through it. I stepped shakily out from my hiding place.

Skalla froze when he saw me, then a look of love and comfort and relief unfurled across his face as he beheld me. Neither of us spoke. We just looked at each other, happiness stretching and glowing, its own source of light between us even when the sun went down.

CHAPTER SIXTY-TWO
Skallagrim

I assumed that neither Suvi nor Jolakaia would be interested in taking part in the kinds of Bohnebregg wedding ceremonies I'd grown up witnessing, because those tended to involve a lot of wrestling and weapons. So, instead, we were married in the way of cotton, with a few of Suvi's human traditions thrown in.

It didn't really matter to me how the ceremony went. What customs were involved, or even where we did it. All that mattered was that Suvi was there, that she was happy, and that she was officially my wife by the end of it.

The wedding took place at sunset, and we did it at the house. According to Jolakaia, most Callabarra weddings took place along the banks of the river Bohnebregg instead of at the temple, and that suited me just fine. Jolakaia and I stood on the dock, the river behind us and the house ahead, everything saturated, darkened and brightened, the cool-warm light of dusk blooming all around us. Once, Suvi had told me that humans called this time of day the *golden hour*, and I could certainly see why. The world took on a sacred sort of glow, and when Suvi took her first step out of the house, holiness poured down on me like rain.

My bride was a beacon. A light even when it was not dark. My gaze was fused to her, her beauty striking against my heart not with a hammer, but with a soft little fist that was somehow twice as strong. Her cheeks were pink with colour, her mist-grey eyes shining. Her arm was looped through Zev's. This, apparently, was a human custom. Apparently there was supposed to be an aisle, and someone would walk the bride down it.

There was no aisle here but the straight line of the dock, upon which Jolakaia and I stood at the very end.

Zev kept a good grip on Suvi, and for that I was very grateful. Suvi's newly rounded body made her clumsier, and I watched her tiny bare feet anxiously as if I had not already spent the entire afternoon clearing every single pebble and sharp stick from the very path she walked now.

Suvi was dressed in white, another of her customs, a long, simple, cotton tunic draped over her form. Her stomach pressed insistently outward against the fabric, and that made me hot with pride. In her delicate hand, she held a bouquet of Shara plants and other flowers, and I was suddenly thrown back with heart-rending nostalgia to that time when she'd looked up at me uncertainly in the temple gardens, healing flowers in her hands. She hadn't been sure of me then, hadn't loved me yet, and I remembered how badly I'd just wanted to let go and *break*. Break from the beauty of loving her alongside the pain of not knowing how I could possibly go on without her.

If only that poor Skallagrim could see me now. Because here she was, holding flowers once again, but this time as my bride.

Zev and Suvi walked down the dock. Zev took Suvi's flowers from her, and my bride entwined her fingers with mine. We gazed at each other as Jolakaia began to speak.

"The Mother sees you both and wraps you in cotton." Jolakaia unfolded a very long piece of cotton, dyed the same blue as the river. She and Zev each took an end and rotated in opposite directions around Suvi and me until the cotton was looped around us multiple times.

"Here she binds you," Jolakaia said softly, tucking her end of the cotton into the loose knot draped around us. "And what she binds let nothing, neither man nor metal, break."

"Now what?" I murmured. I said it to Jolakaia, but I was looking at Suvi. I couldn't tear my eye from her upturned face.

"Now, you are married." Jolakaia and Zev both worked to lift the twisted cotton loop upwards over our heads, not unwinding or breaking the flexible ring of it. "Traditionally," Jolakaia went on, folding the cotton loop with the utmost care, "this will be used as a swaddle for the couple's first child, should they choose to have one. It is not to be unwound before then."

My claws went possessively to Suvi's stomach. Tears glittered on her lashes as she covered my hand with both of hers.

"There's one other thing left," Suvi whispered thickly. "A human custom."

"Oh?"

"You kiss me."

Ah, bless the humans for being such a mostly reasonable race, with traditions I could appreciate. I was not sure what I would have done if Suvi wanted me to do something like, oh, I do not know, hoist her up into my arms and toss her into the river.

A kiss, though... A kiss sounded very, very good.

I lowered my snout in a tender arc, pressing the tip of it to Suvi's mouth. Her lips parted instantly, warm, her tongue wet against mine.

When we drew apart, I saw that Zev and Jolakaia had left the dock and were now standing on the shore, holding each other quietly, and I wondered if they were reminiscing about their own wedding.

"So, my wife," I growled. "Now that we are officially married, what would you have us do?"

I thrilled at the heat that turned liquid in her gaze.

"I want to be with my husband," she said. Then, she laughed. "But I think I need to eat something first."

"Come," I said. I wrapped my arm around her thickened waist, supporting her as we walked back up to the house. "I will take care of it. Of you."

I made something simple but hearty and carried it out to where I found her on her seat in the courtyard. The sun had fully set now, and I paused to admire my wife where she sat with her back to me. The silver light was as fine as lace upon her form.

She turned back towards me, her smile fading into something that almost looked like pain when she saw the food in my hands. A tear slipped from her eye – just one – and I wondered if I'd done something wrong. Maybe it was bad luck to eat a meal such as this on your wedding day.

But though that tear remained, she smiled and stood and thanked me.

She reached for the bowl, took the spoon in her hand.

And then Suvi ate her soup.

Thank you so much for reading Suvi and Skalla's story. I truly loved writing this book. But I hope you haven't forgotten about our shifty, sarcastic shadowlands god Sceadulyr, because his story will be next! And if you were curious about Aeshyr, rest assured he will get a book later in the series too. If you want to keep up to date with me and find out when new books are out, sign up to my newsletter at www.ursadaxwriting.com/contact.

Ursa Dax Books
Brides of the Stone Sky Gods
Alien God
Berserker God
Fated Mates of the Sea Sand Warlords
Alien Tyrant
Alien Enemy
Alien Orphan
Alien Reject
Alien Exile
Alien Hunter
Alien Victor
Alien Shield
Alien Keeper
Alien Claw
Alien Heart
Alien Mask
Alien Storm
Alien Hope
Holiday Romances of Elora Station
Chimera for Christmas
Alien Orc for Christmas